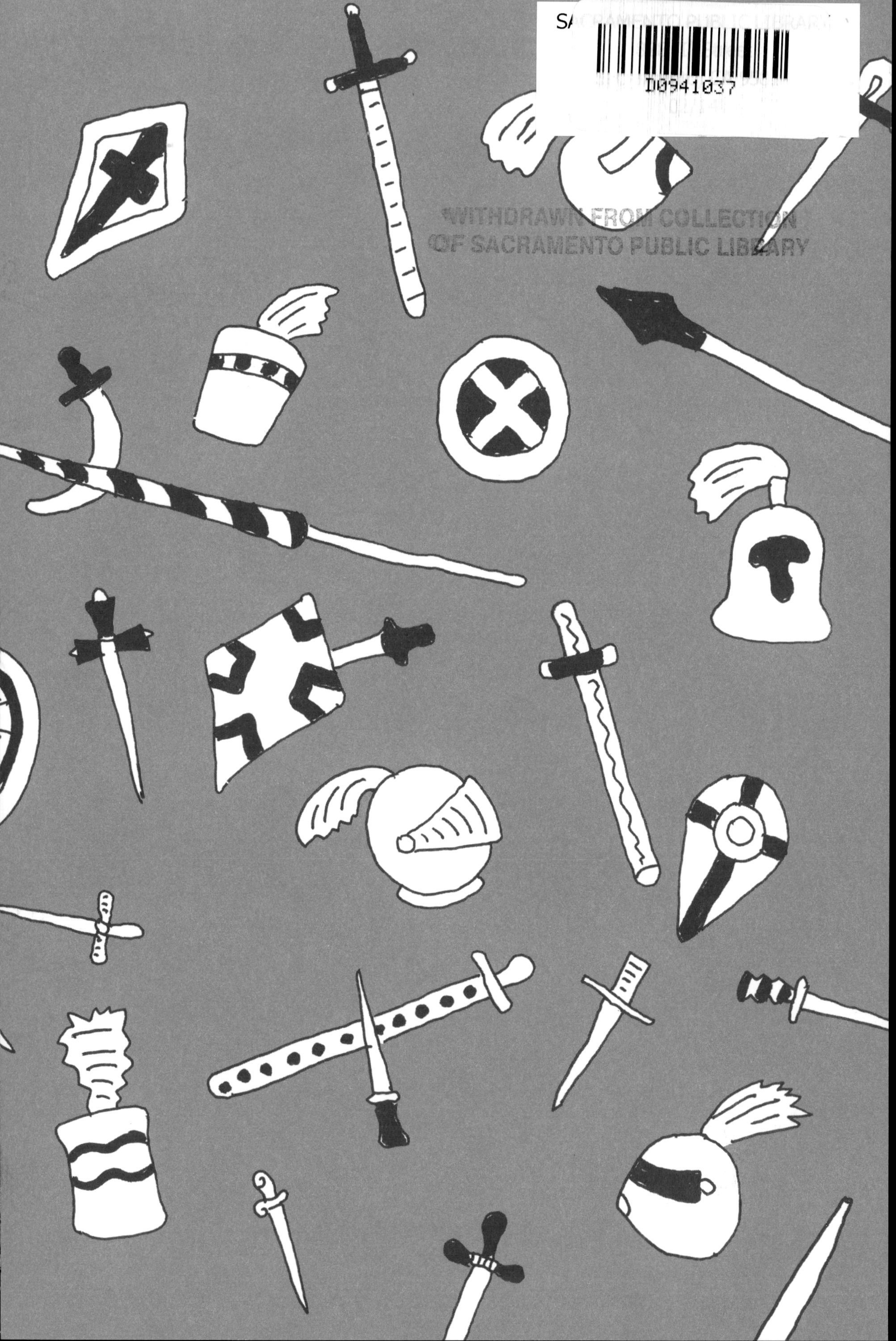

A CONN

BY THE SAME AUTHOR:

DANTE'S DIVINE COMEDY

SEYMOUR: THE OBSESSIVE IMAGES OF SEYMOUR CHWAST

THE CANTERBURY TALES

HOMER'S ODYSSEY

THE PUSH PIN GRAPHIC

MOONRIDE

THE 12 CIRCUS RINGS

THE ALPHABET PARADE

THE LEFT-HANDED DESIGNER

WITH STEVEN HELLER:

GRAPHIC STYLE

ILLUSTRATION: A VISUAL HISTORY

ECTICUT

BY MARK TWAIN

ADAPTED BY
SEYMOUR CHWAST

BLOOMSBURY
NEW YORK
LONDON
NEW DELHI
SYDNEY

YANKEE

COPYRIGHT © 2014 BY SEYMOUR CHWAST

PUBLISHED BY BLOOMSBURY USA, NEW YORK

ALL PAPERS USED BY BLOOMBBURY USA ARE NATURAL
RECYCLABLE PRODUCTS MADE FROM WOOD GROWN
IN WELL-MANAGED FORESTS. THE MANUFACTURING
PROCESSES CONFORM TO THE ENVIRONMENTAL
REGULATIONS OF THE COUNTRY OF ORIGIN.

LIBRARY OF CONGRESS CATALOGING-IN-PUBLICATION
DATA HAS BEEN APPLIED FOR.

ISBN: 978-1-60819-961-7

FIRST U.S. EDITION 2014

1 3 5 7 9 10 8 6 4 2

ART, DESIGN, AND LETTERING BY SEYMOUR CHWAST
PRINTED IN THE U.S.A. BY QUAD/GRAPHICS, TAUNTON

IN KING

ARTHUR

INTRODUCTION

WHILE SIGHTSEEING IN A BRITISH CASTLE, A NINETEENTH-CENTURY NARRATOR (HERE MARK TWAIN) MEETS A STRANGER WHO HANDS HIM A MANUSCRIPT. IT TELLS THE STORY OF THE STRANGER'S ADVENTURES TIME-TRAVELING TO THE ERA OF KING ARTHUR AND HIS ROUND TABLE. THERE WAS NO NEED FOR A TIME MACHINE LIKE THE ONE USED BY H.G. WELLS' TIME TRAVELER— FOR THE CONNECTICUT YANKEE, IT JUST TOOK A HIT ON THE HEAD.

WHAT THE STORYTELLING STRANGER, HANK MORGAN, FOUND ONCE HE AWOKE WAS AN ABSURD FEUDAL SOCIETY, A TYRANNICAL NOBILITY, A CORRUPT AND CRUEL CHURCH, AND KNIGHTS IN ILL-FITTING ARMOR. OUR HERO, A CLEVER ENTRE-PRENEUR, ATTEMPTED TO CREATE A MODERN DEMOCRATIC STATE, COMPLETE WITH TELEPHONES AND GATLING GUNS, IN SIXTH-CENTURY ENGLAND. HE USED HIS KNOWLEDGE OF HISTORY TO "PREDICT" A SOLAR ECLIPSE, FOOLING THE PEOPLE INTO THINKING HE COMMANDED MAGIC. THE SCENE OF KNIGHTS ARRIVING ON HIGH-WHEEL BICYCLES TO SAVE THE LIVES OF MORGAN AND KING ARTHUR IS ONE OF THE FUNNIEST EPISODES IN THIS IMAGI-NATIVE AND EXPLOSIVELY SATIRICAL WORK.

MARK TWAIN, BORN SAMUEL L. CLEMENS IN 1835, IS CONSIDERED BY MANY TO BE AMERICA'S GREATEST WRITER AND HUMORIST. HE WORKED AS A TYPESETTER AND REPORTER, BUT AFTER THE PUBLICATION OF HIS SHORT STORY "THE CELEBRATED JUMPING FROG OF CALAVERAS COUNTY," HE BECAME A SUCCESSFUL WRITER AND PUBLIC SPEAKER. HIS MOST FAMOUS BOOKS ARE *THE ADVENTURES OF TOM SAWYER* AND *THE ADVENTURES OF HUCKLEBERRY FINN*, WHICH SOME CONSIDER "THE GREAT AMER-ICAN NOVEL." THESE CLASSICS HELPED TO DESIGNATE MARK TWAIN AS THE COUNTRY'S MOST FAMOUS LITERARY ICON.

I MUST PERSONALLY THANK THE AUTHOR FOR PROVIDING ME WITH SUCH CHALLENGING MATERIAL FOR GRAPHIC EXPLORATION FOR THIS IS A WONDERFULLY COMIC NOVEL WITH A SERIOUS MESSAGE. WHAT I REALIZED WHILE REREADING TWAIN'S NOVEL AND WORKING ON THIS BOOK IS THAT THE STATE OF MANKIND HAS PROGRESSED VERY LITTLE IN THE PAST THIRTEEN CENTURIES— AND SINCE TWAIN'S TIME, HARDLY AT ALL.

'S COURT

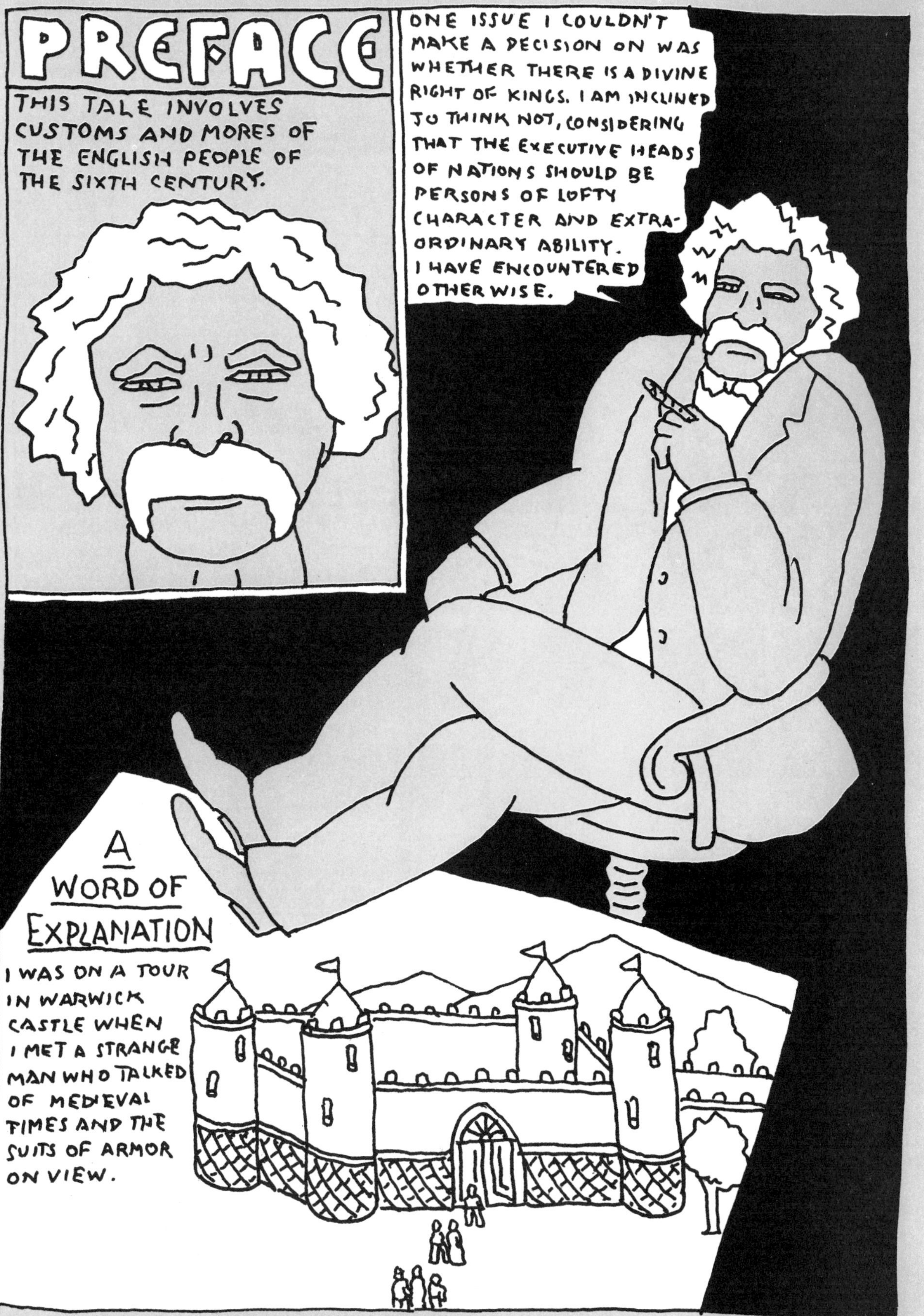
PREFACE
THIS TALE INVOLVES CUSTOMS AND MORES OF THE ENGLISH PEOPLE OF THE SIXTH CENTURY.
ONE ISSUE I COULDN'T MAKE A DECISION ON WAS WHETHER THERE IS A DIVINE RIGHT OF KINGS. I AM INCLINED TO THINK NOT, CONSIDERING THAT THE EXECUTIVE HEADS OF NATIONS SHOULD BE PERSONS OF LOFTY CHARACTER AND EXTRA-ORDINARY ABILITY. I HAVE ENCOUNTERED OTHERWISE.
A WORD OF EXPLANATION
I WAS ON A TOUR IN WARWICK CASTLE WHEN I MET A STRANGE MAN WHO TALKED OF MEDIEVAL TIMES AND THE SUITS OF ARMOR ON VIEW.

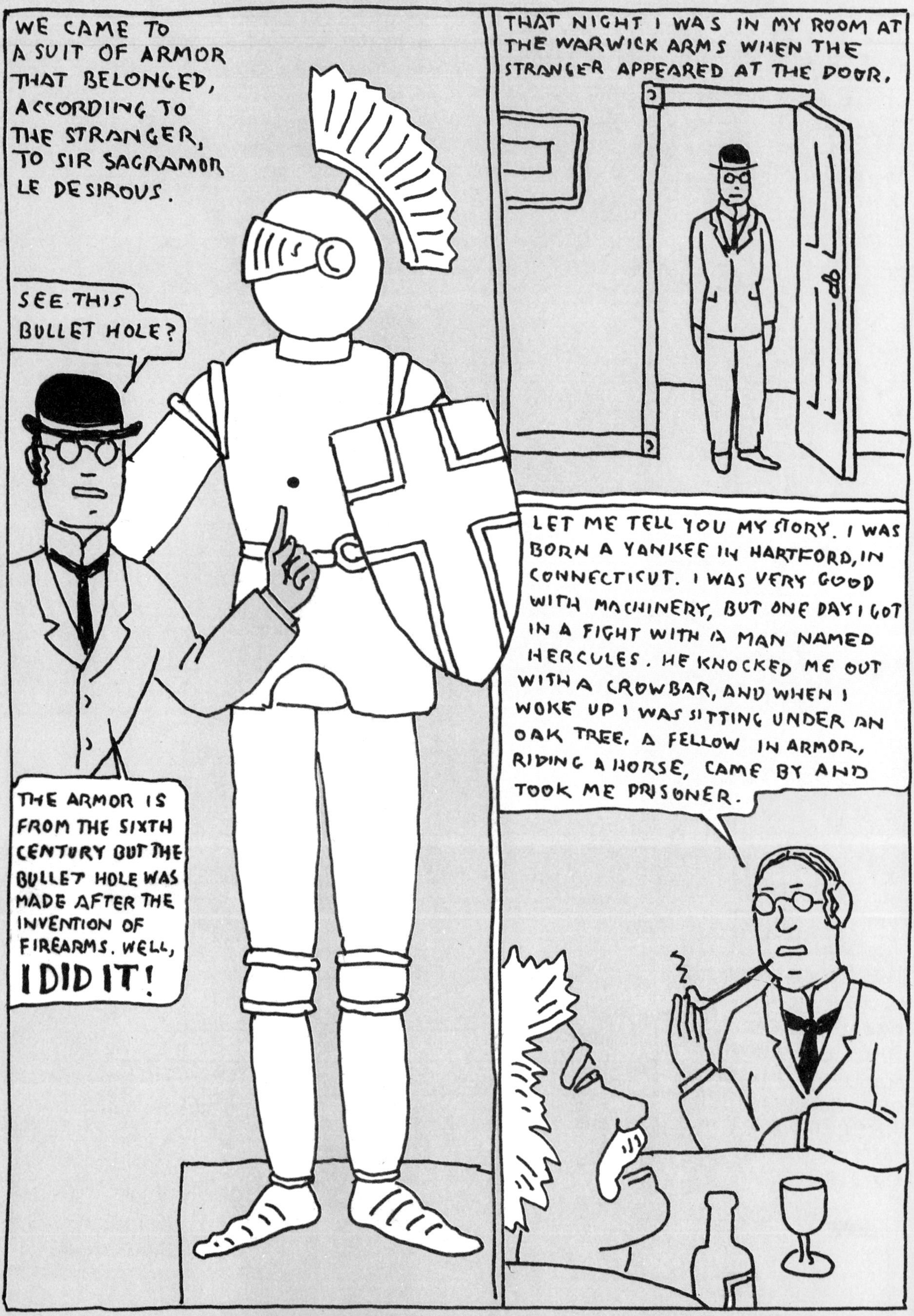
WE CAME TO A SUIT OF ARMOR THAT BELONGED, ACCORDING TO THE STRANGER, TO SIR SAGRAMOR LE DESIROUS.
SEE THIS BULLET HOLE?
THE ARMOR IS FROM THE SIXTH CENTURY BUT THE BULLET HOLE WAS MADE AFTER THE INVENTION OF FIREARMS. WELL, I DID IT!
THAT NIGHT I WAS IN MY ROOM AT THE WARWICK ARMS WHEN THE STRANGER APPEARED AT THE DOOR.
LET ME TELL YOU MY STORY. I WAS BORN A YANKEE IN HARTFORD, IN CONNECTICUT. I WAS VERY GOOD WITH MACHINERY, BUT ONE DAY I GOT IN A FIGHT WITH A MAN NAMED HERCULES. HE KNOCKED ME OUT WITH A CROWBAR, AND WHEN I WOKE UP I WAS SITTING UNDER AN OAK TREE. A FELLOW IN ARMOR, RIDING A HORSE, CAME BY AND TOOK ME PRISONER.

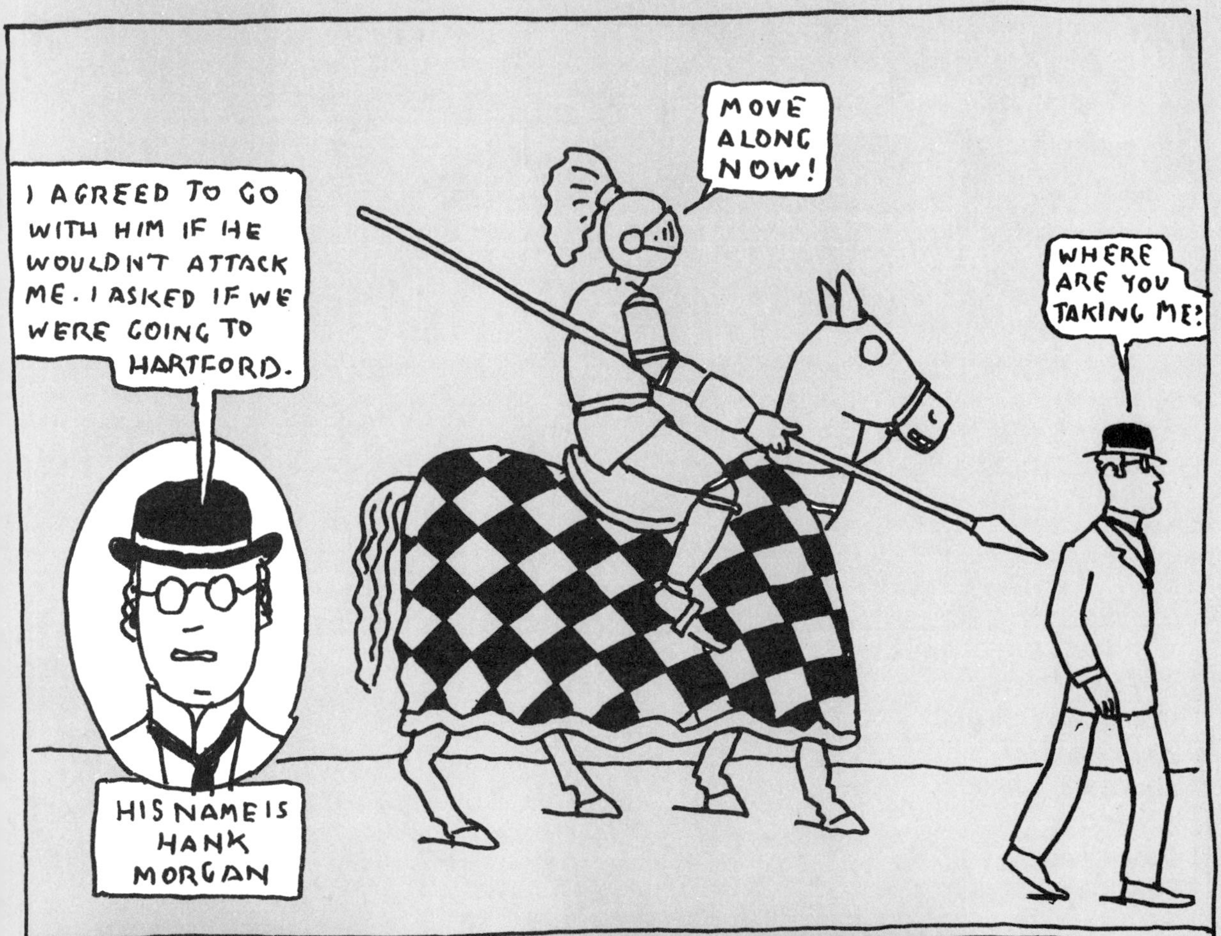
I AGREED TO GO WITH HIM IF HE WOULDN'T ATTACK ME. I ASKED IF WE WERE GOING TO HARTFORD.
MOVE ALONG NOW!
WHERE ARE YOU TAKING ME?
HIS NAME IS HANK MORGAN

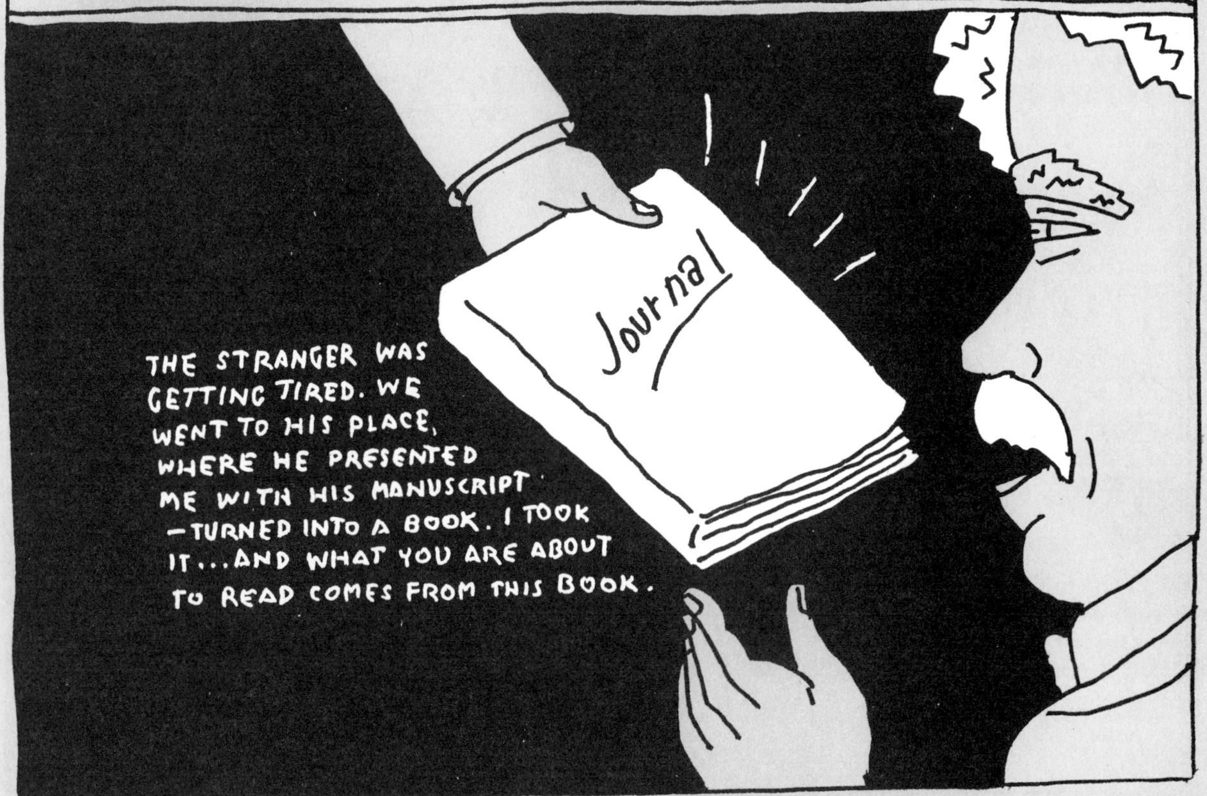
Journal
THE STRANGER WAS GETTING TIRED. WE WENT TO HIS PLACE, WHERE HE PRESENTED ME WITH HIS MANUSCRIPT —TURNED INTO A BOOK. I TOOK IT...AND WHAT YOU ARE ABOUT TO READ COMES FROM THIS BOOK.

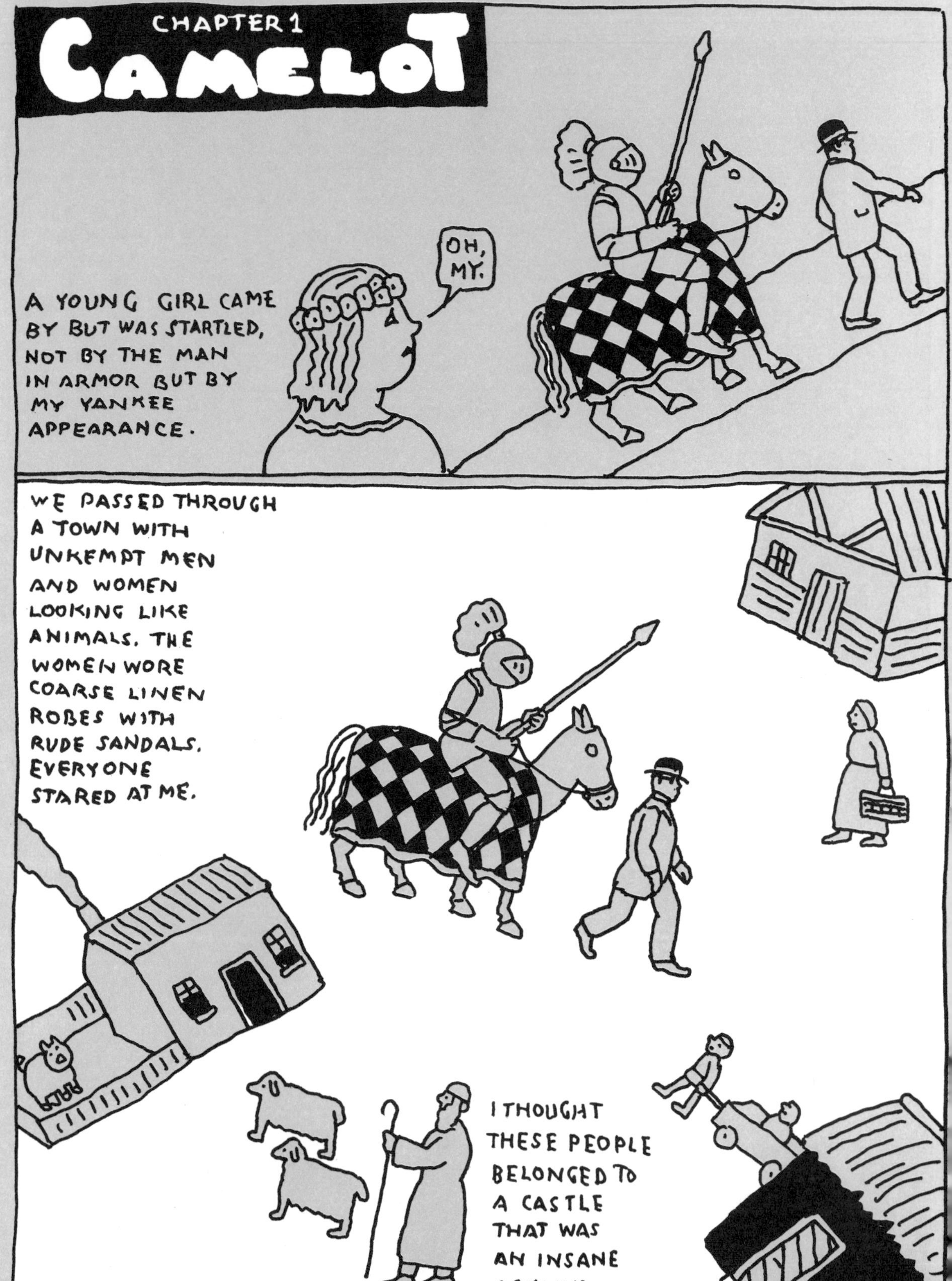
CHAPTER 1
CAMELOT
A YOUNG GIRL CAME BY BUT WAS STARTLED, NOT BY THE MAN IN ARMOR BUT BY MY YANKEE APPEARANCE.
OH, MY.
WE PASSED THROUGH A TOWN WITH UNKEMPT MEN AND WOMEN LOOKING LIKE ANIMALS. THE WOMEN WORE COARSE LINEN ROBES WITH RUDE SANDALS. EVERYONE STARED AT ME.
I THOUGHT THESE PEOPLE BELONGED TO A CASTLE THAT WAS AN INSANE ASYLUM.

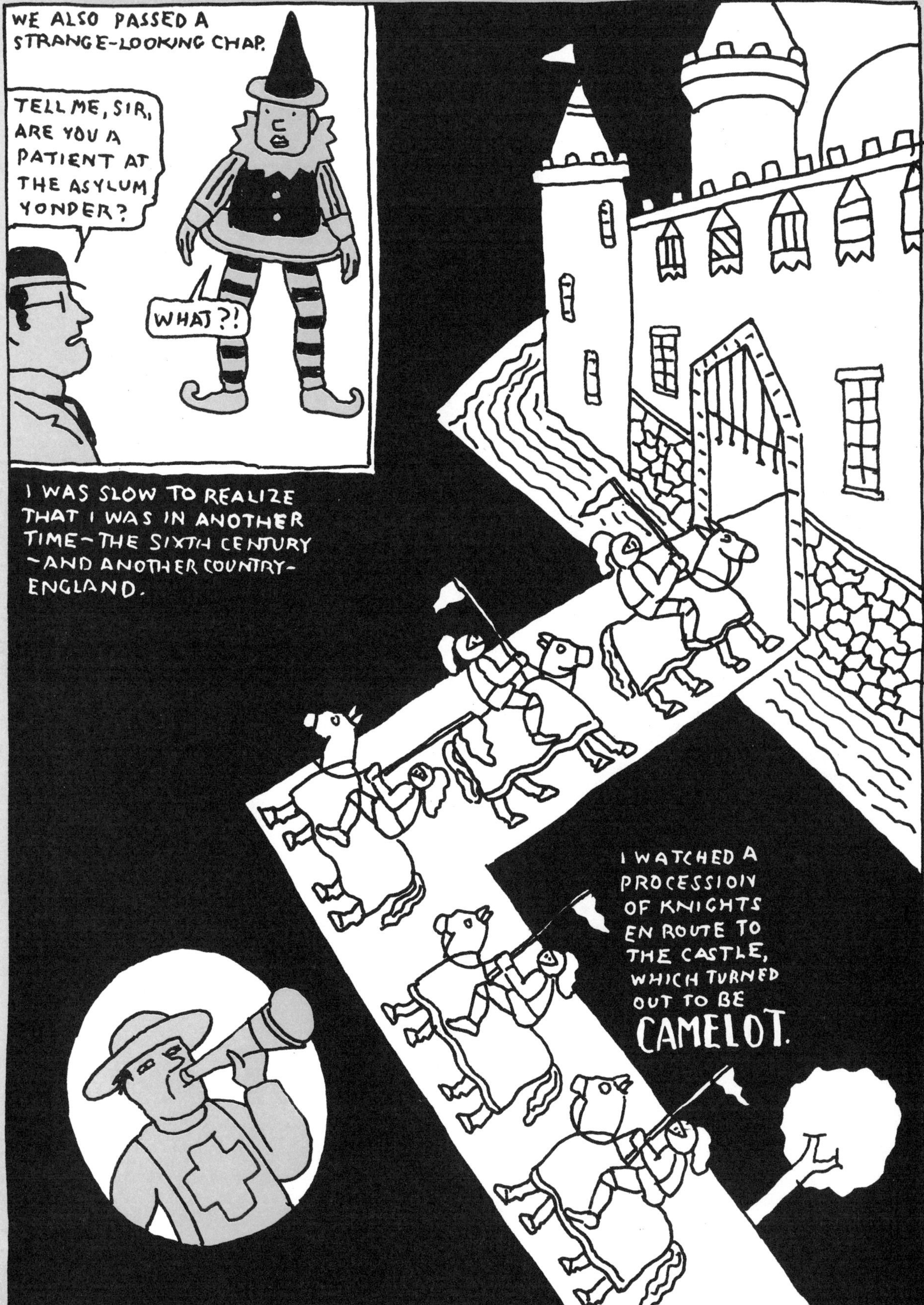
WE ALSO PASSED A STRANGE-LOOKING CHAP.
TELL ME, SIR, ARE YOU A PATIENT AT THE ASYLUM YONDER?
WHAT?!
I WAS SLOW TO REALIZE THAT I WAS IN ANOTHER TIME—THE SIXTH CENTURY—AND ANOTHER COUNTRY—ENGLAND.
I WATCHED A PROCESSION OF KNIGHTS EN ROUTE TO THE CASTLE, WHICH TURNED OUT TO BE CAMELOT.

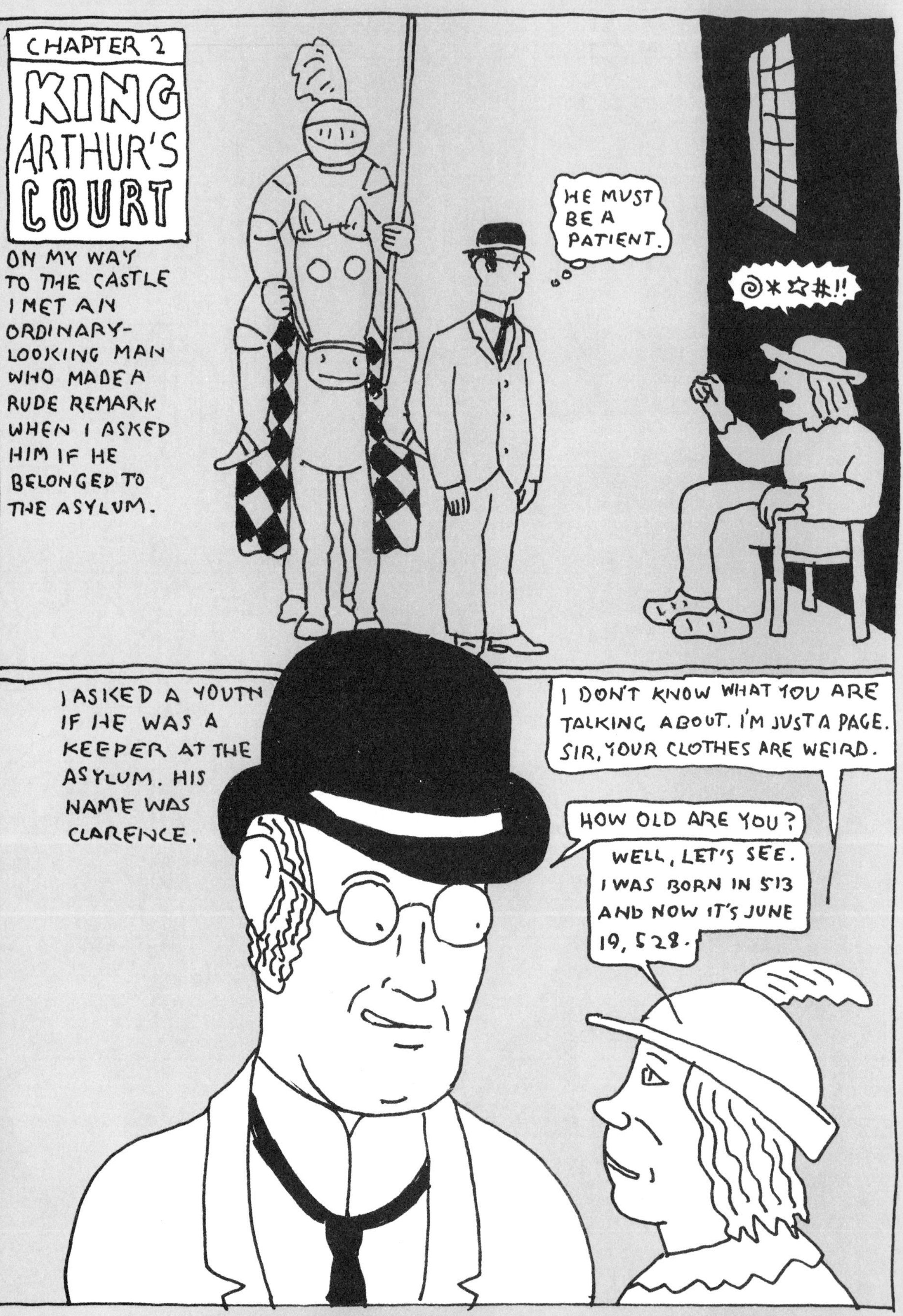
CHAPTER 2
KING ARTHUR'S COURT
ON MY WAY TO THE CASTLE I MET AN ORDINARY-LOOKING MAN WHO MADE A RUDE REMARK WHEN I ASKED HIM IF HE BELONGED TO THE ASYLUM.
HE MUST BE A PATIENT.
@*✩#!!
I ASKED A YOUTH IF HE WAS A KEEPER AT THE ASYLUM. HIS NAME WAS CLARENCE.
I DON'T KNOW WHAT YOU ARE TALKING ABOUT. I'M JUST A PAGE. SIR, YOUR CLOTHES ARE WEIRD.
HOW OLD ARE YOU?
WELL, LET'S SEE. I WAS BORN IN 513 AND NOW IT'S JUNE 19, 528.

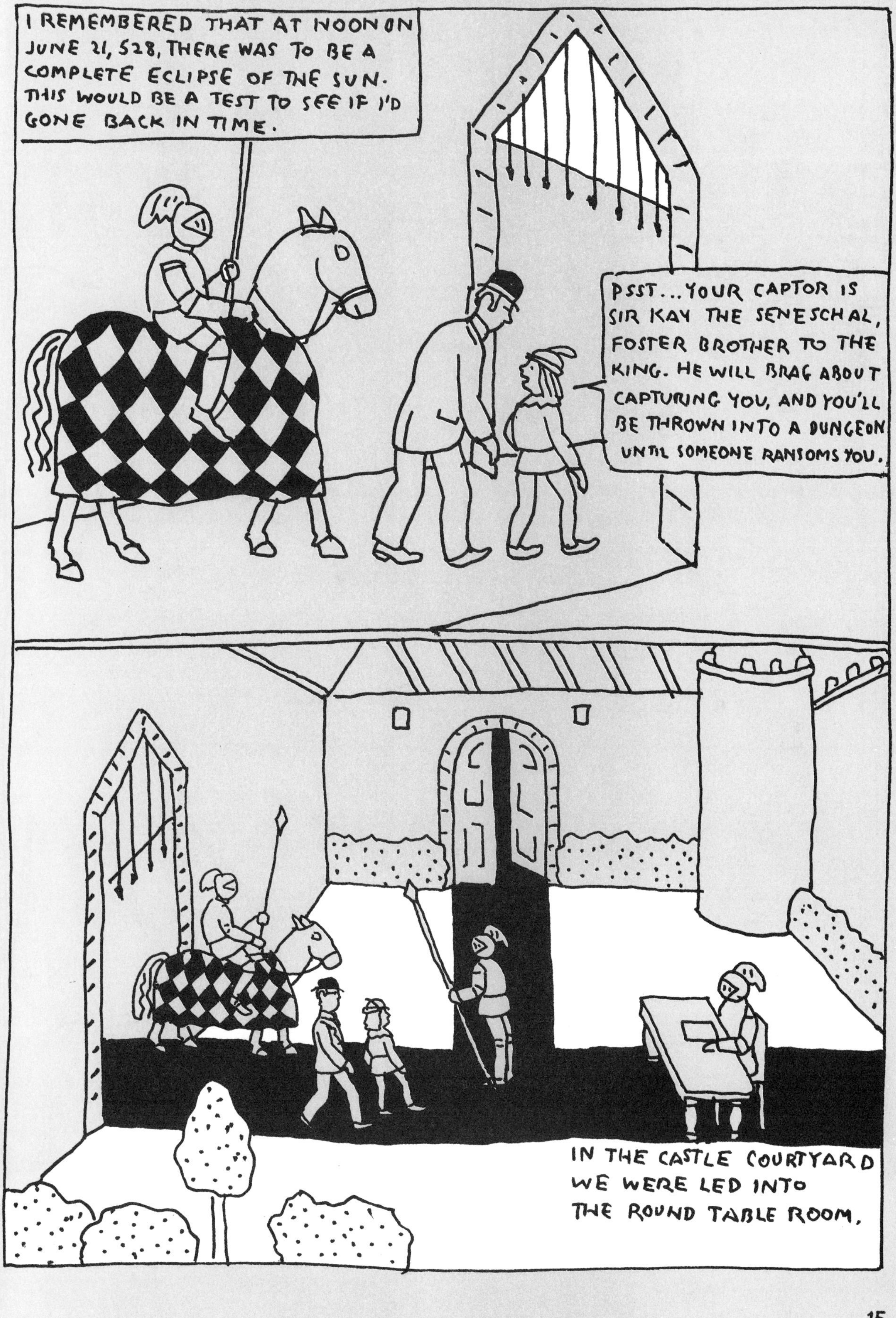
I REMEMBERED THAT AT NOON ON JUNE 21, 528, THERE WAS TO BE A COMPLETE ECLIPSE OF THE SUN. THIS WOULD BE A TEST TO SEE IF I'D GONE BACK IN TIME.
PSST... YOUR CAPTOR IS SIR KAY THE SENESCHAL, FOSTER BROTHER TO THE KING. HE WILL BRAG ABOUT CAPTURING YOU, AND YOU'LL BE THROWN INTO A DUNGEON UNTIL SOMEONE RANSOMS YOU.
IN THE CASTLE COURTYARD WE WERE LED INTO THE ROUND TABLE ROOM.

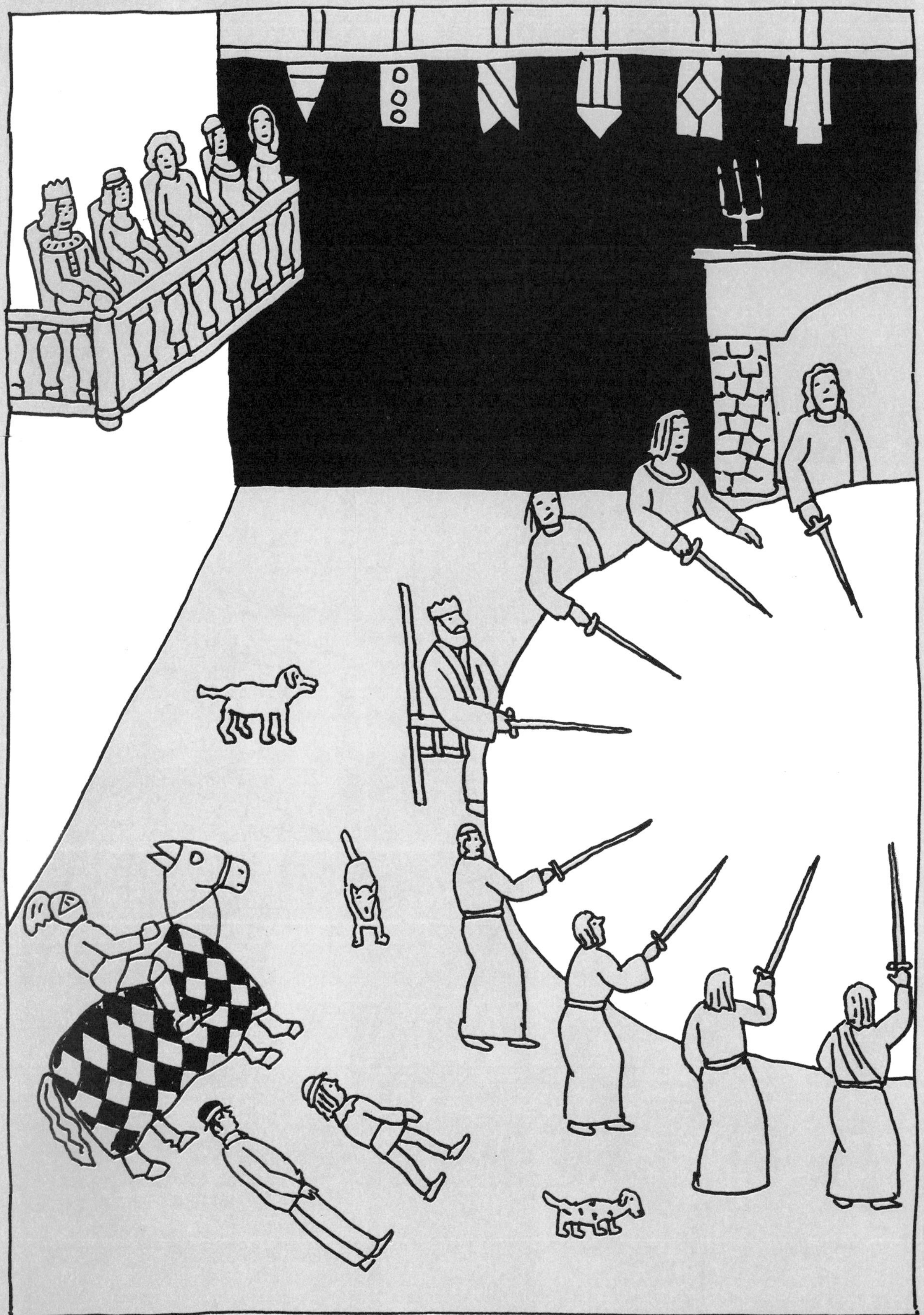

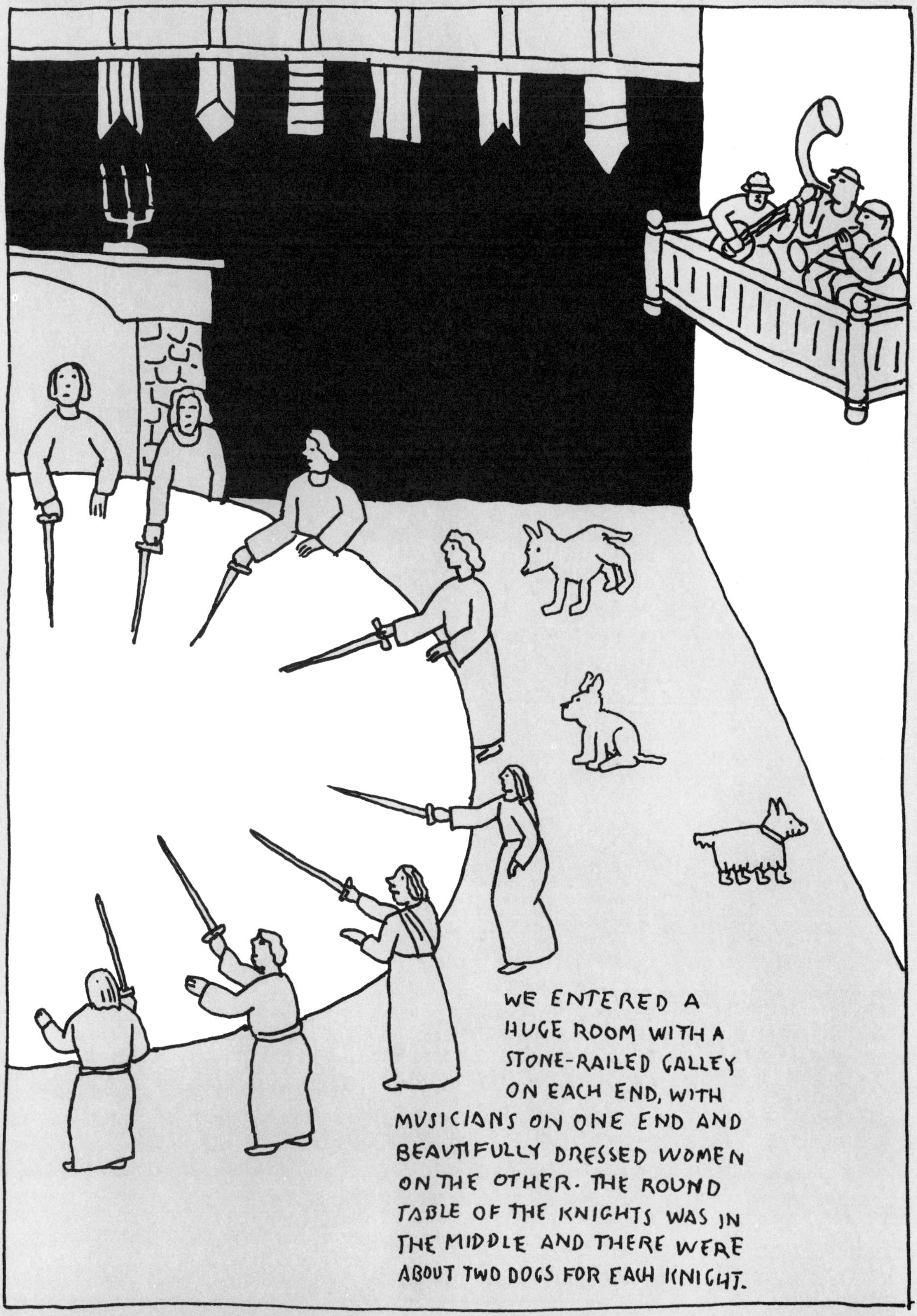
WE ENTERED A HUGE ROOM WITH A STONE-RAILED GALLEY ON EACH END, WITH MUSICIANS ON ONE END AND BEAUTIFULLY DRESSED WOMEN ON THE OTHER. THE ROUND TABLE OF THE KNIGHTS WAS IN THE MIDDLE AND THERE WERE ABOUT TWO DOGS FOR EACH KNIGHT.

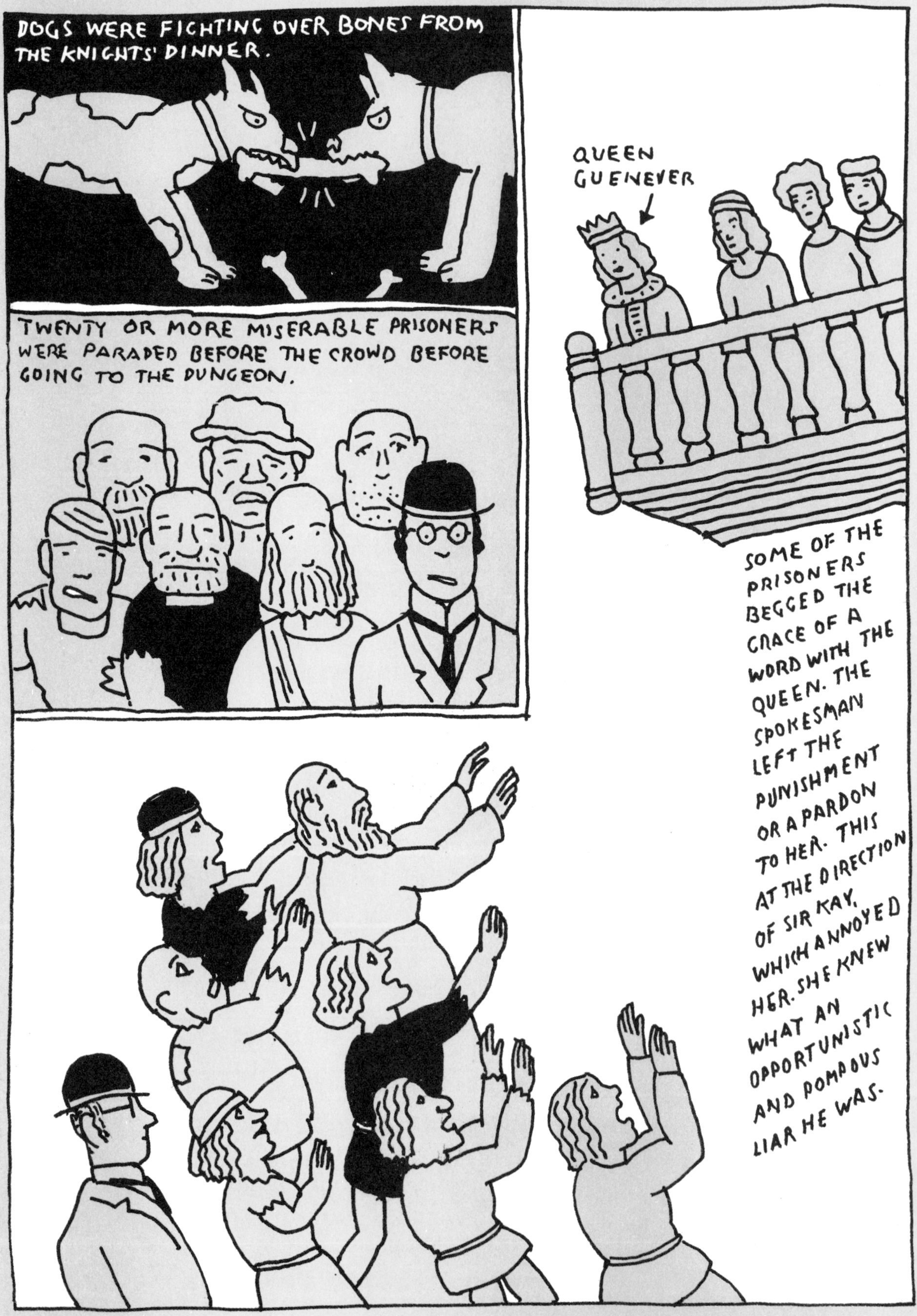
DOGS WERE FIGHTING OVER BONES FROM THE KNIGHTS' DINNER.
TWENTY OR MORE MISERABLE PRISONERS WERE PARADED BEFORE THE CROWD BEFORE GOING TO THE DUNGEON.
QUEEN GUENEVER
SOME OF THE PRISONERS BEGGED THE GRACE OF A WORD WITH THE QUEEN. THE SPOKESMAN LEFT THE PUNISHMENT OR A PARDON TO HER. THIS AT THE DIRECTION OF SIR KAY, WHICH ANNOYED HER. SHE KNEW WHAT AN OPPORTUNISTIC AND POMPOUS LIAR HE WAS.

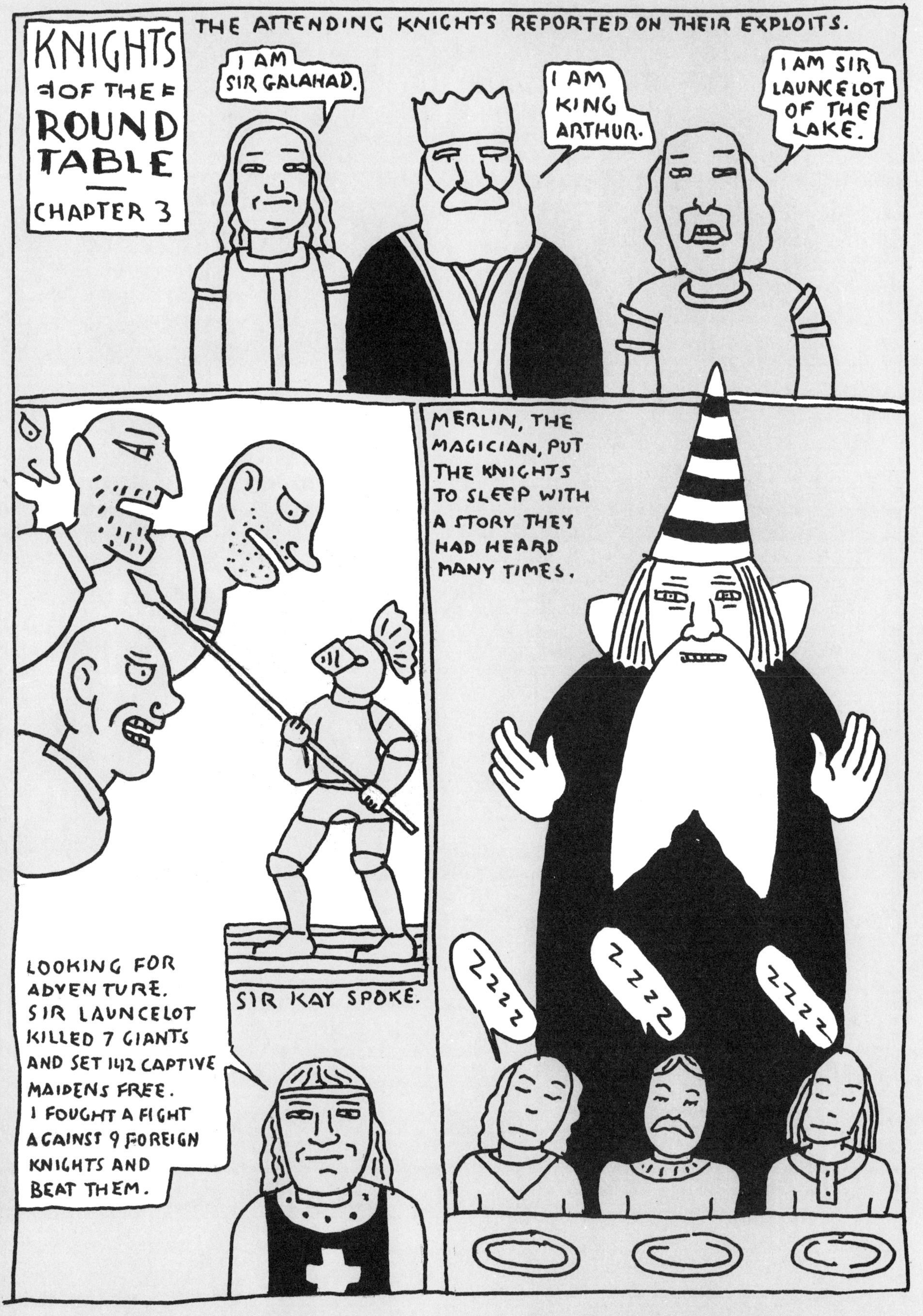
KNIGHTS OF THE ROUND TABLE
CHAPTER 3
THE ATTENDING KNIGHTS REPORTED ON THEIR EXPLOITS.
I AM SIR GALAHAD.
I AM KING ARTHUR.
I AM SIR LAUNCELOT OF THE LAKE.
LOOKING FOR ADVENTURE. SIR LAUNCELOT KILLED 7 GIANTS AND SET 142 CAPTIVE MAIDENS FREE. I FOUGHT A FIGHT AGAINST 9 FOREIGN KNIGHTS AND BEAT THEM.
SIR KAY SPOKE.
MERLIN, THE MAGICIAN, PUT THE KNIGHTS TO SLEEP WITH A STORY THEY HAD HEARD MANY TIMES.
ZZZZ
ZZZZ
ZZZZ

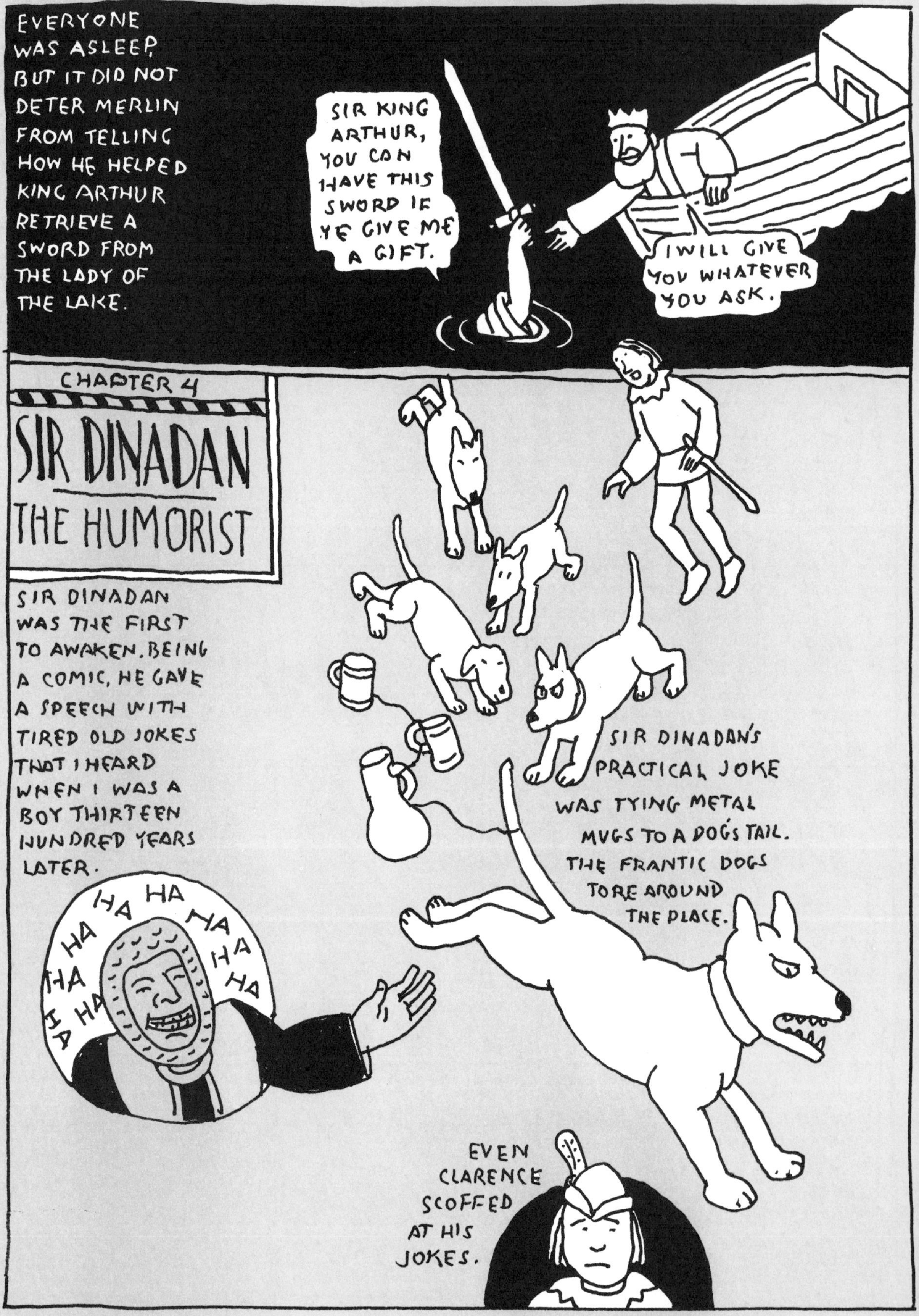
EVERYONE WAS ASLEEP, BUT IT DID NOT DETER MERLIN FROM TELLING HOW HE HELPED KING ARTHUR RETRIEVE A SWORD FROM THE LADY OF THE LAKE.
SIR KING ARTHUR, YOU CAN HAVE THIS SWORD IF YE GIVE ME A GIFT.
I WILL GIVE YOU WHATEVER YOU ASK.
CHAPTER 4
SIR DINADAN
THE HUMORIST
SIR DINADAN WAS THE FIRST TO AWAKEN. BEING A COMIC, HE GAVE A SPEECH WITH TIRED OLD JOKES THAT I HEARD WHEN I WAS A BOY THIRTEEN HUNDRED YEARS LATER.
HA HA HA HA HA HA HA HA HA HA HA
SIR DINADAN'S PRACTICAL JOKE WAS TYING METAL MUGS TO A DOG'S TAIL. THE FRANTIC DOGS TORE AROUND THE PLACE.
EVEN CLARENCE SCOFFED AT HIS JOKES.

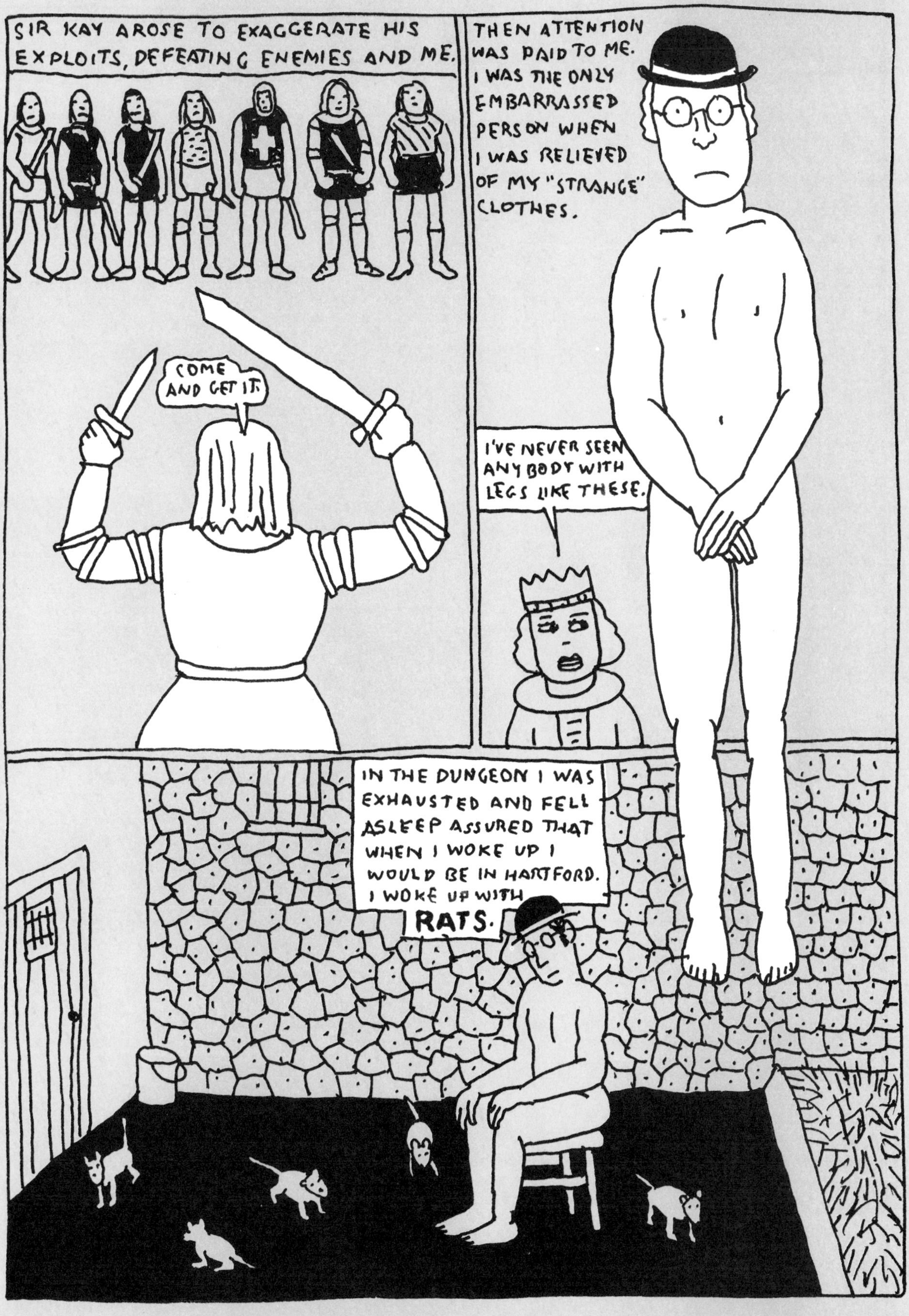
SIR KAY AROSE TO EXAGGERATE HIS EXPLOITS, DEFEATING ENEMIES AND ME.
COME AND GET IT.
THEN ATTENTION WAS PAID TO ME. I WAS THE ONLY EMBARRASSED PERSON WHEN I WAS RELIEVED OF MY "STRANGE" CLOTHES.
I'VE NEVER SEEN ANYBODY WITH LEGS LIKE THESE.
IN THE DUNGEON I WAS EXHAUSTED AND FELL ASLEEP ASSURED THAT WHEN I WOKE UP I WOULD BE IN HARTFORD. I WOKE UP WITH
RATS.

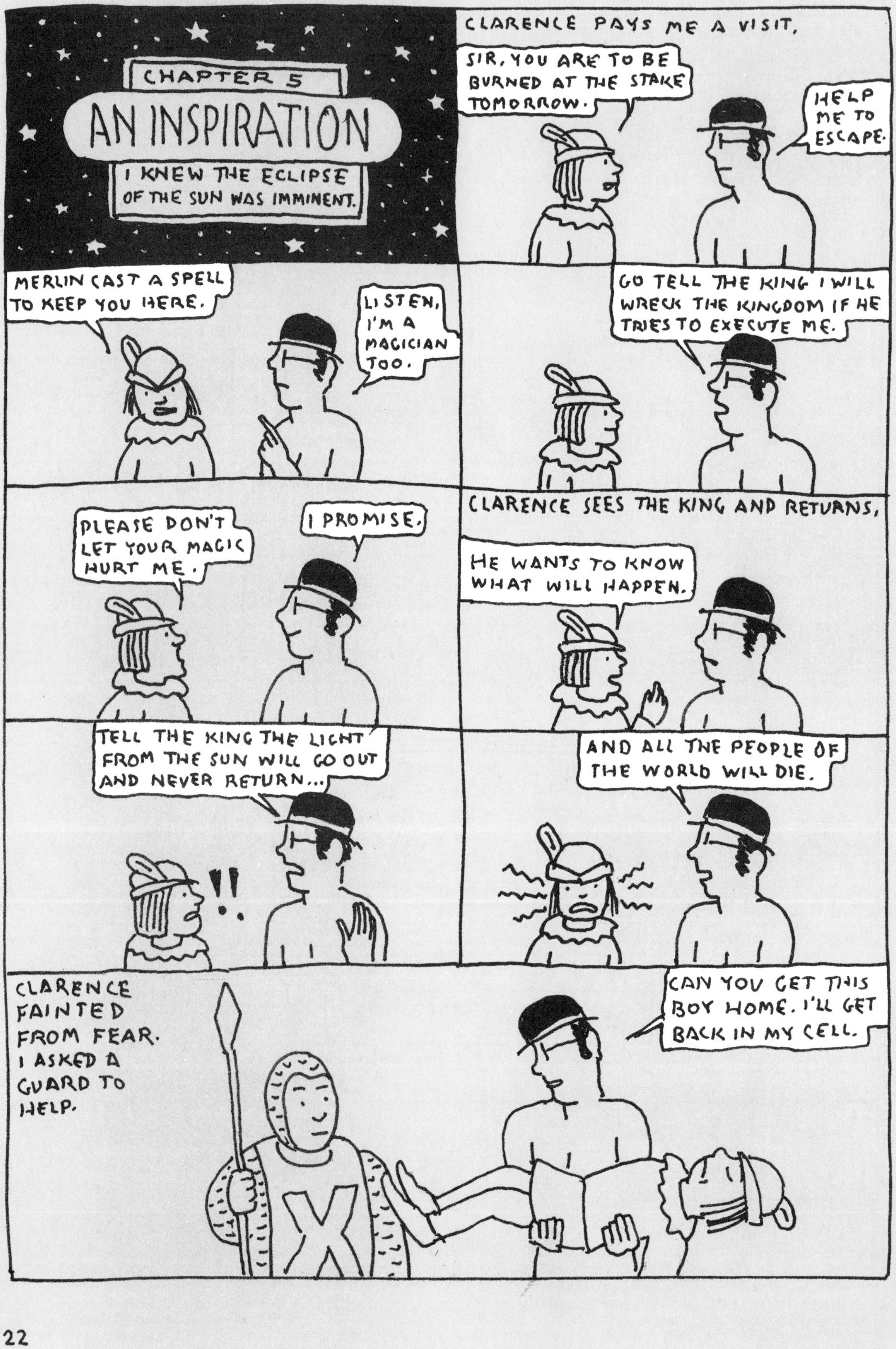
CHAPTER 5
AN INSPIRATION
I KNEW THE ECLIPSE OF THE SUN WAS IMMINENT.
CLARENCE PAYS ME A VISIT,
SIR, YOU ARE TO BE BURNED AT THE STAKE TOMORROW.
HELP ME TO ESCAPE.
MERLIN CAST A SPELL TO KEEP YOU HERE.
LISTEN, I'M A MAGICIAN TOO.
GO TELL THE KING I WILL WRECK THE KINGDOM IF HE TRIES TO EXECUTE ME.
PLEASE DON'T LET YOUR MAGIC HURT ME.
I PROMISE.
CLARENCE SEES THE KING AND RETURNS,
HE WANTS TO KNOW WHAT WILL HAPPEN.
TELL THE KING THE LIGHT FROM THE SUN WILL GO OUT AND NEVER RETURN...
!!
AND ALL THE PEOPLE OF THE WORLD WILL DIE.
CLARENCE FAINTED FROM FEAR. I ASKED A GUARD TO HELP.
CAN YOU GET THIS BOY HOME. I'LL GET BACK IN MY CELL.

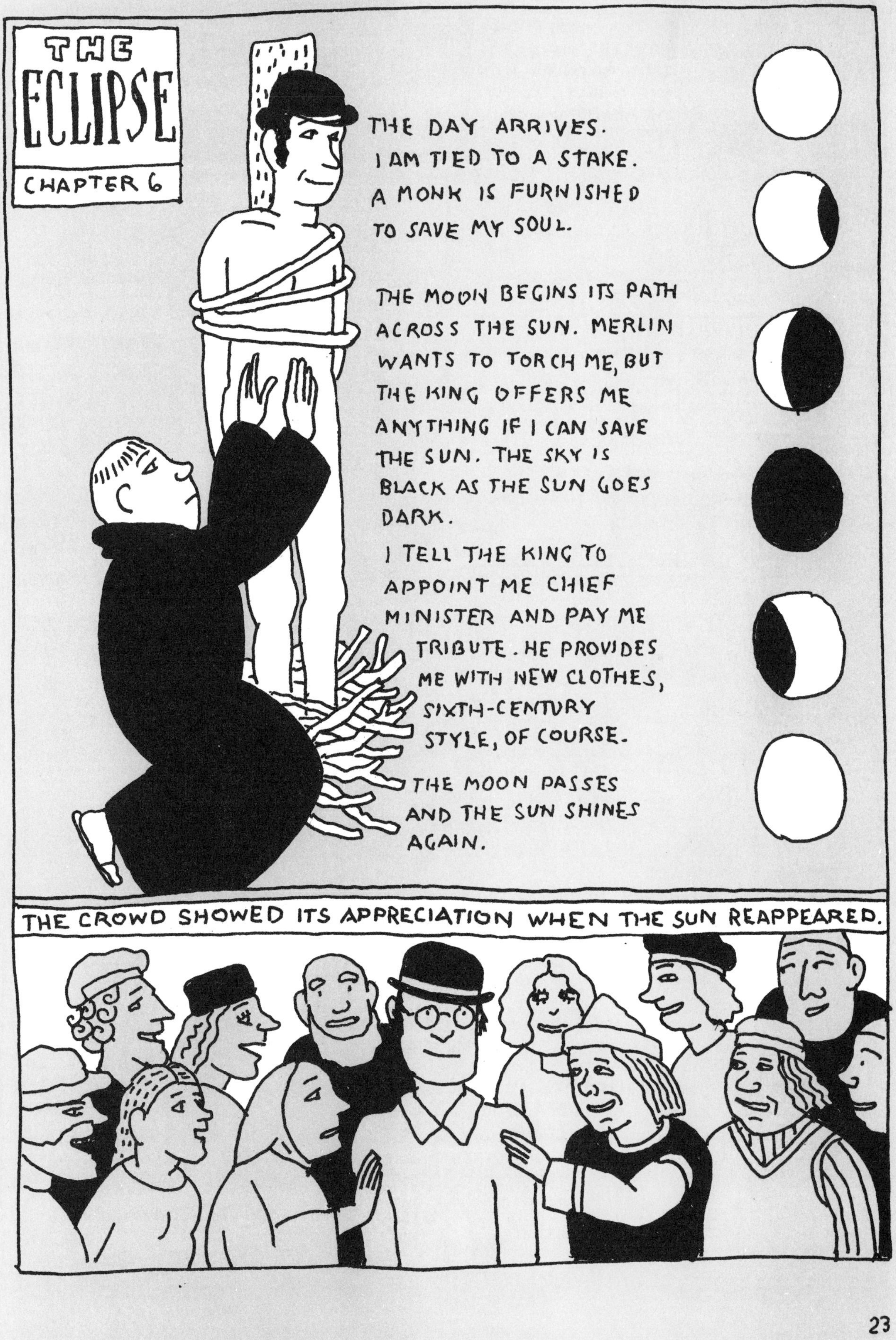
THE ECLIPSE
CHAPTER 6
THE DAY ARRIVES. I AM TIED TO A STAKE. A MONK IS FURNISHED TO SAVE MY SOUL.
THE MOON BEGINS ITS PATH ACROSS THE SUN. MERLIN WANTS TO TORCH ME, BUT THE KING OFFERS ME ANYTHING IF I CAN SAVE THE SUN. THE SKY IS BLACK AS THE SUN GOES DARK.
I TELL THE KING TO APPOINT ME CHIEF MINISTER AND PAY ME TRIBUTE. HE PROVIDES ME WITH NEW CLOTHES, SIXTH-CENTURY STYLE, OF COURSE.
THE MOON PASSES AND THE SUN SHINES AGAIN.
THE CROWD SHOWED ITS APPRECIATION WHEN THE SUN REAPPEARED.

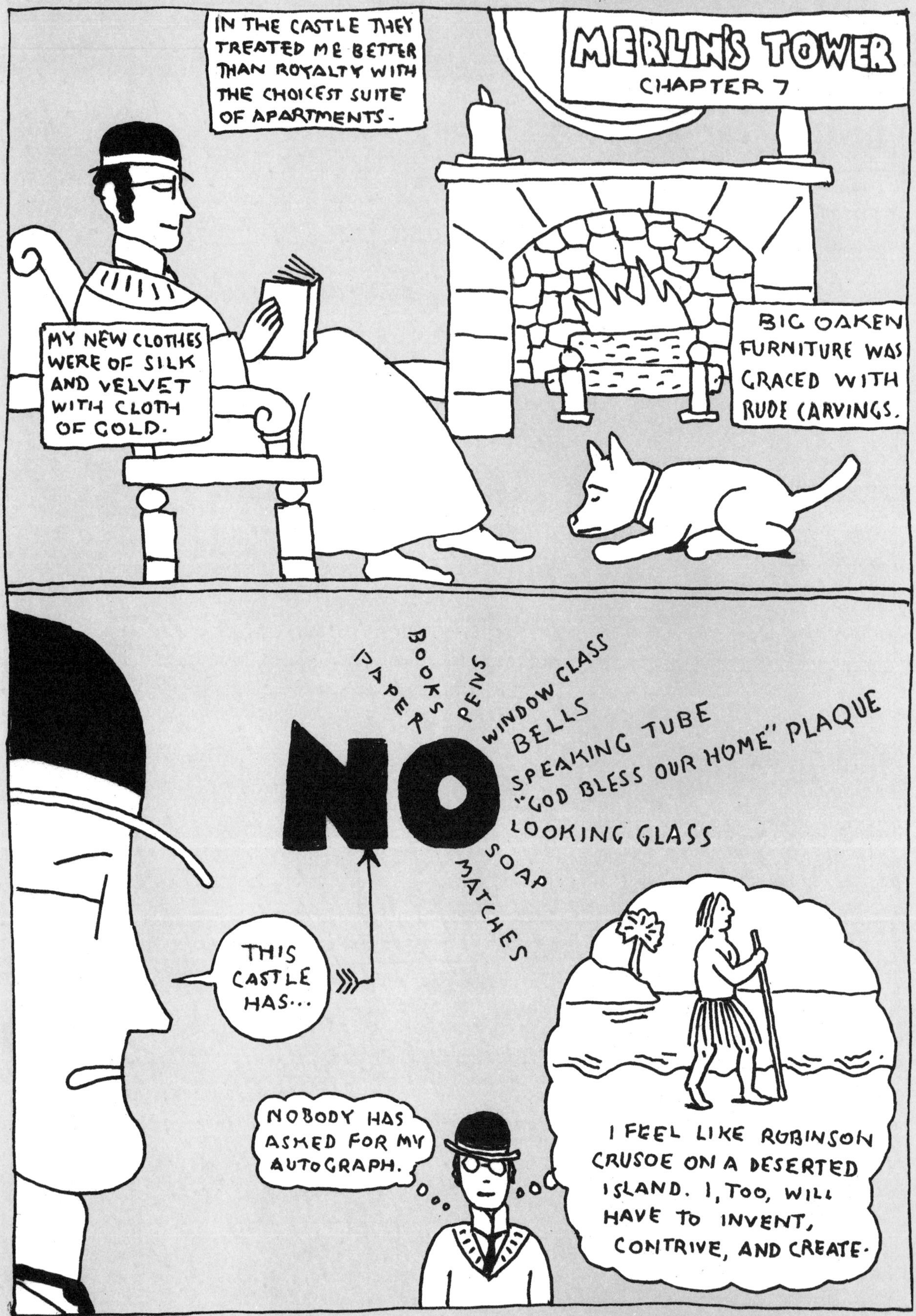
MERLIN'S TOWER
CHAPTER 7
IN THE CASTLE THEY TREATED ME BETTER THAN ROYALTY WITH THE CHOICEST SUITE OF APARTMENTS-
MY NEW CLOTHES WERE OF SILK AND VELVET WITH CLOTH OF GOLD.
BIG OAKEN FURNITURE WAS GRACED WITH RUDE CARVINGS.
THIS CASTLE HAS...
NO
PAPER
BOOKS
PENS
WINDOW GLASS
BELLS
SPEAKING TUBE
"GOD BLESS OUR HOME" PLAQUE
LOOKING GLASS
SOAP
MATCHES
NOBODY HAS ASKED FOR MY AUTOGRAPH.
I FEEL LIKE ROBINSON CRUSOE ON A DESERTED ISLAND. I, TOO, WILL HAVE TO INVENT, CONTRIVE, AND CREATE.

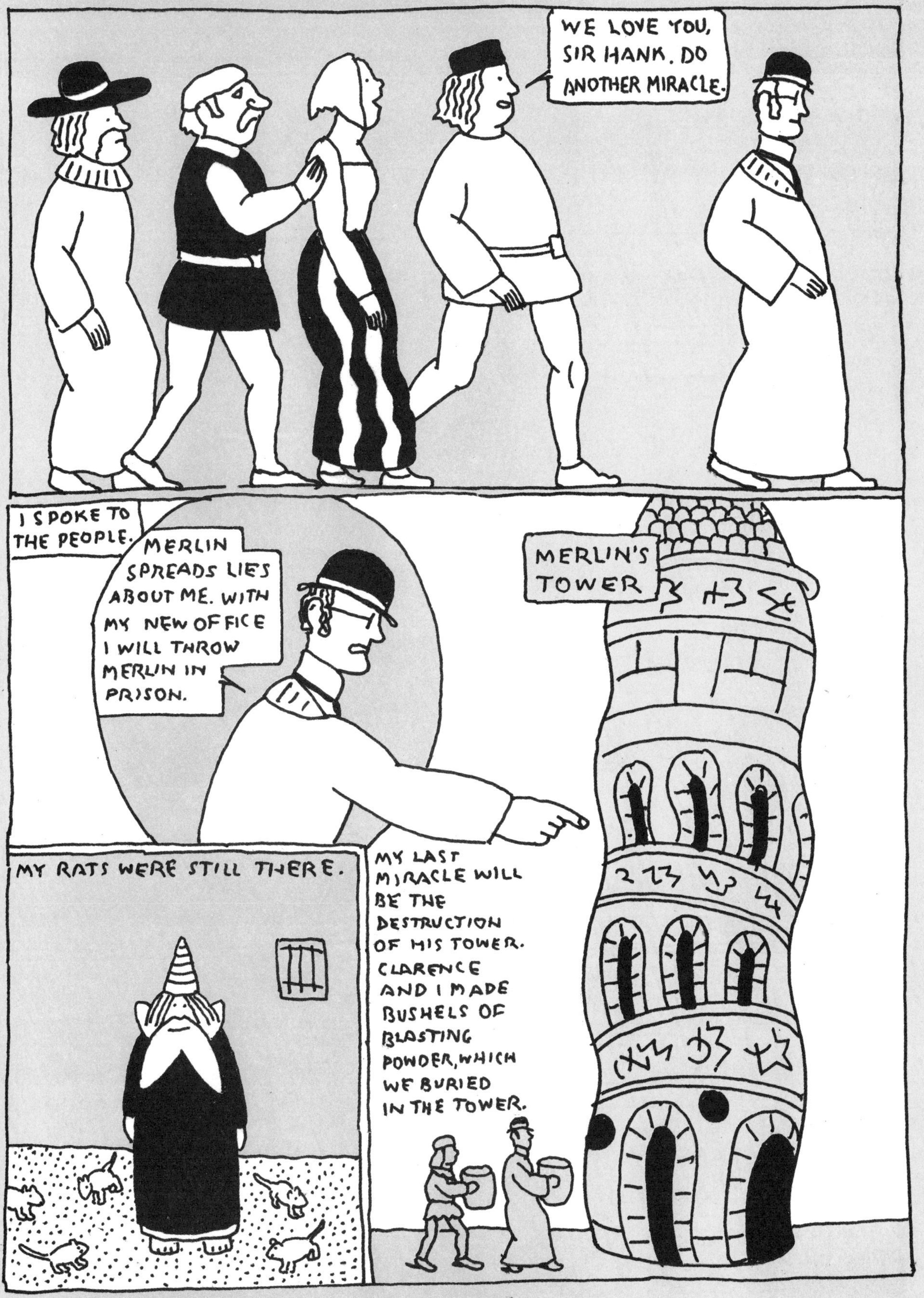
WE LOVE YOU, SIR HANK. DO ANOTHER MIRACLE.
I SPOKE TO THE PEOPLE.
MERLIN SPREADS LIES ABOUT ME. WITH MY NEW OFFICE I WILL THROW MERLIN IN PRISON.
MERLIN'S TOWER
MY RATS WERE STILL THERE.
MY LAST MIRACLE WILL BE THE DESTRUCTION OF HIS TOWER. CLARENCE AND I MADE BUSHELS OF BLASTING POWDER, WHICH WE BURIED IN THE TOWER.

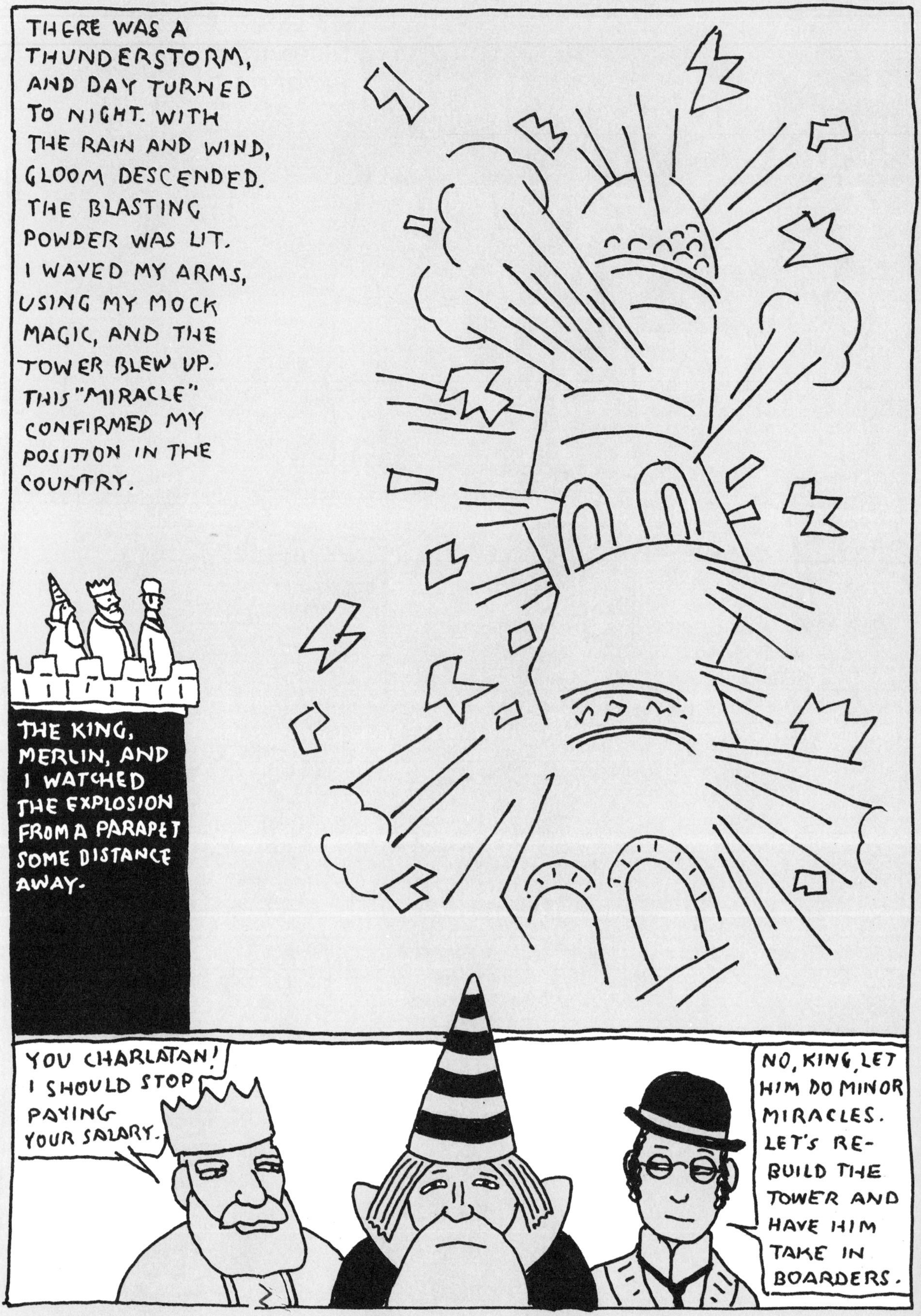
THERE WAS A THUNDERSTORM, AND DAY TURNED TO NIGHT. WITH THE RAIN AND WIND, GLOOM DESCENDED. THE BLASTING POWDER WAS LIT. I WAVED MY ARMS, USING MY MOCK MAGIC, AND THE TOWER BLEW UP. THIS "MIRACLE" CONFIRMED MY POSITION IN THE COUNTRY.
THE KING, MERLIN, AND I WATCHED THE EXPLOSION FROM A PARAPET SOME DISTANCE AWAY.
YOU CHARLATAN! I SHOULD STOP PAYING YOUR SALARY.
NO, KING, LET HIM DO MINOR MIRACLES. LET'S RE-BUILD THE TOWER AND HAVE HIM TAKE IN BOARDERS.

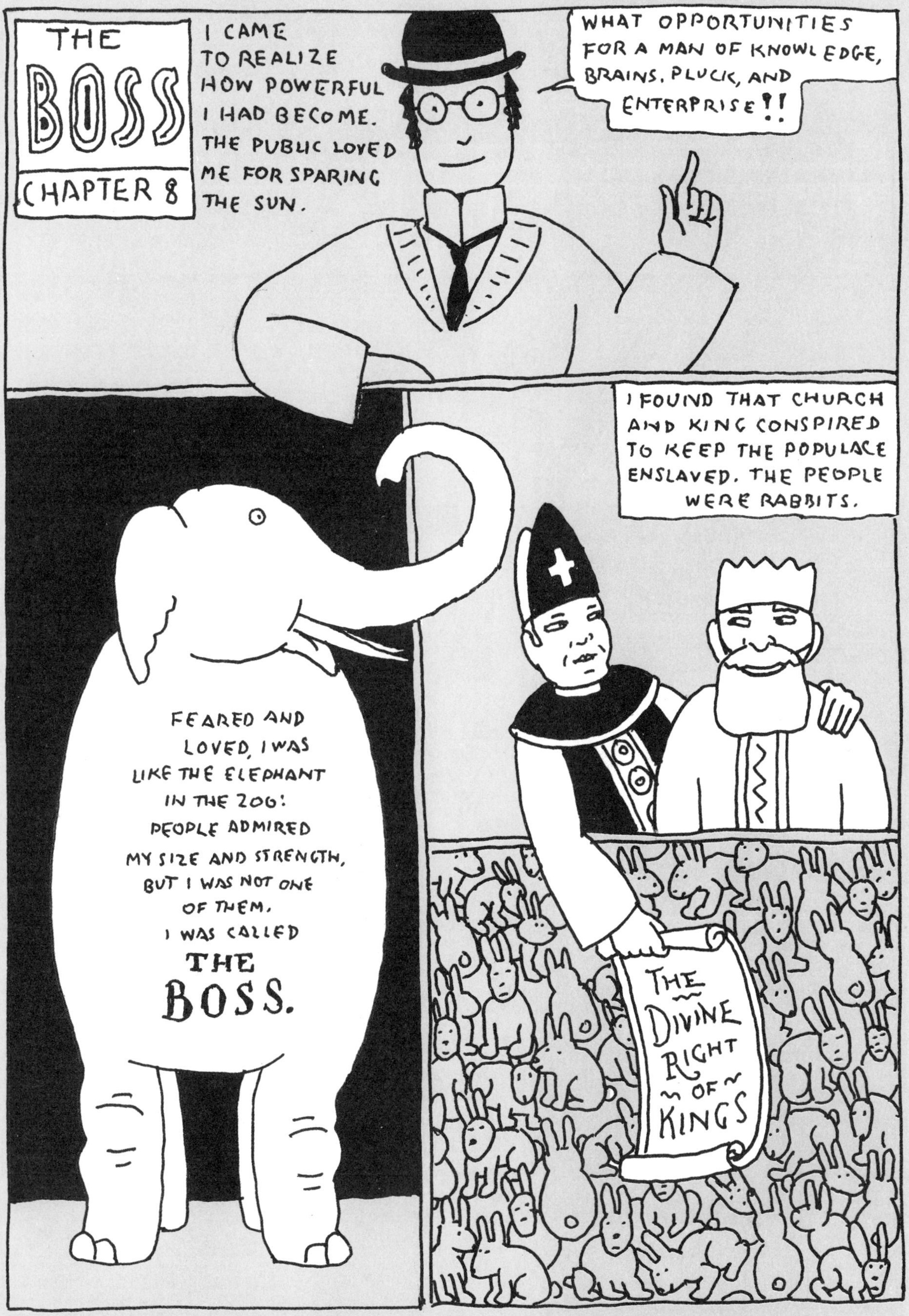
THE BOSS
CHAPTER 8
I CAME TO REALIZE HOW POWERFUL I HAD BECOME. THE PUBLIC LOVED ME FOR SPARING THE SUN.
WHAT OPPORTUNITIES FOR A MAN OF KNOWLEDGE, BRAINS, PLUCK, AND ENTERPRISE!!
FEARED AND LOVED, I WAS LIKE THE ELEPHANT IN THE ZOO: PEOPLE ADMIRED MY SIZE AND STRENGTH, BUT I WAS NOT ONE OF THEM. I WAS CALLED THE BOSS.
I FOUND THAT CHURCH AND KING CONSPIRED TO KEEP THE POPULACE ENSLAVED. THE PEOPLE WERE RABBITS.
THE DIVINE RIGHT OF KINGS

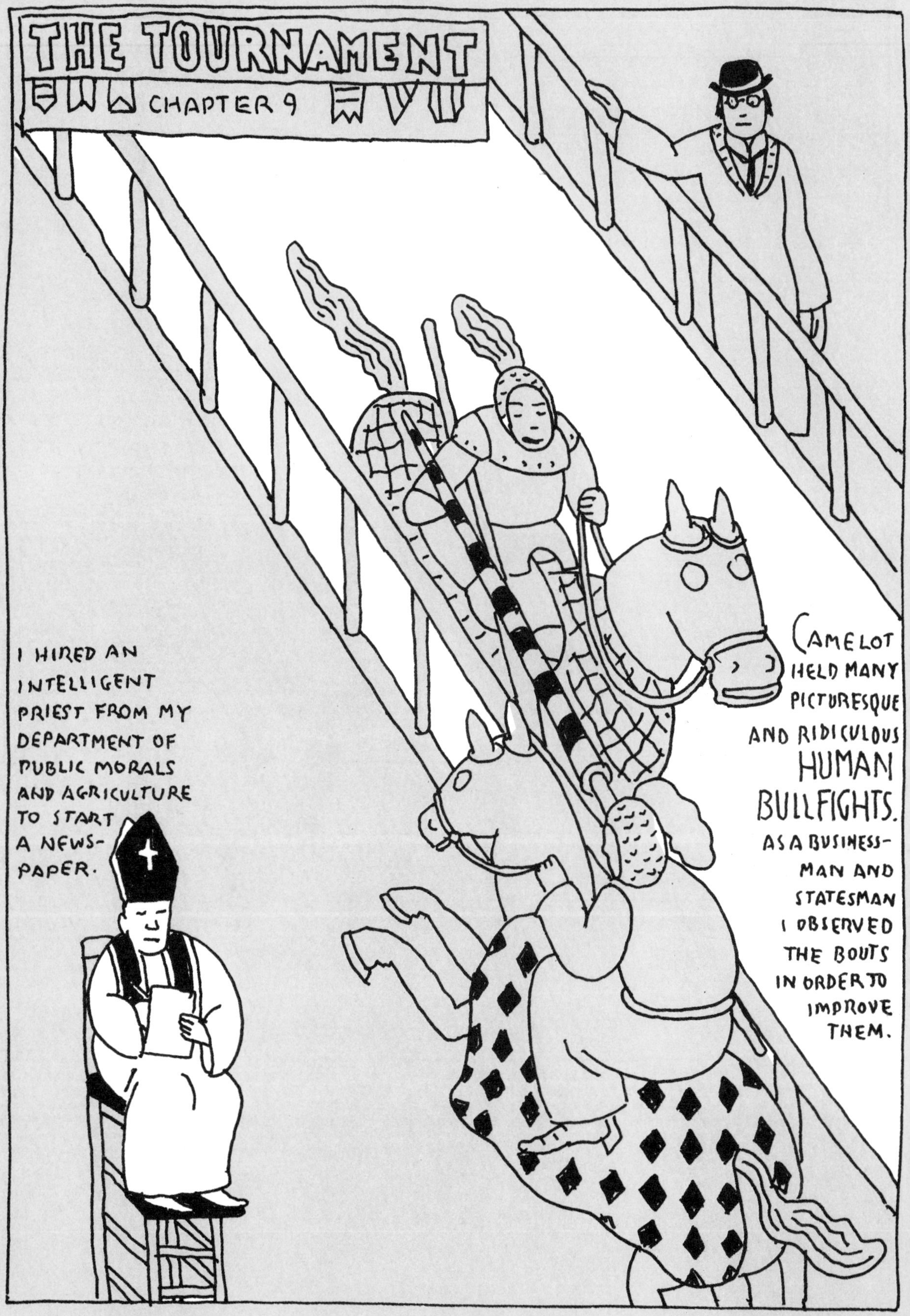
THE TOURNAMENT
CHAPTER 9
I HIRED AN INTELLIGENT PRIEST FROM MY DEPARTMENT OF PUBLIC MORALS AND AGRICULTURE TO START A NEWS-PAPER.
CAMELOT HELD MANY PICTURESQUE AND RIDICULOUS HUMAN BULLFIGHTS. AS A BUSINESS-MAN AND STATESMAN I OBSERVED THE BOUTS IN ORDER TO IMPROVE THEM.

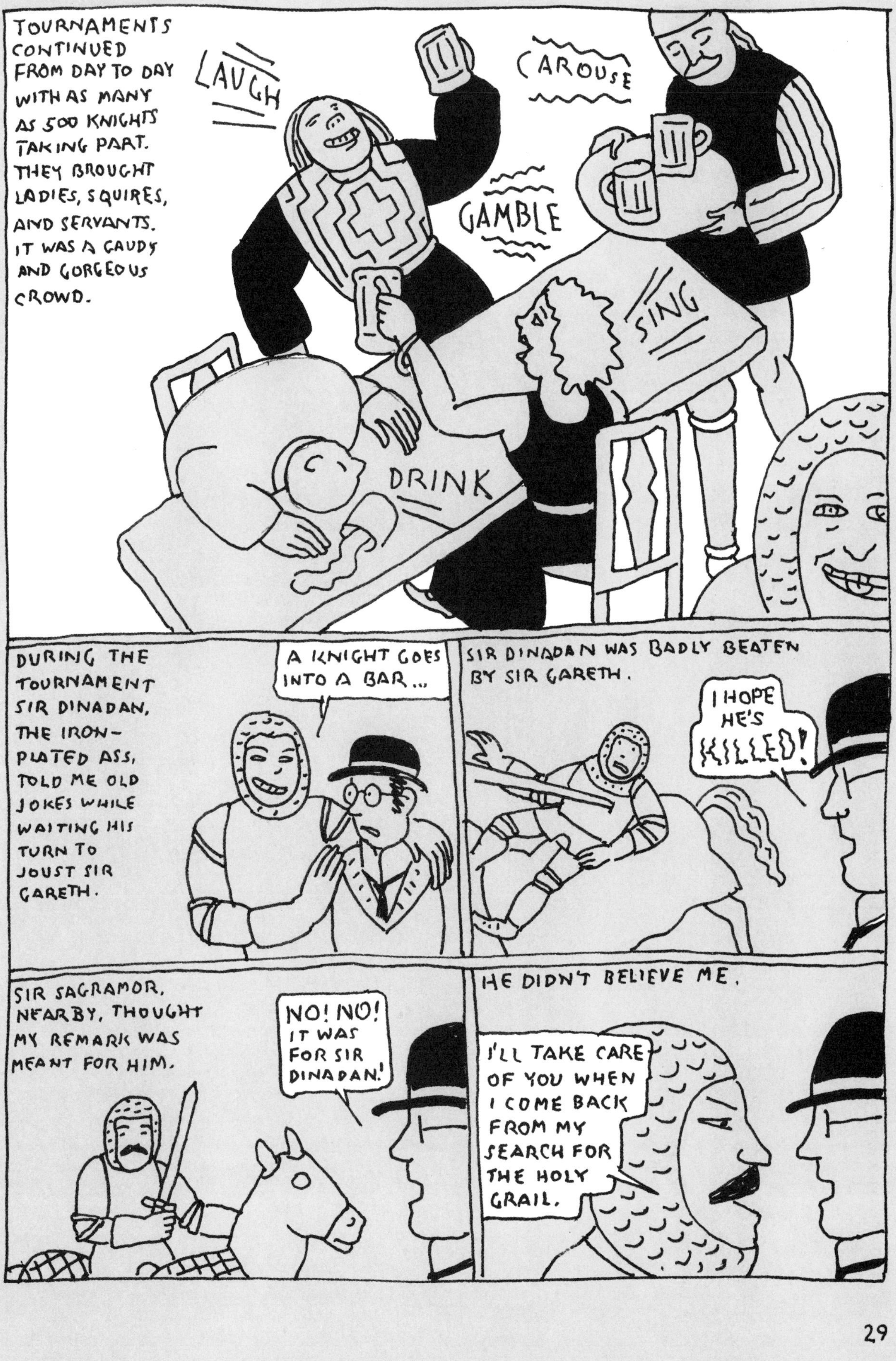
TOURNAMENTS CONTINUED FROM DAY TO DAY WITH AS MANY AS 500 KNIGHTS TAKING PART. THEY BROUGHT LADIES, SQUIRES, AND SERVANTS. IT WAS A GAUDY AND GORGEOUS CROWD.
LAUGH
CAROUSE
GAMBLE
SING
DRINK
DURING THE TOURNAMENT SIR DINADAN, THE IRON-PLATED ASS, TOLD ME OLD JOKES WHILE WAITING HIS TURN TO JOUST SIR GARETH.
A KNIGHT GOES INTO A BAR...
SIR DINADAN WAS BADLY BEATEN BY SIR GARETH.
I HOPE HE'S KILLED!
SIR SAGRAMOR, NEARBY, THOUGHT MY REMARK WAS MEANT FOR HIM.
NO! NO! IT WAS FOR SIR DINADAN!
HE DIDN'T BELIEVE ME.
I'LL TAKE CARE OF YOU WHEN I COME BACK FROM MY SEARCH FOR THE HOLY GRAIL.

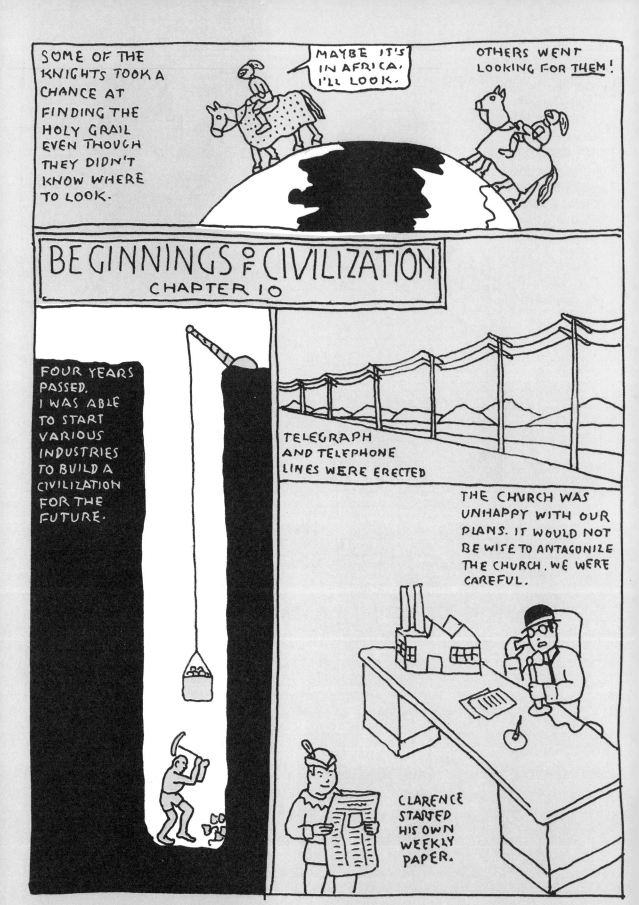

SOME OF THE KNIGHTS TOOK A CHANCE AT FINDING THE HOLY GRAIL EVEN THOUGH THEY DIDN'T KNOW WHERE TO LOOK.

MAYBE IT'S IN AFRICA, I'LL LOOK.

OTHERS WENT LOOKING FOR THEM!

BEGINNINGS OF CIVILIZATION
CHAPTER 10

FOUR YEARS PASSED. I WAS ABLE TO START VARIOUS INDUSTRIES TO BUILD A CIVILIZATION FOR THE FUTURE.

TELEGRAPH AND TELEPHONE LINES WERE ERECTED

THE CHURCH WAS UNHAPPY WITH OUR PLANS. IT WOULD NOT BE WISE TO ANTAGONIZE THE CHURCH. WE WERE CAREFUL.

CLARENCE STARTED HIS OWN WEEKLY PAPER.

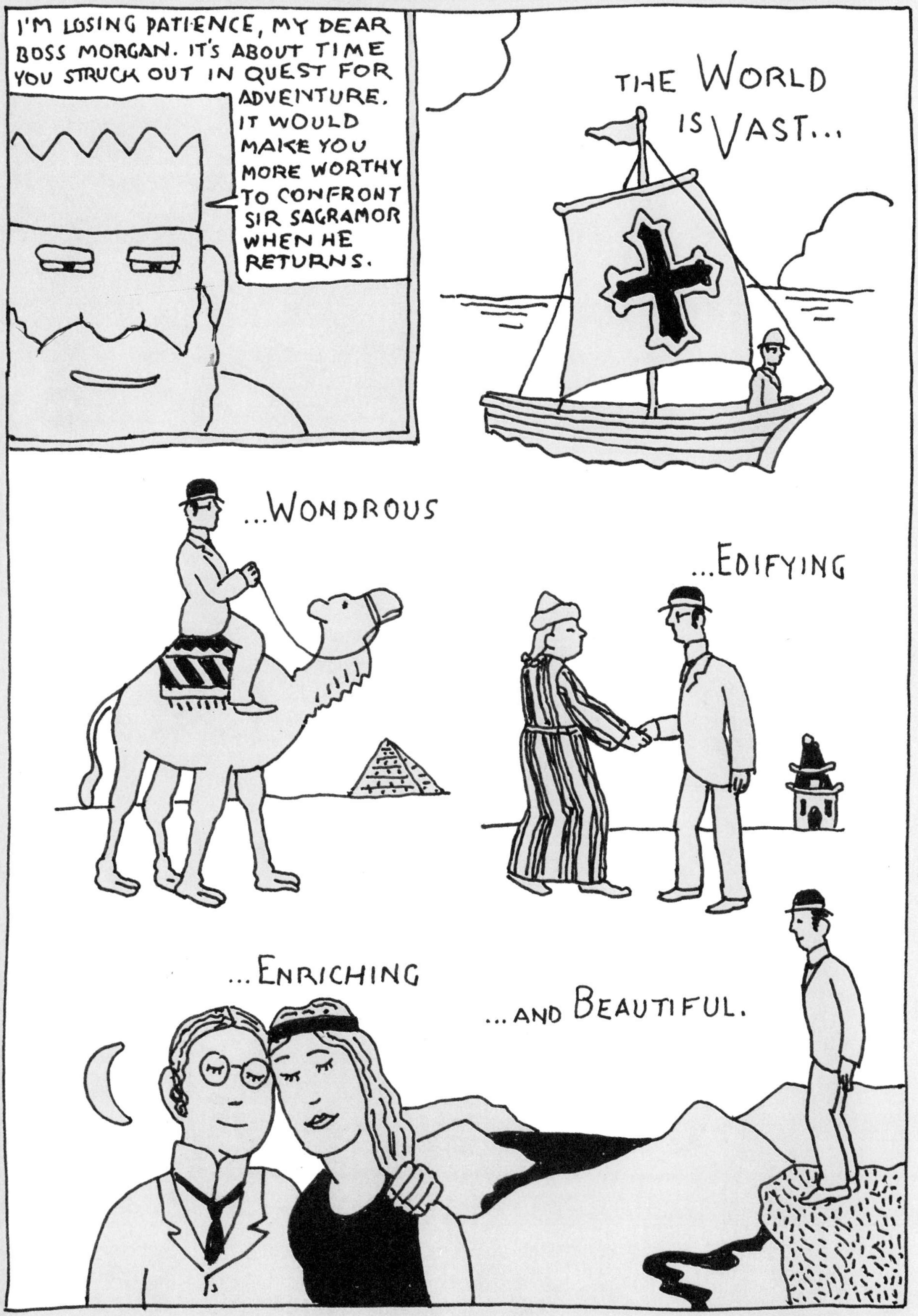
I'M LOSING PATIENCE, MY DEAR BOSS MORGAN. IT'S ABOUT TIME YOU STRUCK OUT IN QUEST FOR ADVENTURE. IT WOULD MAKE YOU MORE WORTHY TO CONFRONT SIR SAGRAMOR WHEN HE RETURNS.
THE WORLD IS VAST...
...WONDROUS
...EDIFYING
...ENRICHING
...AND BEAUTIFUL.

THE YANKEE IN SEARCH OF ADVENTURES

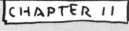
CHAPTER 11

THE KING AND KNIGHTS OF THE ROUND TABLE HEARD TALES. MOSTLY LIES, ABOUT DAMSELS BEING HELD PRISONER BY A SCOUNDREL, USUALLY A GIANT. THEY WOULD ACT ON THESE TALL TALES.

HEH! HEH!

I WAS APPOINTED THE JOB WHEN A YOUNG LADY SHOWED UP WHO CLAIMED TO BE A MISTRESS OF HER CASTLE AND WAS HELD CAPTIVE WITH 44 OTHER YOUNG AND BEAUTIFUL GIRLS FOR 26 YEARS.

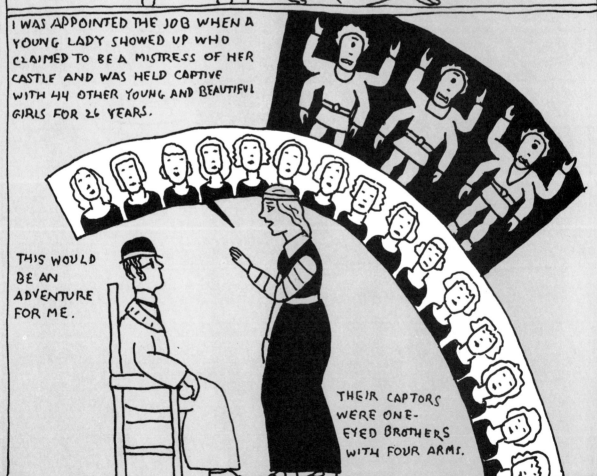

THIS WOULD BE AN ADVENTURE FOR ME.

THEIR CAPTORS WERE ONE-EYED BROTHERS WITH FOUR ARMS.

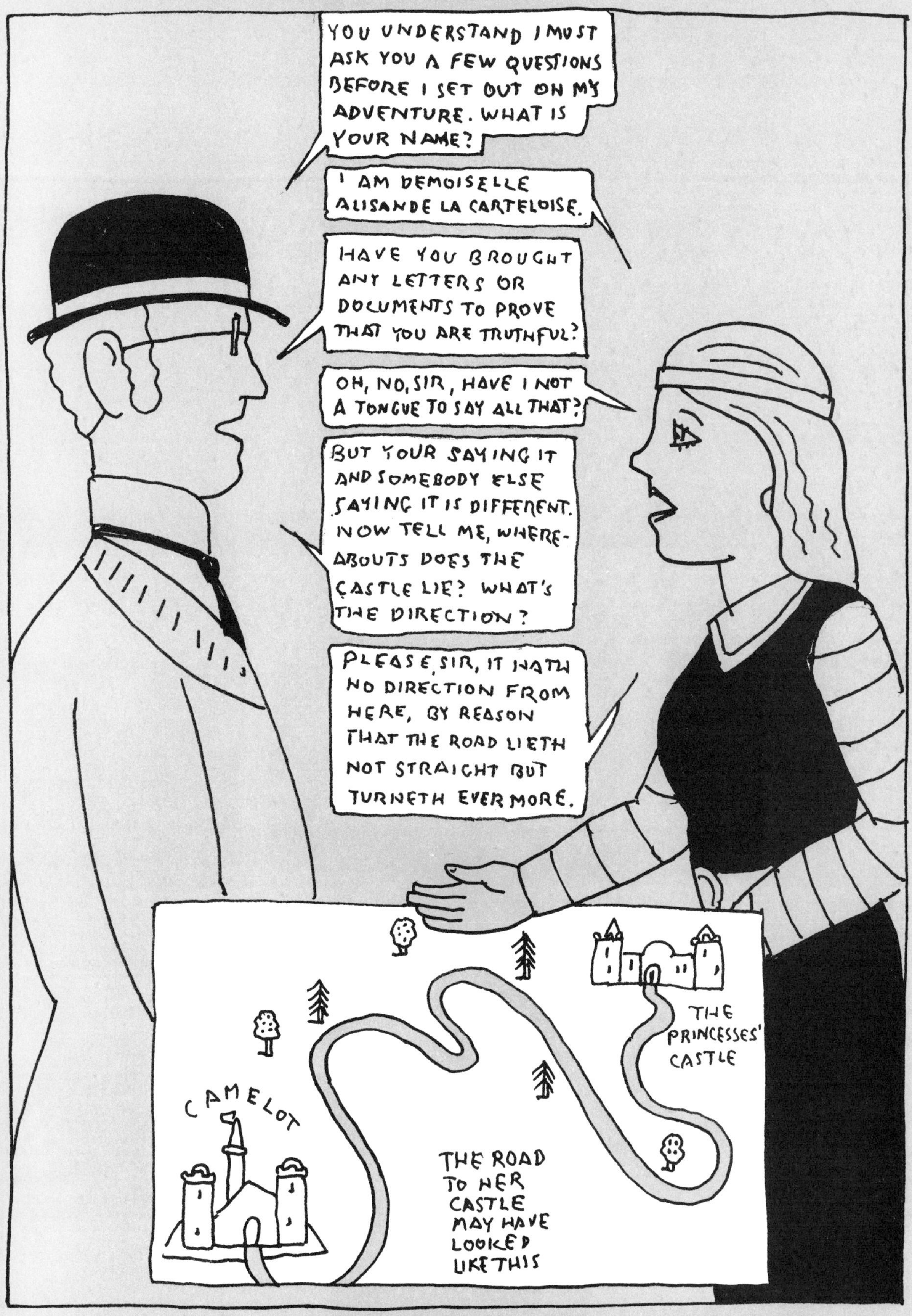
YOU UNDERSTAND I MUST ASK YOU A FEW QUESTIONS BEFORE I SET OUT ON MY ADVENTURE. WHAT IS YOUR NAME?
I AM DEMOISELLE ALISANDE LA CARTELOISE.
HAVE YOU BROUGHT ANY LETTERS OR DOCUMENTS TO PROVE THAT YOU ARE TRUTHFUL?
OH, NO, SIR, HAVE I NOT A TONGUE TO SAY ALL THAT?
BUT YOUR SAYING IT AND SOMEBODY ELSE SAYING IT IS DIFFERENT. NOW TELL ME, WHEREABOUTS DOES THE CASTLE LIE? WHAT'S THE DIRECTION?
PLEASE, SIR, IT HATH NO DIRECTION FROM HERE, BY REASON THAT THE ROAD LIETH NOT STRAIGHT BUT TURNETH EVERMORE.
CAMELOT
THE PRINCESSES' CASTLE
THE ROAD TO HER CASTLE MAY HAVE LOOKED LIKE THIS

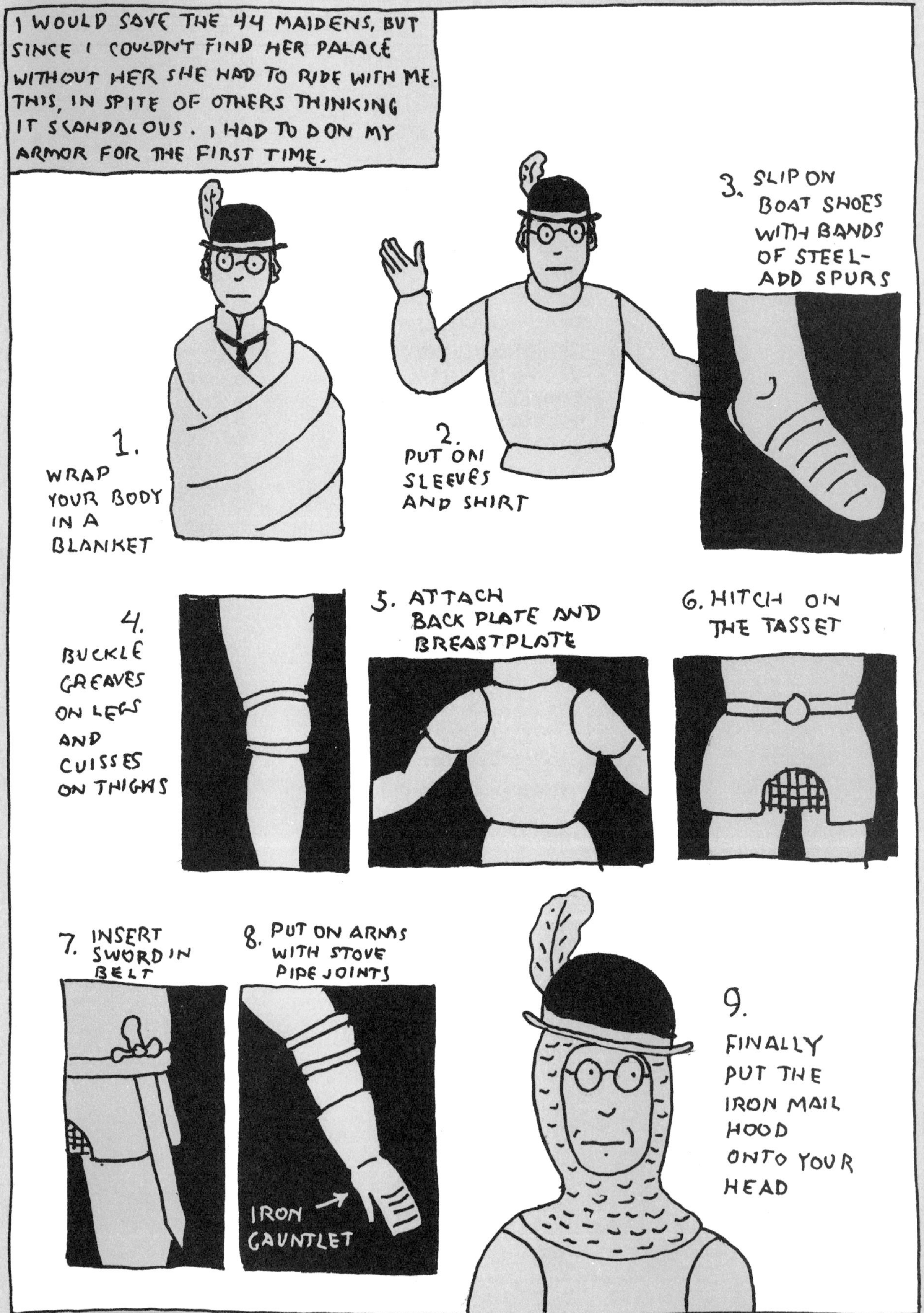
I WOULD SAVE THE 44 MAIDENS, BUT SINCE I COULDN'T FIND HER PALACE WITHOUT HER SHE HAD TO RIDE WITH ME. THIS, IN SPITE OF OTHERS THINKING IT SCANDALOUS. I HAD TO DON MY ARMOR FOR THE FIRST TIME.
1. WRAP YOUR BODY IN A BLANKET
2. PUT ON SLEEVES AND SHIRT
3. SLIP ON BOAT SHOES WITH BANDS OF STEEL- ADD SPURS
4. BUCKLE GREAVES ON LEGS AND CUISSES ON THIGHS
5. ATTACH BACK PLATE AND BREASTPLATE
6. HITCH ON THE TASSET
7. INSERT SWORD IN BELT
8. PUT ON ARMS WITH STOVE PIPE JOINTS
IRON GAUNTLET
9. FINALLY PUT THE IRON MAIL HOOD ONTO YOUR HEAD

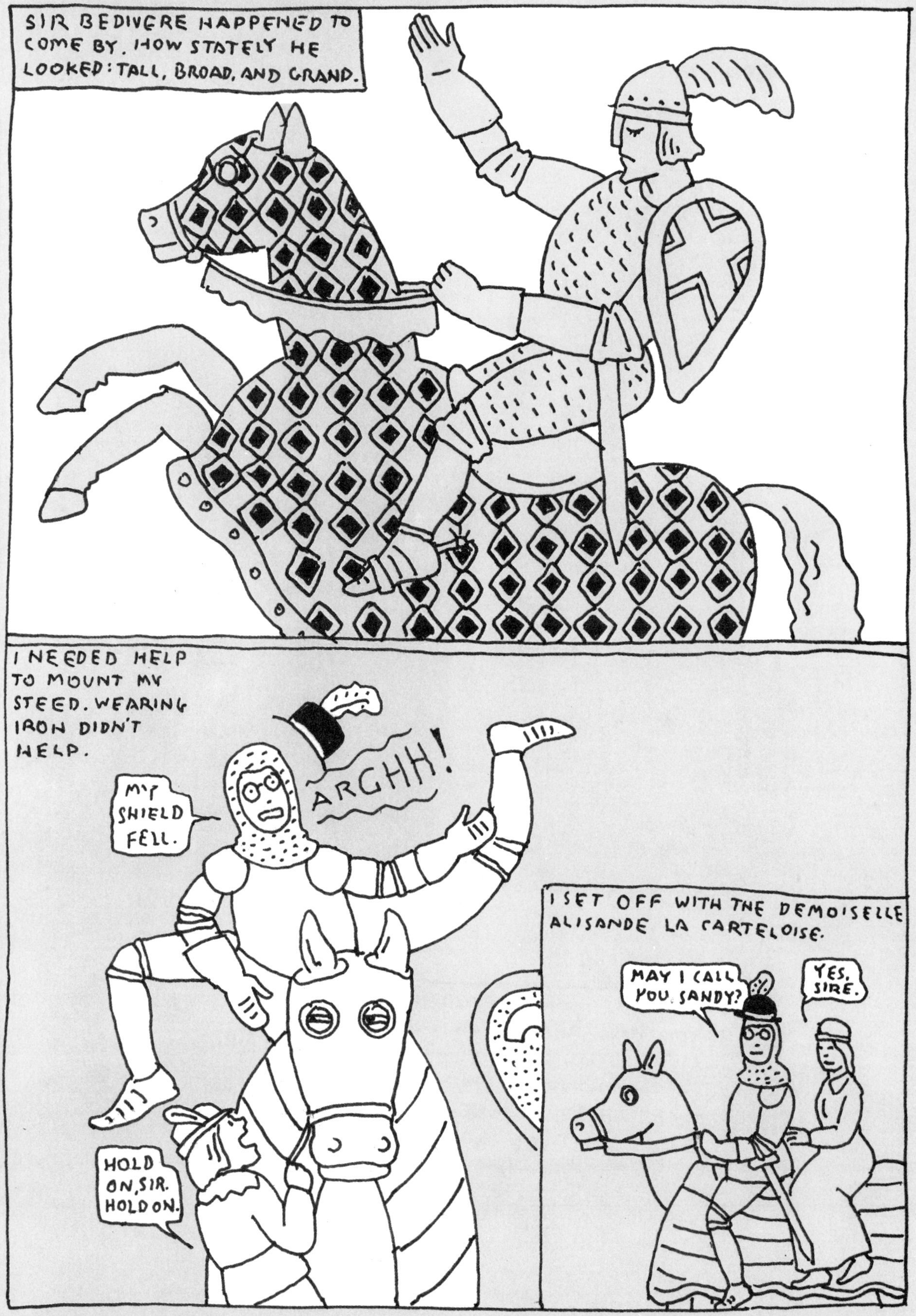
SIR BEDIVERE HAPPENED TO COME BY. HOW STATELY HE LOOKED: TALL, BROAD, AND GRAND.
I NEEDED HELP TO MOUNT MY STEED. WEARING IRON DIDN'T HELP.
MY SHIELD FELL.
ARGHH!
HOLD ON, SIR. HOLD ON.
I SET OFF WITH THE DEMOISELLE ALISANDE LA CARTELOISE.
MAY I CALL YOU SANDY?
YES, SIRE.

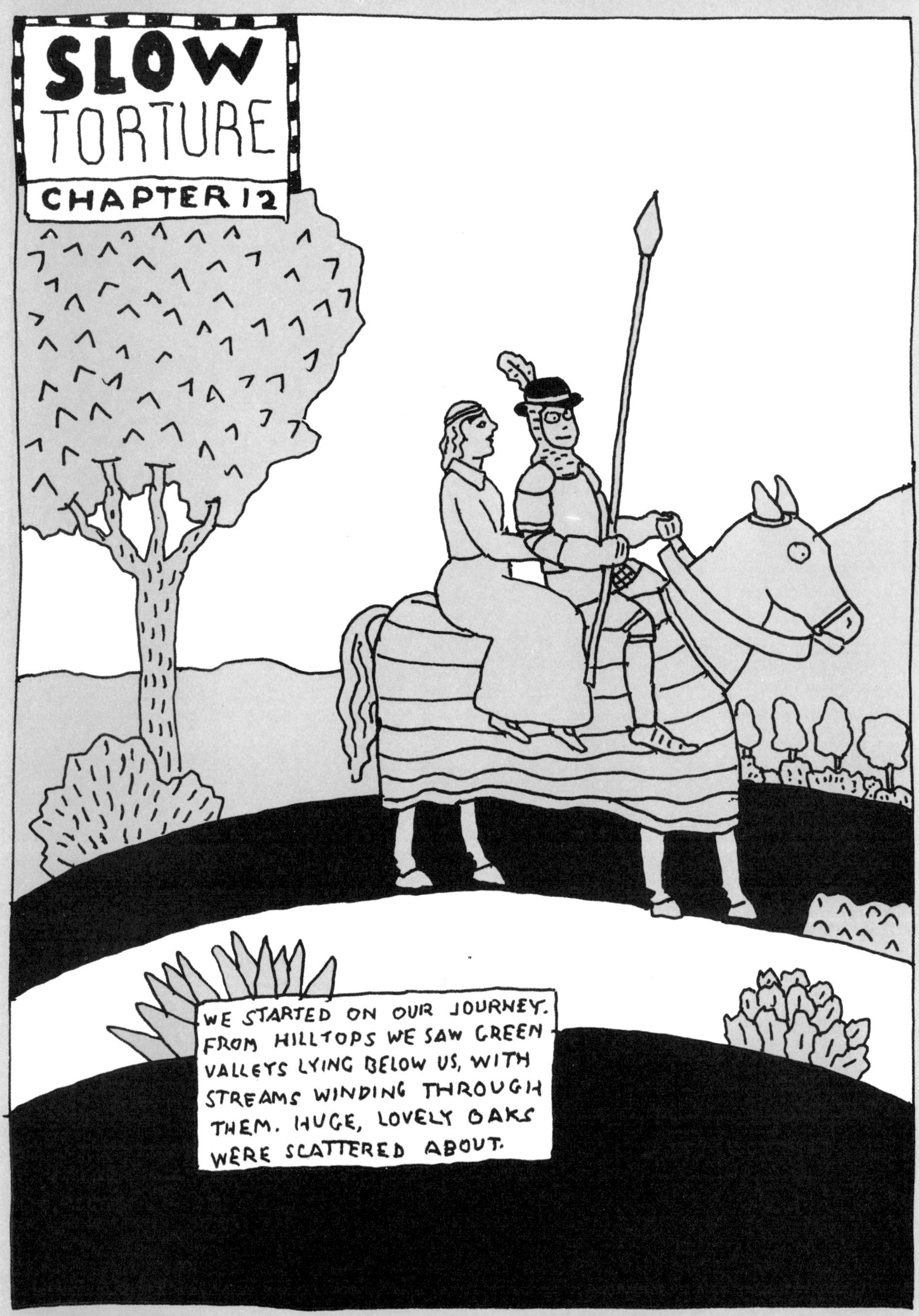
SLOW TORTURE
CHAPTER 12
WE STARTED ON OUR JOURNEY. FROM HILLTOPS WE SAW GREEN VALLEYS LYING BELOW US, WITH STREAMS WINDING THROUGH THEM. HUGE, LOVELY OAKS WERE SCATTERED ABOUT.

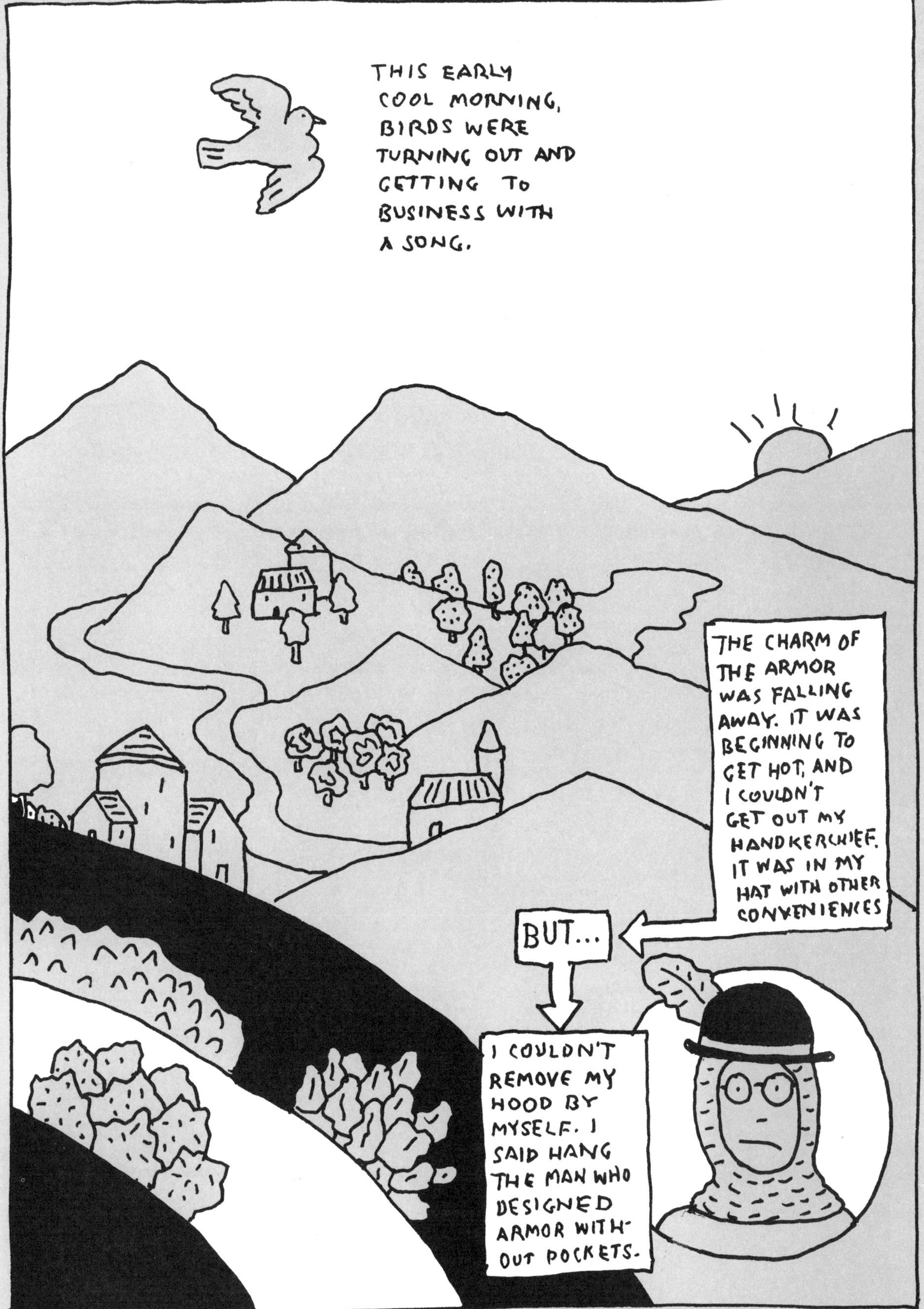
THIS EARLY COOL MORNING, BIRDS WERE TURNING OUT AND GETTING TO BUSINESS WITH A SONG.
THE CHARM OF THE ARMOR WAS FALLING AWAY. IT WAS BEGINNING TO GET HOT, AND I COULDN'T GET OUT MY HANDKERCHIEF. IT WAS IN MY HAT WITH OTHER CONVENIENCES
BUT...
I COULDN'T REMOVE MY HOOD BY MYSELF. I SAID HANG THE MAN WHO DESIGNED ARMOR WITH-OUT POCKETS.

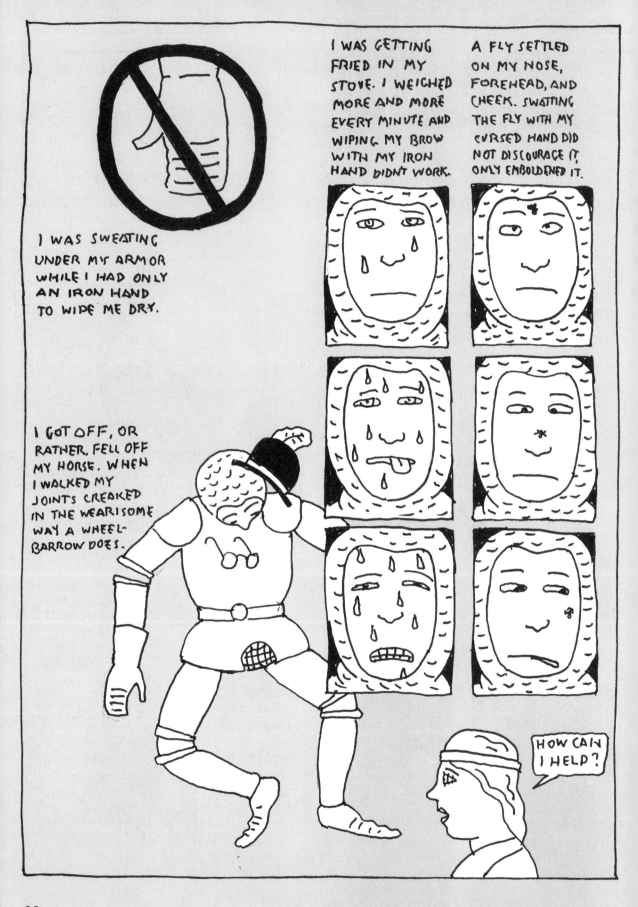

I WAS SWEATING UNDER MY ARMOR WHILE I HAD ONLY AN IRON HAND TO WIPE ME DRY.

I GOT OFF, OR RATHER, FELL OFF MY HORSE. WHEN I WALKED MY JOINTS CREAKED IN THE WEARISOME WAY A WHEELBARROW DOES.

I WAS GETTING FRIED IN MY STOVE. I WEIGHED MORE AND MORE EVERY MINUTE AND WIPING MY BROW WITH MY IRON HAND DIDN'T WORK.

A FLY SETTLED ON MY NOSE, FOREHEAD, AND CHEEK. SWATTING THE FLY WITH MY CURSED HAND DID NOT DISCOURAGE IT, ONLY EMBOLDENED IT.

HOW CAN I HELP?

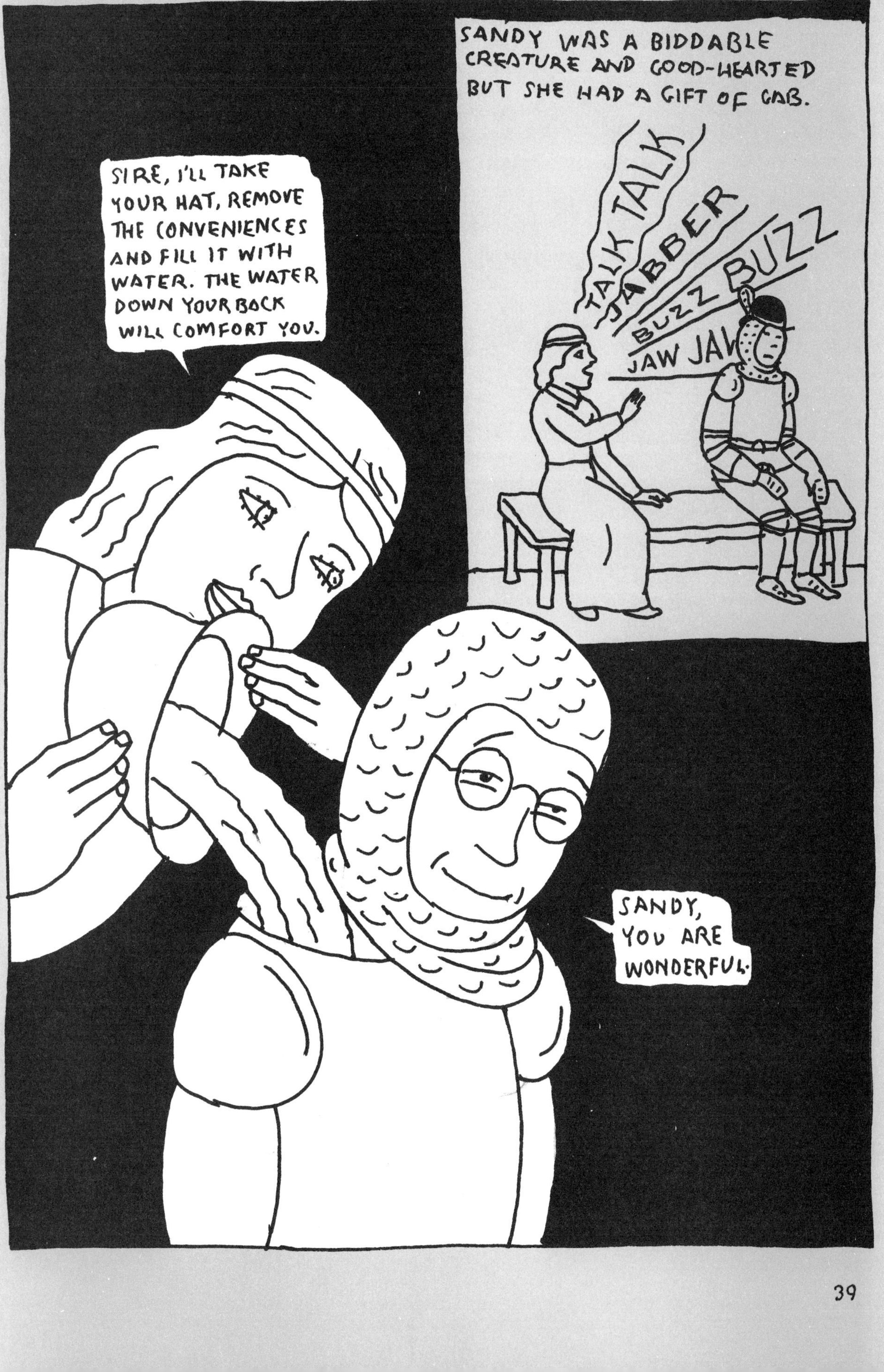
SANDY WAS A BIDDABLE CREATURE AND GOOD-HEARTED BUT SHE HAD A GIFT OF GAB.
TALK TALK
JABBER
BUZZ BUZZ
JAW JAW
SIRE, I'LL TAKE YOUR HAT, REMOVE THE CONVENIENCES AND FILL IT WITH WATER. THE WATER DOWN YOUR BACK WILL COMFORT YOU.
SANDY, YOU ARE WONDERFUL.

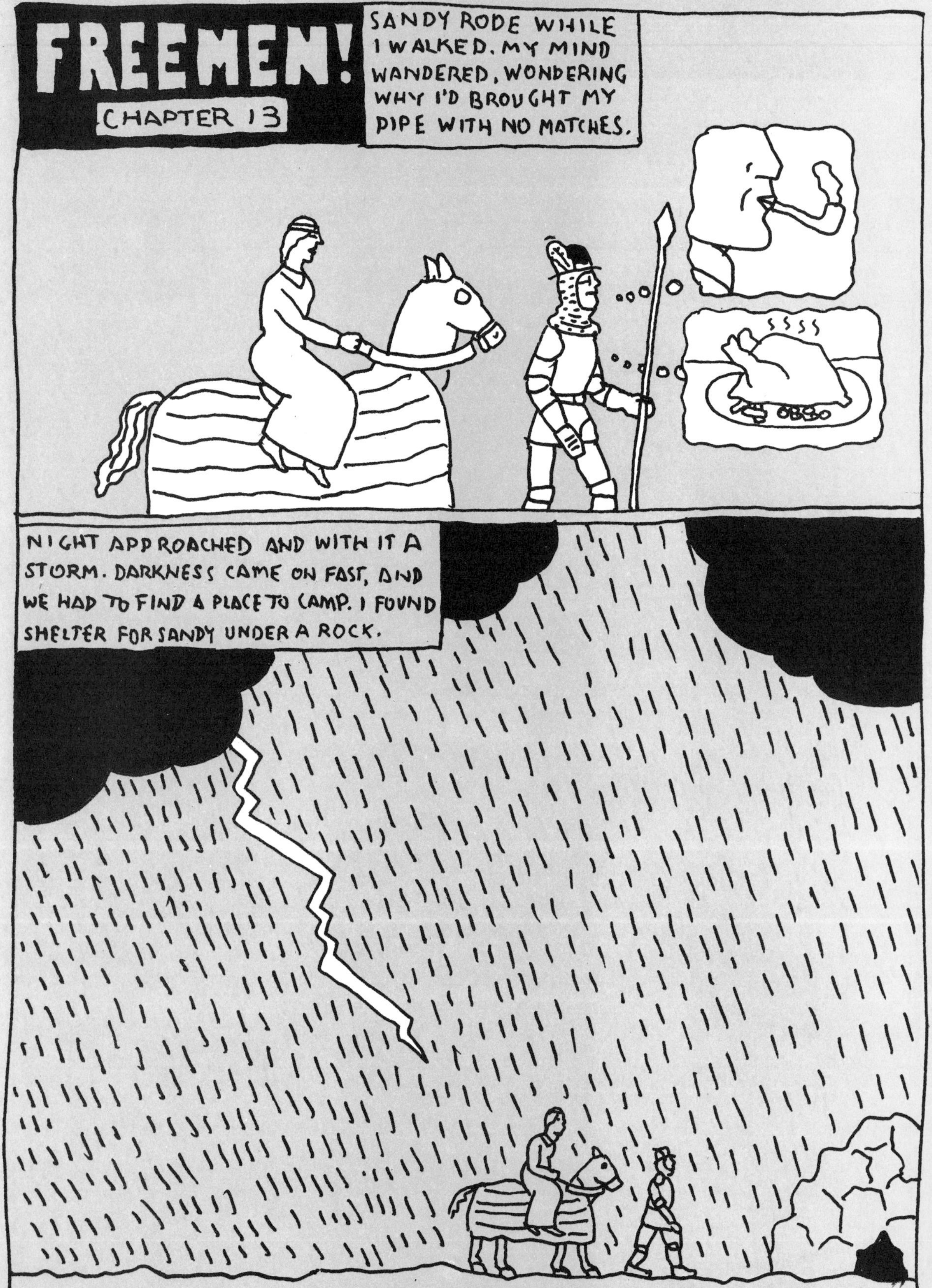
FREEMEN!
CHAPTER 13
SANDY RODE WHILE I WALKED. MY MIND WANDERED, WONDERING WHY I'D BROUGHT MY PIPE WITH NO MATCHES.
NIGHT APPROACHED AND WITH IT A STORM. DARKNESS CAME ON FAST, AND WE HAD TO FIND A PLACE TO CAMP. I FOUND SHELTER FOR SANDY UNDER A ROCK.

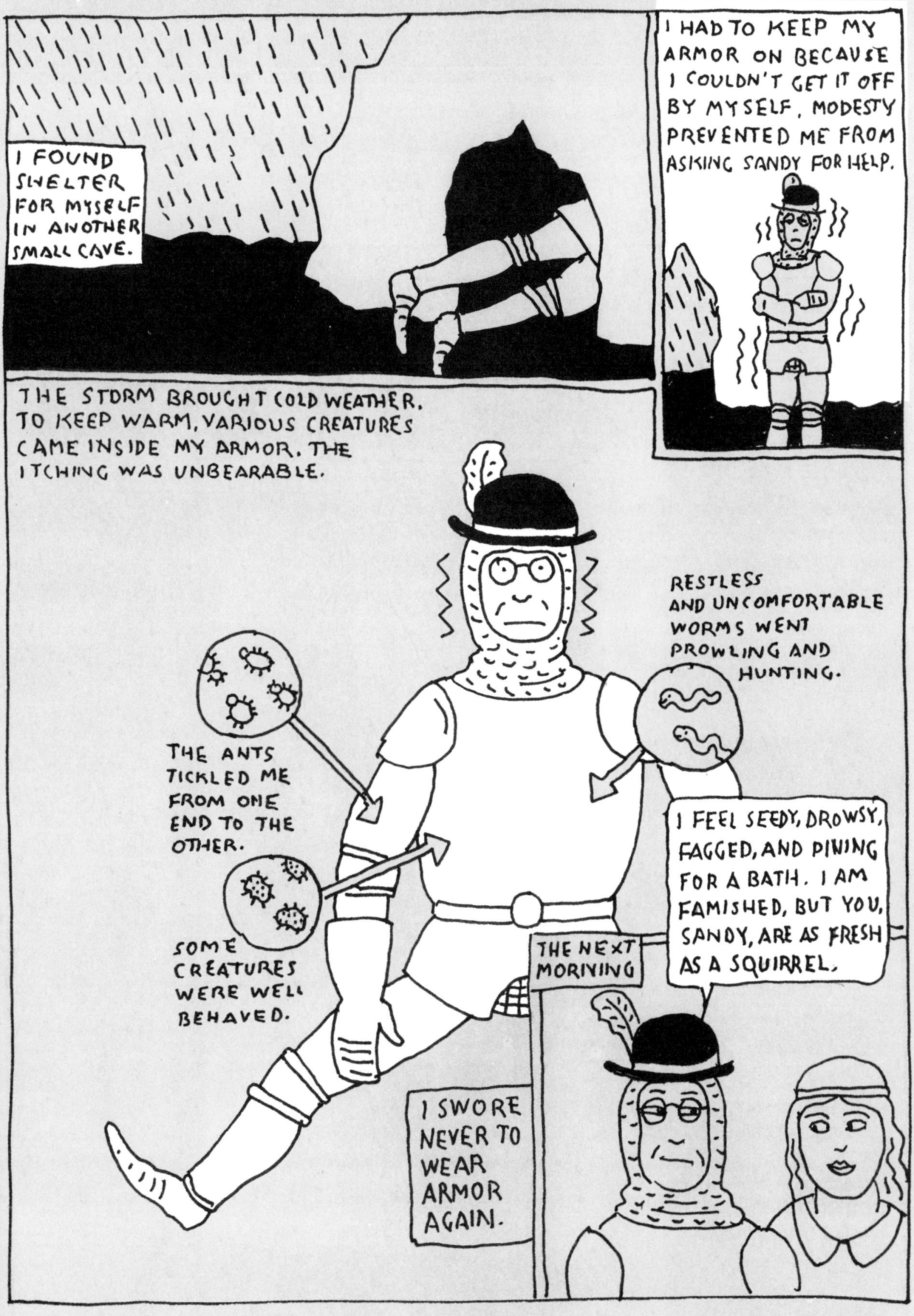
I FOUND SHELTER FOR MYSELF IN ANOTHER SMALL CAVE.
I HAD TO KEEP MY ARMOR ON BECAUSE I COULDN'T GET IT OFF BY MYSELF. MODESTY PREVENTED ME FROM ASKING SANDY FOR HELP.
THE STORM BROUGHT COLD WEATHER. TO KEEP WARM, VARIOUS CREATURES CAME INSIDE MY ARMOR. THE ITCHING WAS UNBEARABLE.
RESTLESS AND UNCOMFORTABLE WORMS WENT PROWLING AND HUNTING.
THE ANTS TICKLED ME FROM ONE END TO THE OTHER.
SOME CREATURES WERE WELL BEHAVED.
THE NEXT MORNING
I FEEL SEEDY, DROWSY, FAGGED, AND PINING FOR A BATH. I AM FAMISHED, BUT YOU, SANDY, ARE AS FRESH AS A SQUIRREL.
I SWORE NEVER TO WEAR ARMOR AGAIN.

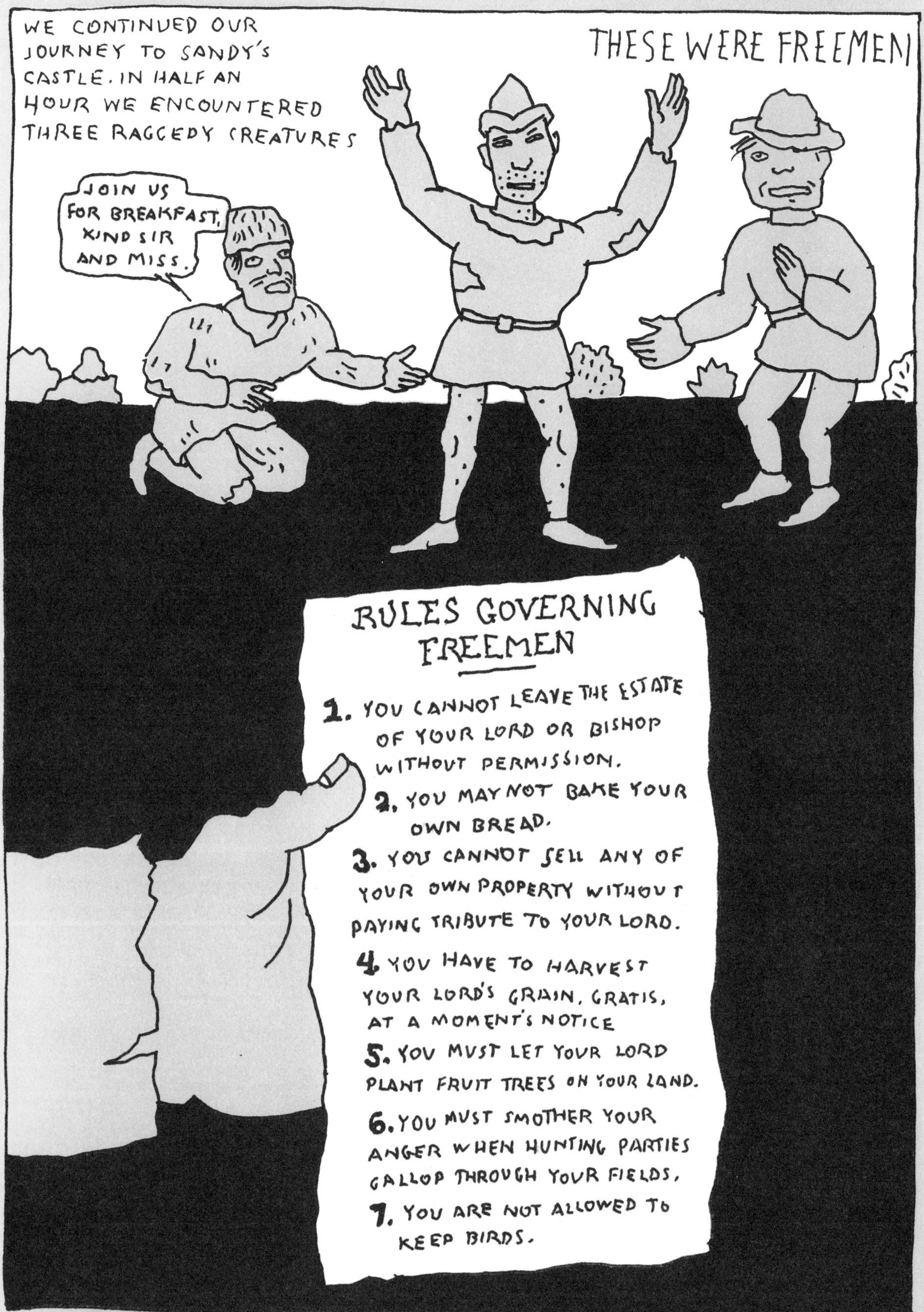

WE CONTINUED OUR JOURNEY TO SANDY'S CASTLE. IN HALF AN HOUR WE ENCOUNTERED THREE RAGGEDY CREATURES
THESE WERE FREEMEN
JOIN US FOR BREAKFAST, KIND SIR AND MISS.
RULES GOVERNING FREEMEN
1. YOU CANNOT LEAVE THE ESTATE OF YOUR LORD OR BISHOP WITHOUT PERMISSION.
2. YOU MAY NOT BAKE YOUR OWN BREAD.
3. YOU CANNOT SELL ANY OF YOUR OWN PROPERTY WITHOUT PAYING TRIBUTE TO YOUR LORD.
4. YOU HAVE TO HARVEST YOUR LORD'S GRAIN, GRATIS, AT A MOMENT'S NOTICE
5. YOU MUST LET YOUR LORD PLANT FRUIT TREES ON YOUR LAND.
6. YOU MUST SMOTHER YOUR ANGER WHEN HUNTING PARTIES GALLOP THROUGH YOUR FIELDS.
7. YOU ARE NOT ALLOWED TO KEEP BIRDS.

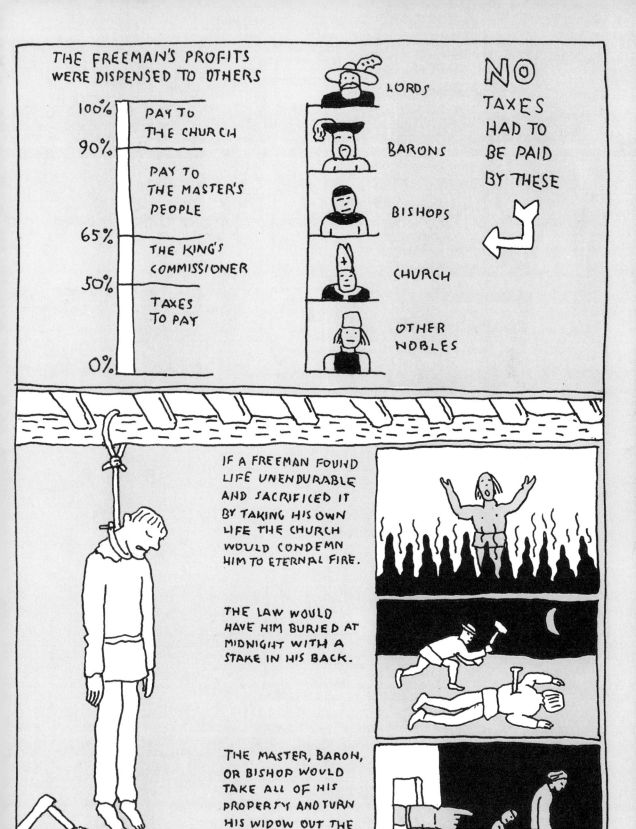

THE FREEMAN'S PROFITS WERE DISPENSED TO OTHERS

100%	PAY TO THE CHURCH
90%	
	PAY TO THE MASTER'S PEOPLE
65%	
	THE KING'S COMMISSIONER
50%	
	TAXES TO PAY
0%	

LORDS
BARONS
BISHOPS
CHURCH
OTHER NOBLES

NO TAXES HAD TO BE PAID BY THESE

IF A FREEMAN FOUND LIFE UNENDURABLE AND SACRIFICED IT BY TAKING HIS OWN LIFE THE CHURCH WOULD CONDEMN HIM TO ETERNAL FIRE.

THE LAW WOULD HAVE HIM BURIED AT MIDNIGHT WITH A STAKE IN HIS BACK.

THE MASTER, BARON, OR BISHOP WOULD TAKE ALL OF HIS PROPERTY AND TURN HIS WIDOW OUT THE DOOR.

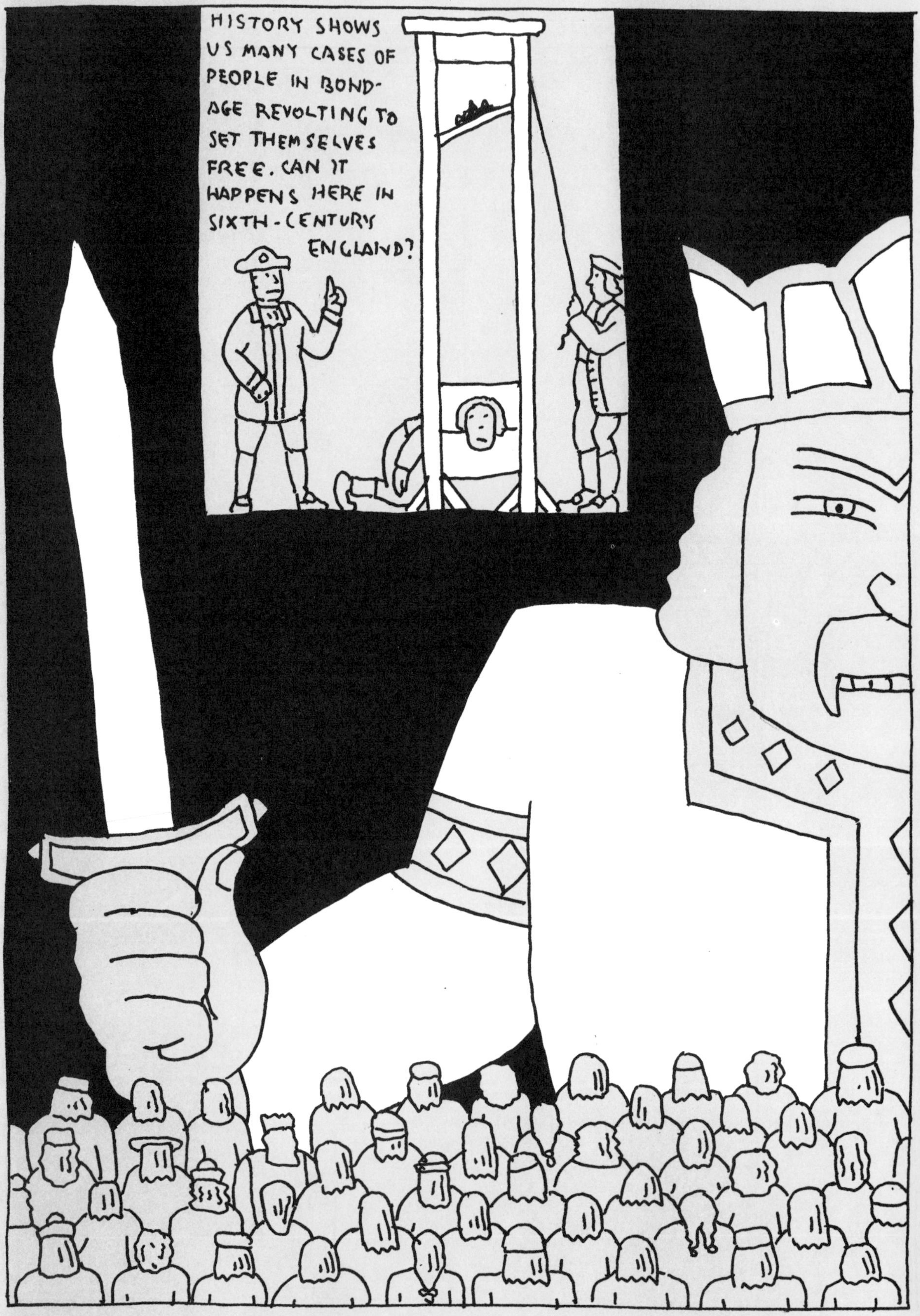
HISTORY SHOWS US MANY CASES OF PEOPLE IN BONDAGE REVOLTING TO SET THEMSELVES FREE. CAN IT HAPPENS HERE IN SIXTH-CENTURY ENGLAND?

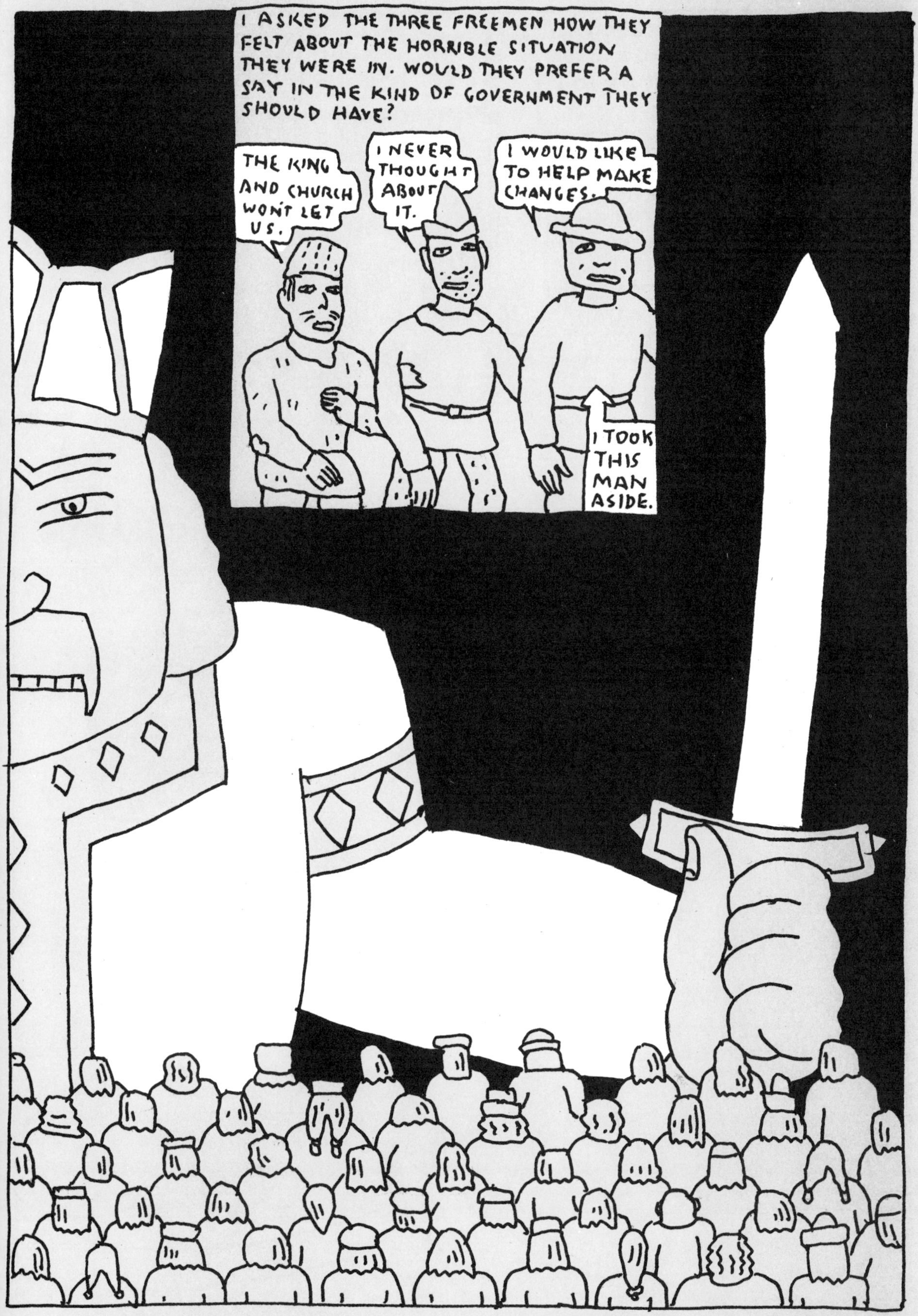
I ASKED THE THREE FREEMEN HOW THEY FELT ABOUT THE HORRIBLE SITUATION THEY WERE IN. WOULD THEY PREFER A SAY IN THE KIND OF GOVERNMENT THEY SHOULD HAVE?
THE KING AND CHURCH WON'T LET US.
I NEVER THOUGHT ABOUT IT.
I WOULD LIKE TO HELP MAKE CHANGES.
I TOOK THIS MAN ASIDE.

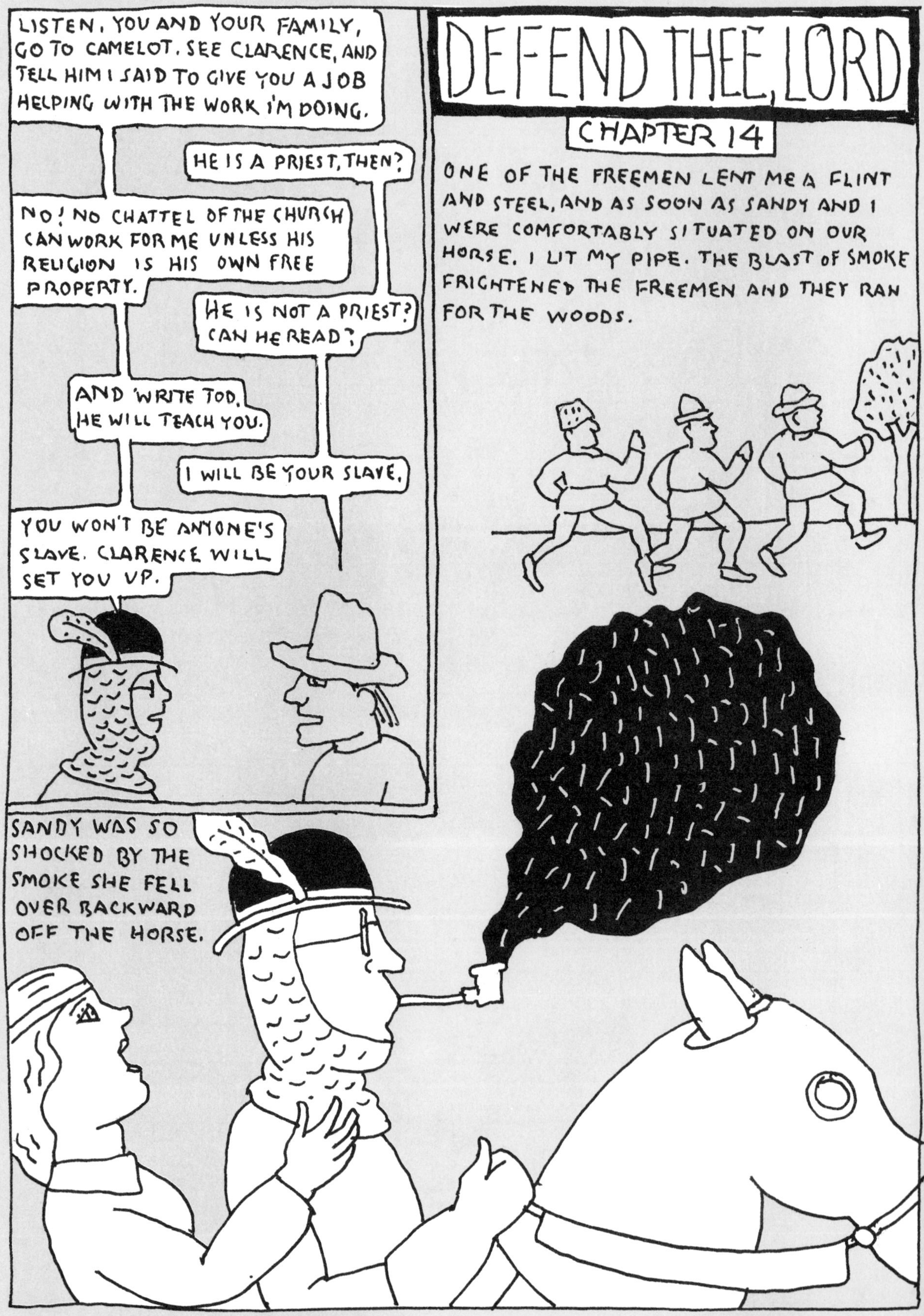
LISTEN. YOU AND YOUR FAMILY, GO TO CAMELOT. SEE CLARENCE, AND TELL HIM I SAID TO GIVE YOU A JOB HELPING WITH THE WORK I'M DOING.
HE IS A PRIEST, THEN?
NO! NO CHATTEL OF THE CHURCH CAN WORK FOR ME UNLESS HIS RELIGION IS HIS OWN FREE PROPERTY.
HE IS NOT A PRIEST? CAN HE READ?
AND WRITE TOO. HE WILL TEACH YOU.
I WILL BE YOUR SLAVE.
YOU WON'T BE ANYONE'S SLAVE. CLARENCE WILL SET YOU UP.
DEFEND THEE, LORD
CHAPTER 14
ONE OF THE FREEMEN LENT ME A FLINT AND STEEL, AND AS SOON AS SANDY AND I WERE COMFORTABLY SITUATED ON OUR HORSE, I LIT MY PIPE. THE BLAST OF SMOKE FRIGHTENED THE FREEMEN AND THEY RAN FOR THE WOODS.
SANDY WAS SO SHOCKED BY THE SMOKE SHE FELL OVER BACKWARD OFF THE HORSE.

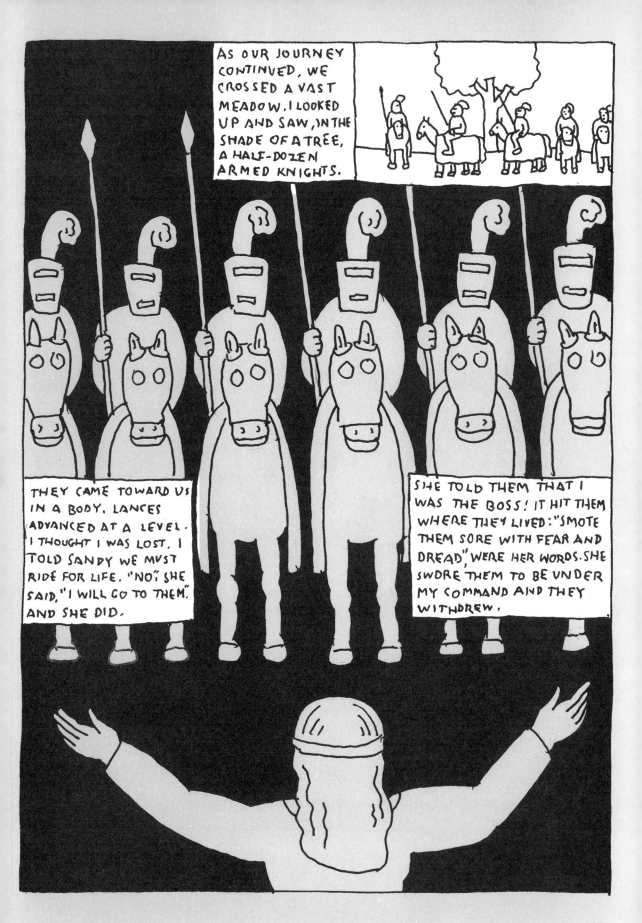

AS OUR JOURNEY CONTINUED, WE CROSSED A VAST MEADOW. I LOOKED UP AND SAW, IN THE SHADE OF A TREE, A HALF-DOZEN ARMED KNIGHTS.

THEY CAME TOWARD US IN A BODY, LANCES ADVANCED AT A LEVEL. I THOUGHT I WAS LOST. I TOLD SANDY WE MUST RIDE FOR LIFE. "NO," SHE SAID, "I WILL GO TO THEM." AND SHE DID.

SHE TOLD THEM THAT I WAS THE BOSS! IT HIT THEM WHERE THEY LIVED: "SMOTE THEM SORE WITH FEAR AND DREAD," WERE HER WORDS. SHE SWORE THEM TO BE UNDER MY COMMAND AND THEY WITHDREW.

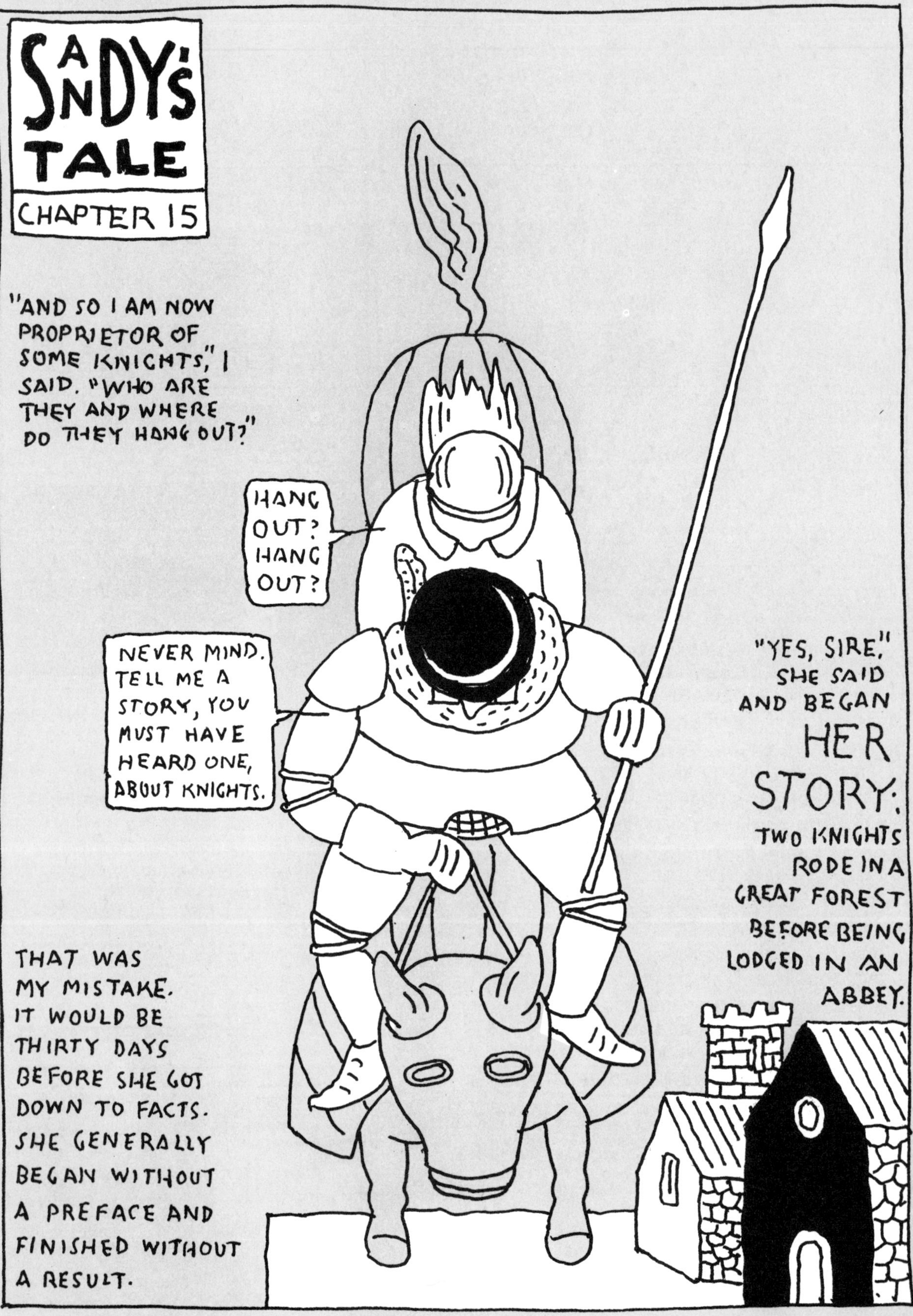
SANDY'S TALE
CHAPTER 15
"AND SO I AM NOW PROPRIETOR OF SOME KNIGHTS," I SAID. "WHO ARE THEY AND WHERE DO THEY HANG OUT?"
HANG OUT? HANG OUT?
NEVER MIND. TELL ME A STORY, YOU MUST HAVE HEARD ONE, ABOUT KNIGHTS.
"YES, SIRE," SHE SAID AND BEGAN HER STORY:
TWO KNIGHTS RODE IN A GREAT FOREST BEFORE BEING LODGED IN AN ABBEY.
THAT WAS MY MISTAKE. IT WOULD BE THIRTY DAYS BEFORE SHE GOT DOWN TO FACTS. SHE GENERALLY BEGAN WITHOUT A PREFACE AND FINISHED WITHOUT A RESULT.

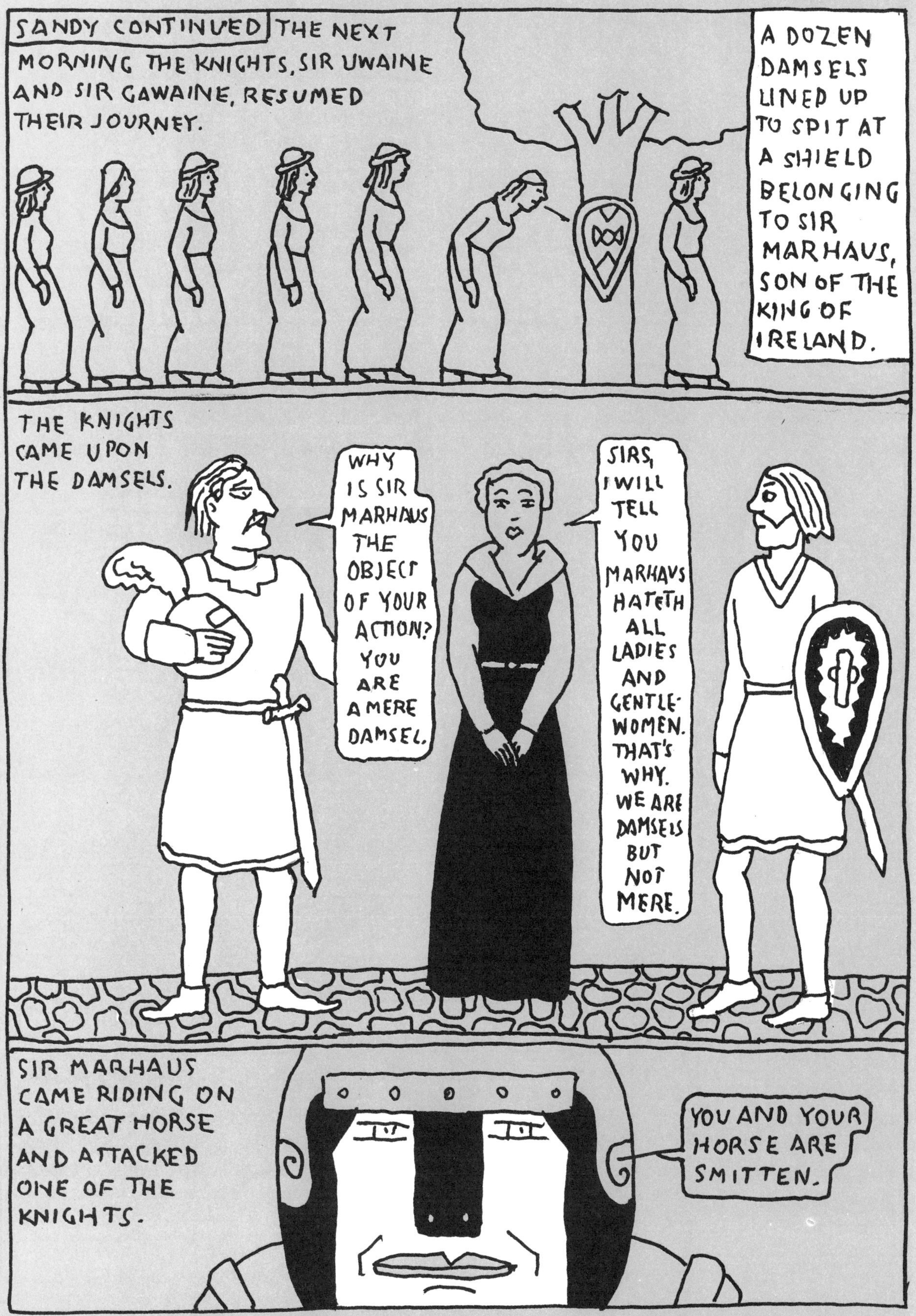
SANDY CONTINUED
THE NEXT MORNING THE KNIGHTS, SIR UWAINE AND SIR GAWAINE, RESUMED THEIR JOURNEY.
A DOZEN DAMSELS LINED UP TO SPIT AT A SHIELD BELONGING TO SIR MARHAUS, SON OF THE KING OF IRELAND.
THE KNIGHTS CAME UPON THE DAMSELS.
WHY IS SIR MARHAUS THE OBJECT OF YOUR ACTION? YOU ARE A MERE DAMSEL.
SIRS, I WILL TELL YOU MARHAUS HATETH ALL LADIES AND GENTLE-WOMEN. THAT'S WHY. WE ARE DAMSELS BUT NOT MERE.
SIR MARHAUS CAME RIDING ON A GREAT HORSE AND ATTACKED ONE OF THE KNIGHTS.
YOU AND YOUR HORSE ARE SMITTEN.

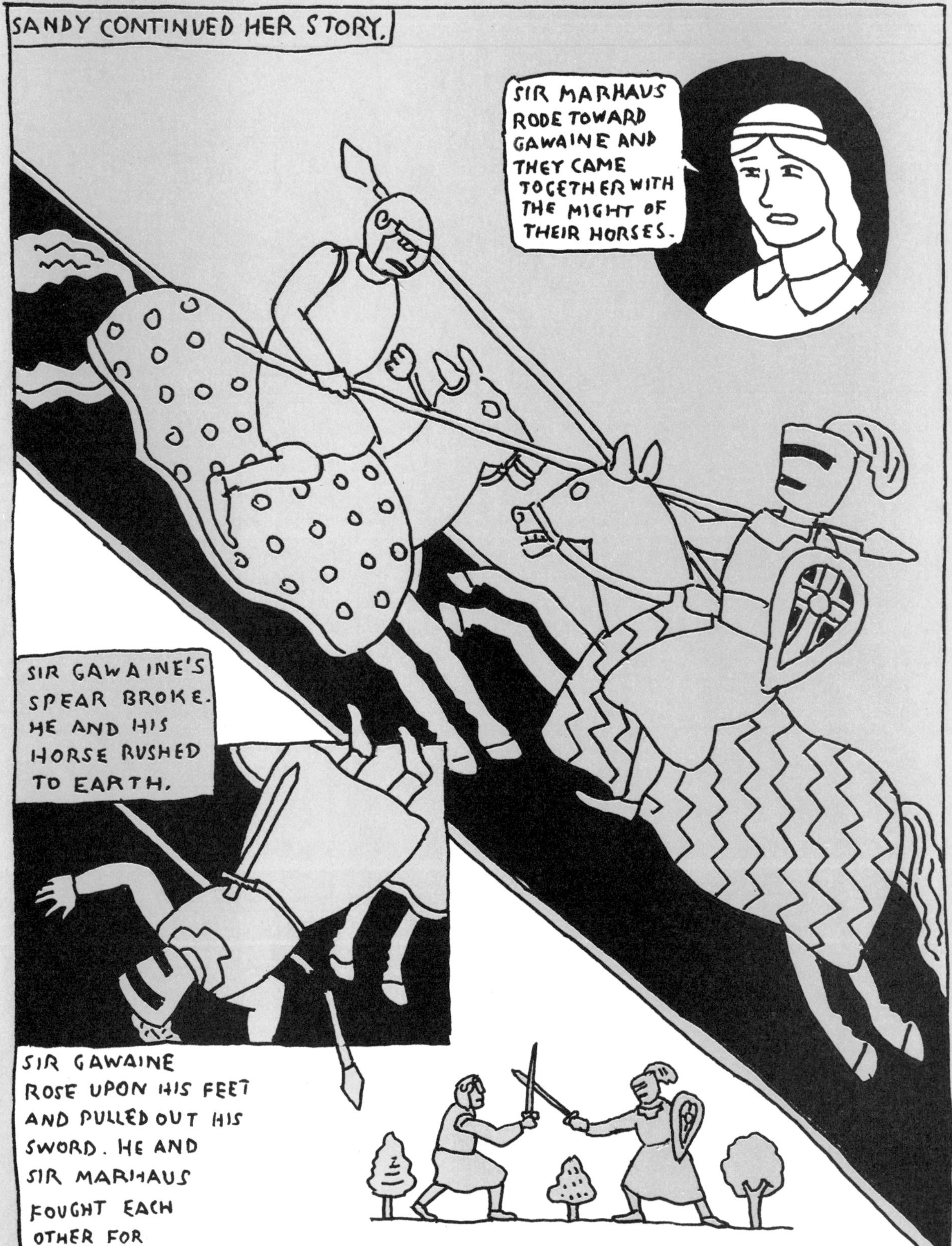
SANDY CONTINUED HER STORY.
SIR MARHAUS RODE TOWARD GAWAINE AND THEY CAME TOGETHER WITH THE MIGHT OF THEIR HORSES.
SIR GAWAINE'S SPEAR BROKE. HE AND HIS HORSE RUSHED TO EARTH.
SIR GAWAINE ROSE UPON HIS FEET AND PULLED OUT HIS SWORD. HE AND SIR MARHAUS FOUGHT EACH OTHER FOR THREE HOURS.

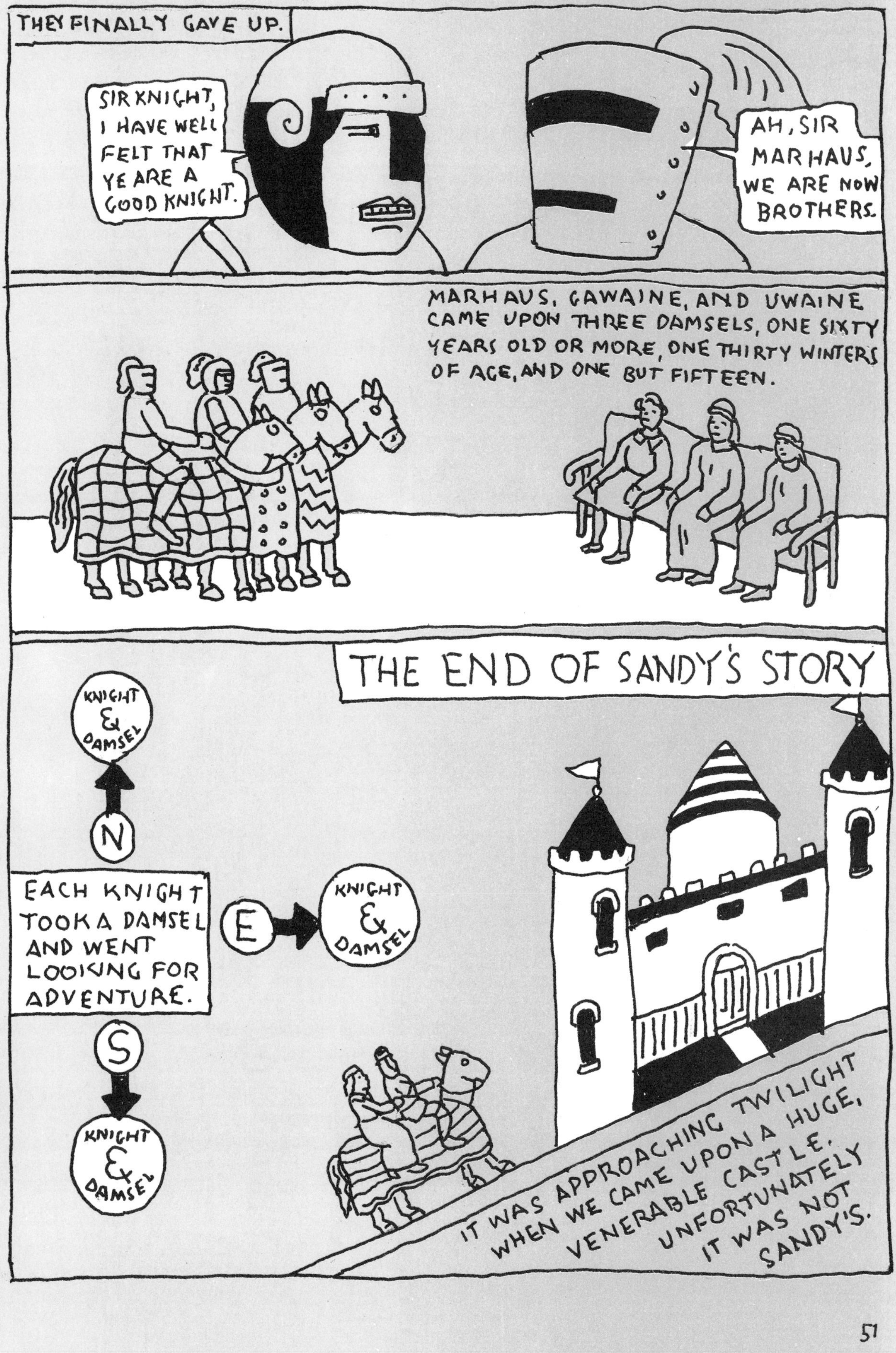
THEY FINALLY GAVE UP.
SIR KNIGHT, I HAVE WELL FELT THAT YE ARE A GOOD KNIGHT.
AH, SIR MARHAUS, WE ARE NOW BROTHERS.
MARHAUS, GAWAINE, AND UWAINE CAME UPON THREE DAMSELS, ONE SIXTY YEARS OLD OR MORE, ONE THIRTY WINTERS OF AGE, AND ONE BUT FIFTEEN.
THE END OF SANDY'S STORY
KNIGHT & DAMSEL
N
EACH KNIGHT TOOK A DAMSEL AND WENT LOOKING FOR ADVENTURE.
E
KNIGHT & DAMSEL
S
KNIGHT & DAMSEL
IT WAS APPROACHING TWILIGHT WHEN WE CAME UPON A HUGE, VENERABLE CASTLE. UNFORTUNATELY IT WAS NOT SANDY'S.

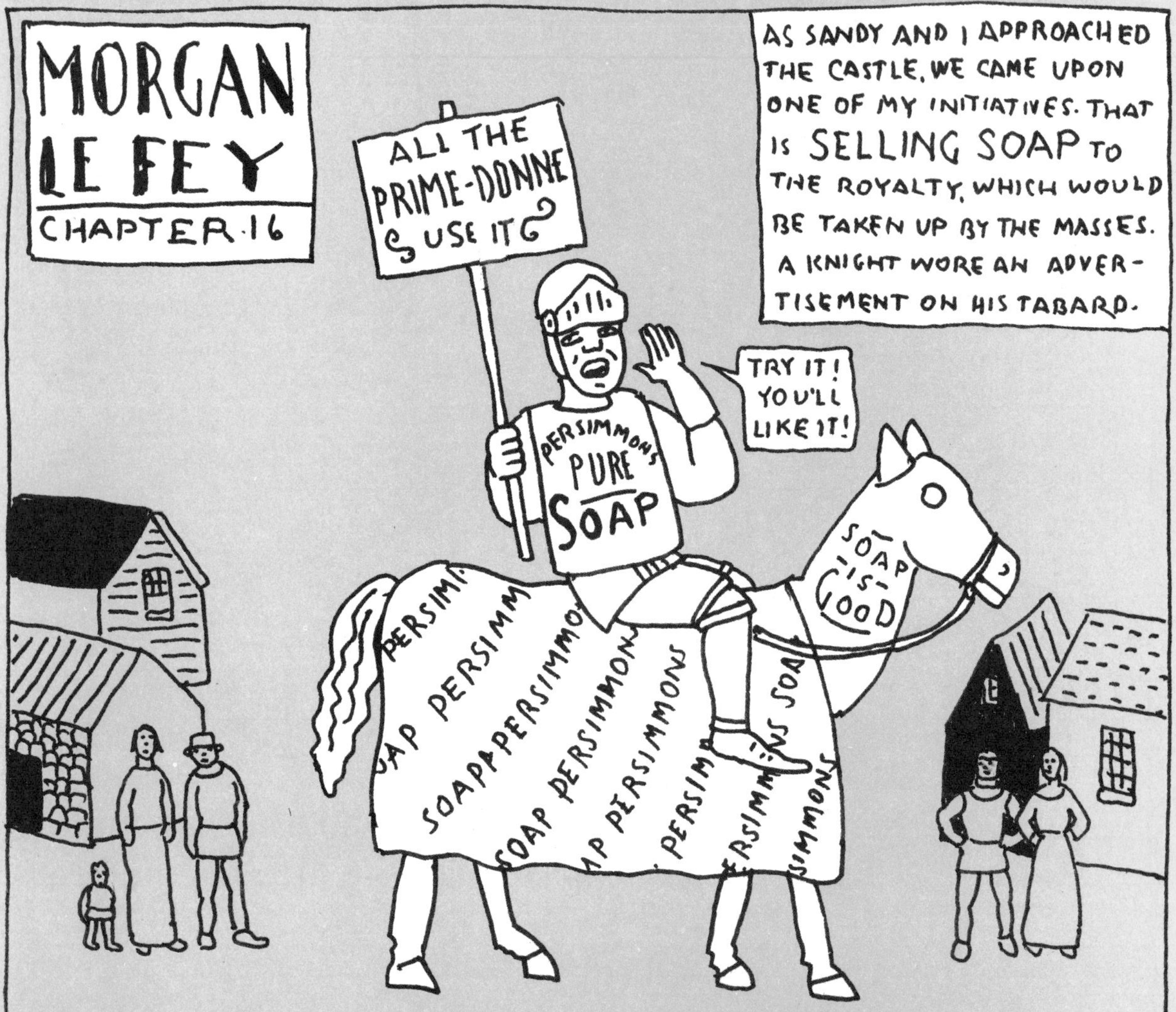
MORGAN LE FEY
CHAPTER 16
AS SANDY AND I APPROACHED THE CASTLE, WE CAME UPON ONE OF MY INITIATIVES. THAT IS SELLING SOAP TO THE ROYALTY, WHICH WOULD BE TAKEN UP BY THE MASSES. A KNIGHT WORE AN ADVERTISEMENT ON HIS TABARD.
ALL THE PRIME-DONNE USE IT
TRY IT! YOU'LL LIKE IT!
PERSIMMONS PURE SOAP
SOAP IS GOOD

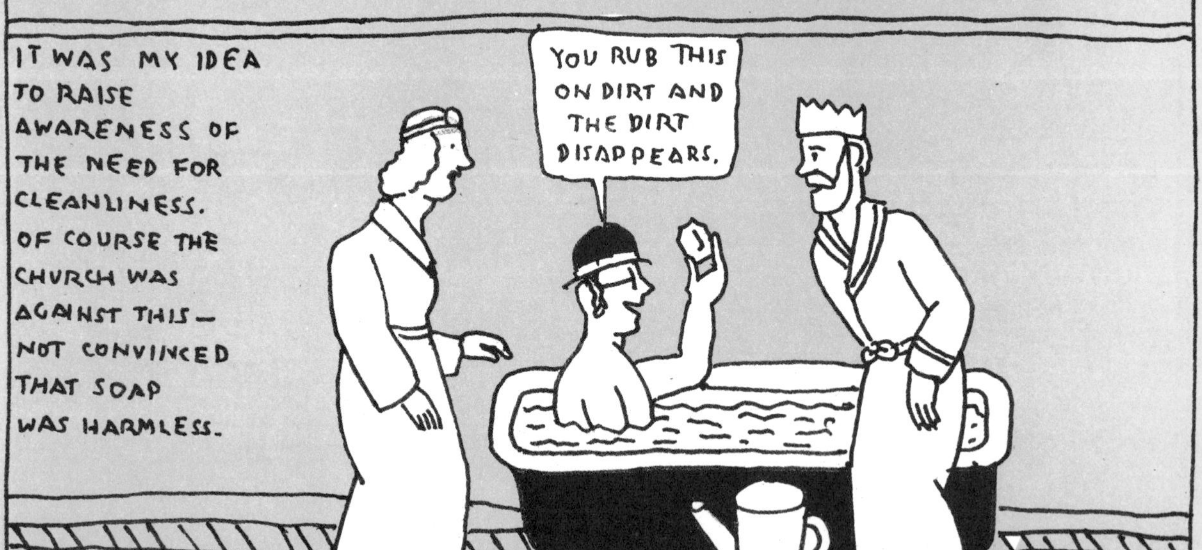
IT WAS MY IDEA TO RAISE AWARENESS OF THE NEED FOR CLEANLINESS. OF COURSE THE CHURCH WAS AGAINST THIS— NOT CONVINCED THAT SOAP WAS HARMLESS.
YOU RUB THIS ON DIRT AND THE DIRT DISAPPEARS.

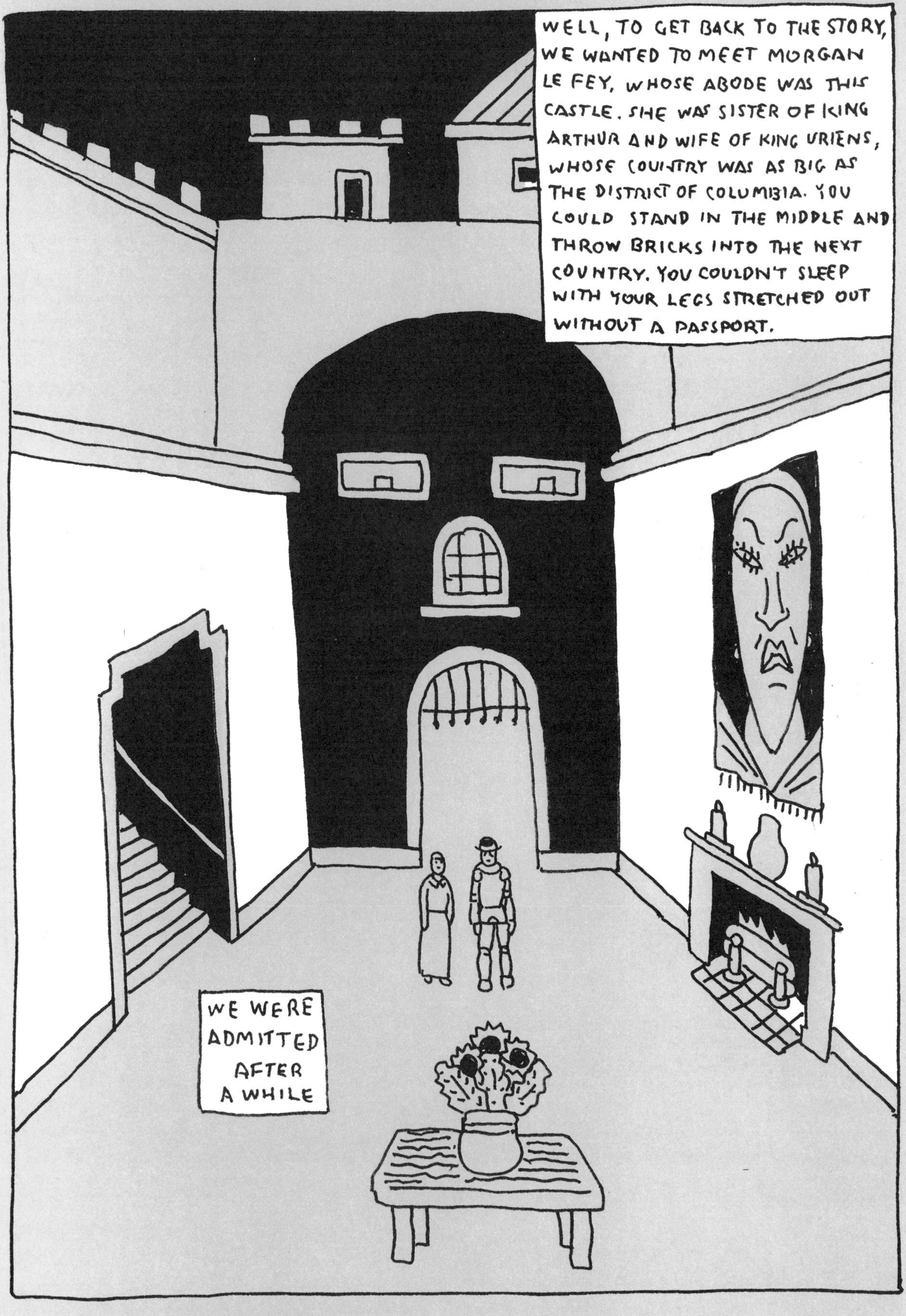
WELL, TO GET BACK TO THE STORY, WE WANTED TO MEET MORGAN LE FEY, WHOSE ABODE WAS THIS CASTLE. SHE WAS SISTER OF KING ARTHUR AND WIFE OF KING URIENS, WHOSE COUNTRY WAS AS BIG AS THE DISTRICT OF COLUMBIA. YOU COULD STAND IN THE MIDDLE AND THROW BRICKS INTO THE NEXT COUNTRY. YOU COULDN'T SLEEP WITH YOUR LEGS STRETCHED OUT WITHOUT A PASSPORT.
WE WERE ADMITTED AFTER A WHILE

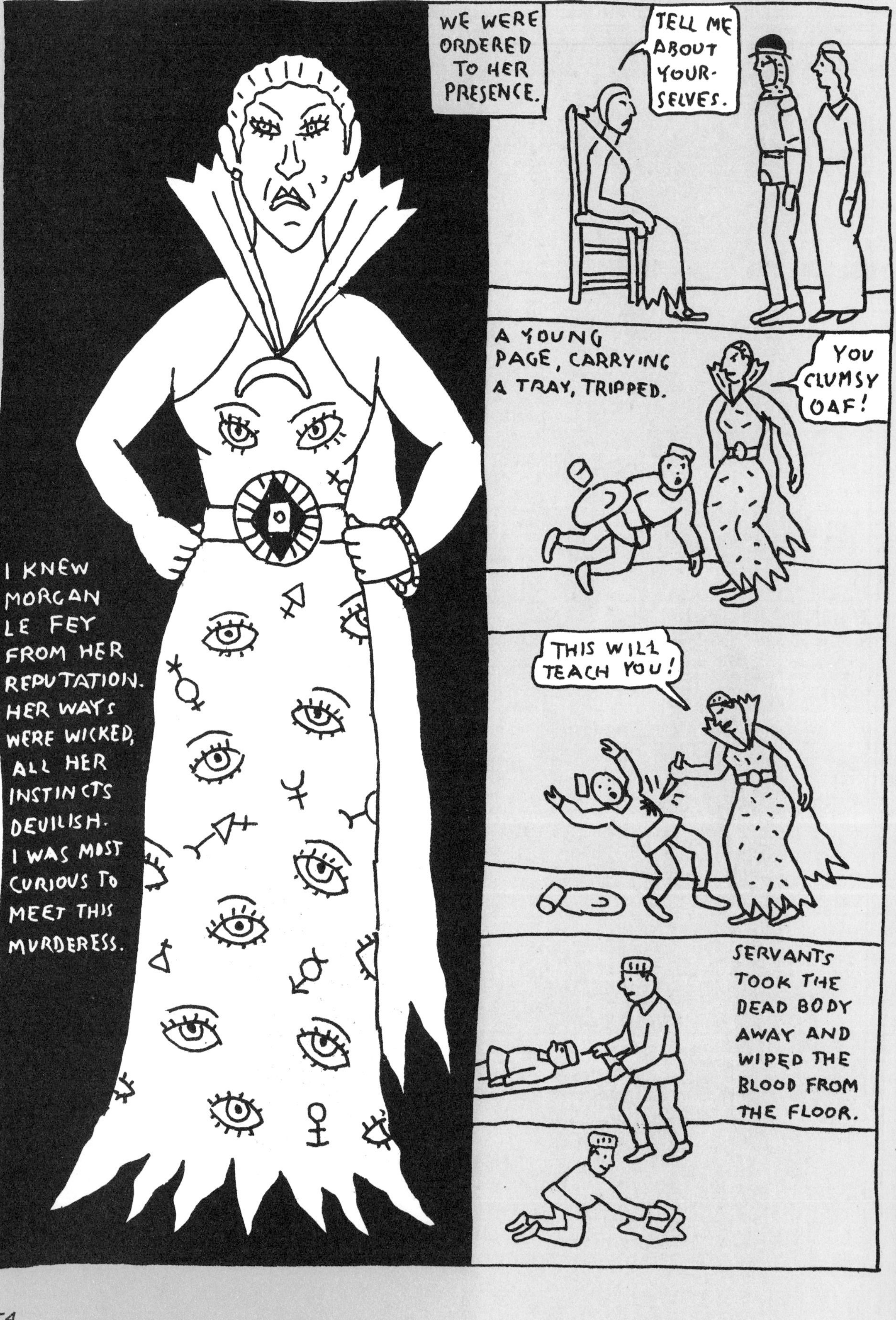
I KNEW MORGAN LE FEY FROM HER REPUTATION. HER WAYS WERE WICKED, ALL HER INSTINCTS DEVILISH. I WAS MOST CURIOUS TO MEET THIS MURDERESS.
WE WERE ORDERED TO HER PRESENCE.
TELL ME ABOUT YOURSELVES.
A YOUNG PAGE, CARRYING A TRAY, TRIPPED.
YOU CLUMSY OAF!
THIS WILL TEACH YOU!
SERVANTS TOOK THE DEAD BODY AWAY AND WIPED THE BLOOD FROM THE FLOOR.

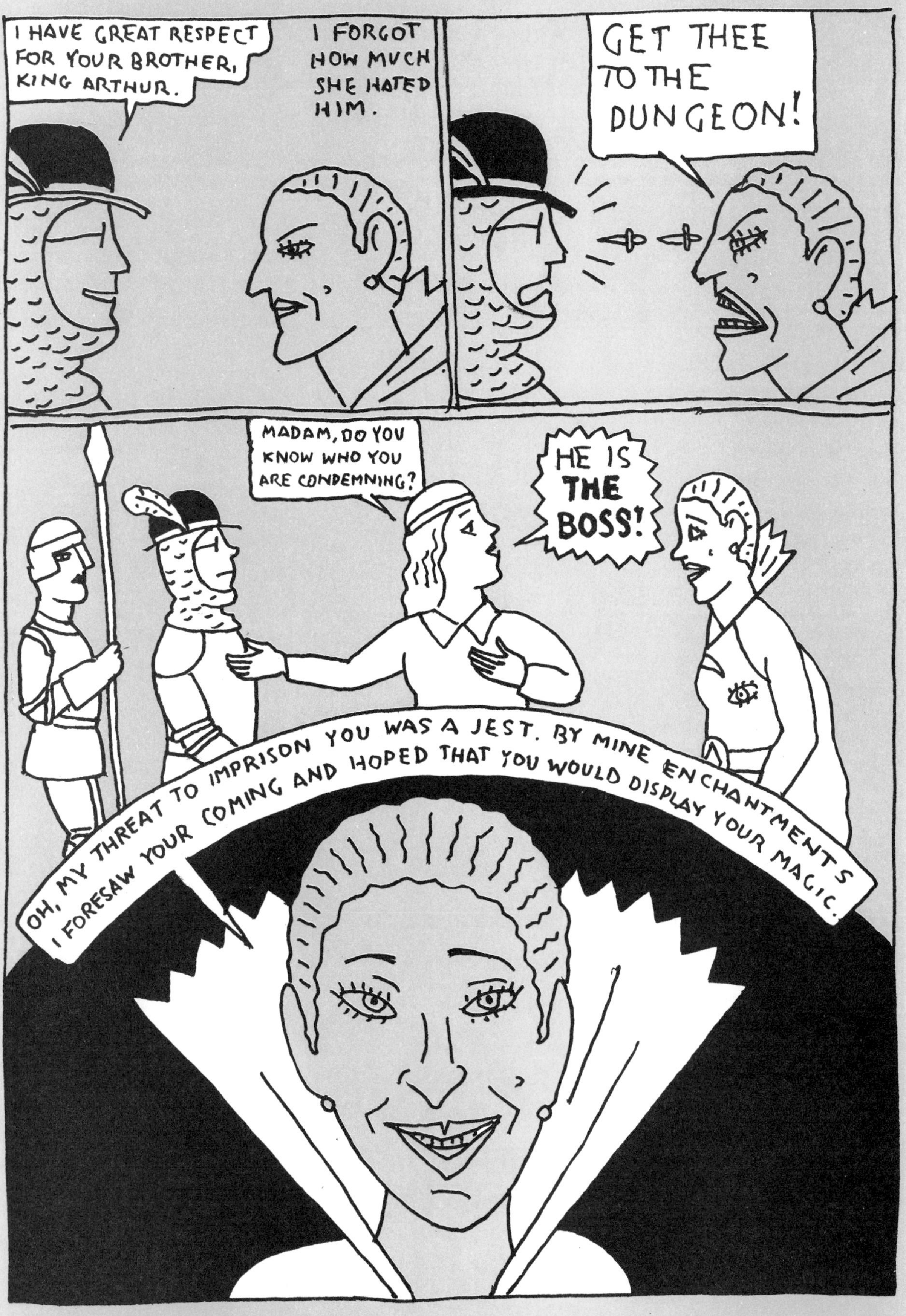

I HAVE GREAT RESPECT FOR YOUR BROTHER, KING ARTHUR.
I FORGOT HOW MUCH SHE HATED HIM.
GET THEE TO THE DUNGEON!
MADAM, DO YOU KNOW WHO YOU ARE CONDEMNING?
HE IS **THE BOSS!**
OH, MY THREAT TO IMPRISON YOU WAS A JEST. BY MINE ENCHANTMENTS I FORESAW YOUR COMING AND HOPED THAT YOU WOULD DISPLAY YOUR MAGIC.

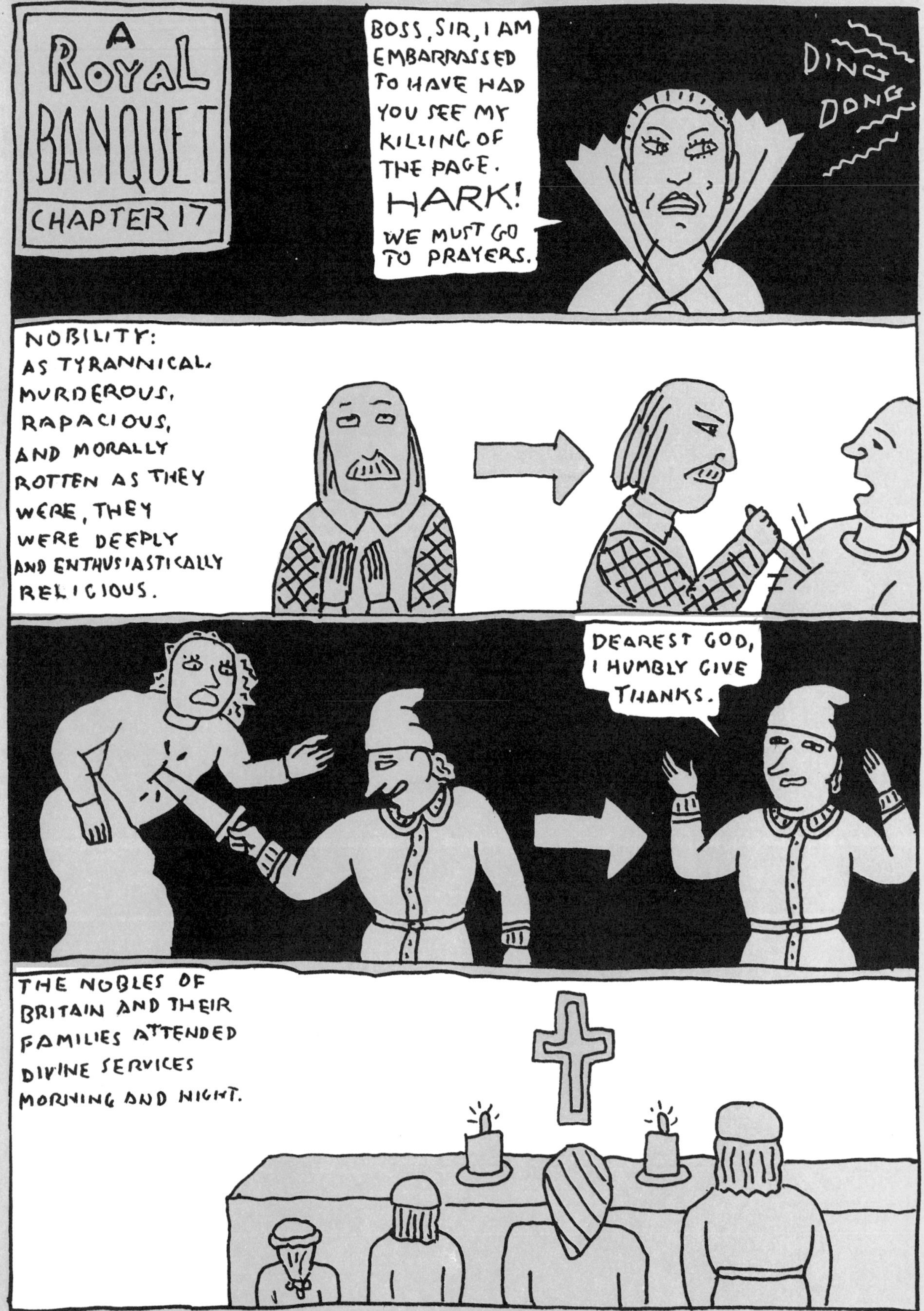
A ROYAL BANQUET
CHAPTER 17
BOSS, SIR, I AM EMBARRASSED TO HAVE HAD YOU SEE MY KILLING OF THE PAGE. HARK! WE MUST GO TO PRAYERS.
DING DONG
NOBILITY: AS TYRANNICAL, MURDEROUS, RAPACIOUS, AND MORALLY ROTTEN AS THEY WERE, THEY WERE DEEPLY AND ENTHUSIASTICALLY RELIGIOUS.
DEAREST GOD, I HUMBLY GIVE THANKS.
THE NOBLES OF BRITAIN AND THEIR FAMILIES ATTENDED DIVINE SERVICES MORNING AND NIGHT.

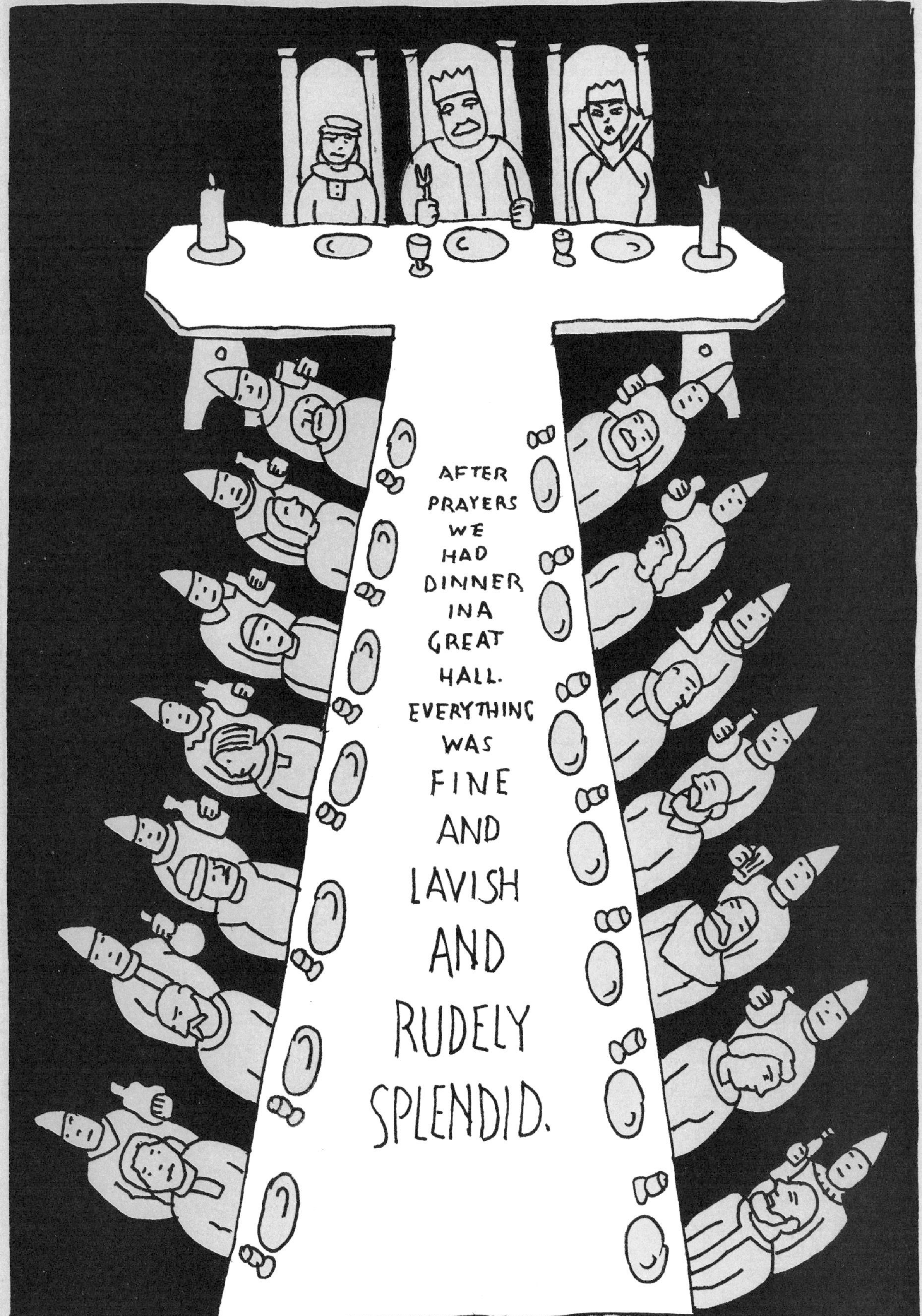
AFTER PRAYERS WE HAD DINNER IN A GREAT HALL. EVERYTHING WAS FINE AND LAVISH AND RUDELY SPLENDID.

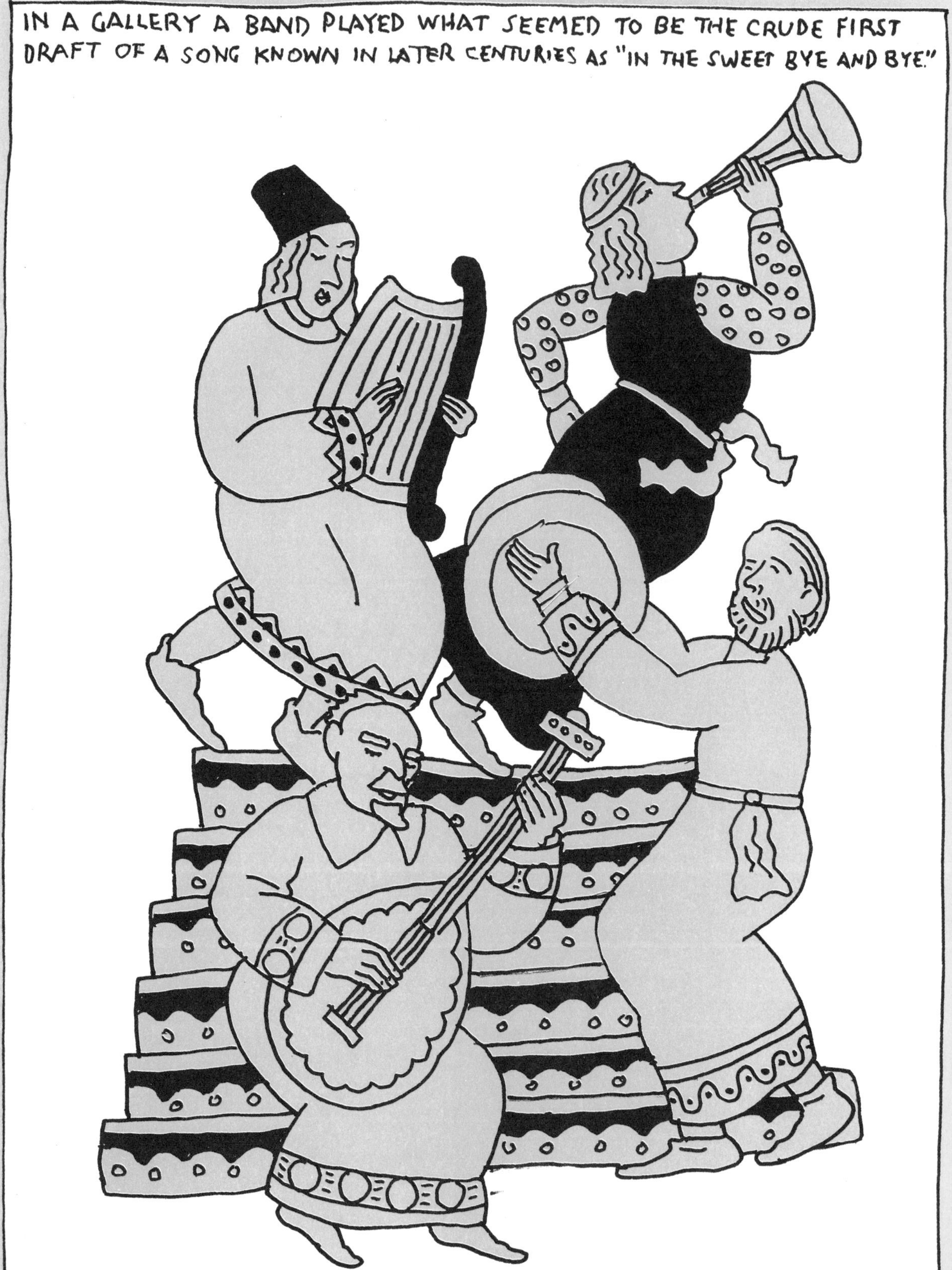
IN A GALLERY A BAND PLAYED WHAT SEEMED TO BE THE CRUDE FIRST DRAFT OF A SONG KNOWN IN LATER CENTURIES AS "IN THE SWEET BYE AND BYE."

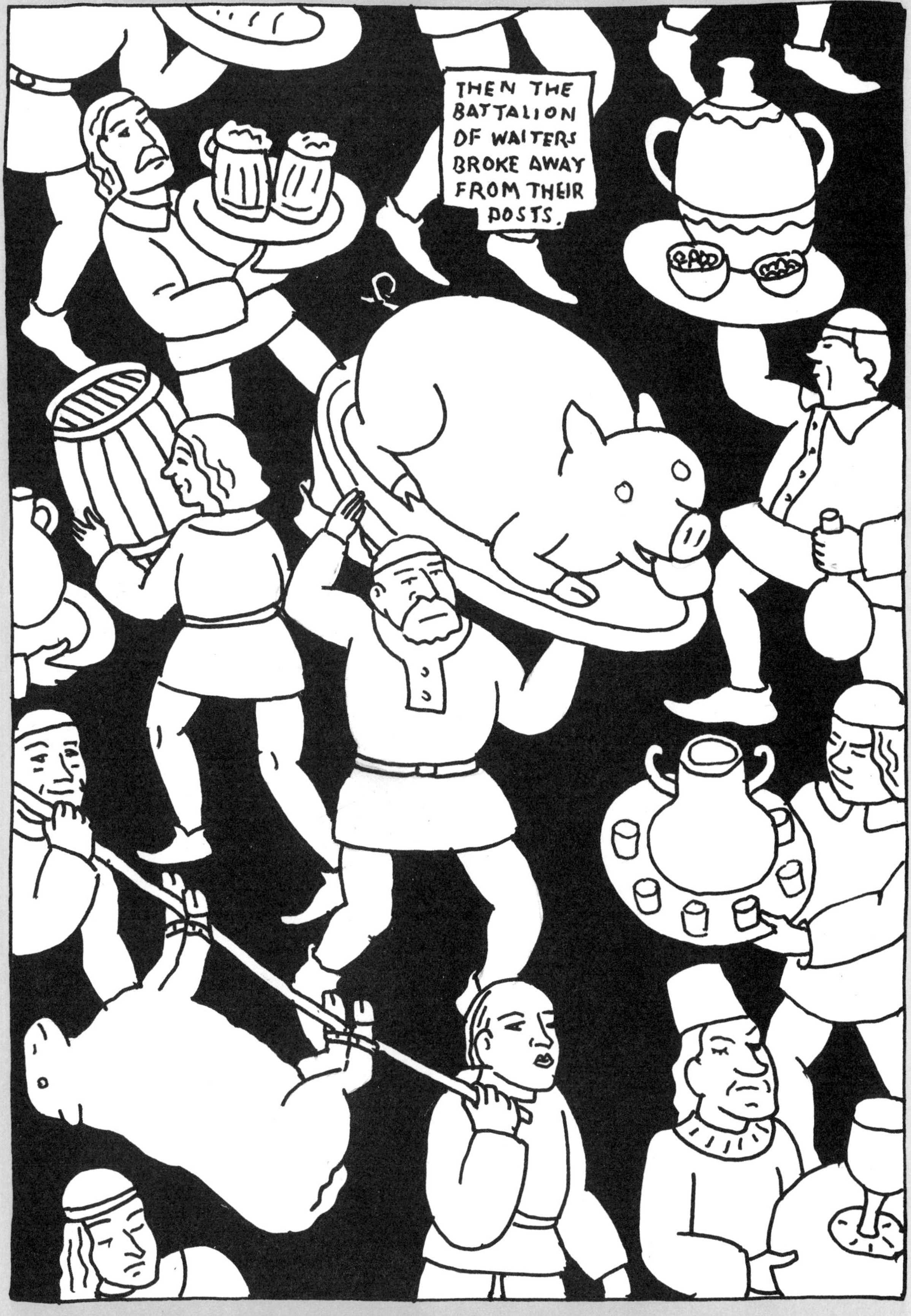
THEN THE BATTALION OF WAITERS BROKE AWAY FROM THEIR POSTS.

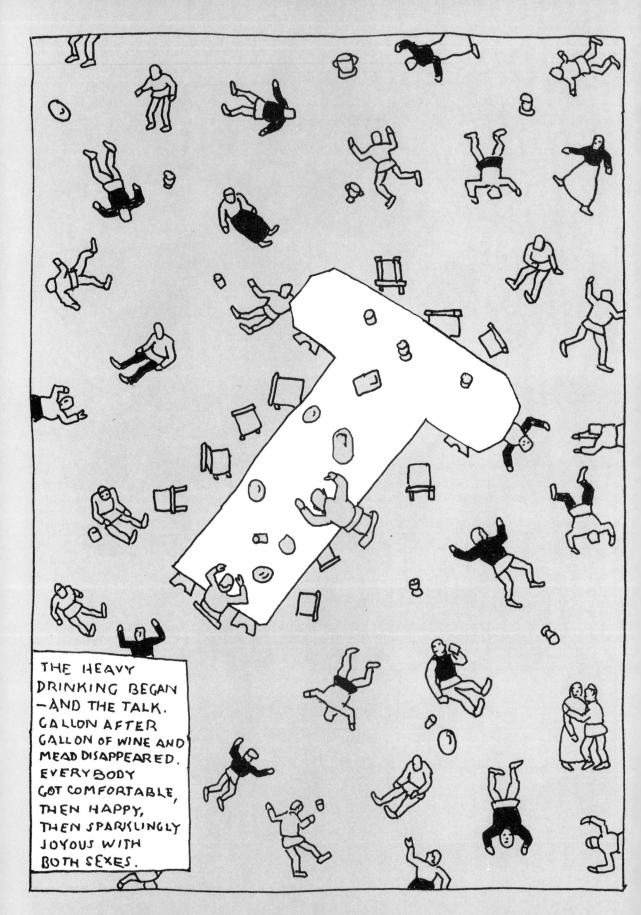

THE HEAVY
DRINKING BEGAN
—AND THE TALK.
GALLON AFTER
GALLON OF WINE AND
MEAD DISAPPEARED.
EVERYBODY
GOT COMFORTABLE,
THEN HAPPY,
THEN SPARKLINGLY
JOYOUS WITH
BOTH SEXES.

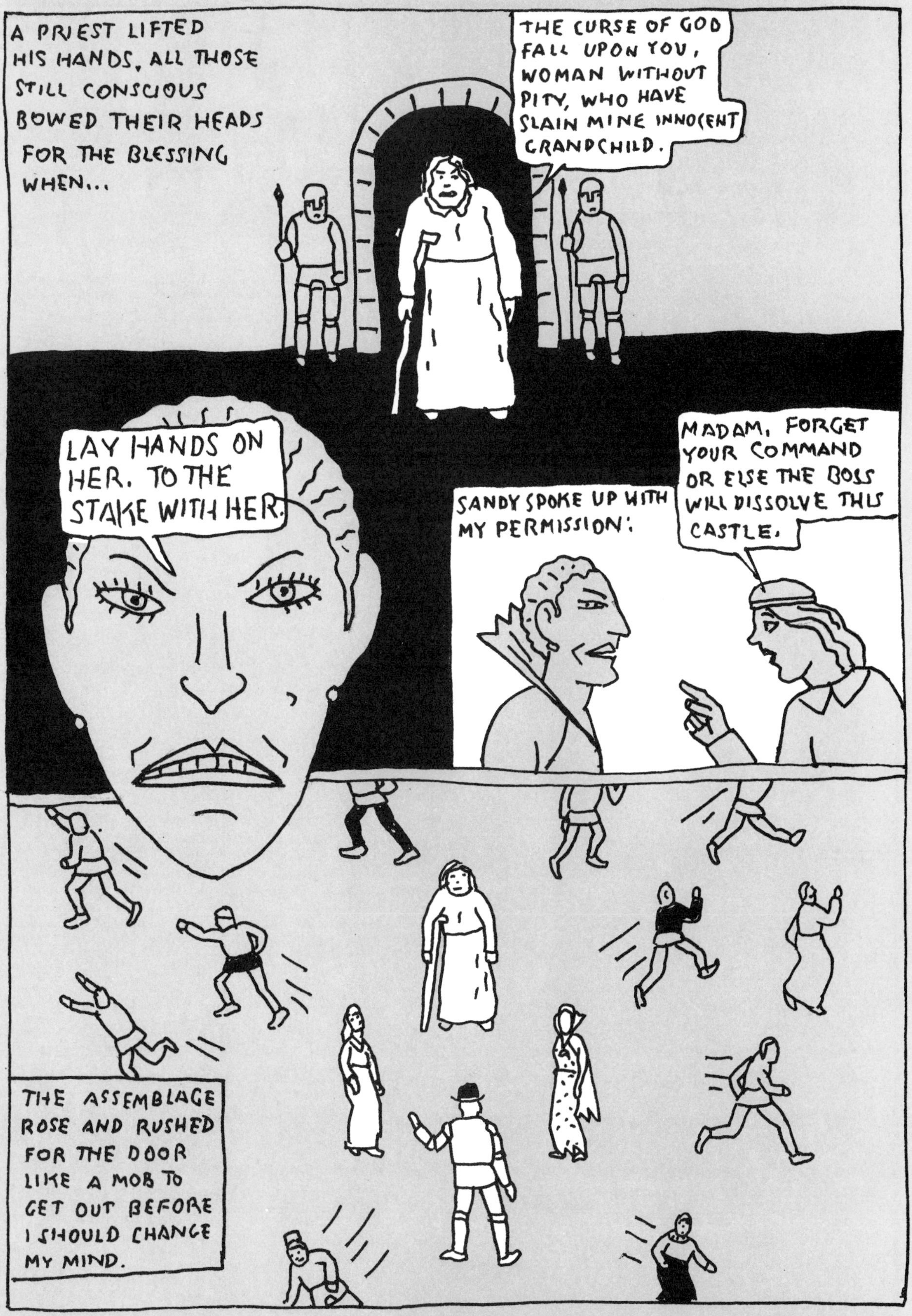
A PRIEST LIFTED HIS HANDS, ALL THOSE STILL CONSCIOUS BOWED THEIR HEADS FOR THE BLESSING WHEN...
THE CURSE OF GOD FALL UPON YOU, WOMAN WITHOUT PITY, WHO HAVE SLAIN MINE INNOCENT GRANDCHILD.
LAY HANDS ON HER. TO THE STAKE WITH HER.
SANDY SPOKE UP WITH MY PERMISSION:
MADAM, FORGET YOUR COMMAND OR ELSE THE BOSS WILL DISSOLVE THIS CASTLE.
THE ASSEMBLAGE ROSE AND RUSHED FOR THE DOOR LIKE A MOB TO GET OUT BEFORE I SHOULD CHANGE MY MIND.

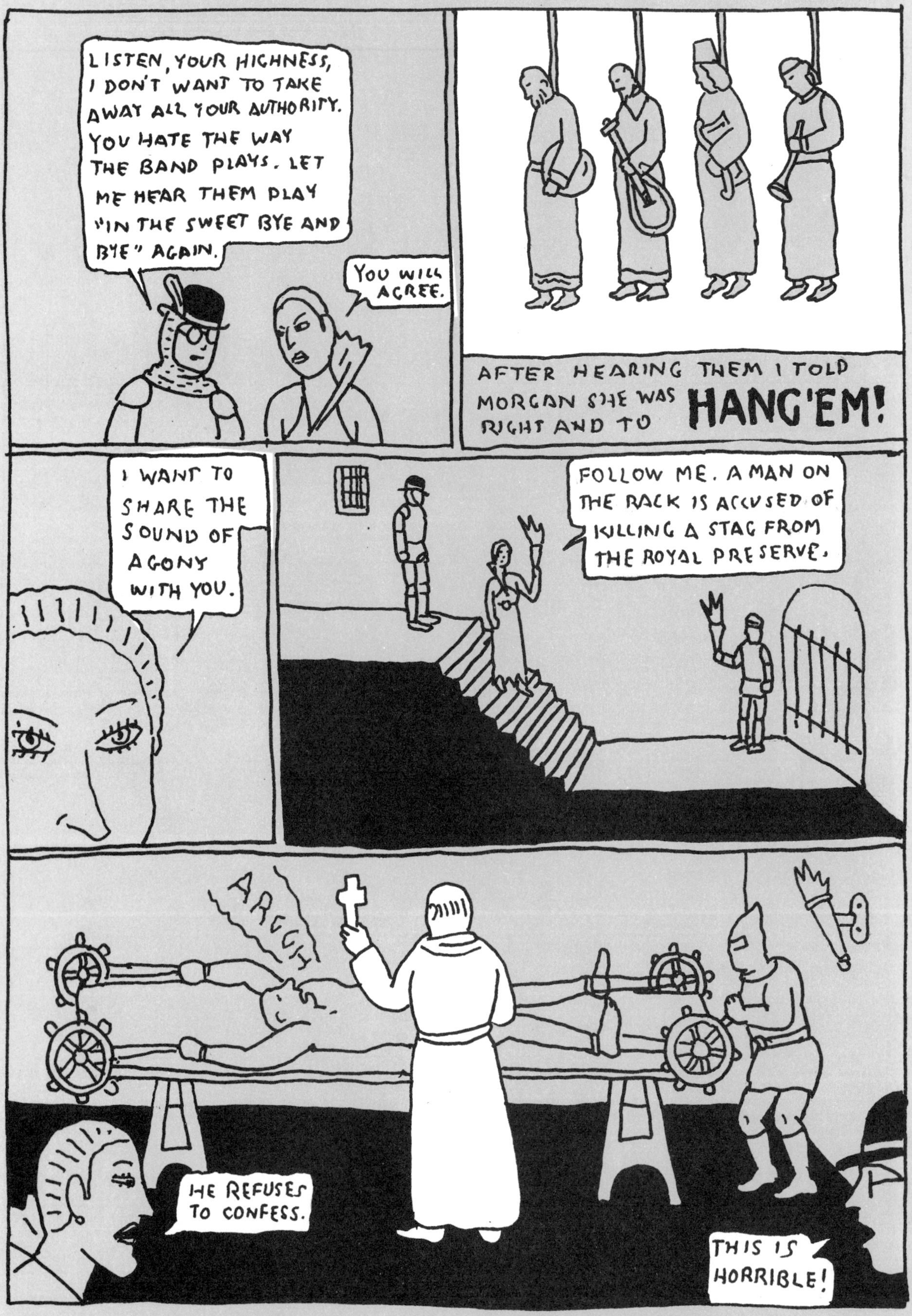
LISTEN, YOUR HIGHNESS, I DON'T WANT TO TAKE AWAY ALL YOUR AUTHORITY. YOU HATE THE WAY THE BAND PLAYS. LET ME HEAR THEM PLAY "IN THE SWEET BYE AND BYE" AGAIN.
YOU WILL AGREE.
AFTER HEARING THEM I TOLD MORGAN SHE WAS RIGHT AND TO HANG'EM!
I WANT TO SHARE THE SOUND OF AGONY WITH YOU.
FOLLOW ME. A MAN ON THE RACK IS ACCUSED OF KILLING A STAG FROM THE ROYAL PRESERVE.
ARGGH
HE REFUSES TO CONFESS.
THIS IS HORRIBLE!

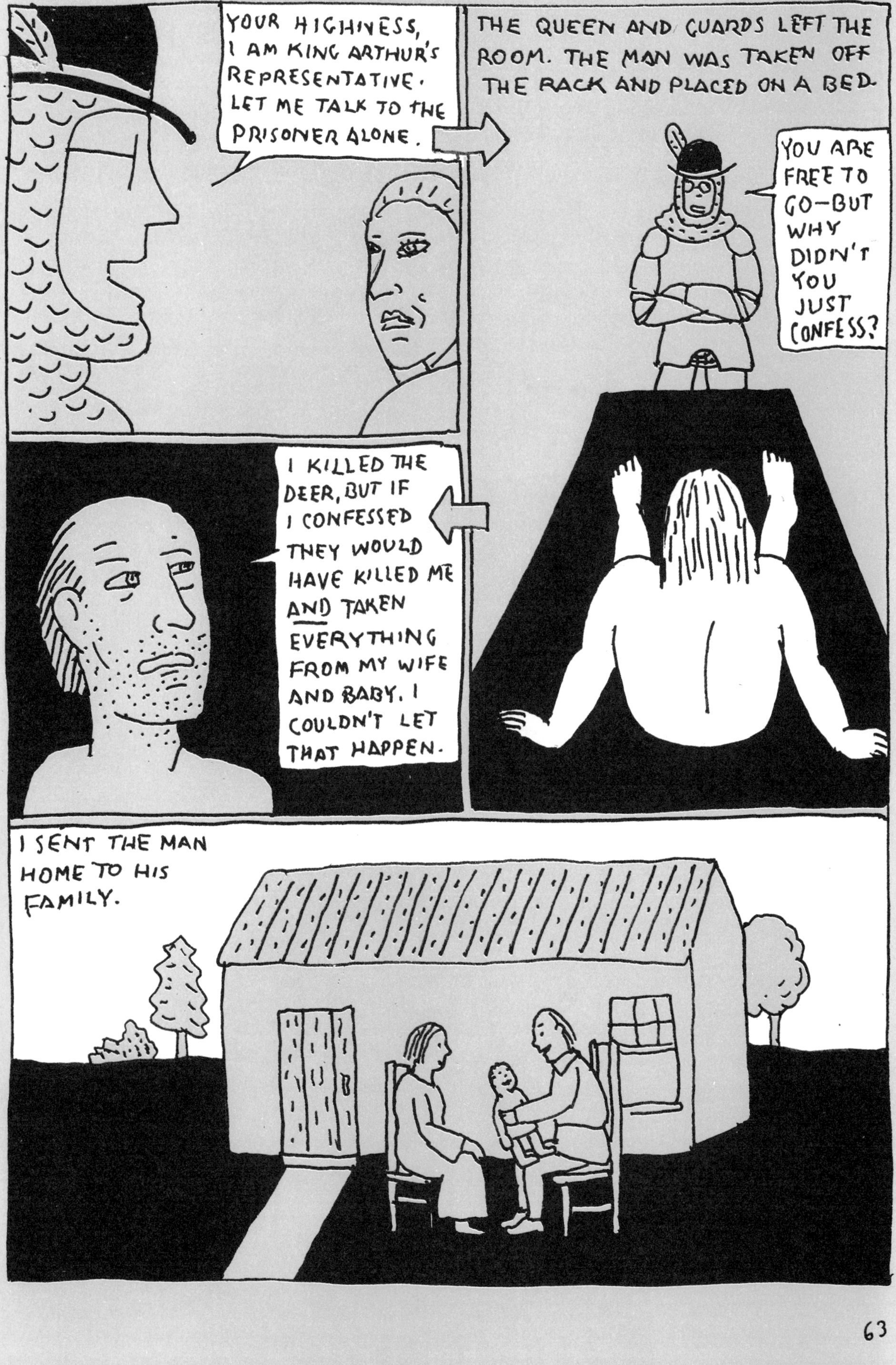
YOUR HIGHNESS, I AM KING ARTHUR'S REPRESENTATIVE. LET ME TALK TO THE PRISONER ALONE.
THE QUEEN AND GUARDS LEFT THE ROOM. THE MAN WAS TAKEN OFF THE RACK AND PLACED ON A BED.
YOU ARE FREE TO GO—BUT WHY DIDN'T YOU JUST CONFESS?
I KILLED THE DEER, BUT IF I CONFESSED THEY WOULD HAVE KILLED ME AND TAKEN EVERYTHING FROM MY WIFE AND BABY. I COULDN'T LET THAT HAPPEN.
I SENT THE MAN HOME TO HIS FAMILY.

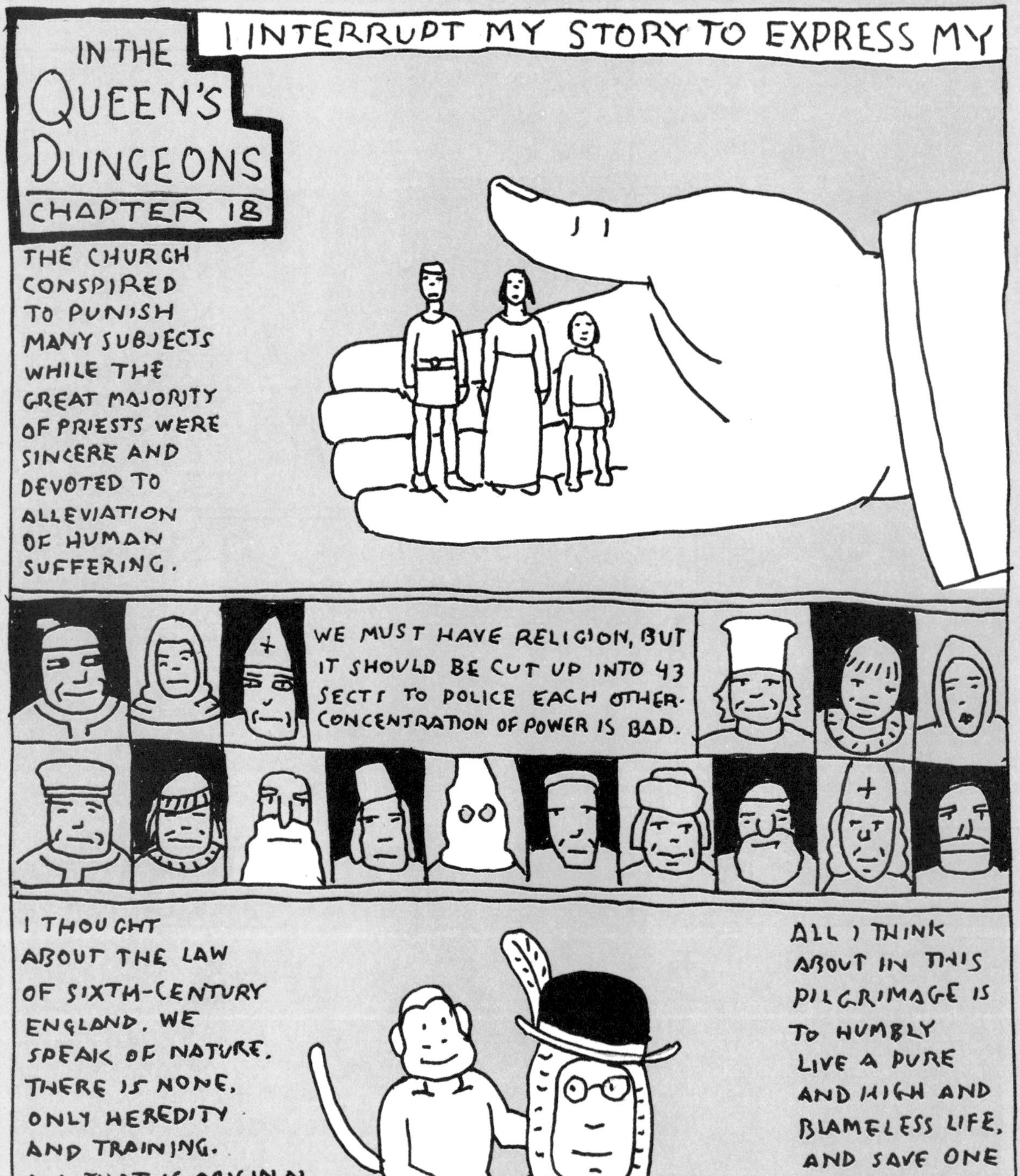
IN THE QUEEN'S DUNGEONS
CHAPTER 18
I INTERRUPT MY STORY TO EXPRESS MY
THE CHURCH CONSPIRED TO PUNISH MANY SUBJECTS WHILE THE GREAT MAJORITY OF PRIESTS WERE SINCERE AND DEVOTED TO ALLEVIATION OF HUMAN SUFFERING.
WE MUST HAVE RELIGION, BUT IT SHOULD BE CUT UP INTO 43 SECTS TO POLICE EACH OTHER. CONCENTRATION OF POWER IS BAD.
I THOUGHT ABOUT THE LAW OF SIXTH-CENTURY ENGLAND. WE SPEAK OF NATURE. THERE IS NONE, ONLY HEREDITY AND TRAINING. ALL THAT IS ORIGINAL IN US CAN BE HIDDEN BY THE POINT OF A NEEDLE, THE REST BEING ATOMS FROM ANCESTORS STRETCHING BACK A BILLION YEARS TO THE ADAM - CLAM OR GRASS-HOPPER OR MONKEY.
ALL I THINK ABOUT IN THIS PILGRIMAGE IS TO HUMBLY LIVE A PURE AND HIGH AND BLAMELESS LIFE, AND SAVE ONE MICROSCOPIC ATOM IN ME THAT IS TRULY ME.

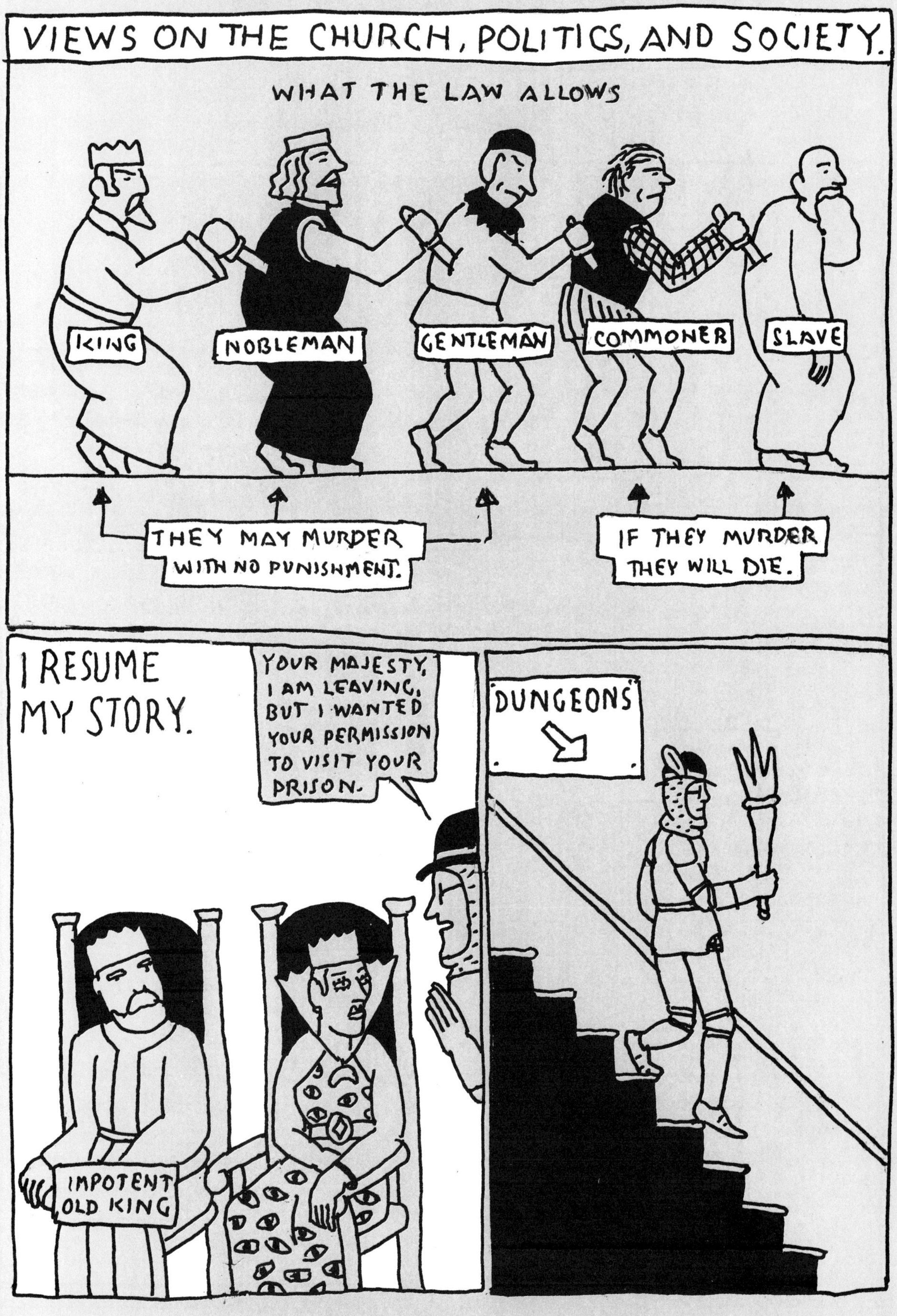

VIEWS ON THE CHURCH, POLITICS, AND SOCIETY.
WHAT THE LAW ALLOWS
KING
NOBLEMAN
GENTLEMAN
COMMONER
SLAVE
THEY MAY MURDER WITH NO PUNISHMENT.
IF THEY MURDER THEY WILL DIE.
I RESUME MY STORY.
YOUR MAJESTY, I AM LEAVING, BUT I WANTED YOUR PERMISSION TO VISIT YOUR PRISON.
IMPOTENT OLD KING
DUNGEONS

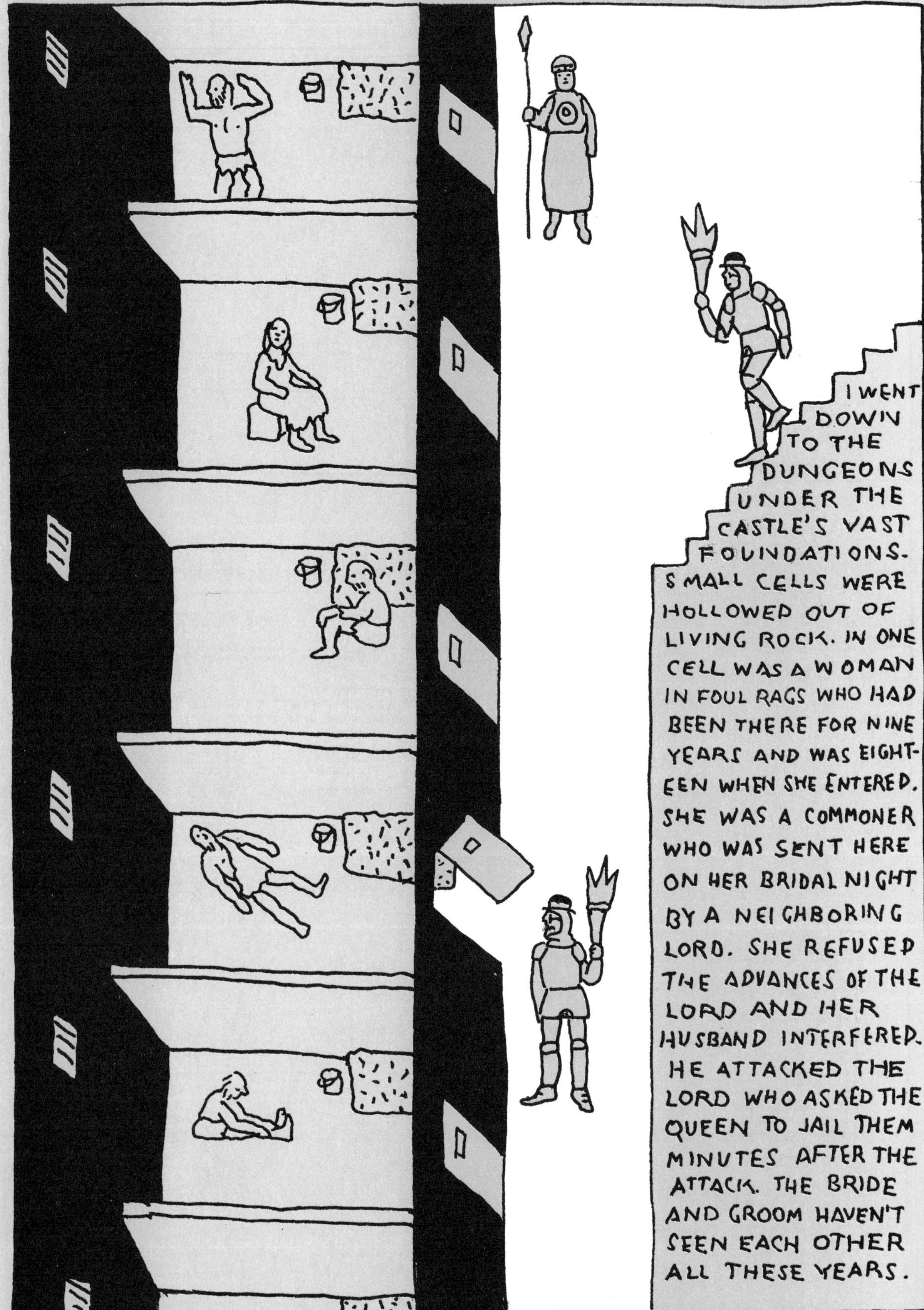
I WENT DOWN TO THE DUNGEONS UNDER THE CASTLE'S VAST FOUNDATIONS- SMALL CELLS WERE HOLLOWED OUT OF LIVING ROCK. IN ONE CELL WAS A WOMAN IN FOUL RAGS WHO HAD BEEN THERE FOR NINE YEARS AND WAS EIGHTEEN WHEN SHE ENTERED. SHE WAS A COMMONER WHO WAS SENT HERE ON HER BRIDAL NIGHT BY A NEIGHBORING LORD. SHE REFUSED THE ADVANCES OF THE LORD AND HER HUSBAND INTERFERED. HE ATTACKED THE LORD WHO ASKED THE QUEEN TO JAIL THEM MINUTES AFTER THE ATTACK. THE BRIDE AND GROOM HAVEN'T SEEN EACH OTHER ALL THESE YEARS.

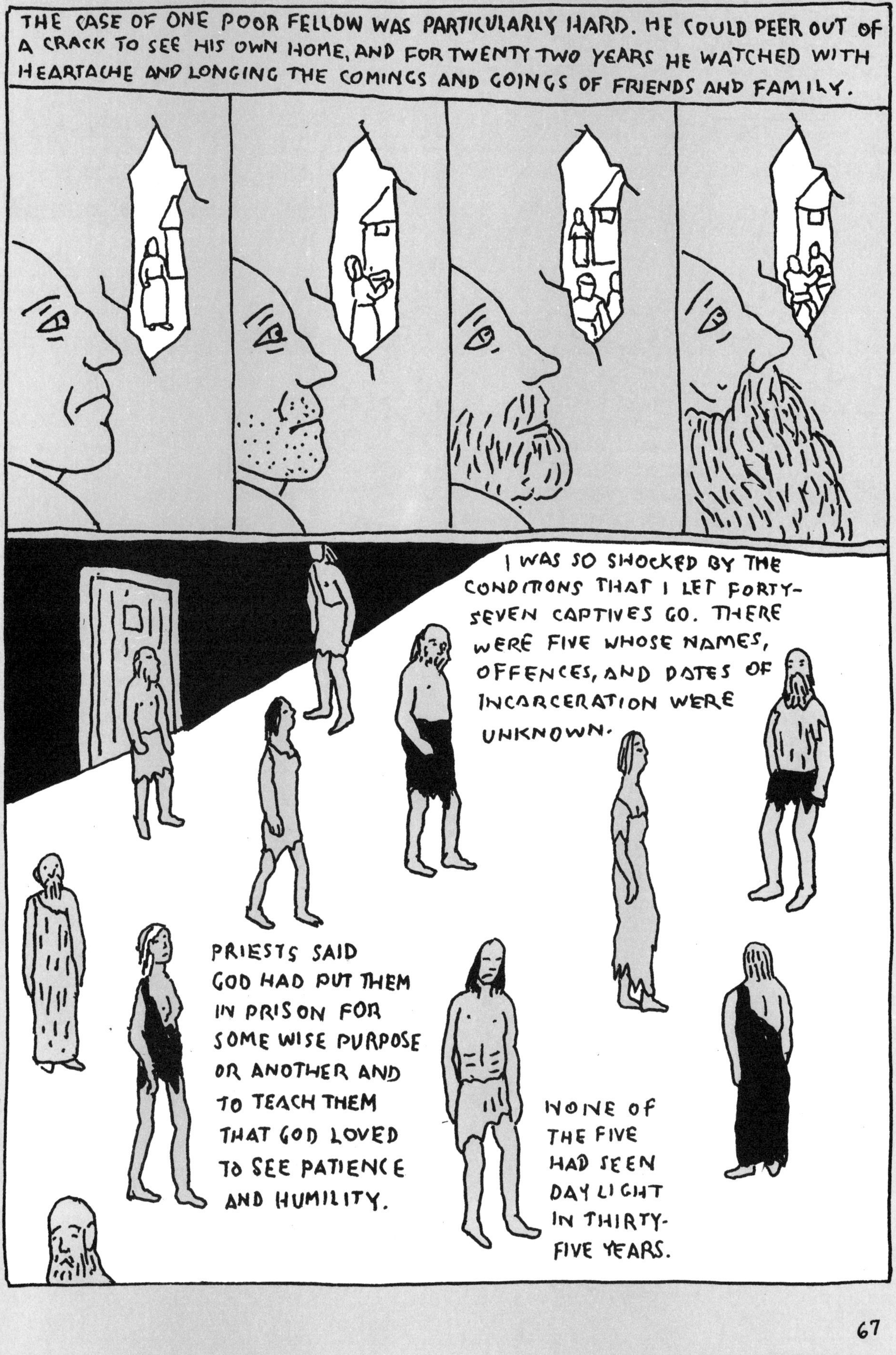
THE CASE OF ONE POOR FELLOW WAS PARTICULARLY HARD. HE COULD PEER OUT OF A CRACK TO SEE HIS OWN HOME, AND FOR TWENTY TWO YEARS HE WATCHED WITH HEARTACHE AND LONGING THE COMINGS AND GOINGS OF FRIENDS AND FAMILY.
I WAS SO SHOCKED BY THE CONDITIONS THAT I LET FORTY-SEVEN CAPTIVES GO. THERE WERE FIVE WHOSE NAMES, OFFENCES, AND DATES OF INCARCERATION WERE UNKNOWN.
PRIESTS SAID GOD HAD PUT THEM IN PRISON FOR SOME WISE PURPOSE OR ANOTHER AND TO TEACH THEM THAT GOD LOVED TO SEE PATIENCE AND HUMILITY.
NONE OF THE FIVE HAD SEEN DAYLIGHT IN THIRTY-FIVE YEARS.

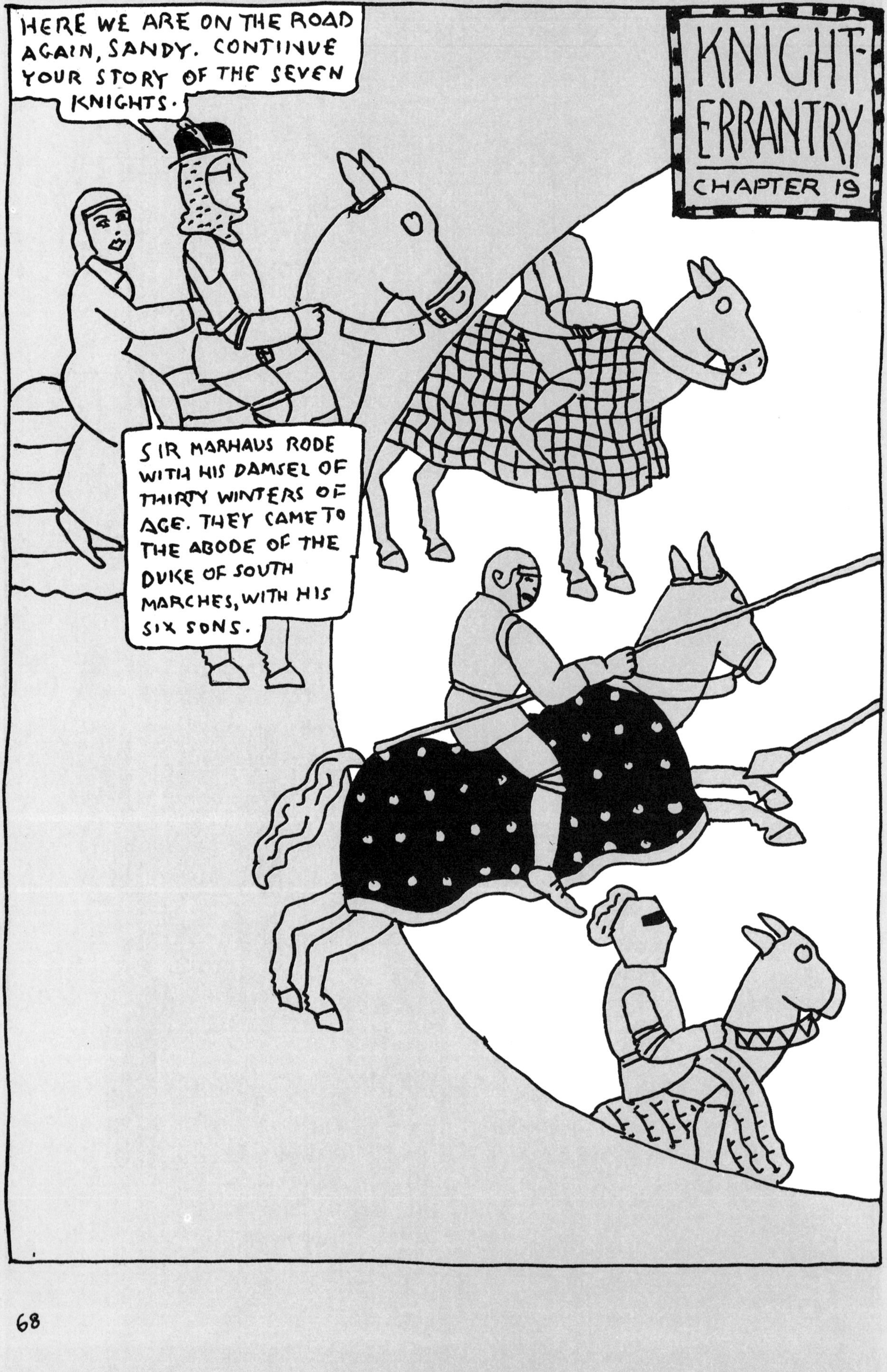
HERE WE ARE ON THE ROAD AGAIN, SANDY. CONTINUE YOUR STORY OF THE SEVEN KNIGHTS.
KNIGHT-ERRANTRY
CHAPTER 19
SIR MARHAUS RODE WITH HIS DAMSEL OF THIRTY WINTERS OF AGE. THEY CAME TO THE ABODE OF THE DUKE OF SOUTH MARCHES, WITH HIS SIX SONS.

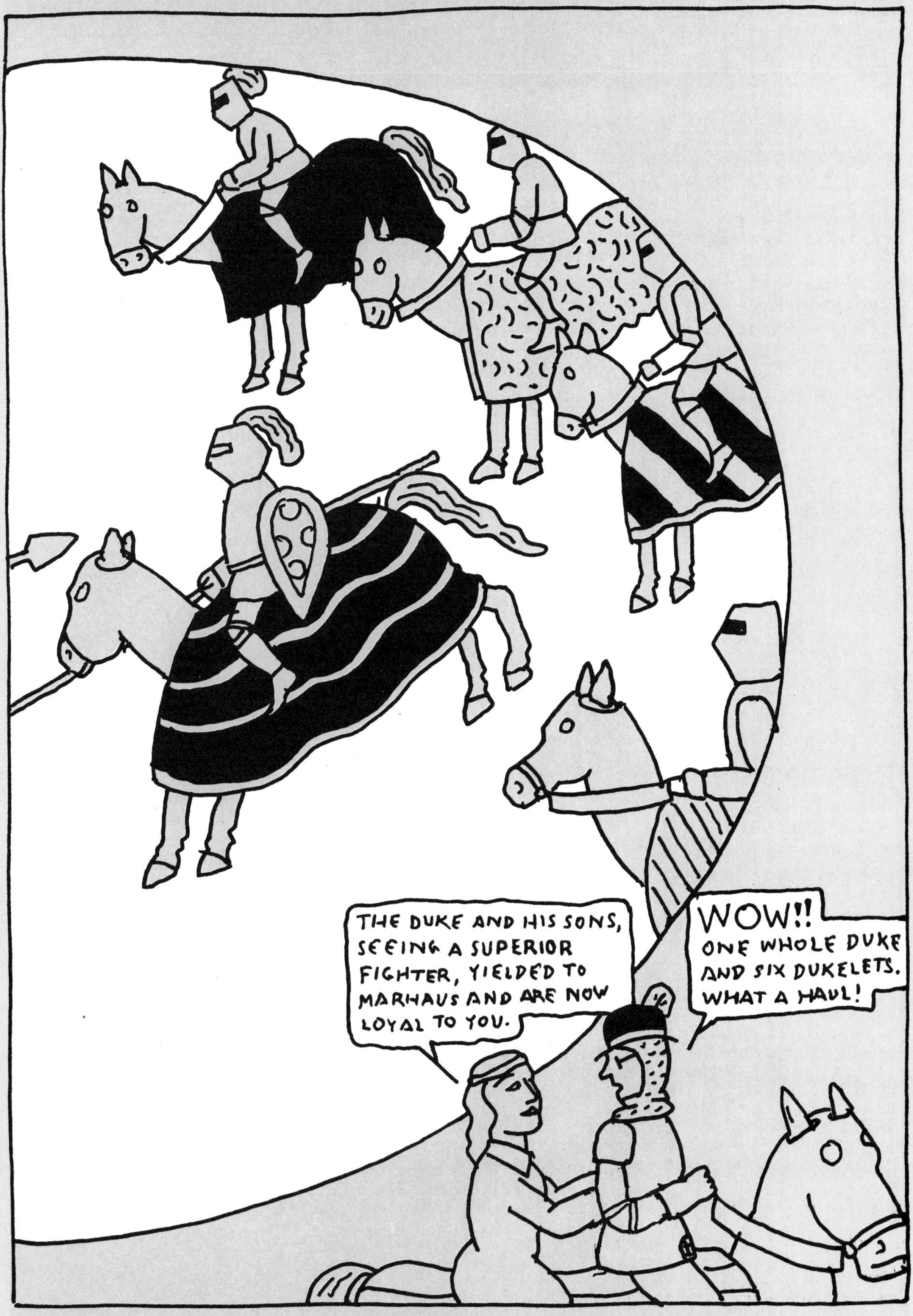
THE DUKE AND HIS SONS, SEEING A SUPERIOR FIGHTER, YIELDED TO MARHAUS AND ARE NOW LOYAL TO YOU.
WOW!! ONE WHOLE DUKE AND SIX DUKELETS. WHAT A HAUL!

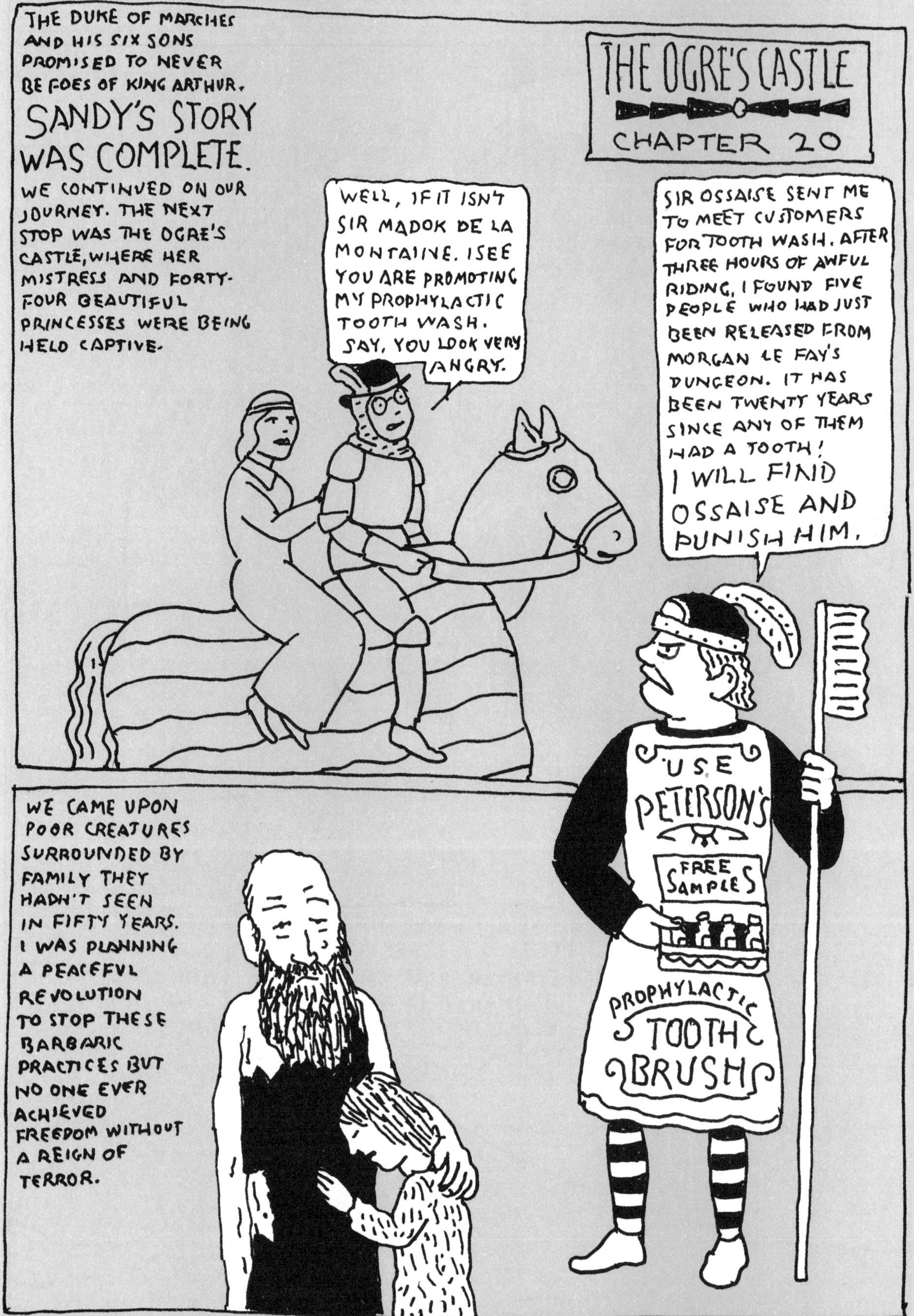
THE DUKE OF MARCHES AND HIS SIX SONS PROMISED TO NEVER BE FOES OF KING ARTHUR.
SANDY'S STORY WAS COMPLETE.
WE CONTINUED ON OUR JOURNEY. THE NEXT STOP WAS THE OGRE'S CASTLE, WHERE HER MISTRESS AND FORTY-FOUR BEAUTIFUL PRINCESSES WERE BEING HELD CAPTIVE.
THE OGRE'S CASTLE
CHAPTER 20
WELL, IF IT ISN'T SIR MADOK DE LA MONTAINE. I SEE YOU ARE PROMOTING MY PROPHYLACTIC TOOTH WASH. SAY, YOU LOOK VERY ANGRY.
SIR OSSAISE SENT ME TO MEET CUSTOMERS FOR TOOTH WASH. AFTER THREE HOURS OF AWFUL RIDING, I FOUND FIVE PEOPLE WHO HAD JUST BEEN RELEASED FROM MORGAN LE FAY'S DUNGEON. IT HAS BEEN TWENTY YEARS SINCE ANY OF THEM HAD A TOOTH! I WILL FIND OSSAISE AND PUNISH HIM.
USE PETERSON'S
FREE SAMPLES
PROPHYLACTIC TOOTH BRUSH
WE CAME UPON POOR CREATURES SURROUNDED BY FAMILY THEY HADN'T SEEN IN FIFTY YEARS. I WAS PLANNING A PEACEFUL REVOLUTION TO STOP THESE BARBARIC PRACTICES BUT NO ONE EVER ACHIEVED FREEDOM WITHOUT A REIGN OF TERROR.

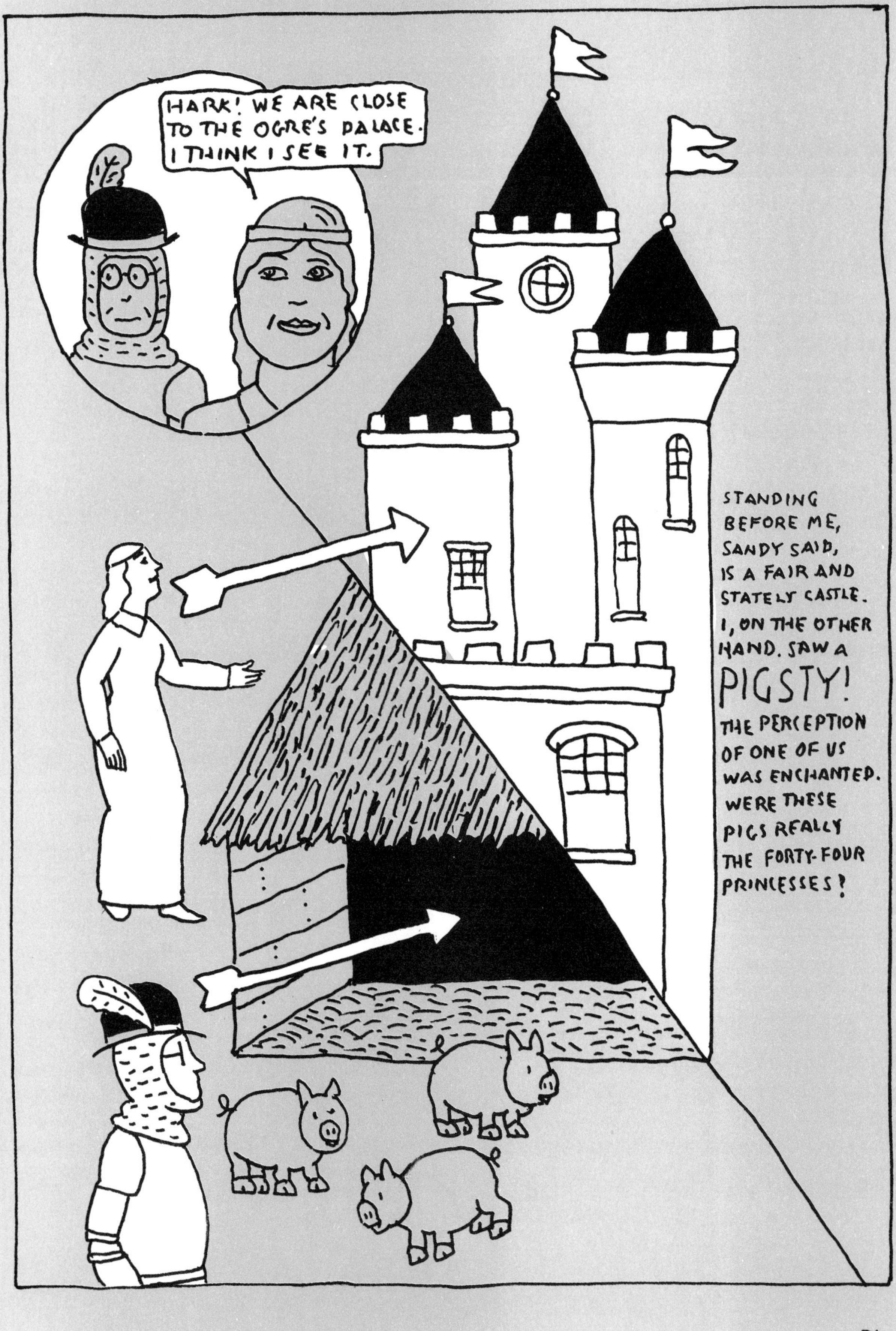
HARK! WE ARE CLOSE TO THE OGRE'S PALACE. I THINK I SEE IT.
STANDING BEFORE ME, SANDY SAID, IS A FAIR AND STATELY CASTLE. I, ON THE OTHER HAND, SAW A PIGSTY! THE PERCEPTION OF ONE OF US WAS ENCHANTED. WERE THESE PIGS REALLY THE FORTY-FOUR PRINCESSES?

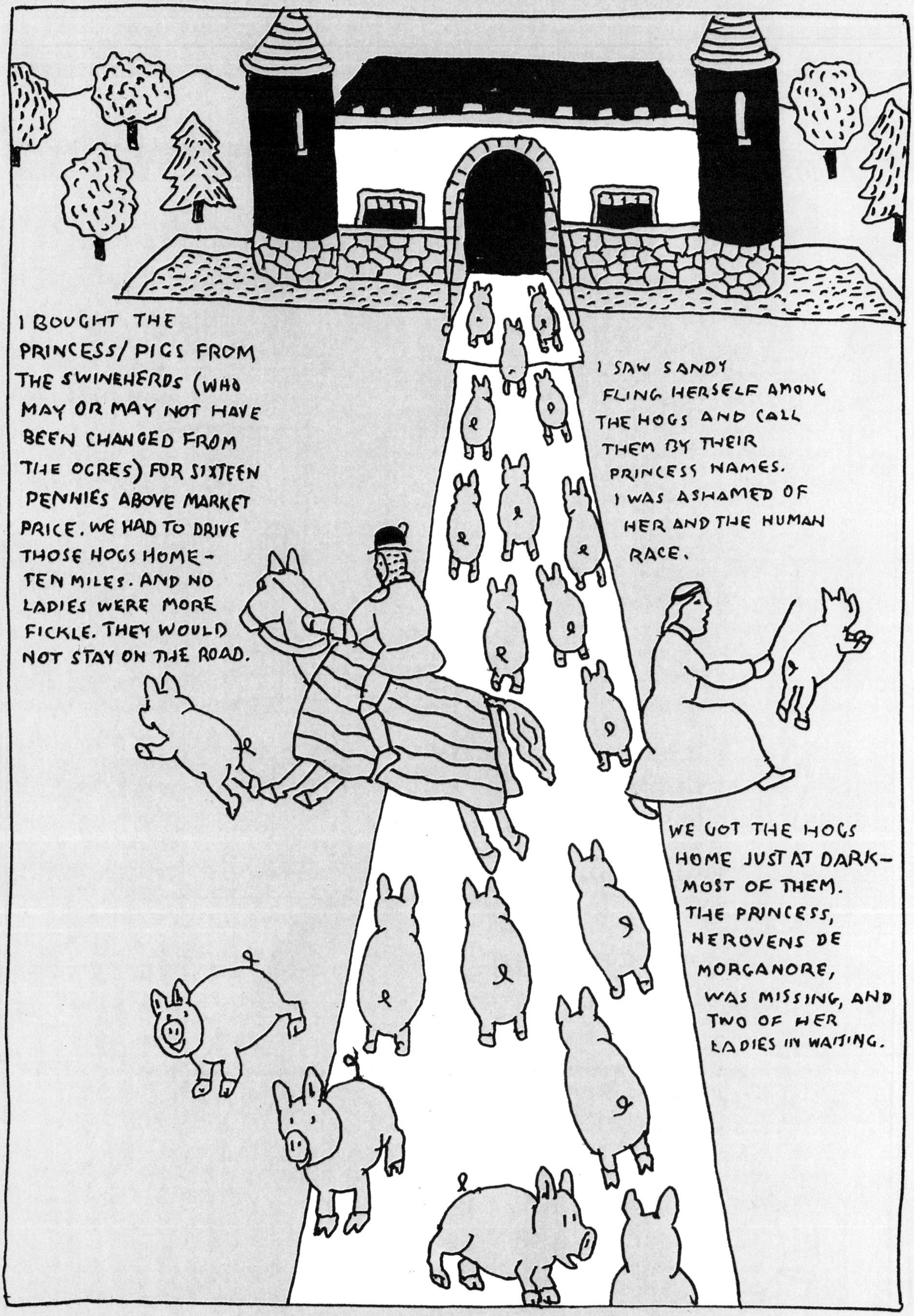
I BOUGHT THE PRINCESS/ PIGS FROM THE SWINEHERDS (WHO MAY OR MAY NOT HAVE BEEN CHANGED FROM THE OGRES) FOR SIXTEEN PENNIES ABOVE MARKET PRICE. WE HAD TO DRIVE THOSE HOGS HOME - TEN MILES. AND NO LADIES WERE MORE FICKLE. THEY WOULD NOT STAY ON THE ROAD.
I SAW SANDY FLING HERSELF AMONG THE HOGS AND CALL THEM BY THEIR PRINCESS NAMES. I WAS ASHAMED OF HER AND THE HUMAN RACE.
WE GOT THE HOGS HOME JUST AT DARK - MOST OF THEM. THE PRINCESS, HEROVENS DE MORGANORE, WAS MISSING, AND TWO OF HER LADIES IN WAITING.

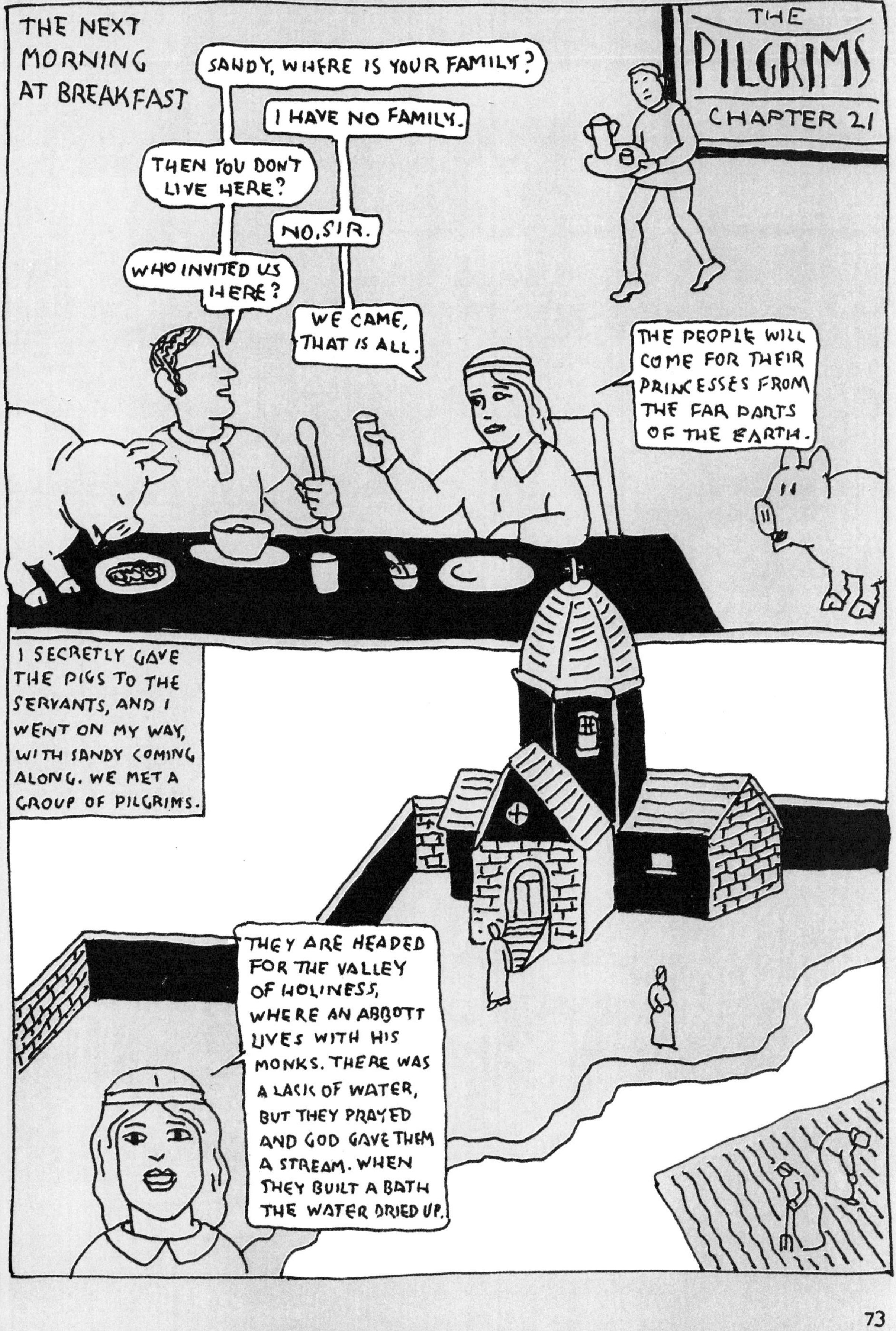
THE PILGRIMS
CHAPTER 21
THE NEXT MORNING AT BREAKFAST
SANDY, WHERE IS YOUR FAMILY?
I HAVE NO FAMILY.
THEN YOU DON'T LIVE HERE?
NO, SIR.
WHO INVITED US HERE?
WE CAME, THAT IS ALL.
THE PEOPLE WILL COME FOR THEIR PRINCESSES FROM THE FAR PARTS OF THE EARTH.
I SECRETLY GAVE THE PIGS TO THE SERVANTS, AND I WENT ON MY WAY, WITH SANDY COMING ALONG. WE MET A GROUP OF PILGRIMS.
THEY ARE HEADED FOR THE VALLEY OF HOLINESS, WHERE AN ABBOTT LIVES WITH HIS MONKS. THERE WAS A LACK OF WATER, BUT THEY PRAYED AND GOD GAVE THEM A STREAM. WHEN THEY BUILT A BATH THE WATER DRIED UP.

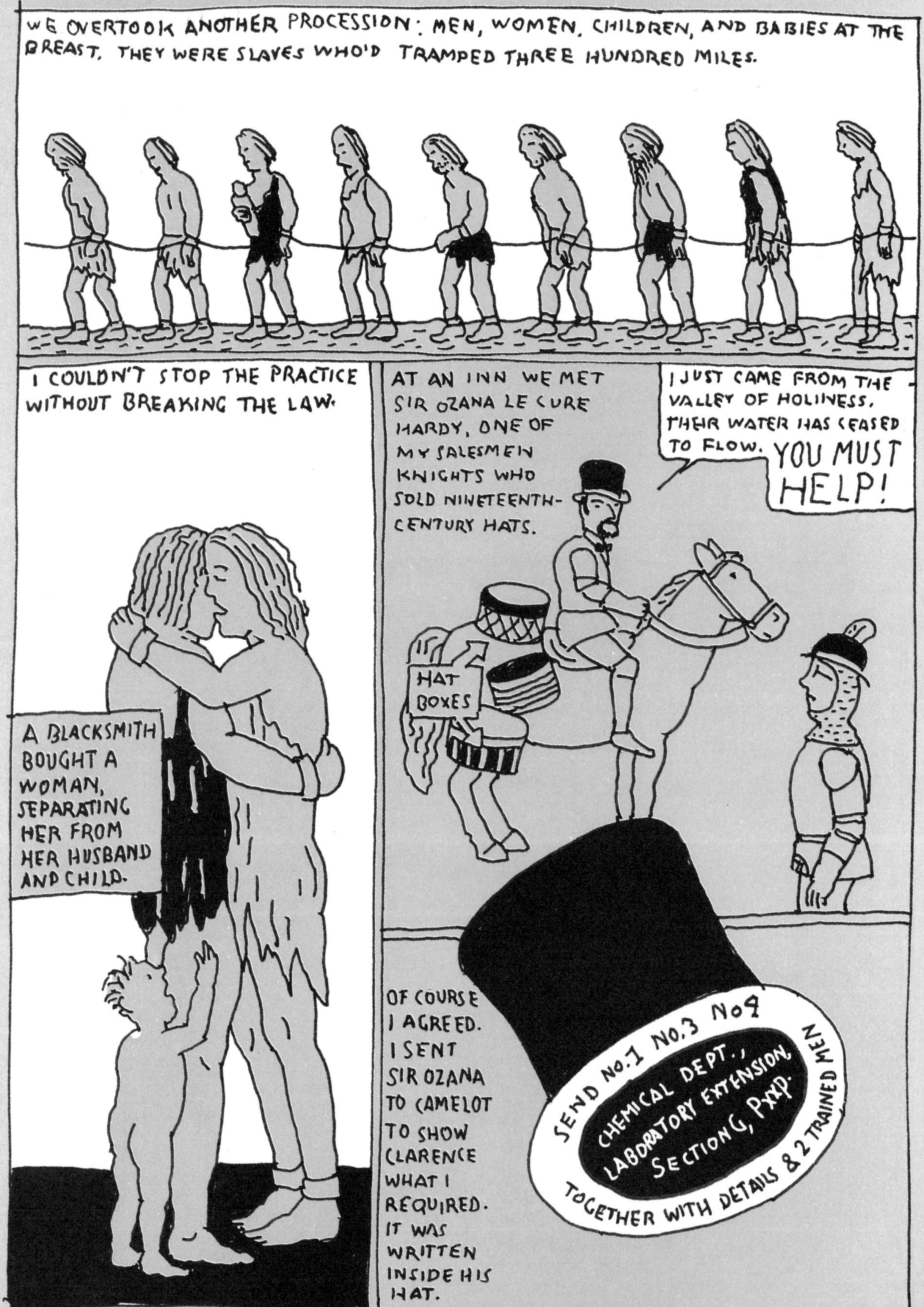
WE OVERTOOK ANOTHER PROCESSION: MEN, WOMEN, CHILDREN, AND BABIES AT THE BREAST. THEY WERE SLAVES WHO'D TRAMPED THREE HUNDRED MILES.
I COULDN'T STOP THE PRACTICE WITHOUT BREAKING THE LAW.
A BLACKSMITH BOUGHT A WOMAN, SEPARATING HER FROM HER HUSBAND AND CHILD.
AT AN INN WE MET SIR OZANA LE CURE HARDY, ONE OF MY SALESMEN KNIGHTS WHO SOLD NINETEENTH-CENTURY HATS.
I JUST CAME FROM THE VALLEY OF HOLINESS. THEIR WATER HAS CEASED TO FLOW. YOU MUST HELP!
HAT BOXES
OF COURSE I AGREED. I SENT SIR OZANA TO CAMELOT TO SHOW CLARENCE WHAT I REQUIRED. IT WAS WRITTEN INSIDE HIS HAT.
SEND No. 1 No. 3 No 4
CHEMICAL DEPT., LABORATORY EXTENSION, SECTION G, Pxxp.
TOGETHER WITH DETAILS & 2 TRAINED MEN

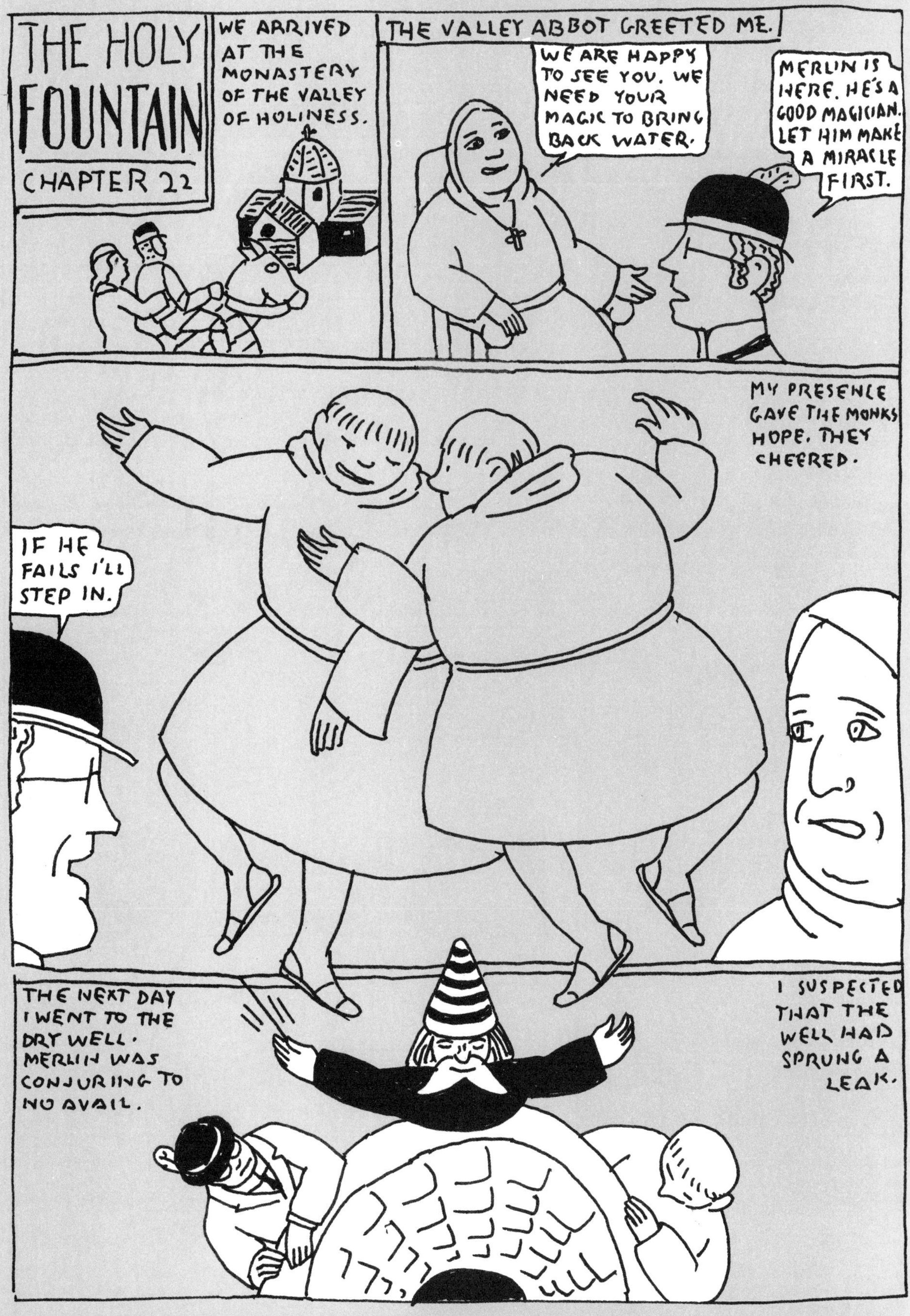
THE HOLY FOUNTAIN
CHAPTER 22
WE ARRIVED AT THE MONASTERY OF THE VALLEY OF HOLINESS.
THE VALLEY ABBOT GREETED ME.
WE ARE HAPPY TO SEE YOU. WE NEED YOUR MAGIC TO BRING BACK WATER.
MERLIN IS HERE. HE'S A GOOD MAGICIAN. LET HIM MAKE A MIRACLE FIRST.
MY PRESENCE GAVE THE MONKS HOPE. THEY CHEERED.
IF HE FAILS I'LL STEP IN.
THE NEXT DAY I WENT TO THE DRY WELL. MERLIN WAS CONJURING TO NO AVAIL.
I SUSPECTED THAT THE WELL HAD SPRUNG A LEAK.

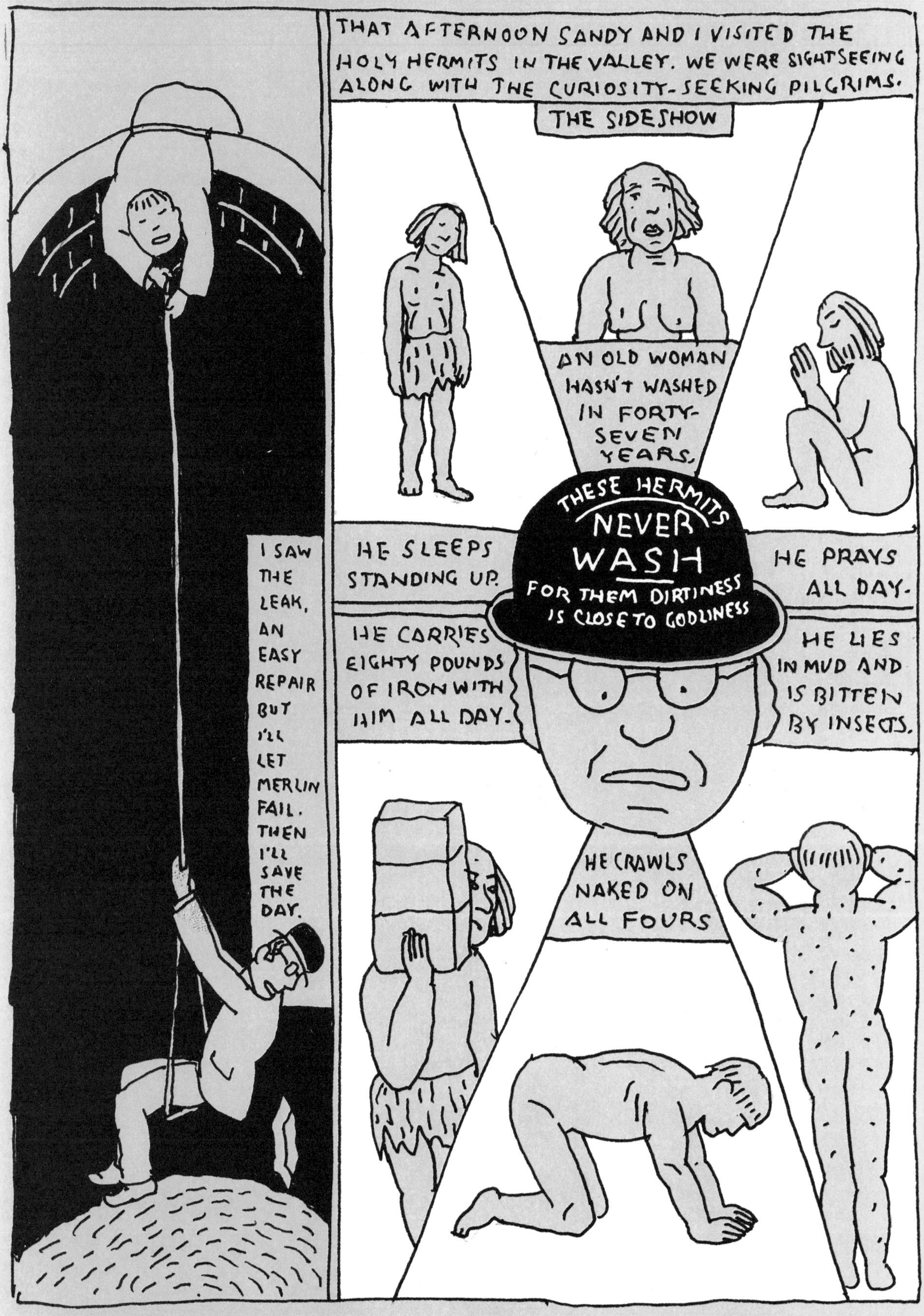

I SAW THE LEAK, AN EASY REPAIR BUT I'LL LET MERLIN FAIL. THEN I'LL SAVE THE DAY.
THAT AFTERNOON SANDY AND I VISITED THE HOLY HERMITS IN THE VALLEY. WE WERE SIGHTSEEING ALONG WITH THE CURIOSITY-SEEKING PILGRIMS.
THE SIDESHOW
AN OLD WOMAN HASN'T WASHED IN FORTY-SEVEN YEARS.
HE SLEEPS STANDING UP.
THESE HERMITS NEVER WASH FOR THEM DIRTINESS IS CLOSE TO GODLINESS
HE PRAYS ALL DAY.
HE CARRIES EIGHTY POUNDS OF IRON WITH HIM ALL DAY.
HE LIES IN MUD AND IS BITTEN BY INSECTS.
HE CRAWLS NAKED ON ALL FOURS

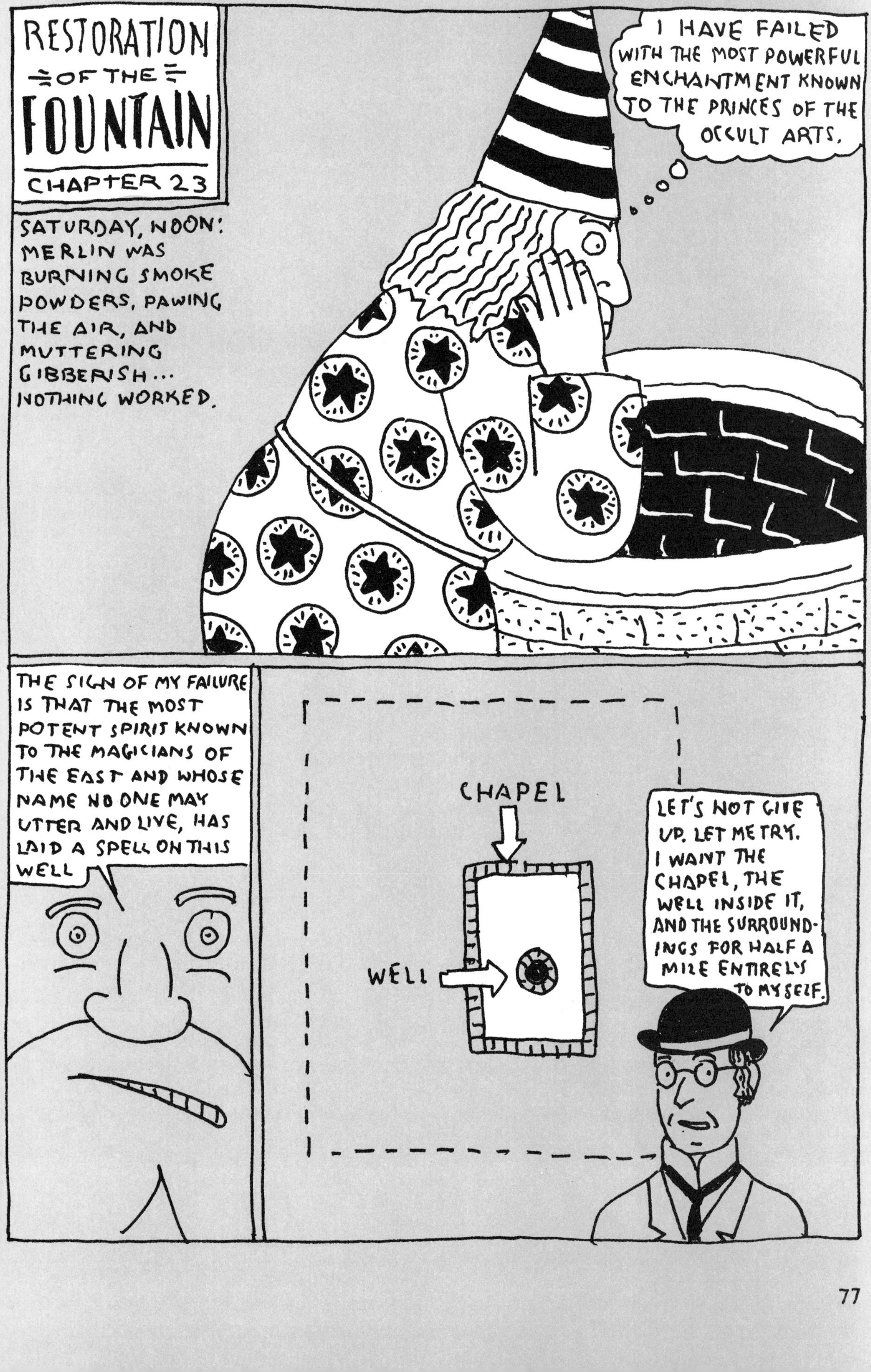
RESTORATION OF THE FOUNTAIN
CHAPTER 23
SATURDAY, NOON: MERLIN WAS BURNING SMOKE POWDERS, PAWING THE AIR, AND MUTTERING GIBBERISH... NOTHING WORKED.
I HAVE FAILED WITH THE MOST POWERFUL ENCHANTMENT KNOWN TO THE PRINCES OF THE OCCULT ARTS.
THE SIGN OF MY FAILURE IS THAT THE MOST POTENT SPIRIS KNOWN TO THE MAGICIANS OF THE EAST AND WHOSE NAME NO ONE MAY UTTER AND LIVE, HAS LAID A SPELL ON THIS WELL
CHAPEL
WELL
LET'S NOT GIVE UP. LET ME TRY. I WANT THE CHAPEL, THE WELL INSIDE IT, AND THE SURROUNDINGS FOR HALF A MILE ENTIRELY TO MYSELF.

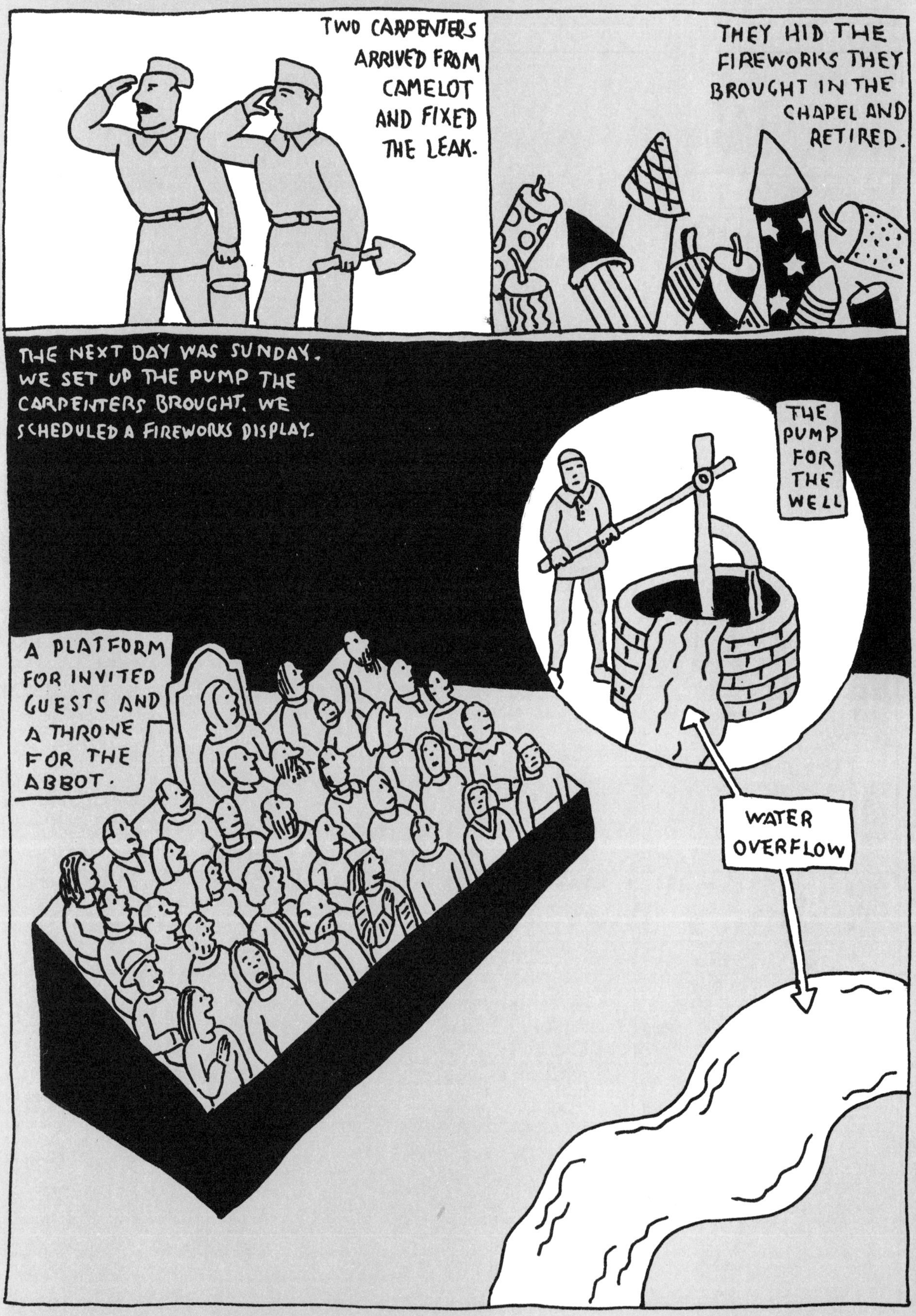
TWO CARPENTERS ARRIVED FROM CAMELOT AND FIXED THE LEAK.
THEY HID THE FIREWORKS THEY BROUGHT IN THE CHAPEL AND RETIRED.
THE NEXT DAY WAS SUNDAY. WE SET UP THE PUMP THE CARPENTERS BROUGHT. WE SCHEDULED A FIREWORKS DISPLAY.
THE PUMP FOR THE WELL
A PLATFORM FOR INVITED GUESTS AND A THRONE FOR THE ABBOT.
WATER OVERFLOW

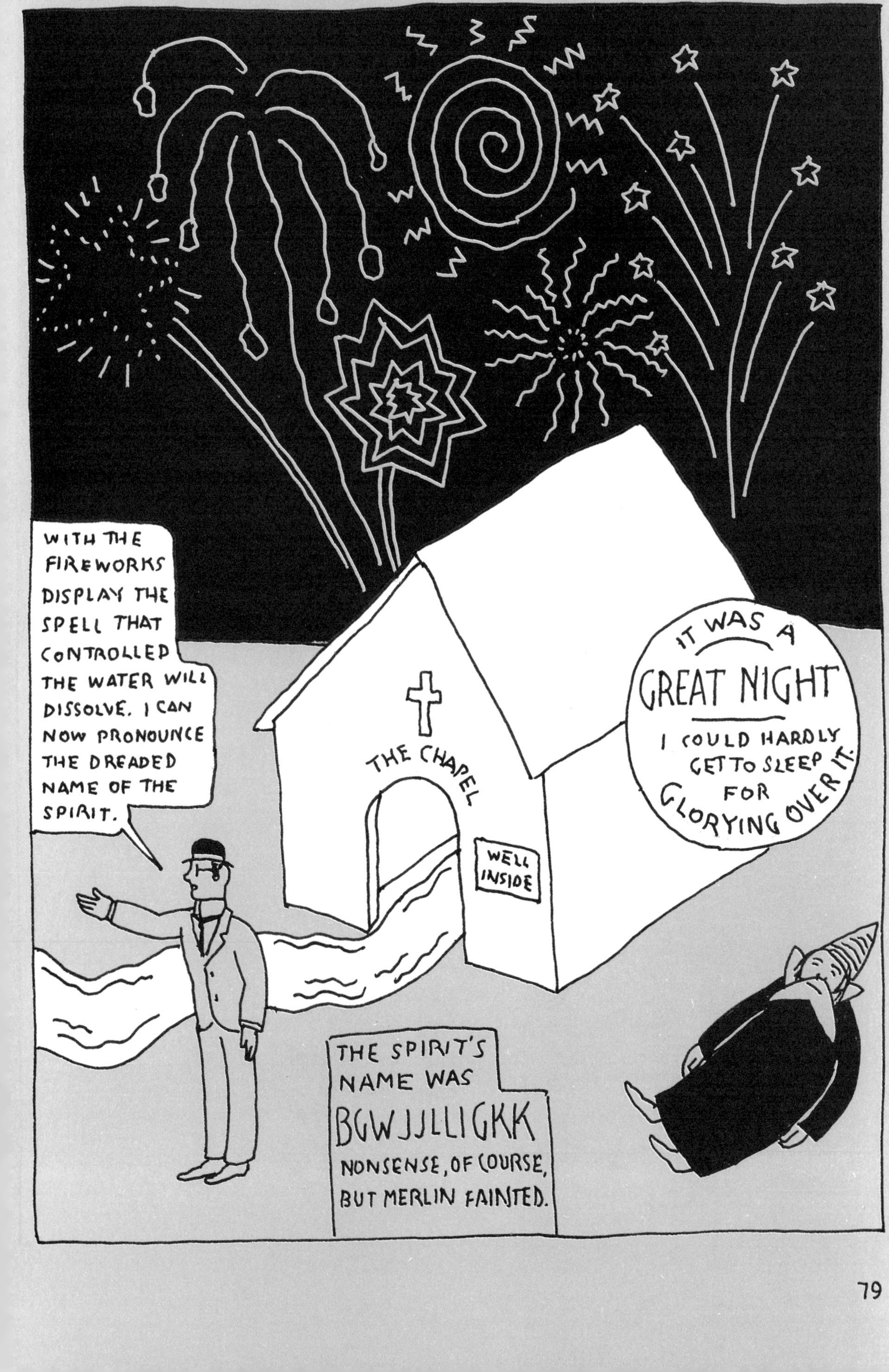
WITH THE FIREWORKS DISPLAY THE SPELL THAT CONTROLLED THE WATER WILL DISSOLVE. I CAN NOW PRONOUNCE THE DREADED NAME OF THE SPIRIT.
THE CHAPEL
WELL INSIDE
IT WAS A GREAT NIGHT I COULD HARDLY GET TO SLEEP FOR GLORYING OVER IT.
THE SPIRIT'S NAME WAS BGWJJLLIGKK NONSENSE, OF COURSE, BUT MERLIN FAINTED.

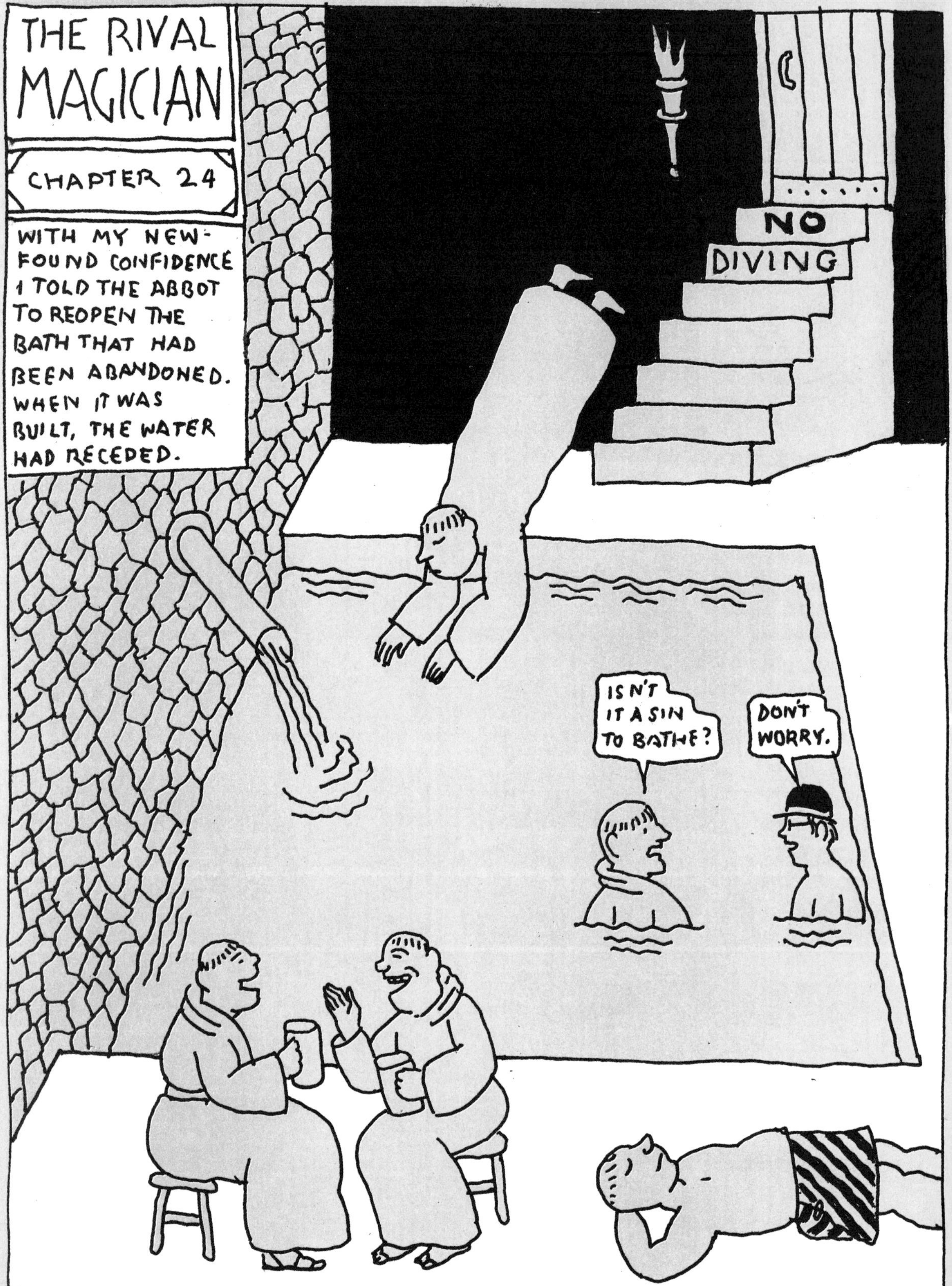
THE RIVAL MAGICIAN
CHAPTER 24
WITH MY NEW-FOUND CONFIDENCE I TOLD THE ABBOT TO REOPEN THE BATH THAT HAD BEEN ABANDONED. WHEN IT WAS BUILT, THE WATER HAD RECEDED.
NO DIVING
ISN'T IT A SIN TO BATHE?
DON'T WORRY.

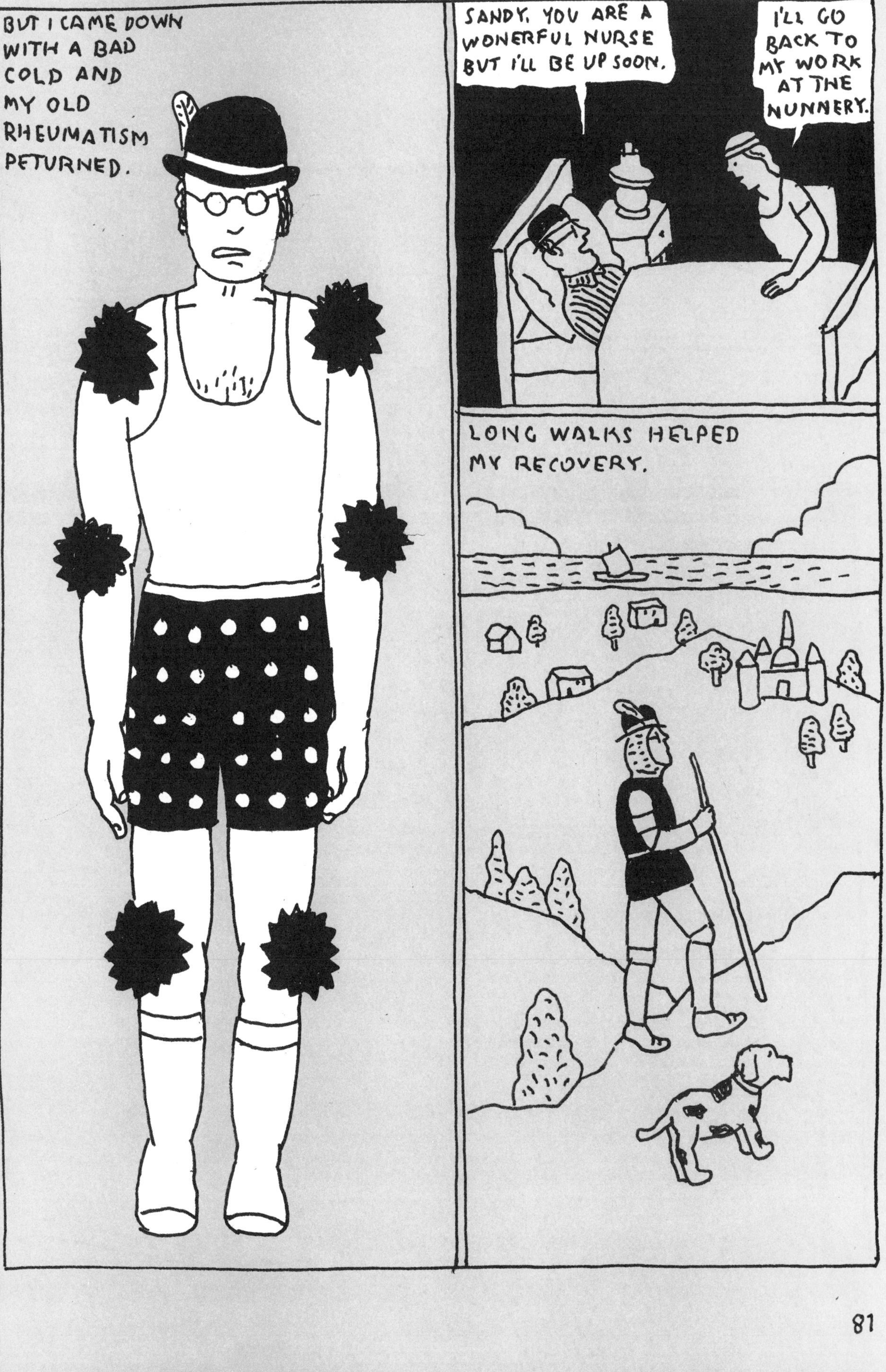
BUT I CAME DOWN WITH A BAD COLD AND MY OLD RHEUMATISM RETURNED.
SANDY, YOU ARE A WONERFUL NURSE BUT I'LL BE UP SOON.
I'LL GO BACK TO MY WORK AT THE NUNNERY.
LONG WALKS HELPED MY RECOVERY.

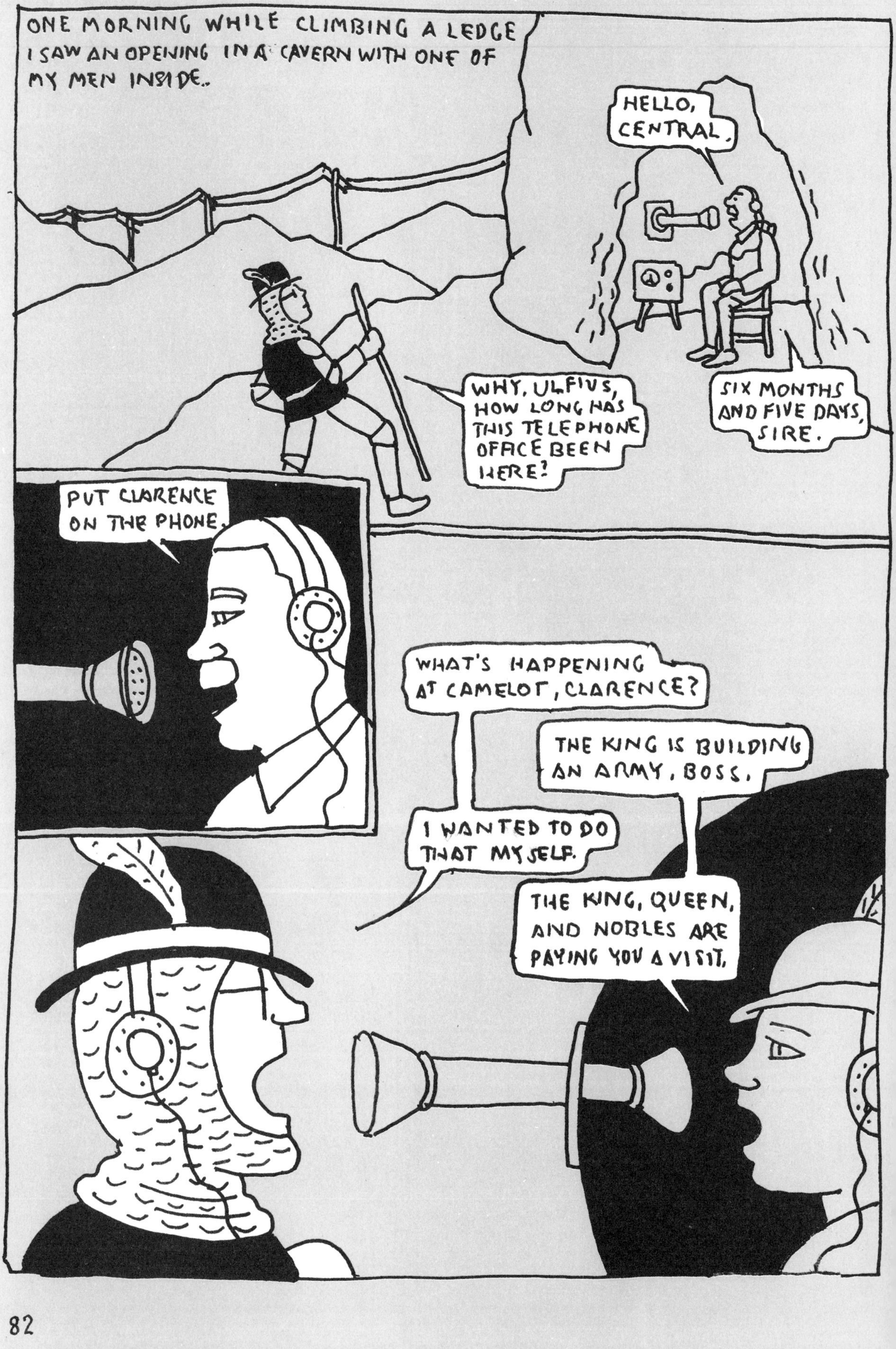
ONE MORNING WHILE CLIMBING A LEDGE I SAW AN OPENING IN A CAVERN WITH ONE OF MY MEN INSIDE..
HELLO, CENTRAL.
WHY, ULFIUS, HOW LONG HAS THIS TELEPHONE OFFICE BEEN HERE?
SIX MONTHS AND FIVE DAYS, SIRE.
PUT CLARENCE ON THE PHONE.
WHAT'S HAPPENING AT CAMELOT, CLARENCE?
THE KING IS BUILDING AN ARMY, BOSS.
I WANTED TO DO THAT MYSELF.
THE KING, QUEEN, AND NOBLES ARE PAYING YOU A VISIT.

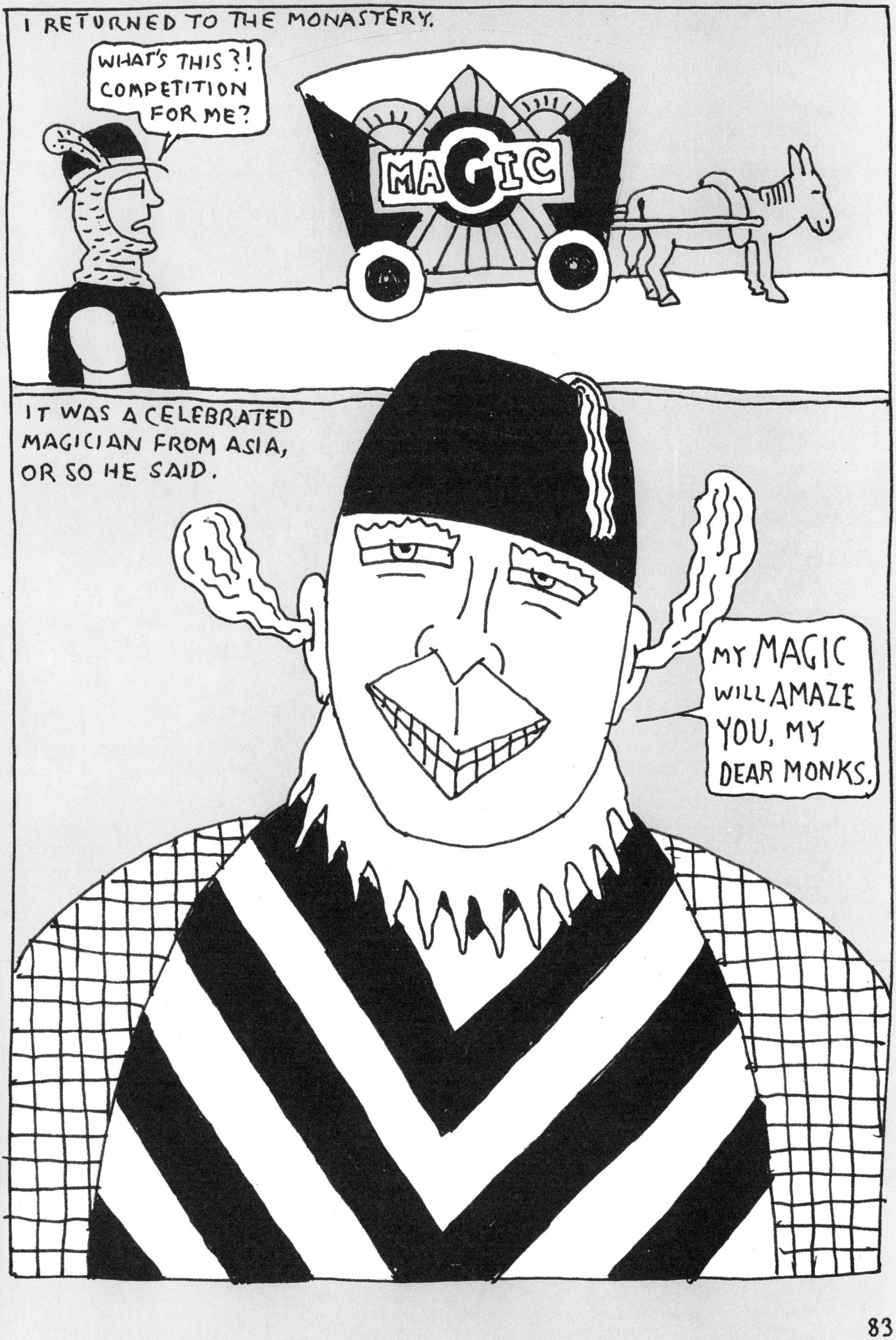
I RETURNED TO THE MONASTERY.
WHAT'S THIS?! COMPETITION FOR ME?
MAGIC
IT WAS A CELEBRATED MAGICIAN FROM ASIA, OR SO HE SAID.
MY MAGIC WILL AMAZE YOU, MY DEAR MONKS.

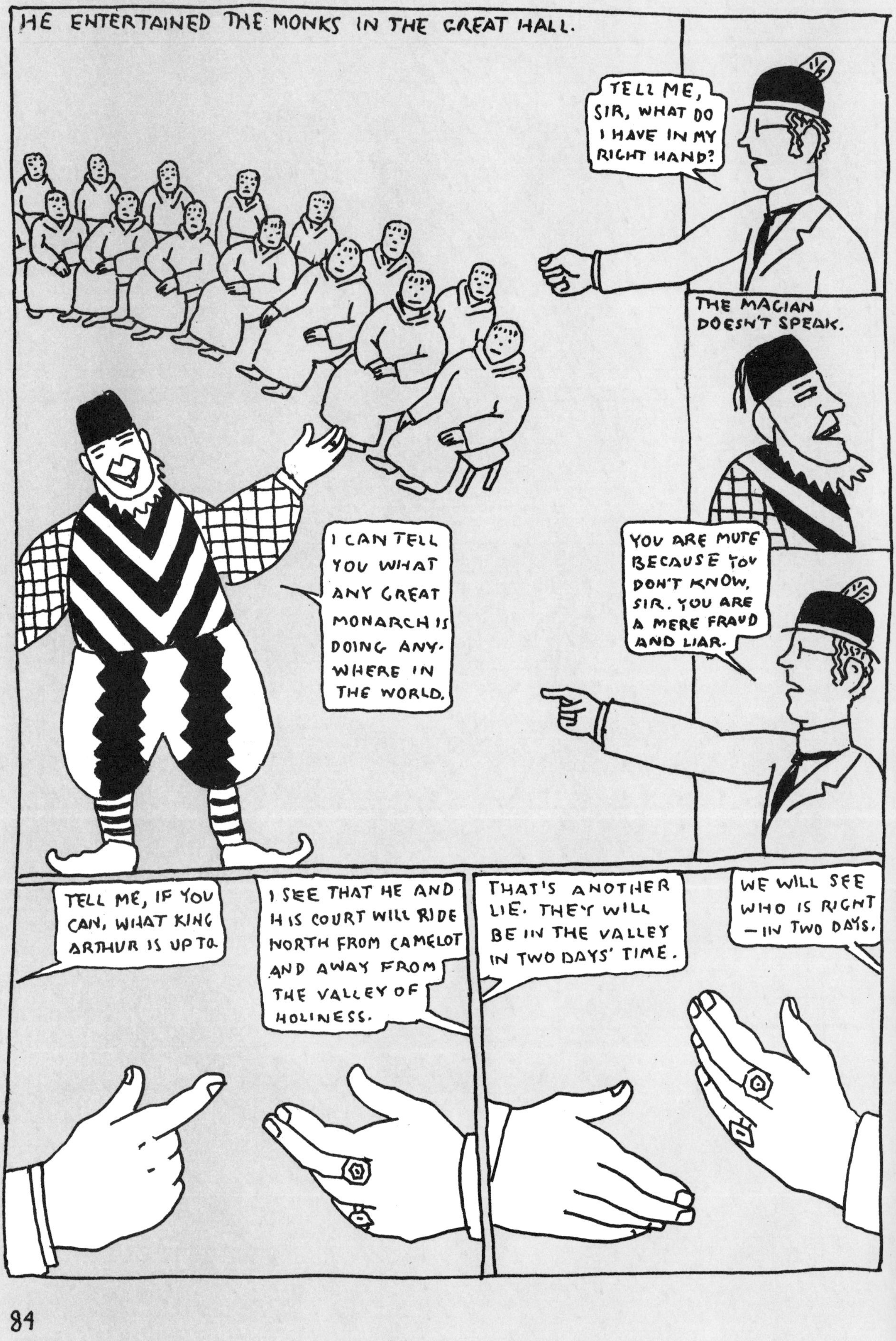
HE ENTERTAINED THE MONKS IN THE GREAT HALL.
TELL ME, SIR, WHAT DO I HAVE IN MY RIGHT HAND?
THE MAGIAN DOESN'T SPEAK.
I CAN TELL YOU WHAT ANY GREAT MONARCH IS DOING ANY-WHERE IN THE WORLD.
YOU ARE MUTE BECAUSE YOU DON'T KNOW, SIR. YOU ARE A MERE FRAUD AND LIAR.
TELL ME, IF YOU CAN, WHAT KING ARTHUR IS UP TO.
I SEE THAT HE AND HIS COURT WILL RIDE NORTH FROM CAMELOT AND AWAY FROM THE VALLEY OF HOLINESS.
THAT'S ANOTHER LIE. THEY WILL BE IN THE VALLEY IN TWO DAYS' TIME.
WE WILL SEE WHO IS RIGHT —IN TWO DAYS.

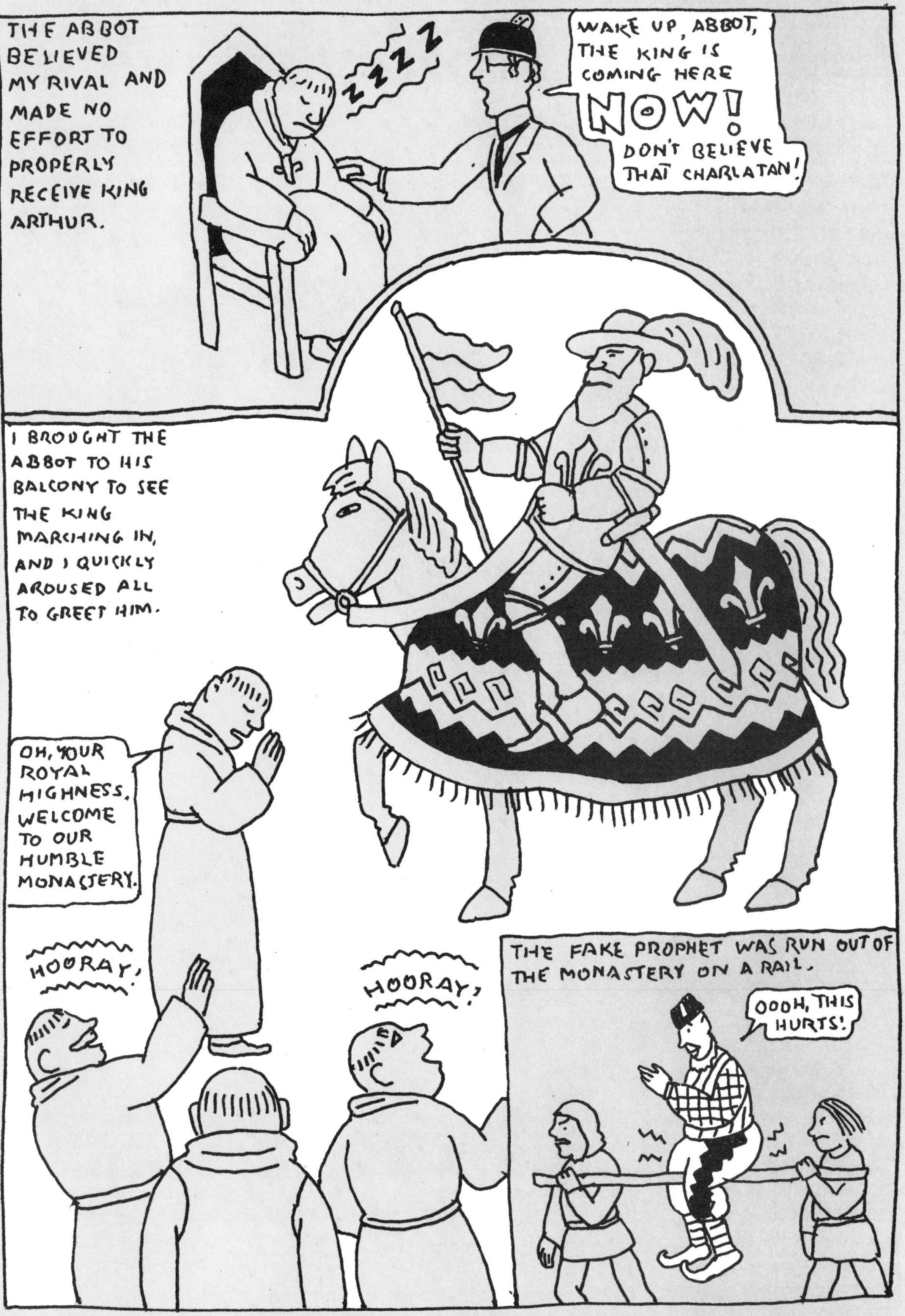
THE ABBOT BELIEVED MY RIVAL AND MADE NO EFFORT TO PROPERLY RECEIVE KING ARTHUR.
ZZZZ
WAKE UP, ABBOT, THE KING IS COMING HERE NOW!
DON'T BELIEVE THAT CHARLATAN!
I BROUGHT THE ABBOT TO HIS BALCONY TO SEE THE KING MARCHING IN, AND I QUICKLY AROUSED ALL TO GREET HIM.
OH, YOUR ROYAL HIGHNESS. WELCOME TO OUR HUMBLE MONASTERY.
HOORAY!
HOORAY!
THE FAKE PROPHET WAS RUN OUT OF THE MONASTERY ON A RAIL.
OOOH, THIS HURTS!

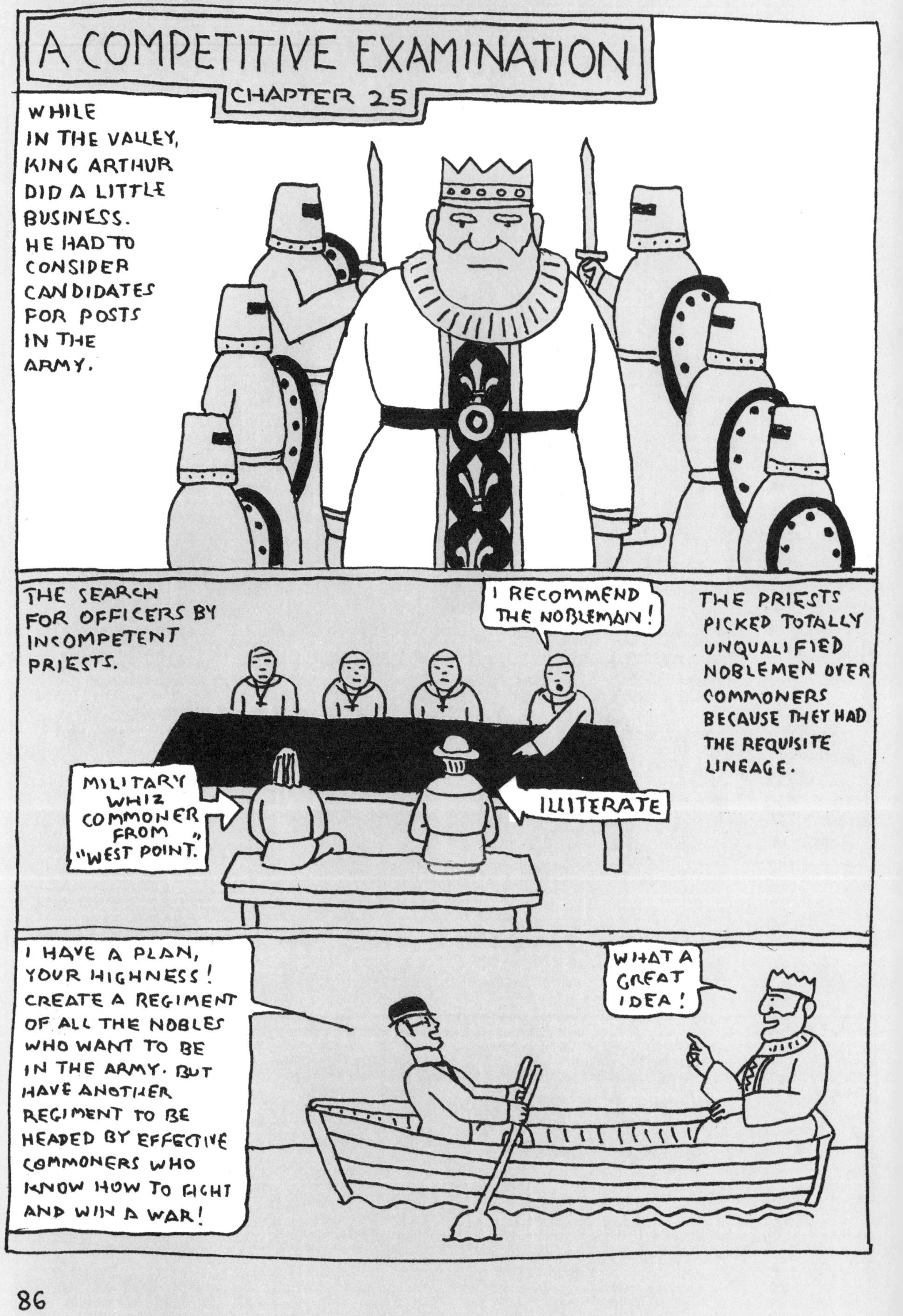
A COMPETITIVE EXAMINATION
CHAPTER 25
WHILE IN THE VALLEY, KING ARTHUR DID A LITTLE BUSINESS. HE HAD TO CONSIDER CANDIDATES FOR POSTS IN THE ARMY.
THE SEARCH FOR OFFICERS BY INCOMPETENT PRIESTS.
I RECOMMEND THE NOBLEMAN!
THE PRIESTS PICKED TOTALLY UNQUALIFIED NOBLEMEN OVER COMMONERS BECAUSE THEY HAD THE REQUISITE LINEAGE.
MILITARY WHIZ COMMONER FROM "WEST POINT."
ILLITERATE
I HAVE A PLAN, YOUR HIGHNESS! CREATE A REGIMENT OF ALL THE NOBLES WHO WANT TO BE IN THE ARMY. BUT HAVE ANOTHER REGIMENT TO BE HEADED BY EFFECTIVE COMMONERS WHO KNOW HOW TO FIGHT AND WIN A WAR!
WHAT A GREAT IDEA!

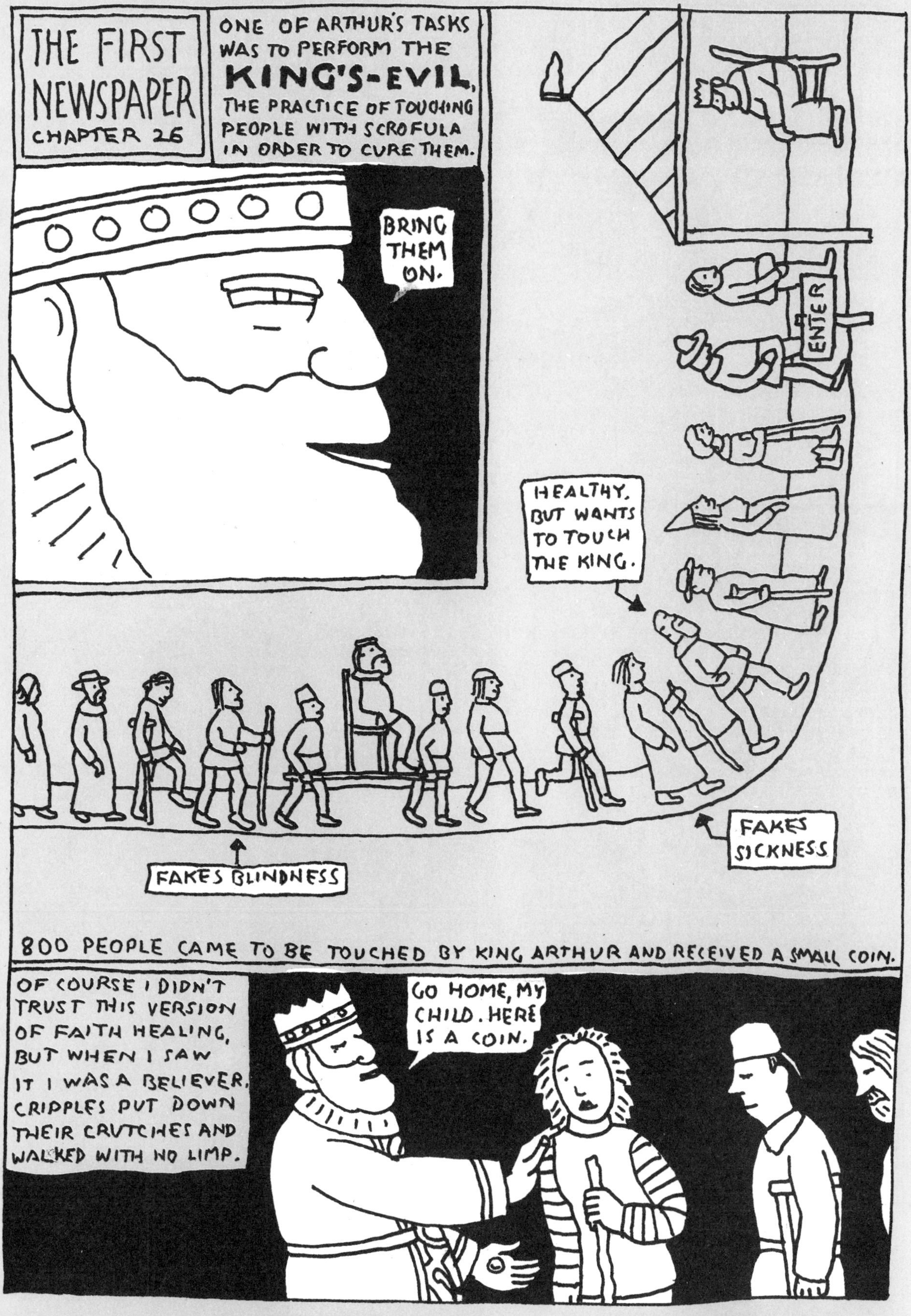

THE FIRST NEWSPAPER
CHAPTER 26
ONE OF ARTHUR'S TASKS WAS TO PERFORM THE KING'S-EVIL, THE PRACTICE OF TOUCHING PEOPLE WITH SCROFULA IN ORDER TO CURE THEM.
BRING THEM ON.
ENTER
HEALTHY, BUT WANTS TO TOUCH THE KING.
FAKES SICKNESS
FAKES BLINDNESS
800 PEOPLE CAME TO BE TOUCHED BY KING ARTHUR AND RECEIVED A SMALL COIN.
OF COURSE I DIDN'T TRUST THIS VERSION OF FAITH HEALING, BUT WHEN I SAW IT I WAS A BELIEVER. CRIPPLES PUT DOWN THEIR CRUTCHES AND WALKED WITH NO LIMP.
GO HOME, MY CHILD. HERE IS A COIN.

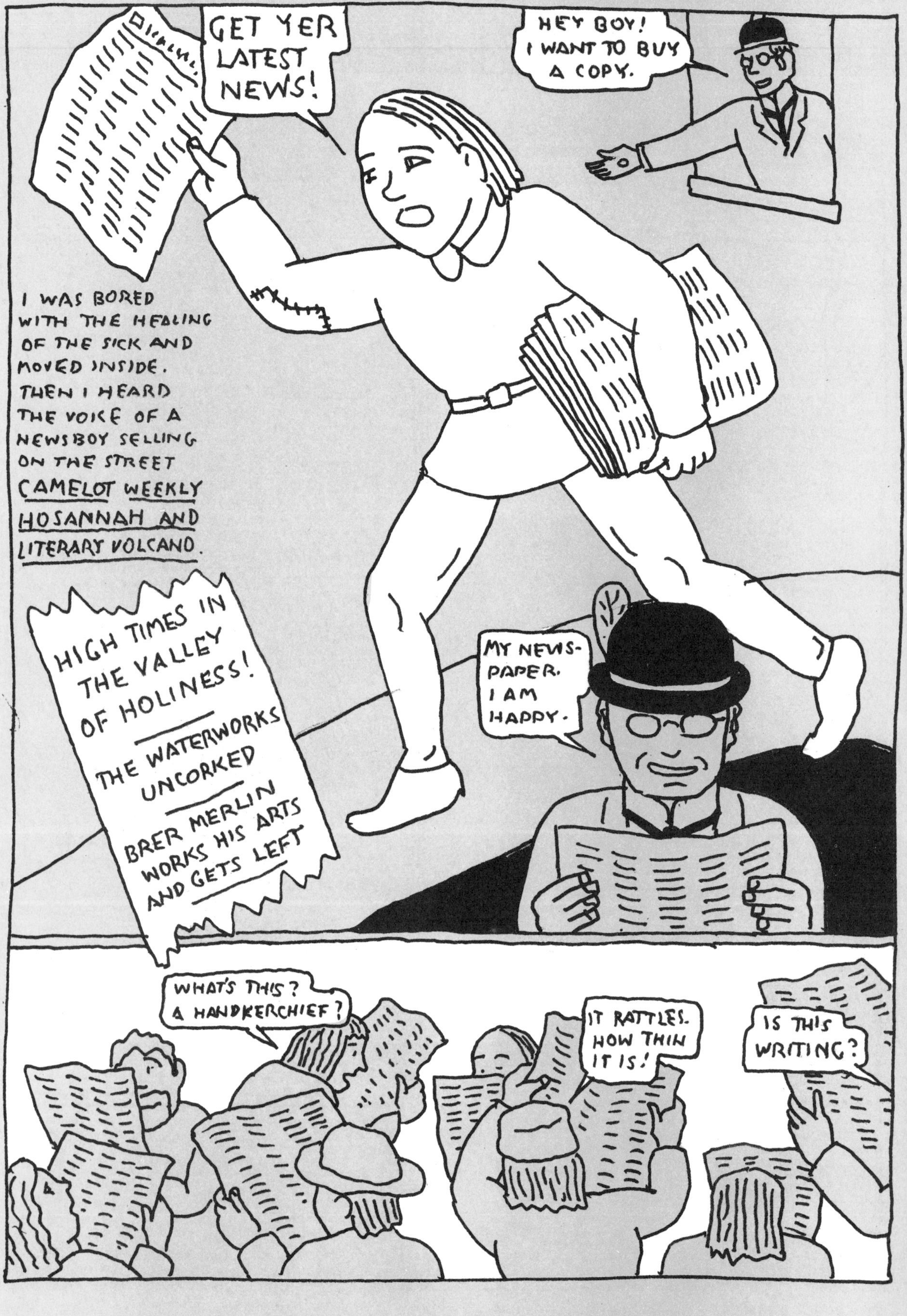

GET YER LATEST NEWS!
HEY BOY! I WANT TO BUY A COPY.
I WAS BORED WITH THE HEALING OF THE SICK AND MOVED INSIDE. THEN I HEARD THE VOICE OF A NEWSBOY SELLING ON THE STREET CAMELOT WEEKLY HOSANNAH AND LITERARY VOLCANO.
HIGH TIMES IN THE VALLEY OF HOLINESS!
THE WATERWORKS UNCORKED
BRER MERLIN WORKS HIS ARTS AND GETS LEFT
MY NEWSPAPER. I AM HAPPY.
WHAT'S THIS? A HANDKERCHIEF?
IT RATTLES. HOW THIN IT IS!
IS THIS WRITING?

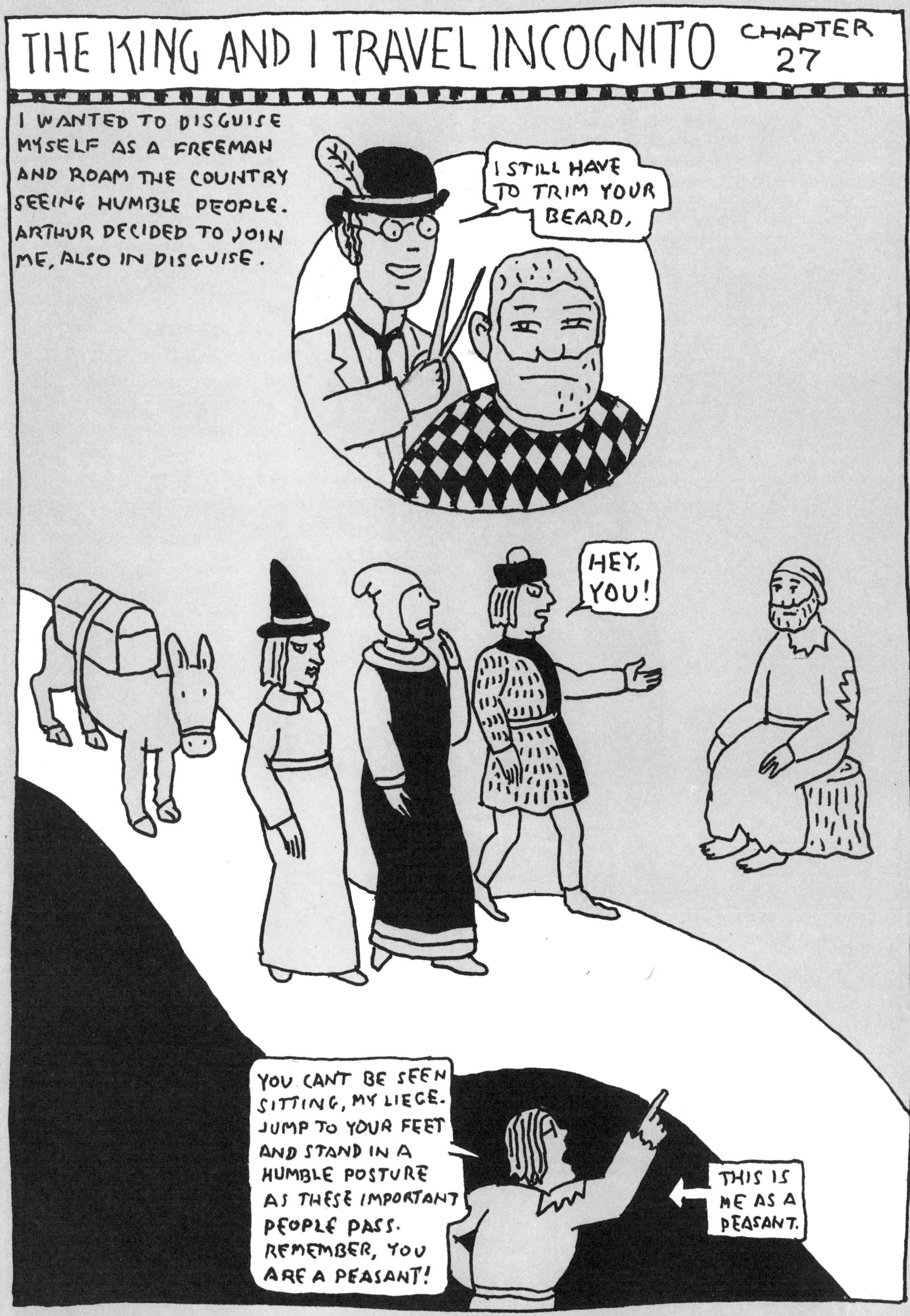
THE KING AND I TRAVEL INCOGNITO
CHAPTER 27
I WANTED TO DISGUISE MYSELF AS A FREEMAN AND ROAM THE COUNTRY SEEING HUMBLE PEOPLE. ARTHUR DECIDED TO JOIN ME, ALSO IN DISGUISE.
I STILL HAVE TO TRIM YOUR BEARD.
HEY, YOU!
YOU CANT BE SEEN SITTING, MY LIEGE. JUMP TO YOUR FEET AND STAND IN A HUMBLE POSTURE AS THESE IMPORTANT PEOPLE PASS. REMEMBER, YOU ARE A PEASANT!
THIS IS ME AS A PEASANT.

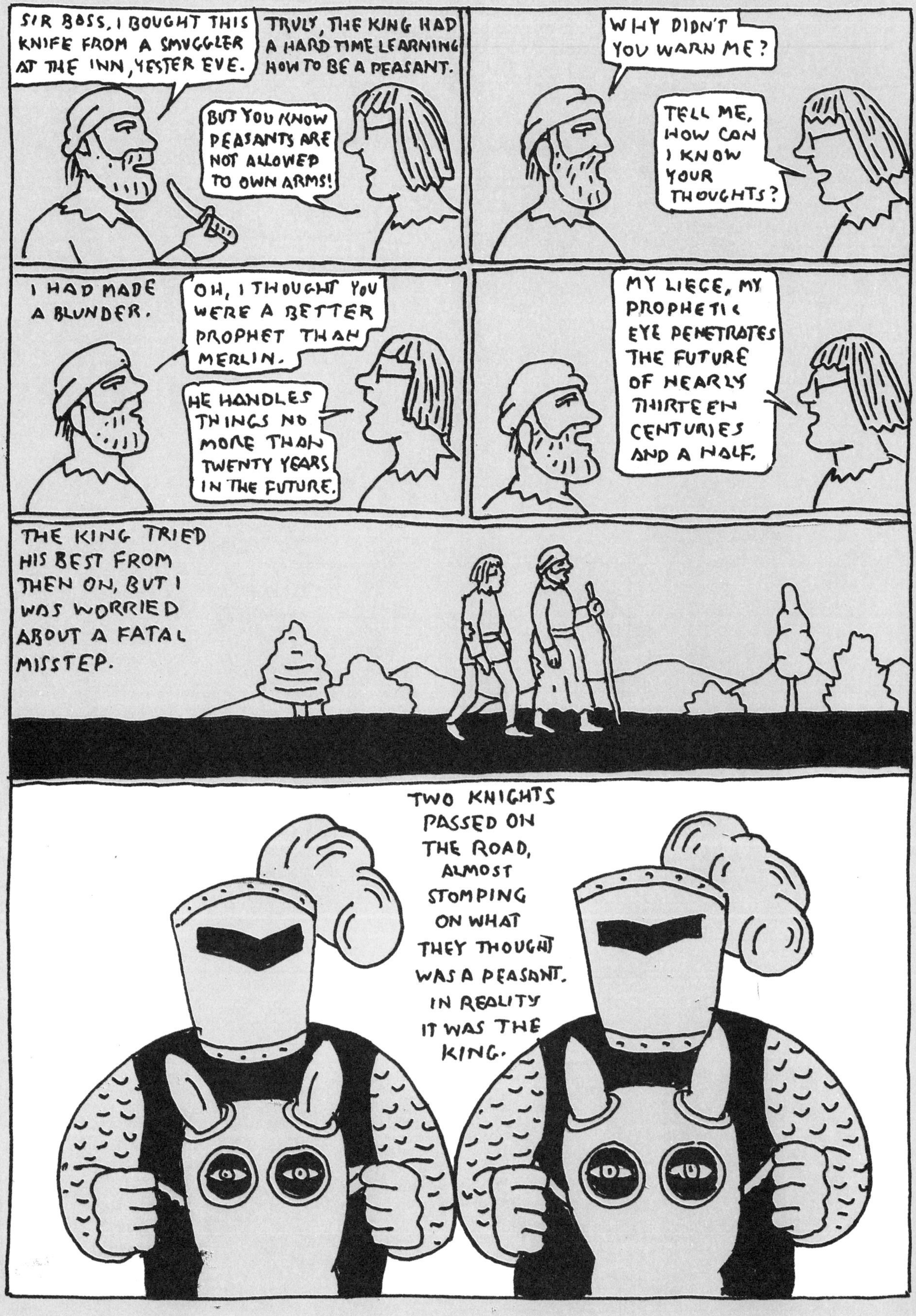
SIR BOSS, I BOUGHT THIS KNIFE FROM A SMUGGLER AT THE INN, YESTER EVE.
TRULY, THE KING HAD A HARD TIME LEARNING HOW TO BE A PEASANT.
BUT YOU KNOW PEASANTS ARE NOT ALLOWED TO OWN ARMS!
WHY DIDN'T YOU WARN ME?
TELL ME, HOW CAN I KNOW YOUR THOUGHTS?
I HAD MADE A BLUNDER.
OH, I THOUGHT YOU WERE A BETTER PROPHET THAN MERLIN.
HE HANDLES THINGS NO MORE THAN TWENTY YEARS IN THE FUTURE.
MY LIEGE, MY PROPHETIC EYE PENETRATES THE FUTURE OF NEARLY THIRTEEN CENTURIES AND A HALF.
THE KING TRIED HIS BEST FROM THEN ON, BUT I WAS WORRIED ABOUT A FATAL MISSTEP.
TWO KNIGHTS PASSED ON THE ROAD, ALMOST STOMPING ON WHAT THEY THOUGHT WAS A PEASANT. IN REALITY IT WAS THE KING.

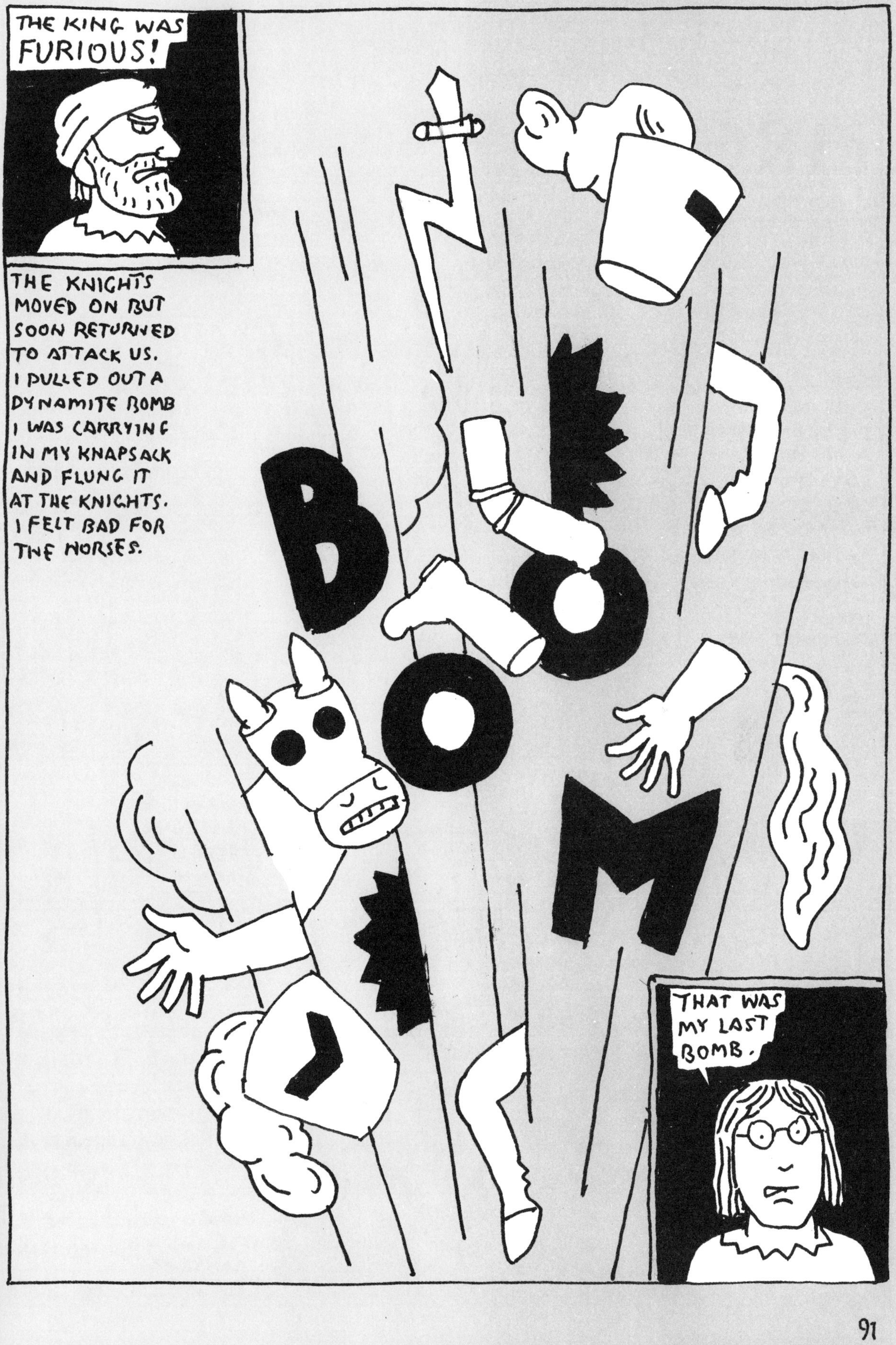
THE KING WAS FURIOUS!
THE KNIGHTS MOVED ON BUT SOON RETURNED TO ATTACK US. I PULLED OUT A DYNAMITE BOMB I WAS CARRYING IN MY KNAPSACK AND FLUNG IT AT THE KNIGHTS. I FELT BAD FOR THE HORSES.
BOOOM
THAT WAS MY LAST BOMB.

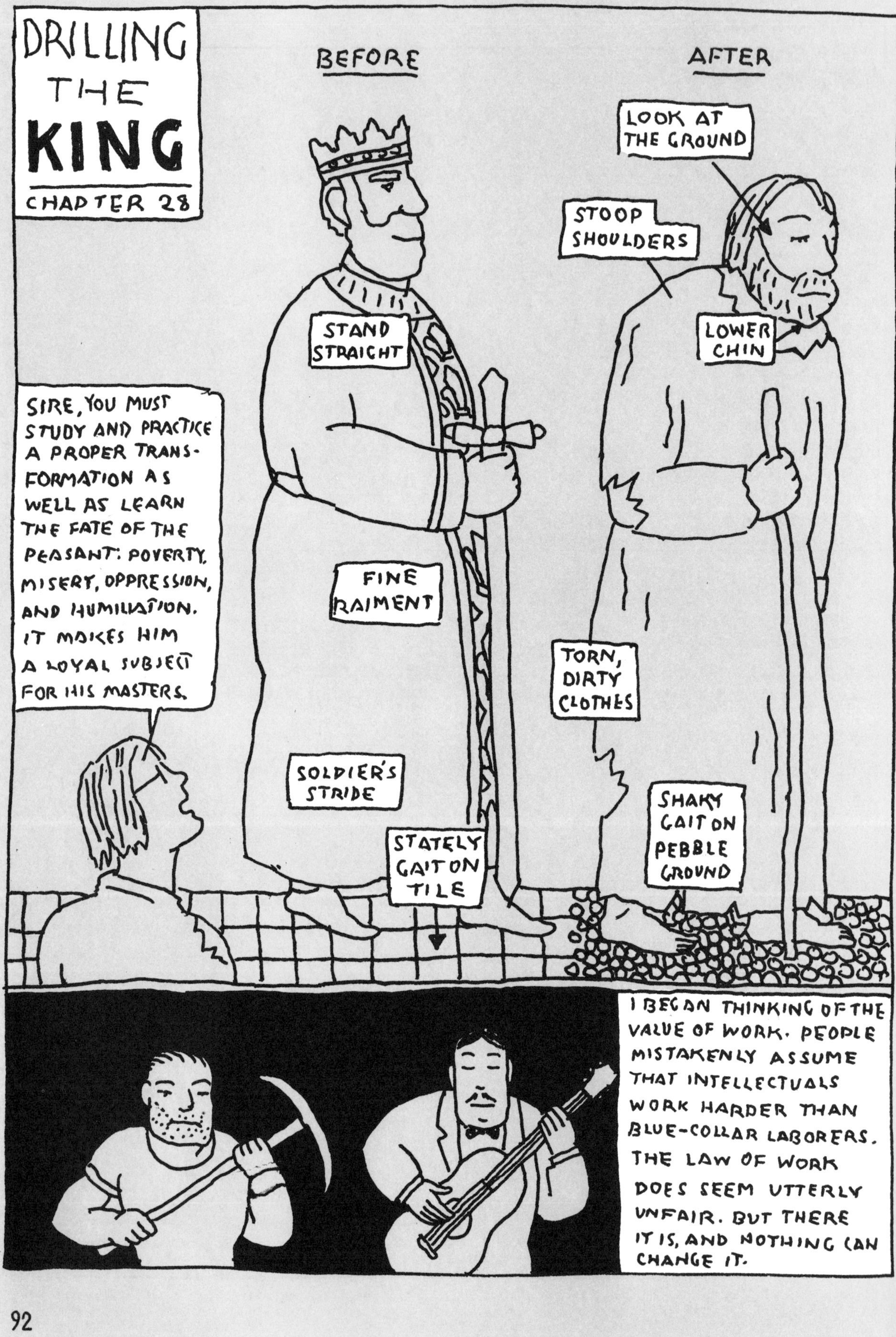
DRILLING THE KING
CHAPTER 28
BEFORE
AFTER
SIRE, YOU MUST STUDY AND PRACTICE A PROPER TRANS-FORMATION AS WELL AS LEARN THE FATE OF THE PEASANT: POVERTY, MISERY, OPPRESSION, AND HUMILIATION. IT MAKES HIM A LOYAL SUBJECT FOR HIS MASTERS.
STAND STRAIGHT
FINE RAIMENT
SOLDIER'S STRIDE
STATELY GAIT ON TILE
LOOK AT THE GROUND
STOOP SHOULDERS
LOWER CHIN
TORN, DIRTY CLOTHES
SHAKY GAIT ON PEBBLE GROUND
I BEGAN THINKING OF THE VALUE OF WORK. PEOPLE MISTAKENLY ASSUME THAT INTELLECTUALS WORK HARDER THAN BLUE-COLLAR LABORERS. THE LAW OF WORK DOES SEEM UTTERLY UNFAIR. BUT THERE IT IS, AND NOTHING CAN CHANGE IT.

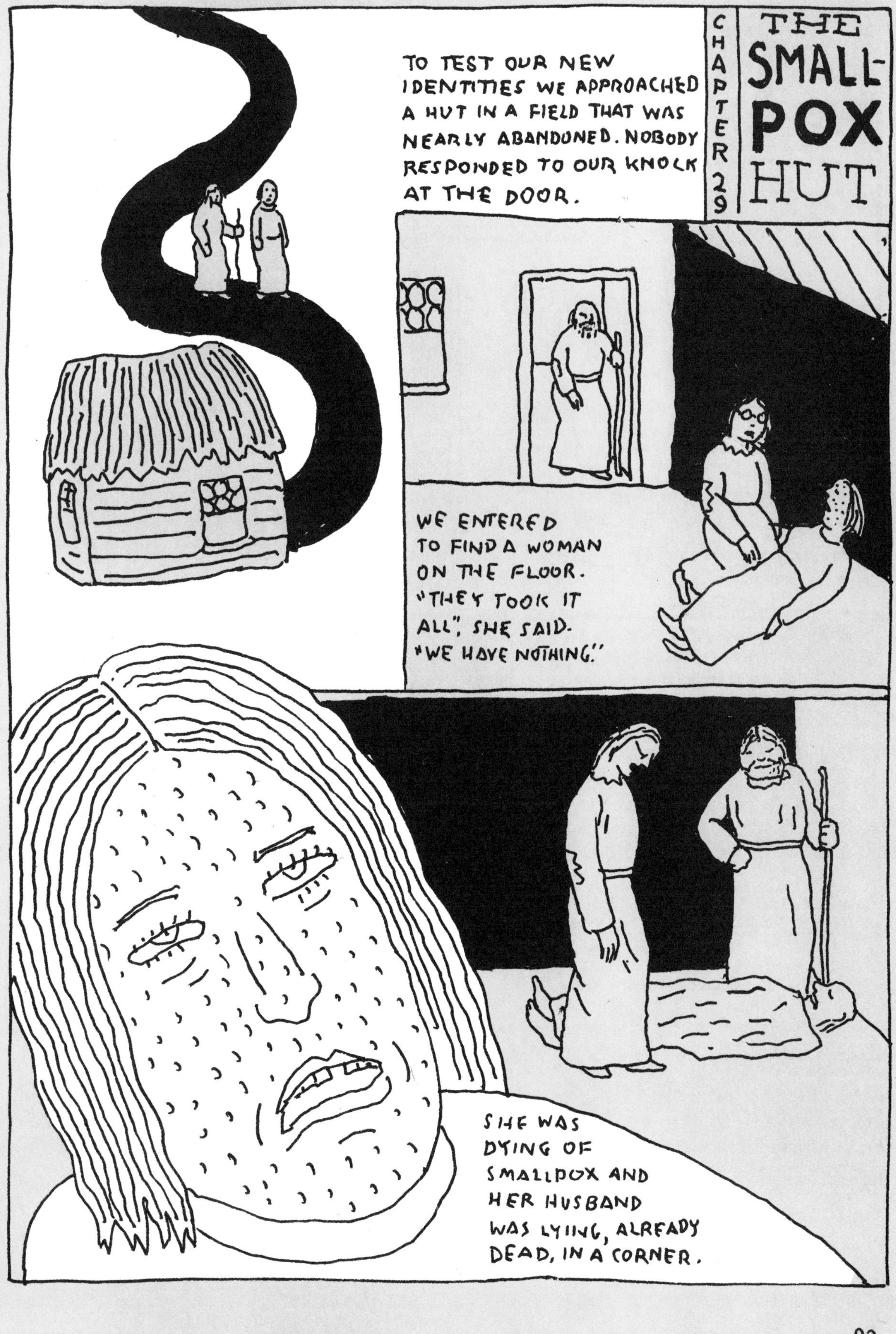
CHAPTER 29
THE SMALLPOX HUT
TO TEST OUR NEW IDENTITIES WE APPROACHED A HUT IN A FIELD THAT WAS NEARLY ABANDONED. NOBODY RESPONDED TO OUR KNOCK AT THE DOOR.
WE ENTERED TO FIND A WOMAN ON THE FLOOR. "THEY TOOK IT ALL", SHE SAID. "WE HAVE NOTHING."
SHE WAS DYING OF SMALLPOX AND HER HUSBAND WAS LYING, ALREADY DEAD, IN A CORNER.

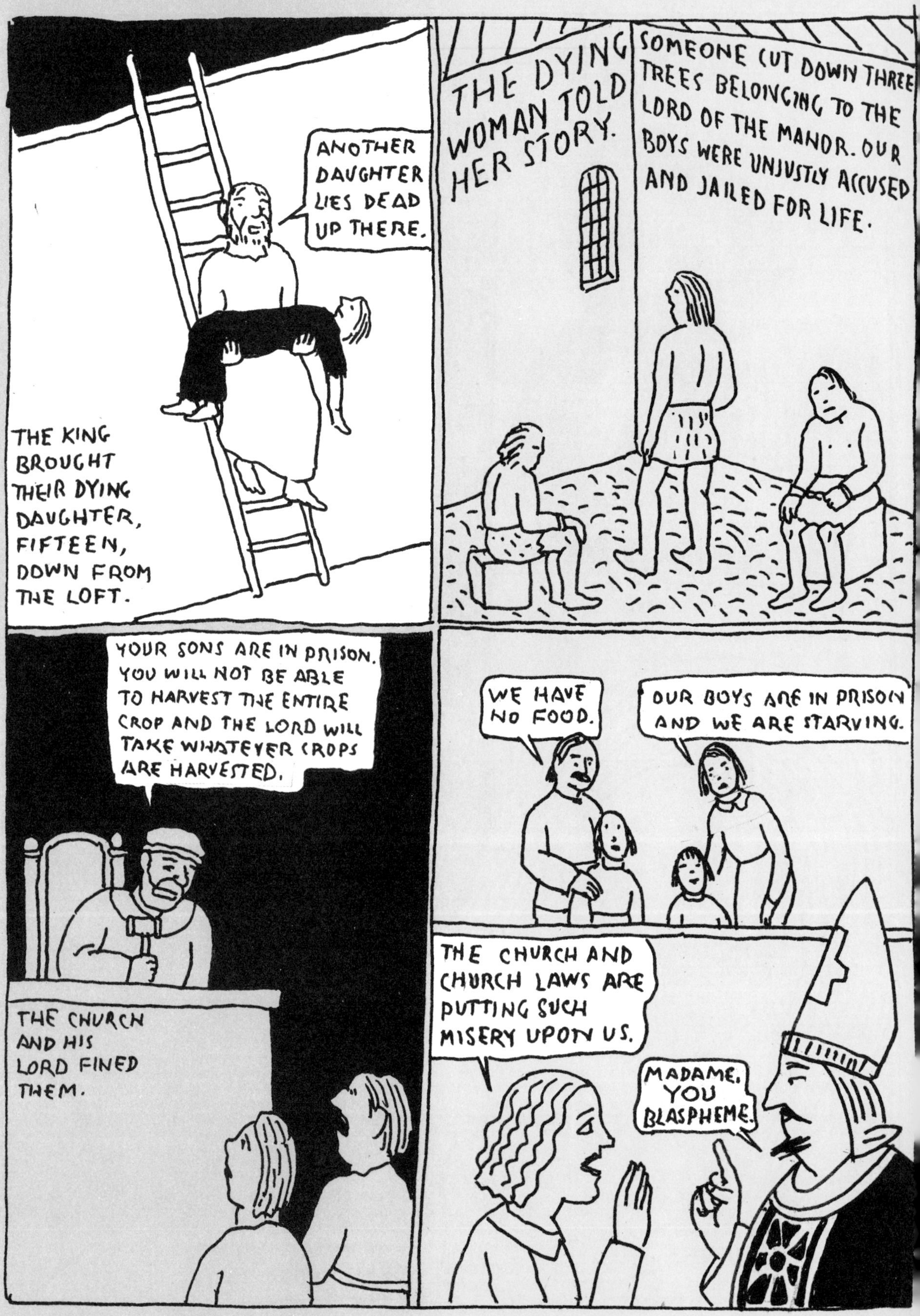
ANOTHER DAUGHTER LIES DEAD UP THERE.
THE KING BROUGHT THEIR DYING DAUGHTER, FIFTEEN, DOWN FROM THE LOFT.
THE DYING WOMAN TOLD HER STORY.
SOMEONE CUT DOWN THREE TREES BELONGING TO THE LORD OF THE MANOR. OUR BOYS WERE UNJUSTLY ACCUSED AND JAILED FOR LIFE.
YOUR SONS ARE IN PRISON. YOU WILL NOT BE ABLE TO HARVEST THE ENTIRE CROP AND THE LORD WILL TAKE WHATEVER CROPS ARE HARVESTED.
THE CHURCH AND HIS LORD FINED THEM.
WE HAVE NO FOOD.
OUR BOYS ARE IN PRISON AND WE ARE STARVING.
THE CHURCH AND CHURCH LAWS ARE PUTTING SUCH MISERY UPON US.
MADAME. YOU BLASPHEME.

THE TRAGEDY • OF THE • MANOR HOUSE

CHAPTER 30

THAT NIGHT THE WOMAN JOINED HER HUSBAND AND DAUGHTERS IN DEATH. THEY COULD NOT HAVE A CHRISTIAN BURIAL OR BE ADMITTED TO CONSECRATED GROUND.

WE HEARD THE THREE BOYS APPROACH THE HOUSE. WE QUICKLY LEFT.

THEY DISCOVERED THE WORST.

THOSE BOYS ESCAPED. WE MUST RE-CAPTURE THEM.

THAT IS NOT JUSTICE, MY LIEGE.

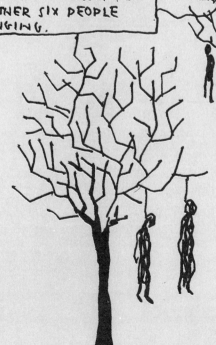

AS WE CONTINUED OUR TOUR WE NOTICED A FIRE IN THE DISTANCE. WE CAME UPON A HANGING. THEN TWO OTHERS WITHIN THE NEXT MILE. WE COUNTED ANOTHER SIX PEOPLE HANGING.

95

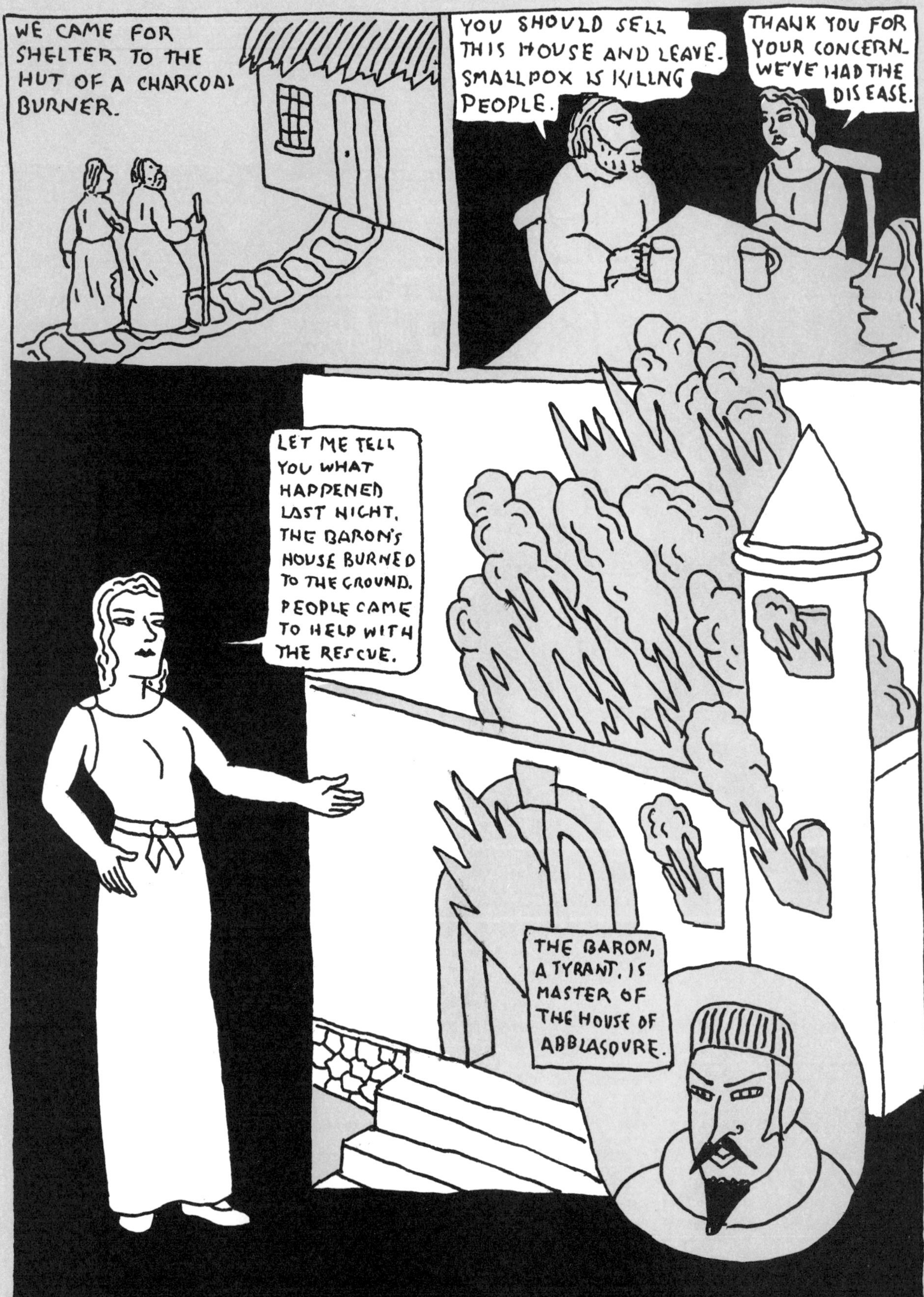
WE CAME FOR SHELTER TO THE HUT OF A CHARCOAL BURNER.
YOU SHOULD SELL THIS HOUSE AND LEAVE. SMALLPOX IS KILLING PEOPLE.
THANK YOU FOR YOUR CONCERN. WE'VE HAD THE DISEASE.
LET ME TELL YOU WHAT HAPPENED LAST NIGHT. THE BARON'S HOUSE BURNED TO THE GROUND. PEOPLE CAME TO HELP WITH THE RESCUE.
THE BARON, A TYRANT, IS MASTER OF THE HOUSE OF ABBLASOURE.

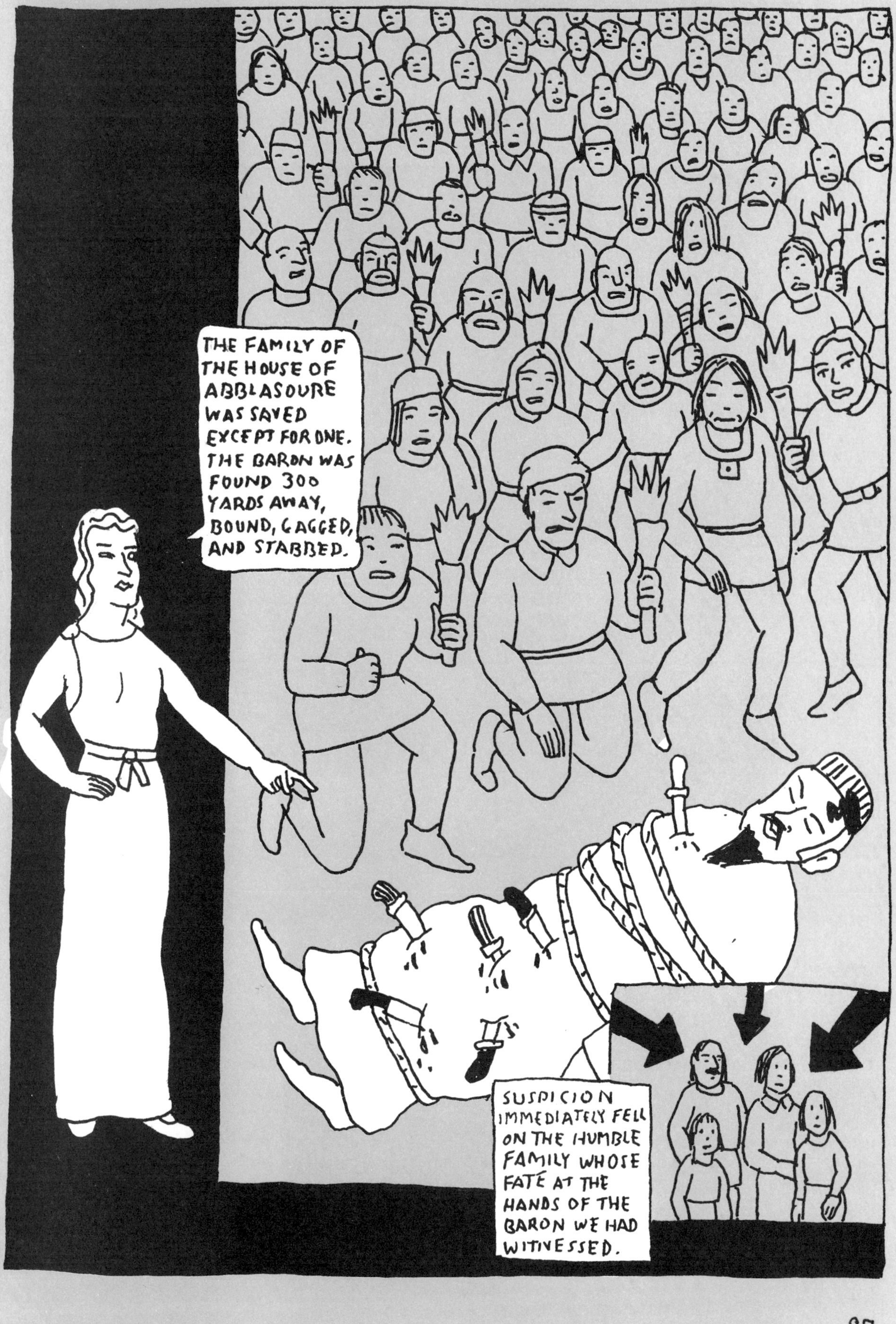
THE FAMILY OF THE HOUSE OF ABBLASOURE WAS SAVED EXCEPT FOR ONE. THE BARON WAS FOUND 300 YARDS AWAY, BOUND, GAGGED, AND STABBED.
SUSPICION IMMEDIATELY FELL ON THE HUMBLE FAMILY WHOSE FATE AT THE HANDS OF THE BARON WE HAD WITNESSED.

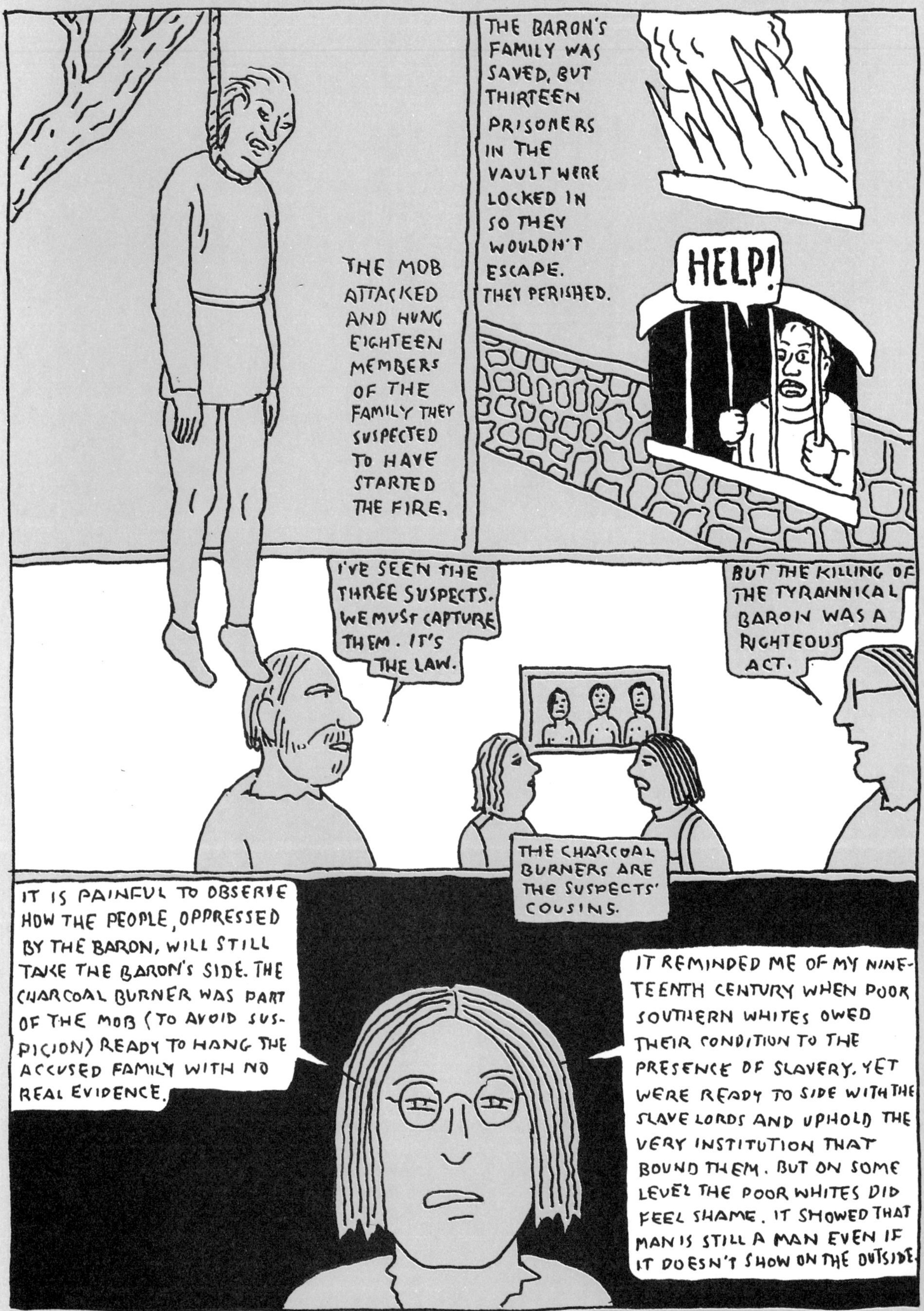
THE MOB ATTACKED AND HUNG EIGHTEEN MEMBERS OF THE FAMILY THEY SUSPECTED TO HAVE STARTED THE FIRE.
THE BARON'S FAMILY WAS SAVED, BUT THIRTEEN PRISONERS IN THE VAULT WERE LOCKED IN SO THEY WOULDN'T ESCAPE. THEY PERISHED.
HELP!
I'VE SEEN THE THREE SUSPECTS. WE MUST CAPTURE THEM. IT'S THE LAW.
BUT THE KILLING OF THE TYRANNICAL BARON WAS A RIGHTEOUS ACT.
THE CHARCOAL BURNERS ARE THE SUSPECTS' COUSINS.
IT IS PAINFUL TO OBSERVE HOW THE PEOPLE, OPPRESSED BY THE BARON, WILL STILL TAKE THE BARON'S SIDE. THE CHARCOAL BURNER WAS PART OF THE MOB (TO AVOID SUSPICION) READY TO HANG THE ACCUSED FAMILY WITH NO REAL EVIDENCE.
IT REMINDED ME OF MY NINETEENTH CENTURY WHEN POOR SOUTHERN WHITES OWED THEIR CONDITION TO THE PRESENCE OF SLAVERY, YET WERE READY TO SIDE WITH THE SLAVE LORDS AND UPHOLD THE VERY INSTITUTION THAT BOUND THEM. BUT ON SOME LEVEL THE POOR WHITES DID FEEL SHAME. IT SHOWED THAT MAN IS STILL A MAN EVEN IF IT DOESN'T SHOW ON THE OUTSIDE.

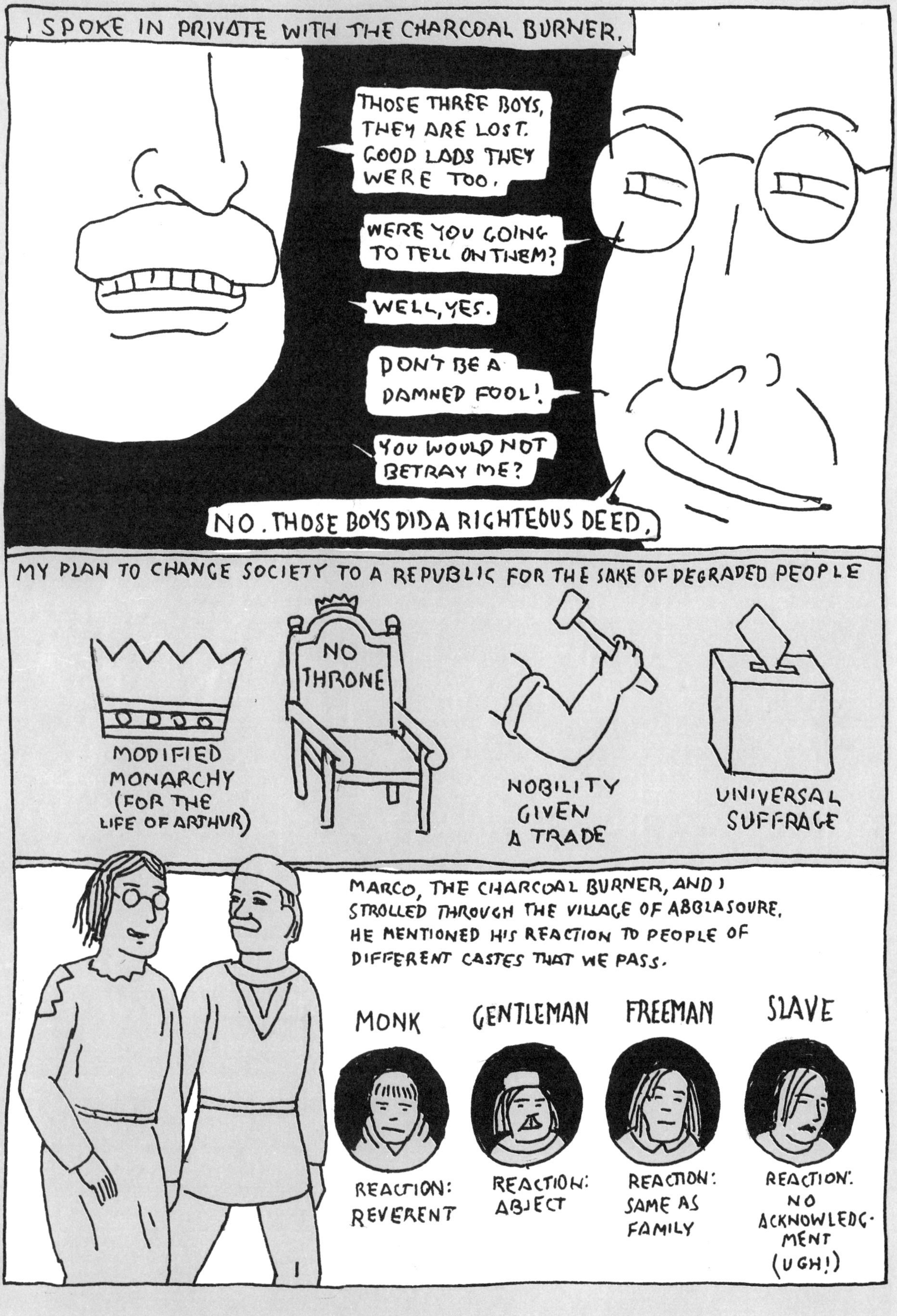

I SPOKE IN PRIVATE WITH THE CHARCOAL BURNER.
THOSE THREE BOYS, THEY ARE LOST. GOOD LADS THEY WERE TOO.
WERE YOU GOING TO TELL ON THEM?
WELL, YES.
DON'T BE A DAMNED FOOL!
YOU WOULD NOT BETRAY ME?
NO. THOSE BOYS DID A RIGHTEOUS DEED.
MY PLAN TO CHANGE SOCIETY TO A REPUBLIC FOR THE SAKE OF DEGRADED PEOPLE
MODIFIED MONARCHY (FOR THE LIFE OF ARTHUR)
NO THRONE
NOBILITY GIVEN A TRADE
UNIVERSAL SUFFRAGE
MARCO, THE CHARCOAL BURNER, AND I STROLLED THROUGH THE VILLAGE OF ABBLASOURE. HE MENTIONED HIS REACTION TO PEOPLE OF DIFFERENT CASTES THAT WE PASS.
MONK
GENTLEMAN
FREEMAN
SLAVE
REACTION: REVERENT
REACTION: ABJECT
REACTION: SAME AS FAMILY
REACTION: NO ACKNOWLEDGMENT (UGH!)

MARCO AND I CONTINUED ALONG IN THE VILLAGE.

LOOK, THESE KIDS ARE LEARNING FROM THE MOB.

AAARG!

MARCO

CHAPTER 31

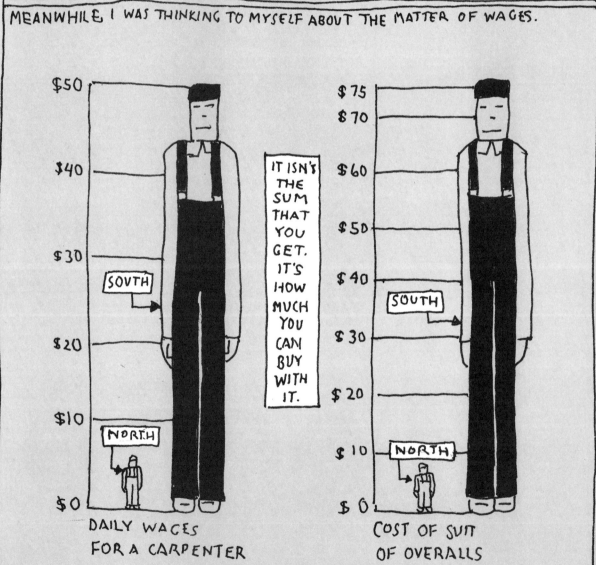

MEANWHILE, I WAS THINKING TO MYSELF ABOUT THE MATTER OF WAGES.

IT ISN'T THE SUM THAT YOU GET. IT'S HOW MUCH YOU CAN BUY WITH IT.

$50
$40
$30
SOUTH
$20
$10
NORTH
$0

DAILY WAGES FOR A CARPENTER

$75
$70
$60
$50
$40
SOUTH
$30
$20
$10
NORTH
$0

COST OF SUIT OF OVERALLS

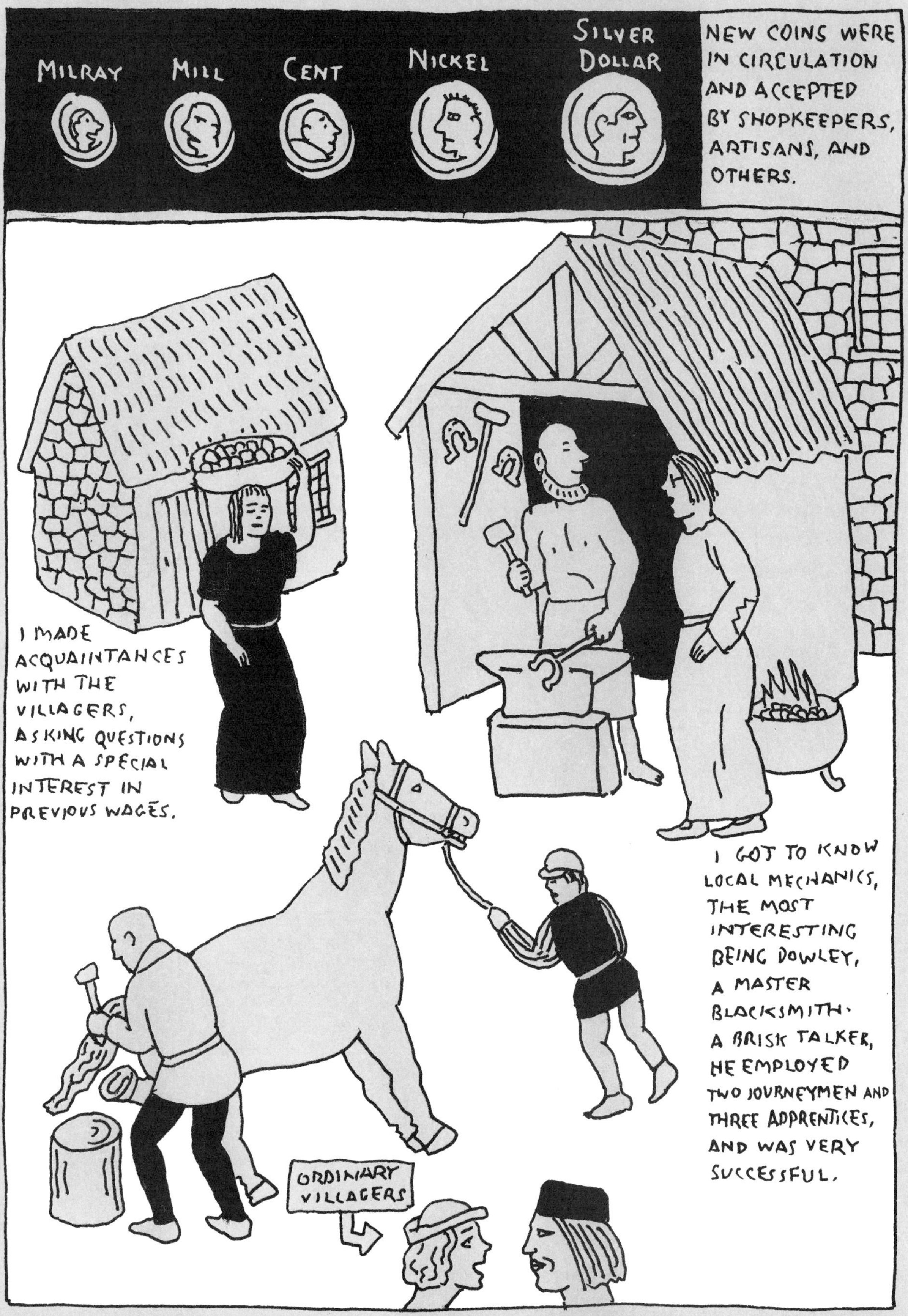
MILRAY
MILL
CENT
NICKEL
SILVER DOLLAR
NEW COINS WERE IN CIRCULATION AND ACCEPTED BY SHOPKEEPERS, ARTISANS, AND OTHERS.
I MADE ACQUAINTANCES WITH THE VILLAGERS, ASKING QUESTIONS WITH A SPECIAL INTEREST IN PREVIOUS WAGES.
I GOT TO KNOW LOCAL MECHANICS, THE MOST INTERESTING BEING DOWLEY, A MASTER BLACKSMITH. A BRISK TALKER, HE EMPLOYED TWO JOURNEYMEN AND THREE APPRENTICES, AND WAS VERY SUCCESSFUL.
ORDINARY VILLAGERS

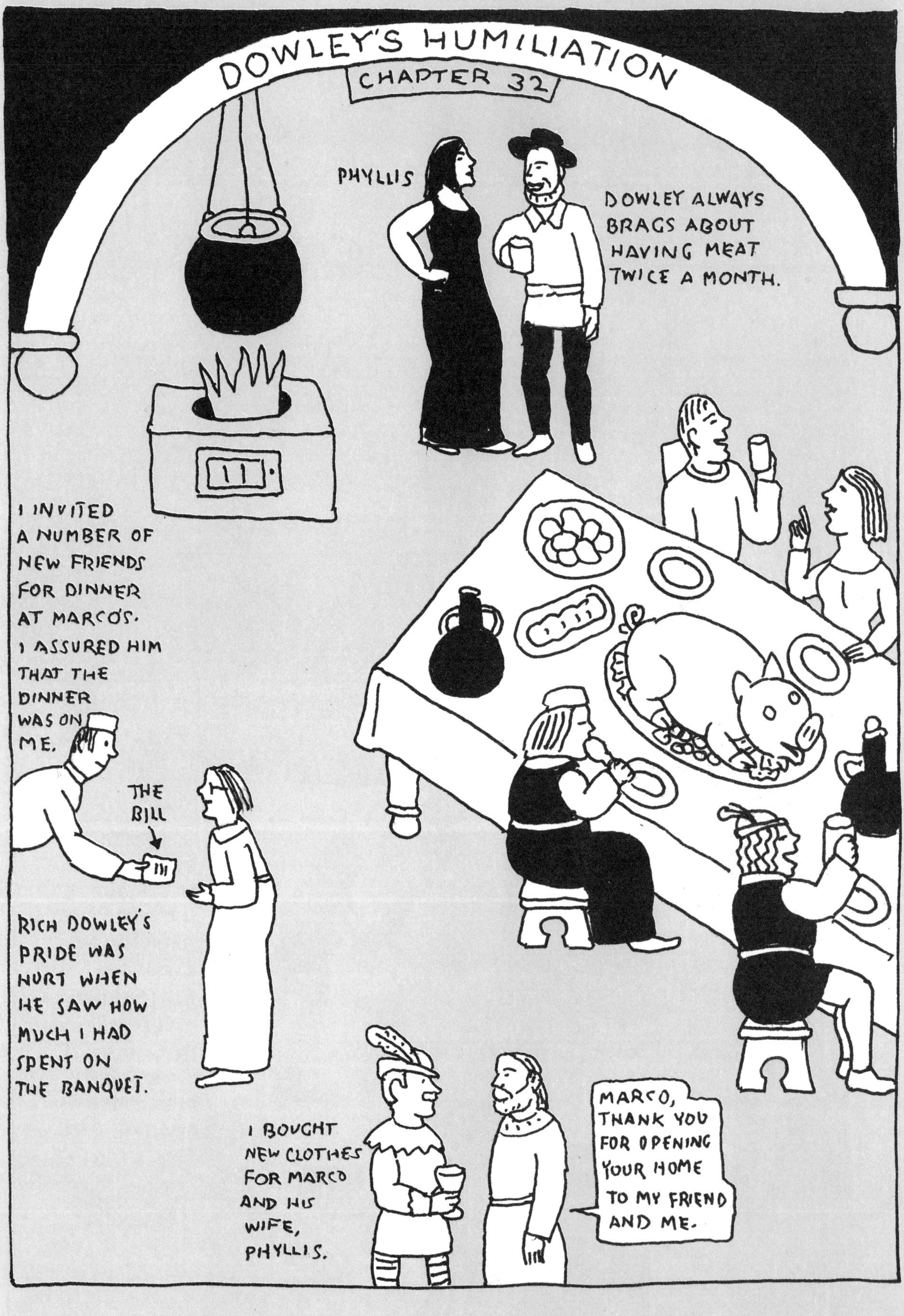
DOWLEY'S HUMILIATION
CHAPTER 32
PHYLLIS
DOWLEY ALWAYS BRAGS ABOUT HAVING MEAT TWICE A MONTH.
I INVITED A NUMBER OF NEW FRIENDS FOR DINNER AT MARCO'S. I ASSURED HIM THAT THE DINNER WAS ON ME.
THE BILL
RICH DOWLEY'S PRIDE WAS HURT WHEN HE SAW HOW MUCH I HAD SPENT ON THE BANQUET.
I BOUGHT NEW CLOTHES FOR MARCO AND HIS WIFE, PHYLLIS.
MARCO, THANK YOU FOR OPENING YOUR HOME TO MY FRIEND AND ME.

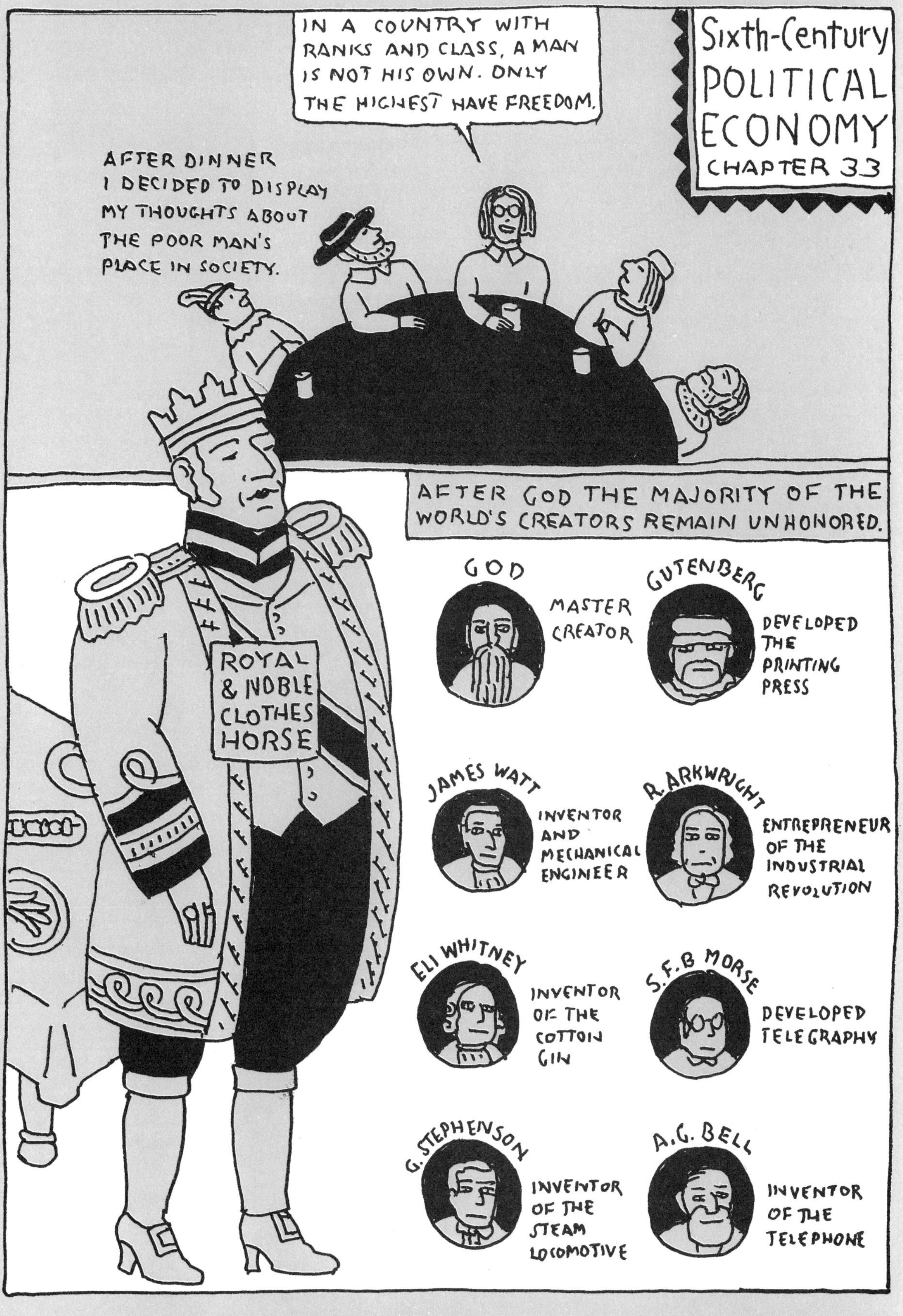
Sixth-Century POLITICAL ECONOMY
CHAPTER 33
AFTER DINNER I DECIDED TO DISPLAY MY THOUGHTS ABOUT THE POOR MAN'S PLACE IN SOCIETY.
IN A COUNTRY WITH RANKS AND CLASS, A MAN IS NOT HIS OWN. ONLY THE HIGHEST HAVE FREEDOM.
AFTER GOD THE MAJORITY OF THE WORLD'S CREATORS REMAIN UNHONORED.
ROYAL & NOBLE CLOTHES HORSE
GOD
MASTER CREATOR
GUTENBERG
DEVELOPED THE PRINTING PRESS
JAMES WATT
INVENTOR AND MECHANICAL ENGINEER
R. ARKWRIGHT
ENTREPRENEUR OF THE INDUSTRIAL REVOLUTION
ELI WHITNEY
INVENTOR OF THE COTTON GIN
S.F.B MORSE
DEVELOPED TELEGRAPHY
G. STEPHENSON
INVENTOR OF THE STEAM LOCOMOTIVE
A.G. BELL
INVENTOR OF THE TELEPHONE

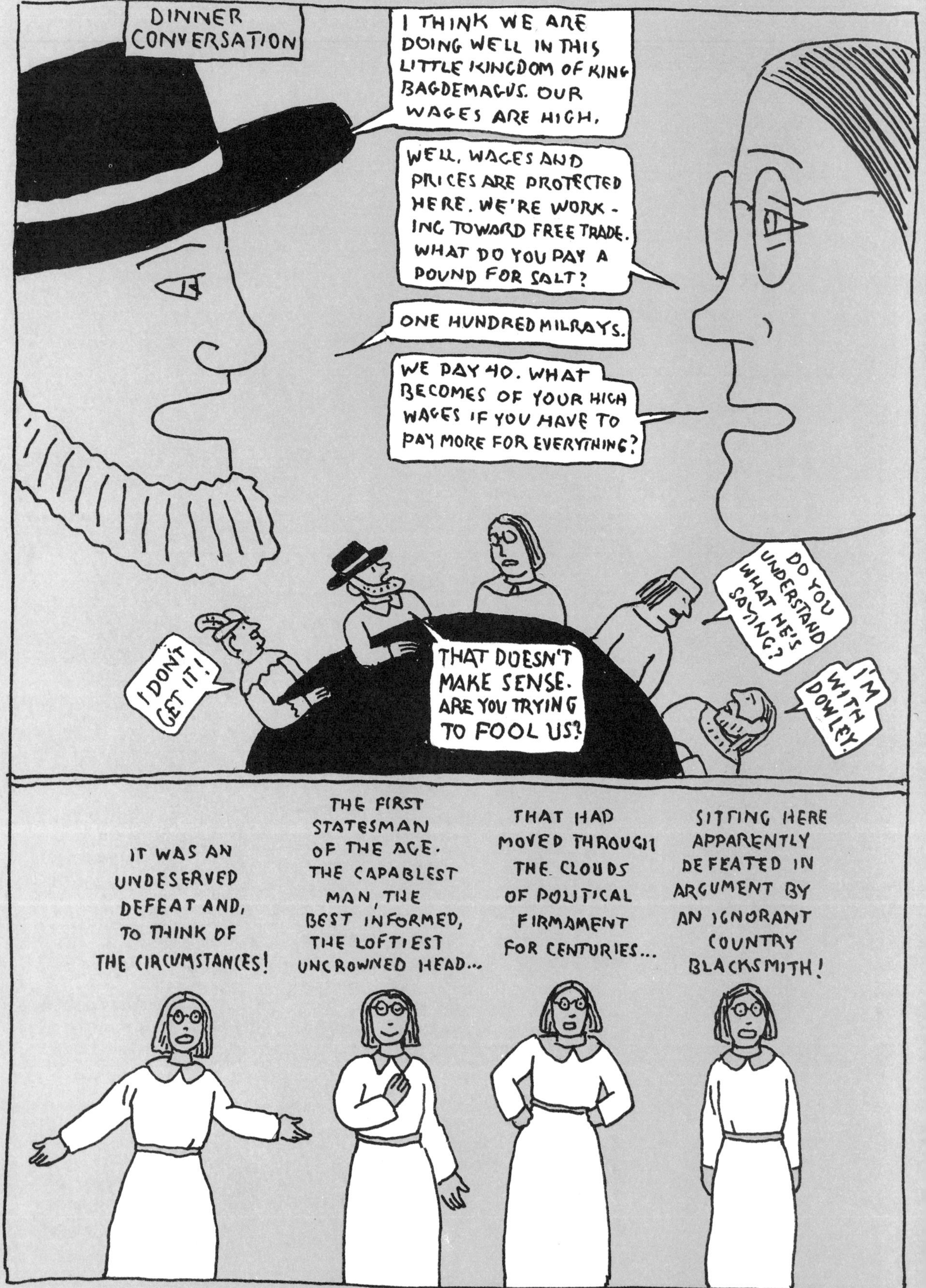
DINNER CONVERSATION
I THINK WE ARE DOING WELL IN THIS LITTLE KINGDOM OF KING BAGDEMAGUS. OUR WAGES ARE HIGH.
WELL, WAGES AND PRICES ARE PROTECTED HERE. WE'RE WORKING TOWARD FREE TRADE. WHAT DO YOU PAY A POUND FOR SALT?
ONE HUNDRED MILRAYS.
WE PAY 40. WHAT BECOMES OF YOUR HIGH WAGES IF YOU HAVE TO PAY MORE FOR EVERYTHING?
I DON'T GET IT!
THAT DOESN'T MAKE SENSE. ARE YOU TRYING TO FOOL US?
DO YOU UNDERSTAND WHAT HE'S SAYING?
I'M WITH DOWLEY.
IT WAS AN UNDESERVED DEFEAT AND, TO THINK OF THE CIRCUMSTANCES!
THE FIRST STATESMAN OF THE AGE. THE CAPABLEST MAN, THE BEST INFORMED, THE LOFTIEST UNCROWNED HEAD...
THAT HAD MOVED THROUGH THE CLOUDS OF POLITICAL FIRMAMENT FOR CENTURIES...
SITTING HERE APPARENTLY DEFEATED IN ARGUMENT BY AN IGNORANT COUNTRY BLACKSMITH!

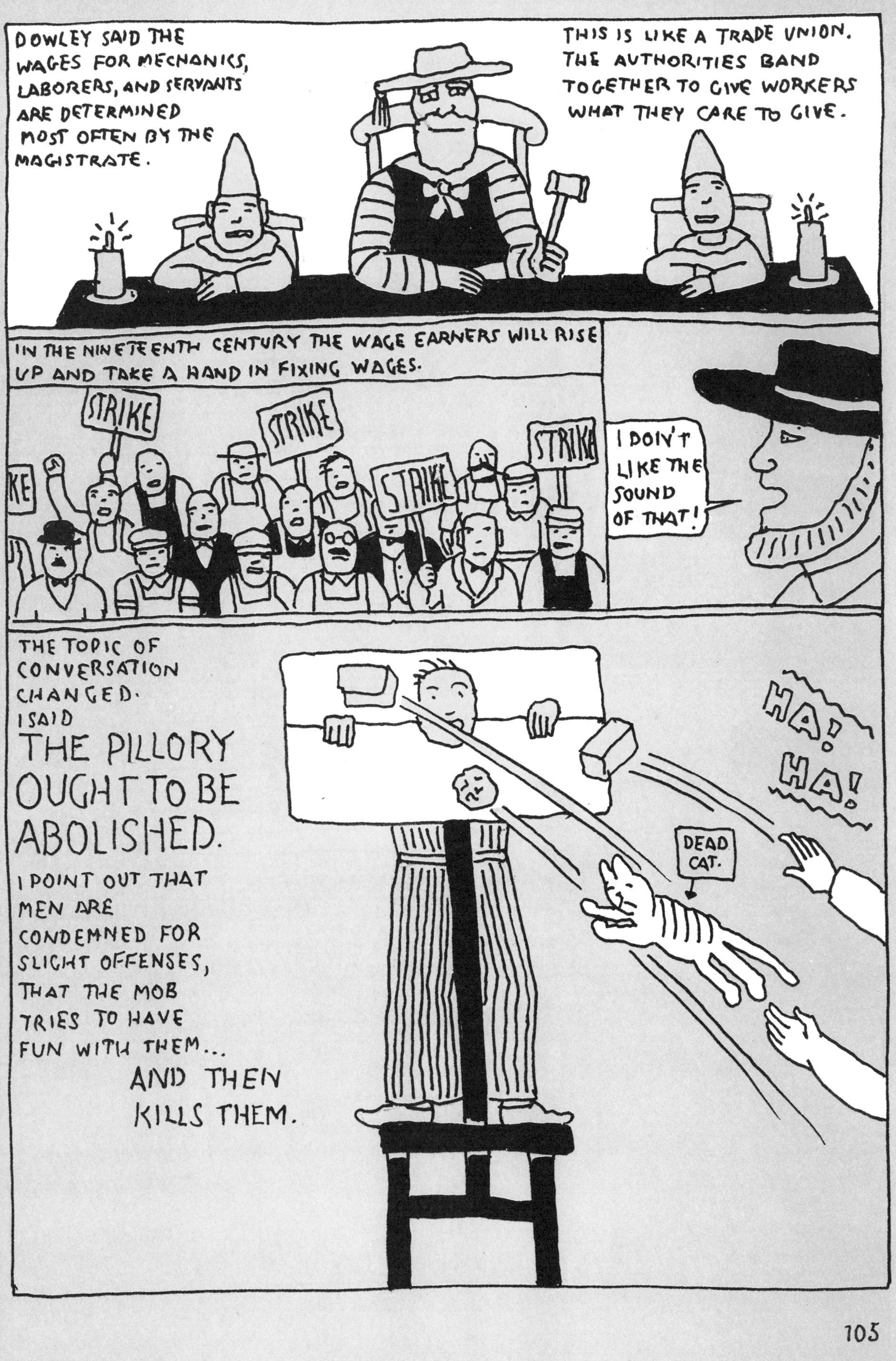
DOWLEY SAID THE WAGES FOR MECHANICS, LABORERS, AND SERVANTS ARE DETERMINED MOST OFTEN BY THE MAGISTRATE.
THIS IS LIKE A TRADE UNION. THE AUTHORITIES BAND TOGETHER TO GIVE WORKERS WHAT THEY CARE TO GIVE.
IN THE NINETEENTH CENTURY THE WAGE EARNERS WILL RISE UP AND TAKE A HAND IN FIXING WAGES.
STRIKE
STRIKE
STRIKE
I DON'T LIKE THE SOUND OF THAT!
THE TOPIC OF CONVERSATION CHANGED. I SAID
THE PILLORY OUGHT TO BE ABOLISHED.
I POINT OUT THAT MEN ARE CONDEMNED FOR SLIGHT OFFENSES, THAT THE MOB TRIES TO HAVE FUN WITH THEM...
AND THEN KILLS THEM.
HA! HA!
DEAD CAT.

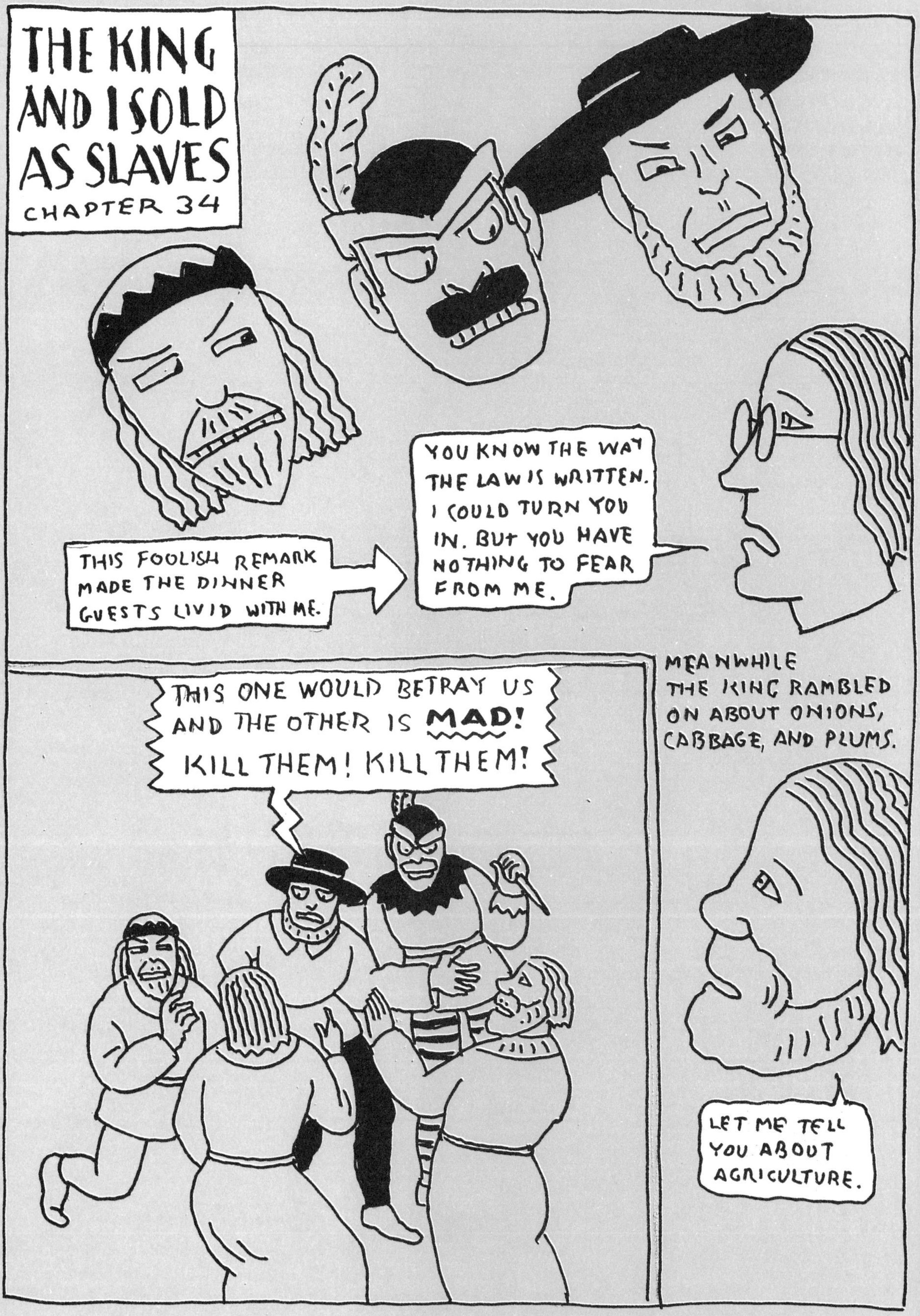
THE KING AND I SOLD AS SLAVES
CHAPTER 34
YOU KNOW THE WAY THE LAW IS WRITTEN. I COULD TURN YOU IN. BUT YOU HAVE NOTHING TO FEAR FROM ME.
THIS FOOLISH REMARK MADE THE DINNER GUESTS LIVID WITH ME.
THIS ONE WOULD BETRAY US AND THE OTHER IS MAD! KILL THEM! KILL THEM!
MEANWHILE THE KING RAMBLED ON ABOUT ONIONS, CABBAGE, AND PLUMS.
LET ME TELL YOU ABOUT AGRICULTURE.

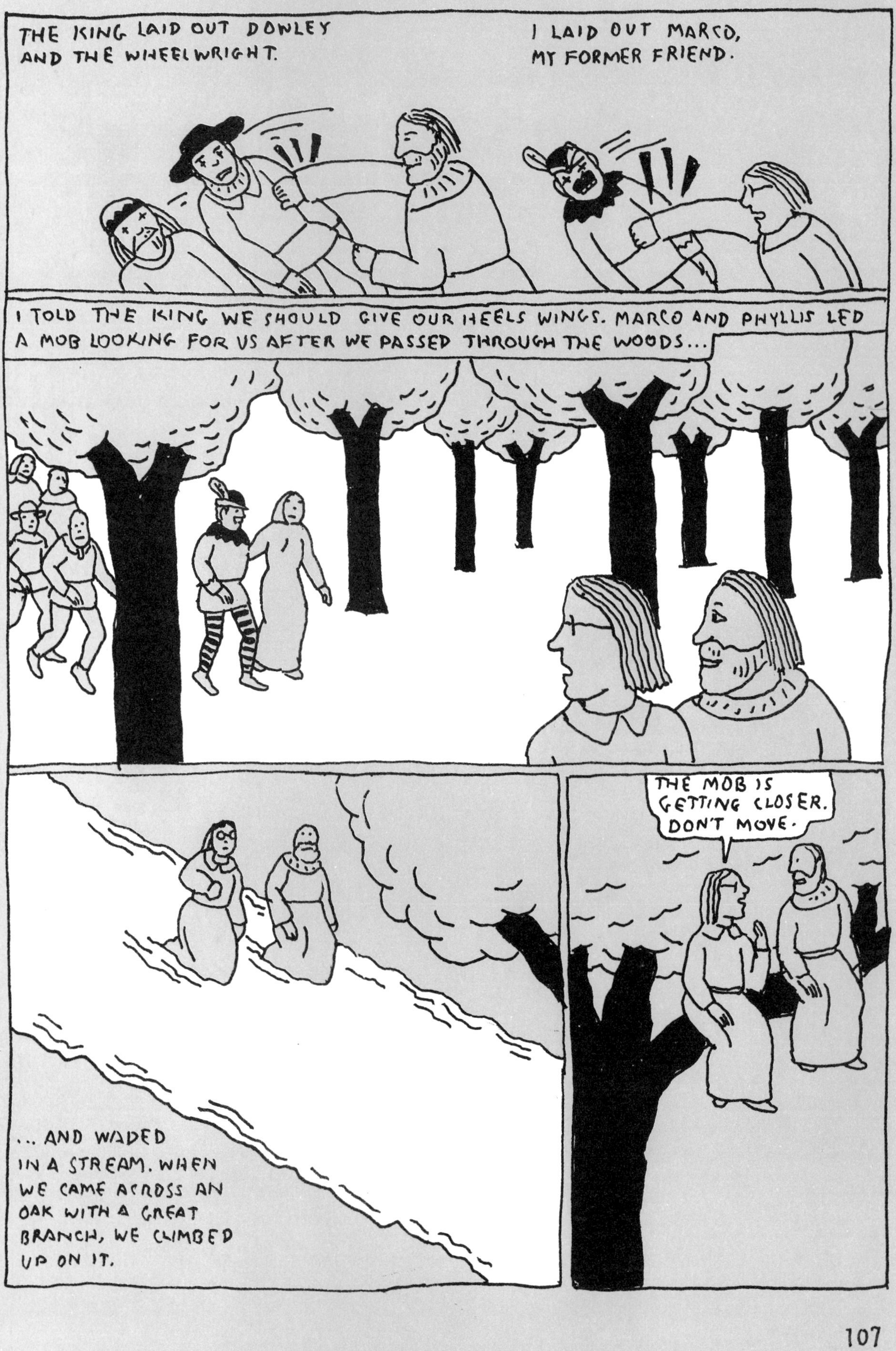
THE KING LAID OUT DOWLEY AND THE WHEELWRIGHT.
I LAID OUT MARCO, MY FORMER FRIEND.
I TOLD THE KING WE SHOULD GIVE OUR HEELS WINGS. MARCO AND PHYLLIS LED A MOB LOOKING FOR US AFTER WE PASSED THROUGH THE WOODS...
... AND WADED IN A STREAM. WHEN WE CAME ACROSS AN OAK WITH A GREAT BRANCH, WE CLIMBED UP ON IT.
THE MOB IS GETTING CLOSER. DON'T MOVE.

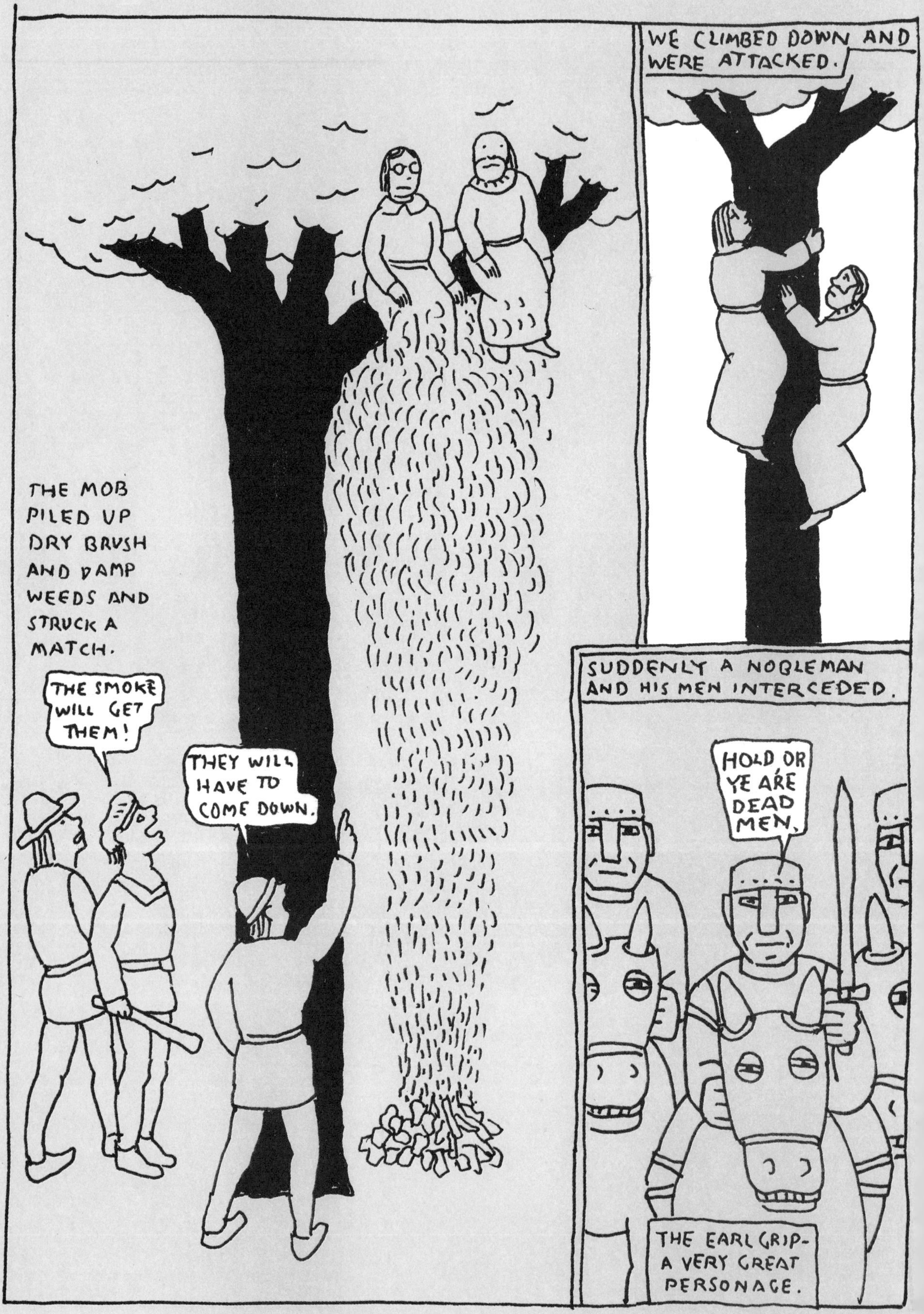
THE MOB PILED UP DRY BRUSH AND DAMP WEEDS AND STRUCK A MATCH.
THE SMOKE WILL GET THEM!
THEY WILL HAVE TO COME DOWN.
WE CLIMBED DOWN AND WERE ATTACKED.
SUDDENLY A NOBLEMAN AND HIS MEN INTERCEDED.
HOLD OR YE ARE DEAD MEN.
THE EARL GRIP- A VERY GREAT PERSONAGE.

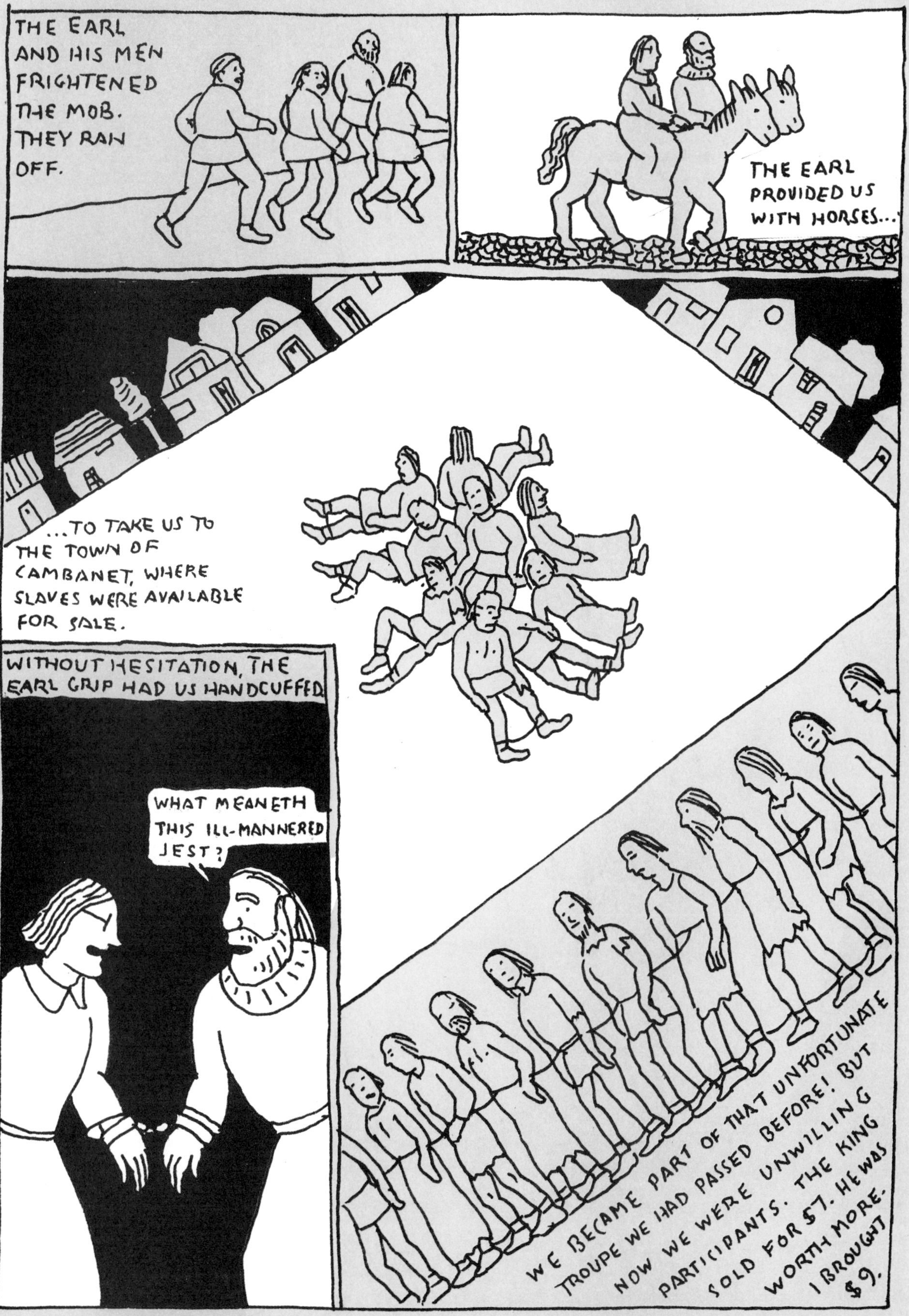
THE EARL AND HIS MEN FRIGHTENED THE MOB. THEY RAN OFF.
THE EARL PROVIDED US WITH HORSES...
...TO TAKE US TO THE TOWN OF CAMBANET, WHERE SLAVES WERE AVAILABLE FOR SALE.
WITHOUT HESITATION, THE EARL GRIP HAD US HANDCUFFED.
WHAT MEANETH THIS ILL-MANNERED JEST?
WE BECAME PART OF THAT UNFORTUNATE TROUPE WE HAD PASSED BEFORE! BUT NOW WE WERE UNWILLING PARTICIPANTS. THE KING SOLD FOR $7. HE WAS WORTH MORE. I BROUGHT $9.

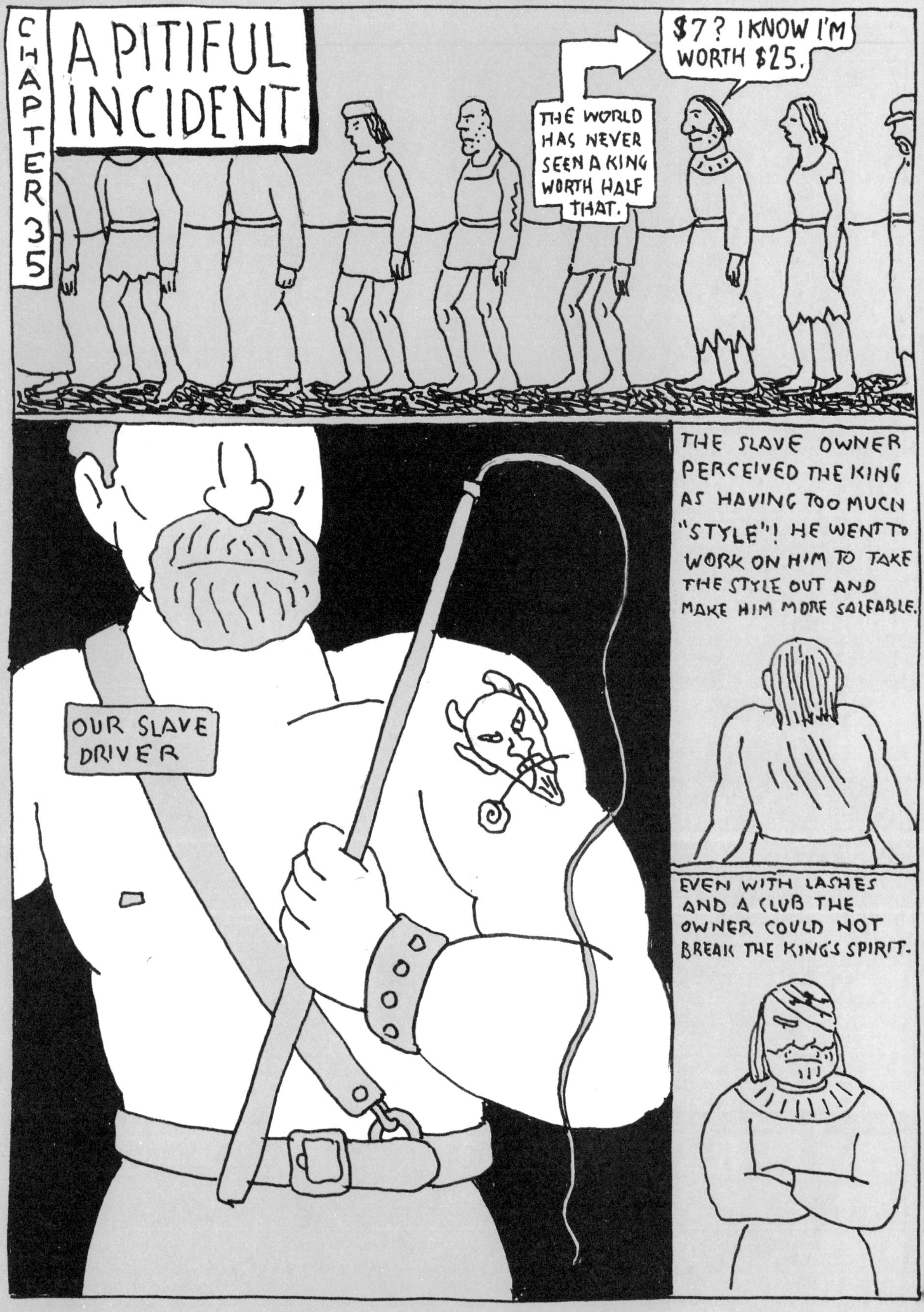
CHAPTER 35
A PITIFUL INCIDENT
THE WORLD HAS NEVER SEEN A KING WORTH HALF THAT.
$7? I KNOW I'M WORTH $25.
OUR SLAVE DRIVER
THE SLAVE OWNER PERCEIVED THE KING AS HAVING TOO MUCH "STYLE"! HE WENT TO WORK ON HIM TO TAKE THE STYLE OUT AND MAKE HIM MORE SALEABLE.
EVEN WITH LASHES AND A CLUB THE OWNER COULD NOT BREAK THE KING'S SPIRIT.

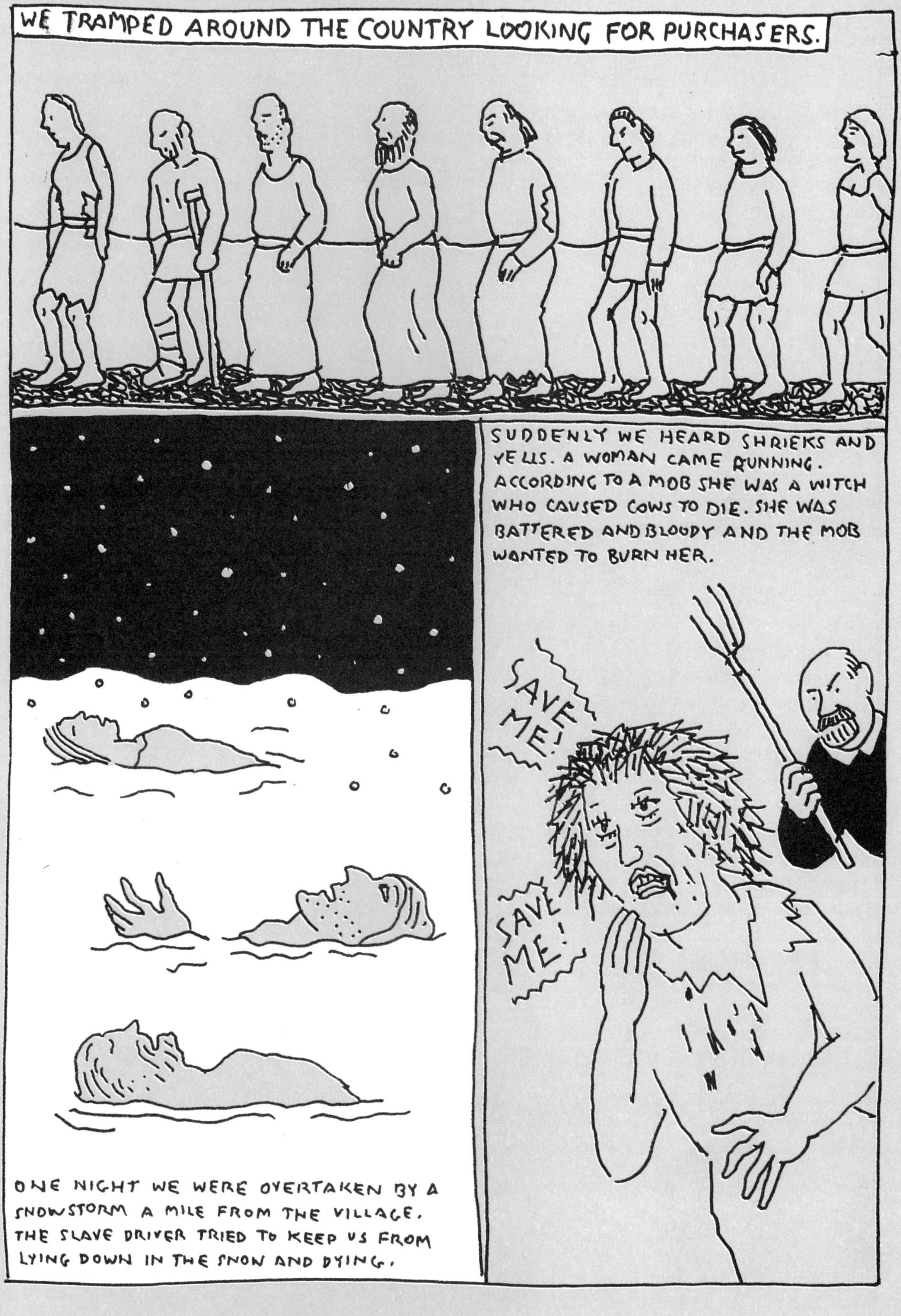
WE TRAMPED AROUND THE COUNTRY LOOKING FOR PURCHASERS.
ONE NIGHT WE WERE OVERTAKEN BY A SNOWSTORM A MILE FROM THE VILLAGE. THE SLAVE DRIVER TRIED TO KEEP US FROM LYING DOWN IN THE SNOW AND DYING.
SUDDENLY WE HEARD SHRIEKS AND YELLS. A WOMAN CAME RUNNING. ACCORDING TO A MOB SHE WAS A WITCH WHO CAUSED COWS TO DIE. SHE WAS BATTERED AND BLOODY AND THE MOB WANTED TO BURN HER.
SAVE ME!
SAVE ME!

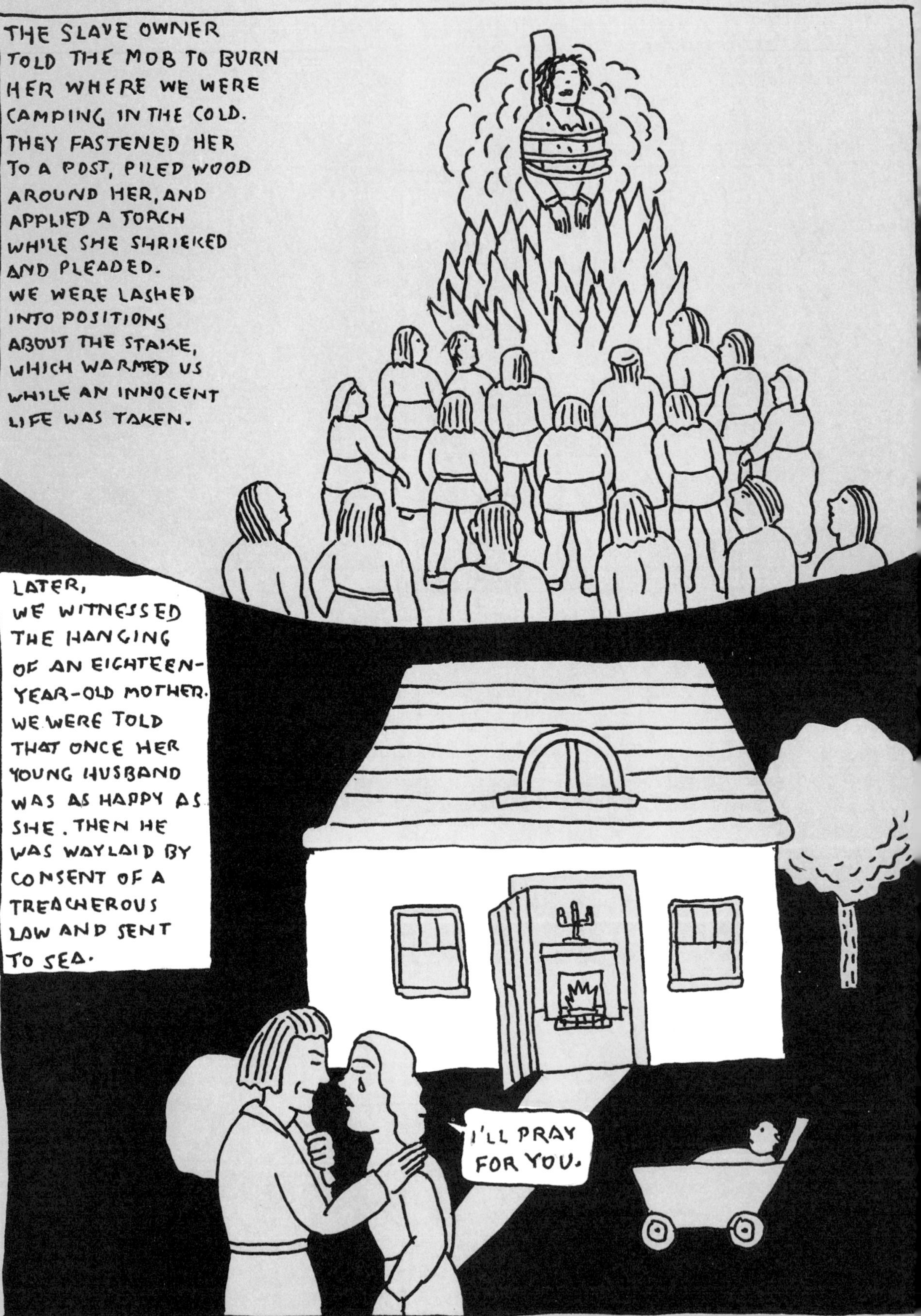
THE SLAVE OWNER TOLD THE MOB TO BURN HER WHERE WE WERE CAMPING IN THE COLD. THEY FASTENED HER TO A POST, PILED WOOD AROUND HER, AND APPLIED A TORCH WHILE SHE SHRIEKED AND PLEADED. WE WERE LASHED INTO POSITIONS ABOUT THE STAKE, WHICH WARMED US WHILE AN INNOCENT LIFE WAS TAKEN.
LATER, WE WITNESSED THE HANGING OF AN EIGHTEEN-YEAR-OLD MOTHER. WE WERE TOLD THAT ONCE HER YOUNG HUSBAND WAS AS HAPPY AS SHE. THEN HE WAS WAYLAID BY CONSENT OF A TREACHEROUS LAW AND SENT TO SEA.
I'LL PRAY FOR YOU.

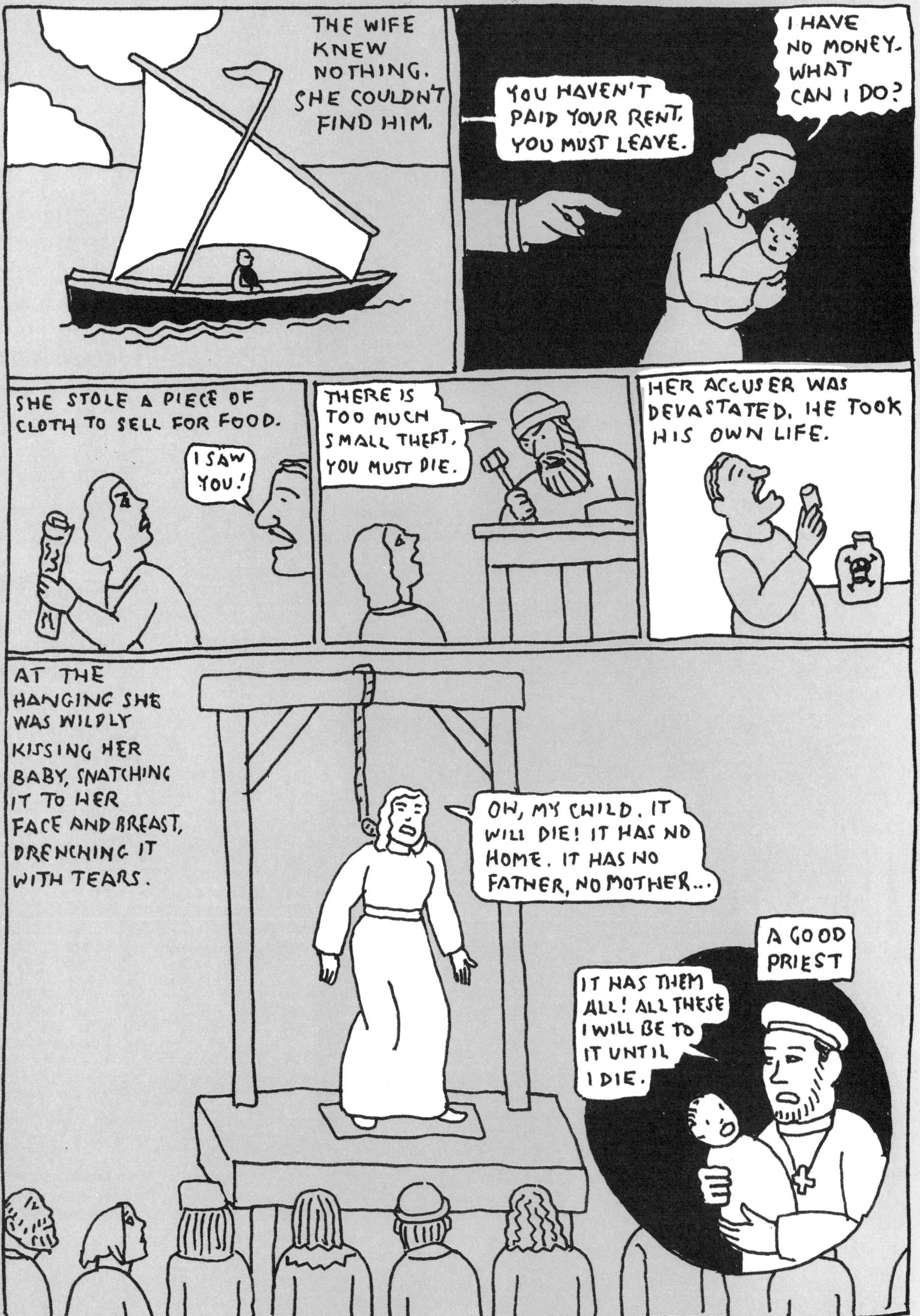
THE WIFE KNEW NOTHING. SHE COULDN'T FIND HIM.
YOU HAVEN'T PAID YOUR RENT. YOU MUST LEAVE.
I HAVE NO MONEY. WHAT CAN I DO?
SHE STOLE A PIECE OF CLOTH TO SELL FOR FOOD.
I SAW YOU!
THERE IS TOO MUCH SMALL THEFT. YOU MUST DIE.
HER ACCUSER WAS DEVASTATED. HE TOOK HIS OWN LIFE.
AT THE HANGING SHE WAS WILDLY KISSING HER BABY, SNATCHING IT TO HER FACE AND BREAST, DRENCHING IT WITH TEARS.
OH, MY CHILD. IT WILL DIE! IT HAS NO HOME. IT HAS NO FATHER, NO MOTHER...
A GOOD PRIEST
IT HAS THEM ALL! ALL THESE I WILL BE TO IT UNTIL I DIE.

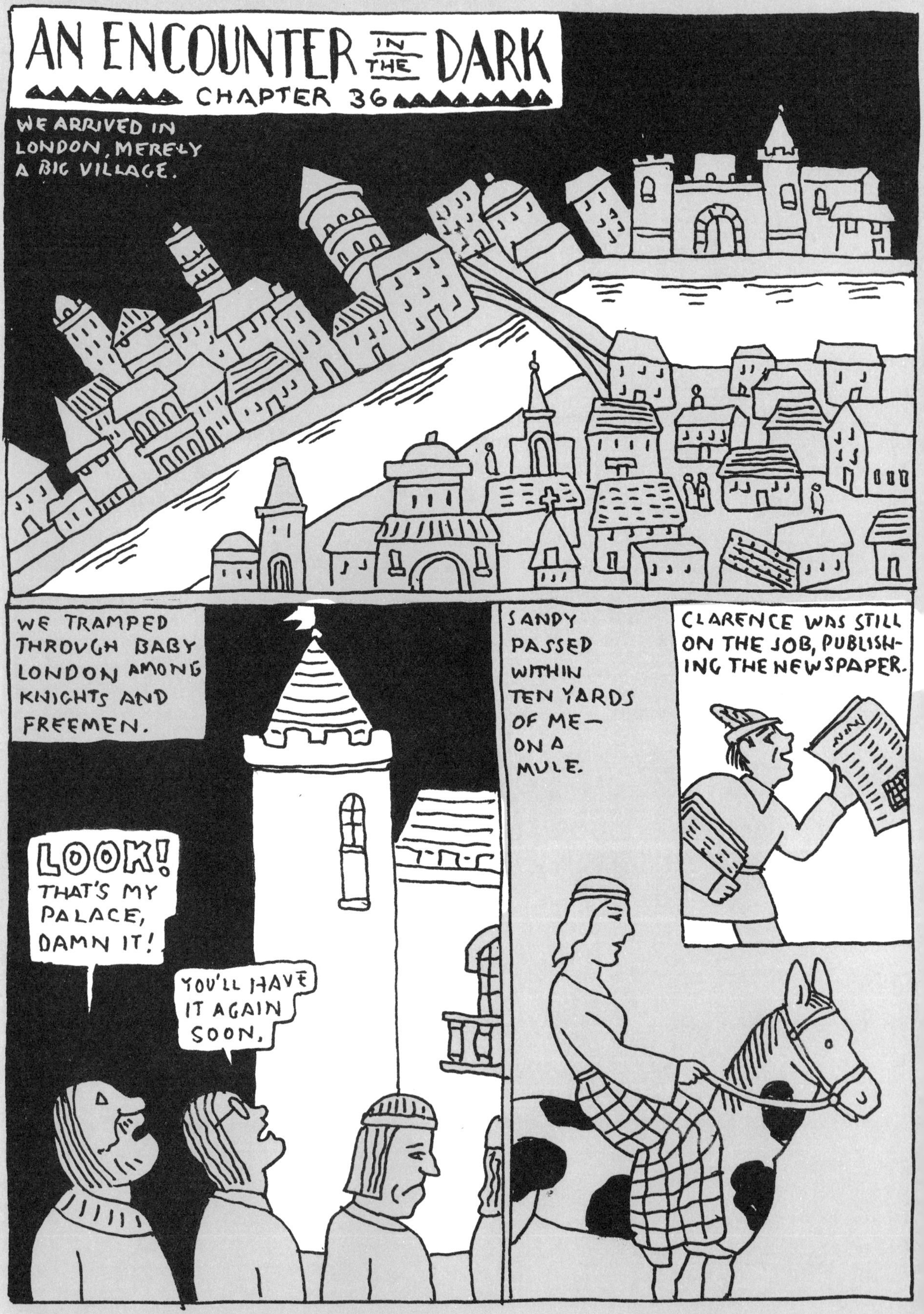
AN ENCOUNTER IN THE DARK
CHAPTER 36
WE ARRIVED IN LONDON, MERELY A BIG VILLAGE.
WE TRAMPED THROUGH BABY LONDON AMONG KNIGHTS AND FREEMEN.
LOOK! THAT'S MY PALACE, DAMN IT!
YOU'LL HAVE IT AGAIN SOON.
SANDY PASSED WITHIN TEN YARDS OF ME— ON A MULE.
CLARENCE WAS STILL ON THE JOB, PUBLISHING THE NEWSPAPER.

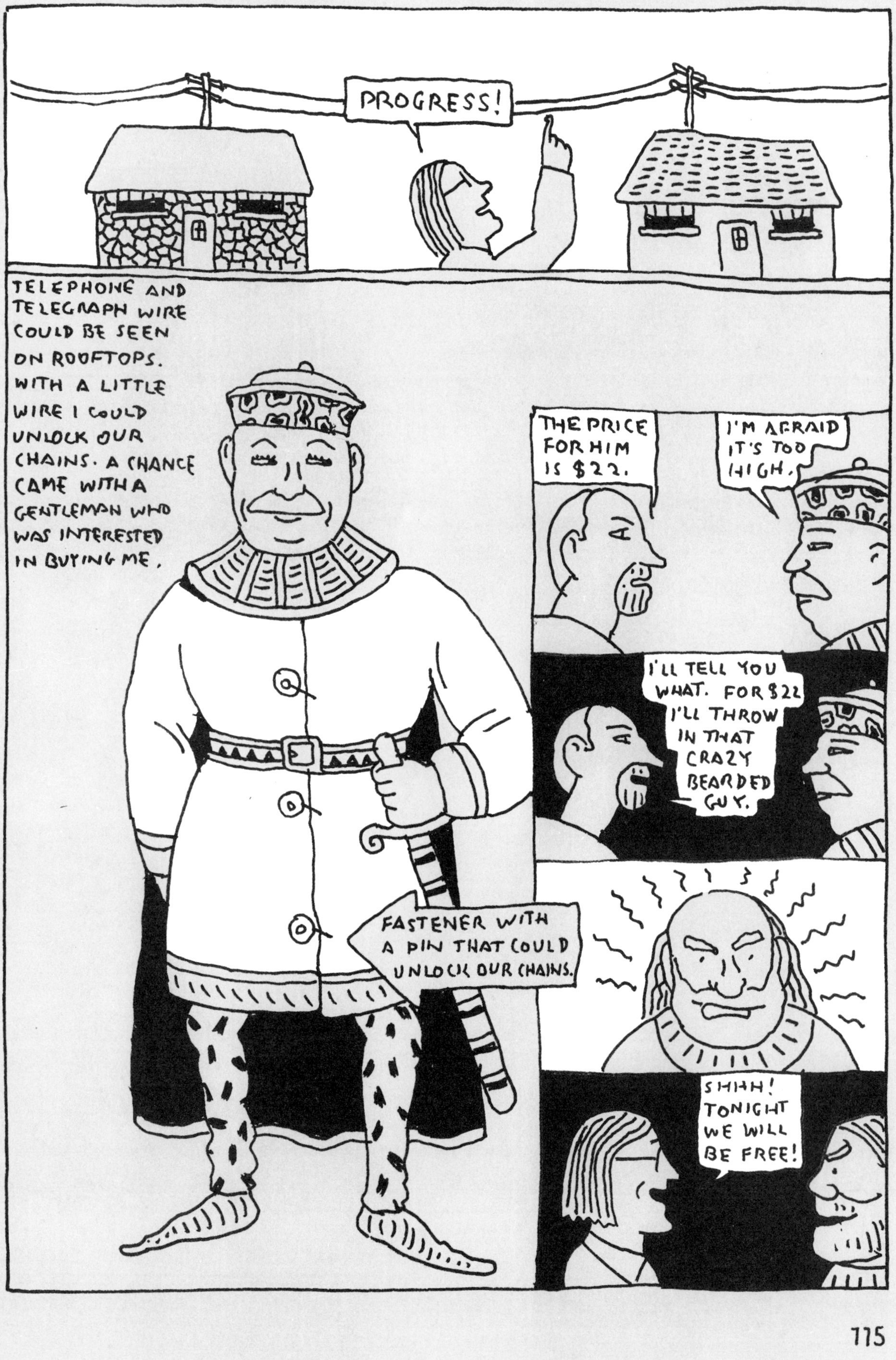
PROGRESS!
TELEPHONE AND TELEGRAPH WIRE COULD BE SEEN ON ROOFTOPS. WITH A LITTLE WIRE I COULD UNLOCK OUR CHAINS. A CHANCE CAME WITH A GENTLEMAN WHO WAS INTERESTED IN BUYING ME.
FASTENER WITH A PIN THAT COULD UNLOCK OUR CHAINS.
THE PRICE FOR HIM IS $22.
I'M AFRAID IT'S TOO HIGH.
I'LL TELL YOU WHAT. FOR $22 I'LL THROW IN THAT CRAZY BEARDED GUY.
SHHH! TONIGHT WE WILL BE FREE!

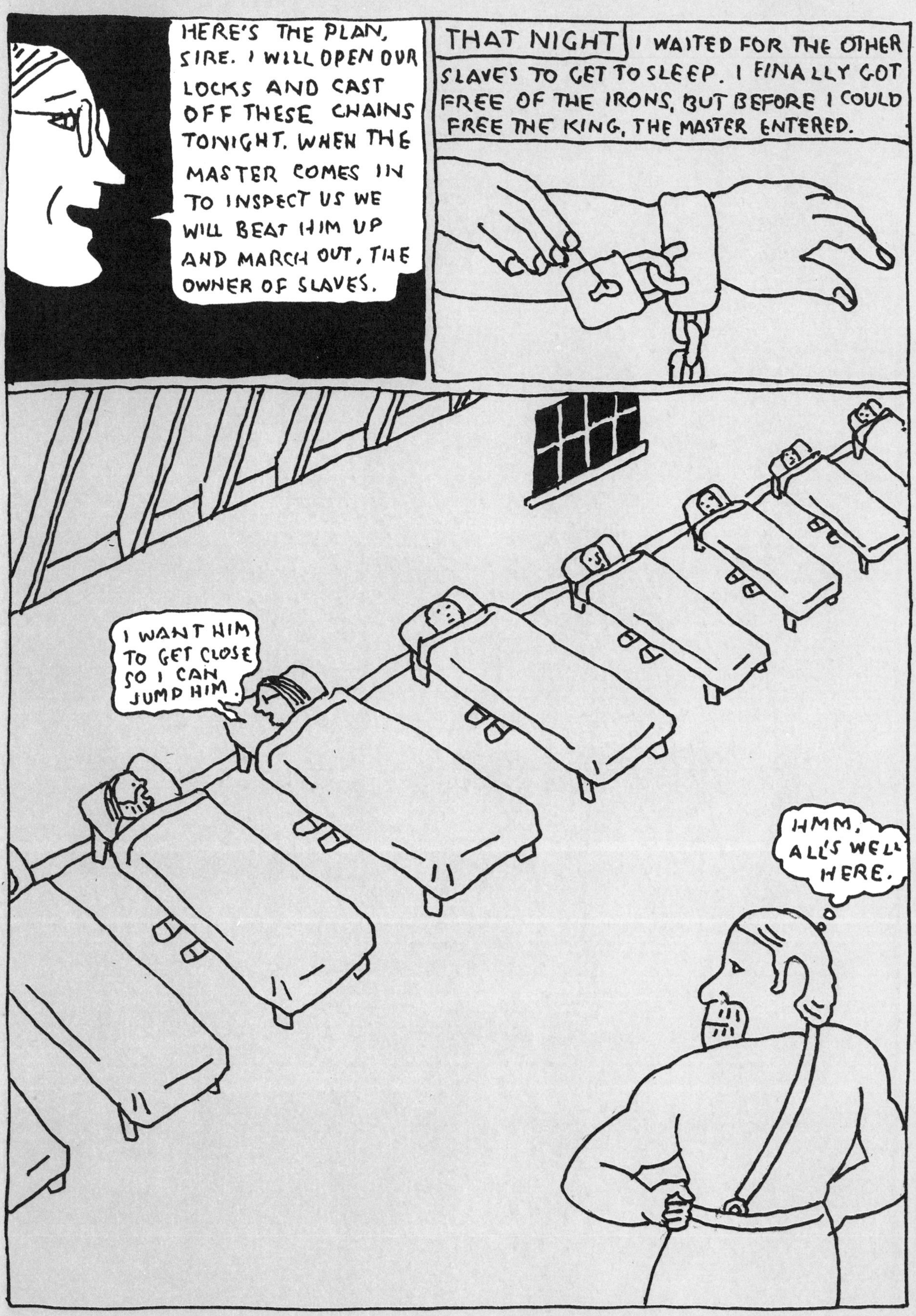
HERE'S THE PLAN, SIRE. I WILL OPEN OUR LOCKS AND CAST OFF THESE CHAINS TONIGHT. WHEN THE MASTER COMES IN TO INSPECT US WE WILL BEAT HIM UP AND MARCH OUT, THE OWNER OF SLAVES.
THAT NIGHT
I WAITED FOR THE OTHER SLAVES TO GET TO SLEEP. I FINALLY GOT FREE OF THE IRONS, BUT BEFORE I COULD FREE THE KING, THE MASTER ENTERED.
I WANT HIM TO GET CLOSE SO I CAN JUMP HIM.
HMM, ALL'S WELL HERE.

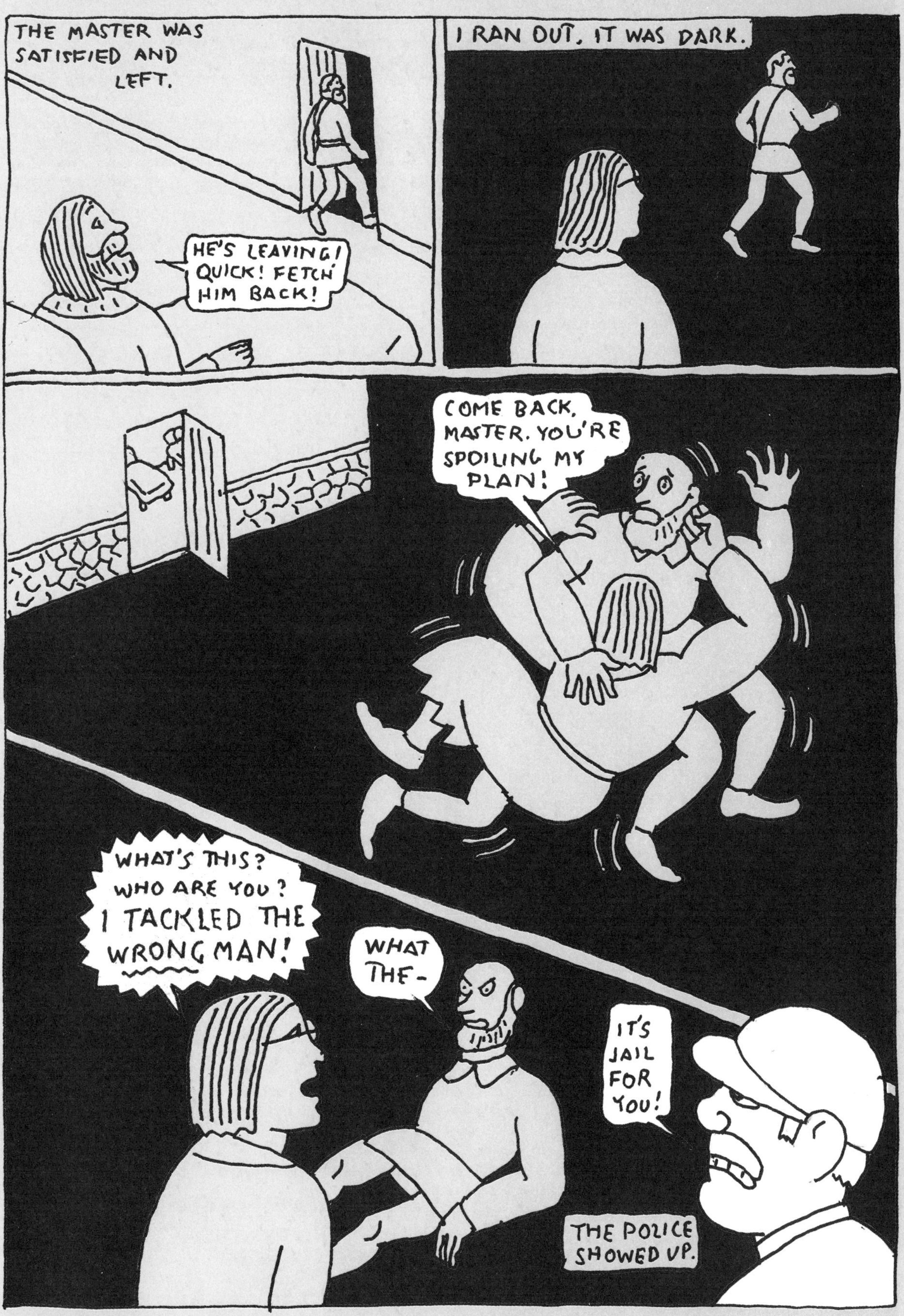
THE MASTER WAS SATISFIED AND LEFT.
HE'S LEAVING! QUICK! FETCH HIM BACK!
I RAN OUT. IT WAS DARK.
COME BACK, MASTER. YOU'RE SPOILING MY PLAN!
WHAT'S THIS? WHO ARE YOU? I TACKLED THE WRONG MAN!
WHAT THE-
IT'S JAIL FOR YOU!
THE POLICE SHOWED UP.

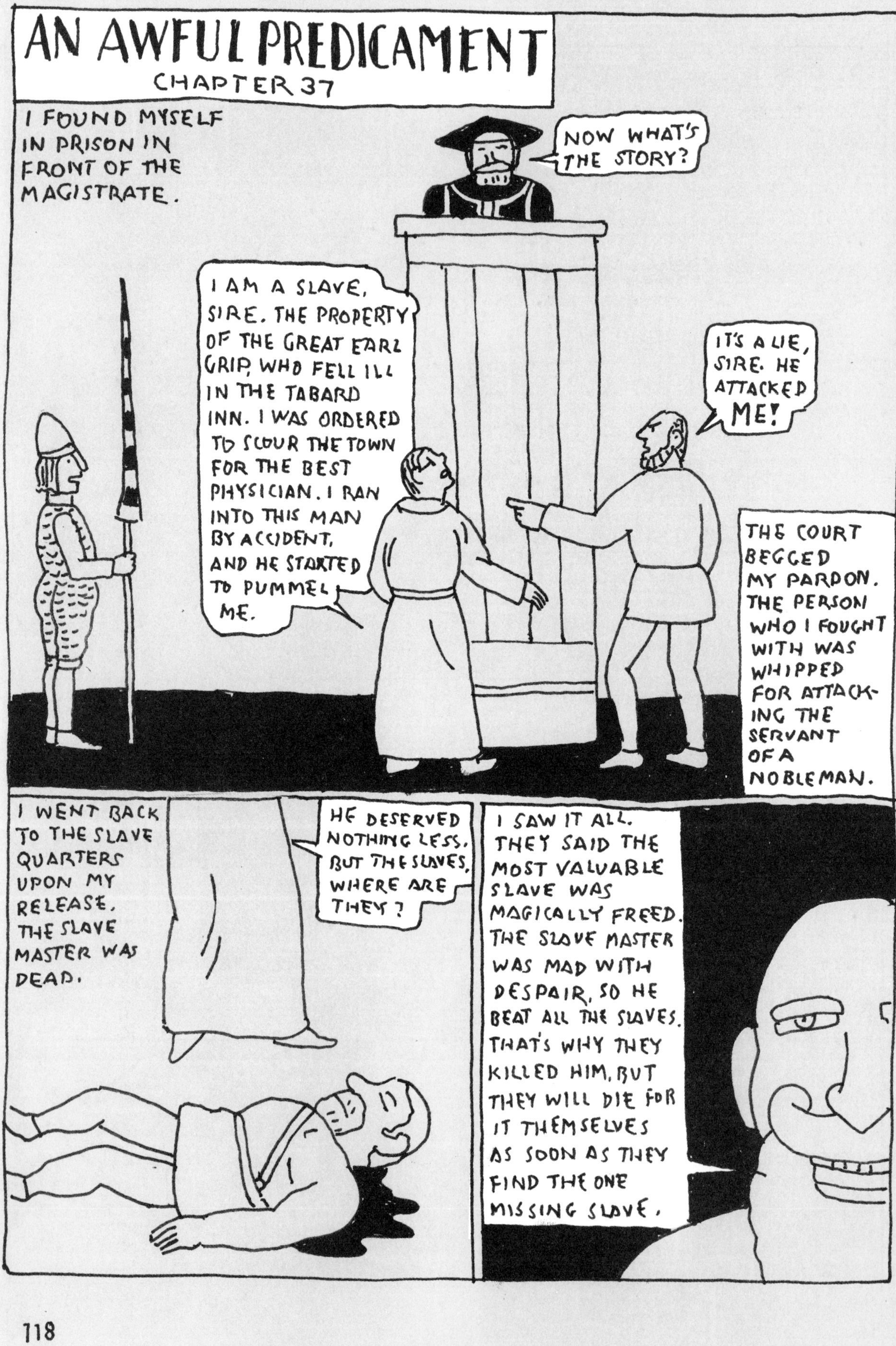
AN AWFUL PREDICAMENT
CHAPTER 37
I FOUND MYSELF IN PRISON IN FRONT OF THE MAGISTRATE.
NOW WHAT'S THE STORY?
I AM A SLAVE, SIRE. THE PROPERTY OF THE GREAT EARL GRIP, WHO FELL ILL IN THE TABARD INN. I WAS ORDERED TO SCOUR THE TOWN FOR THE BEST PHYSICIAN. I RAN INTO THIS MAN BY ACCIDENT, AND HE STARTED TO PUMMEL ME.
IT'S A LIE, SIRE. HE ATTACKED ME!
THE COURT BEGGED MY PARDON. THE PERSON WHO I FOUGHT WITH WAS WHIPPED FOR ATTACKING THE SERVANT OF A NOBLEMAN.
I WENT BACK TO THE SLAVE QUARTERS UPON MY RELEASE. THE SLAVE MASTER WAS DEAD.
HE DESERVED NOTHING LESS. BUT THE SLAVES, WHERE ARE THEY?
I SAW IT ALL. THEY SAID THE MOST VALUABLE SLAVE WAS MAGICALLY FREED. THE SLAVE MASTER WAS MAD WITH DESPAIR, SO HE BEAT ALL THE SLAVES. THAT'S WHY THEY KILLED HIM, BUT THEY WILL DIE FOR IT THEMSELVES AS SOON AS THEY FIND THE ONE MISSING SLAVE.

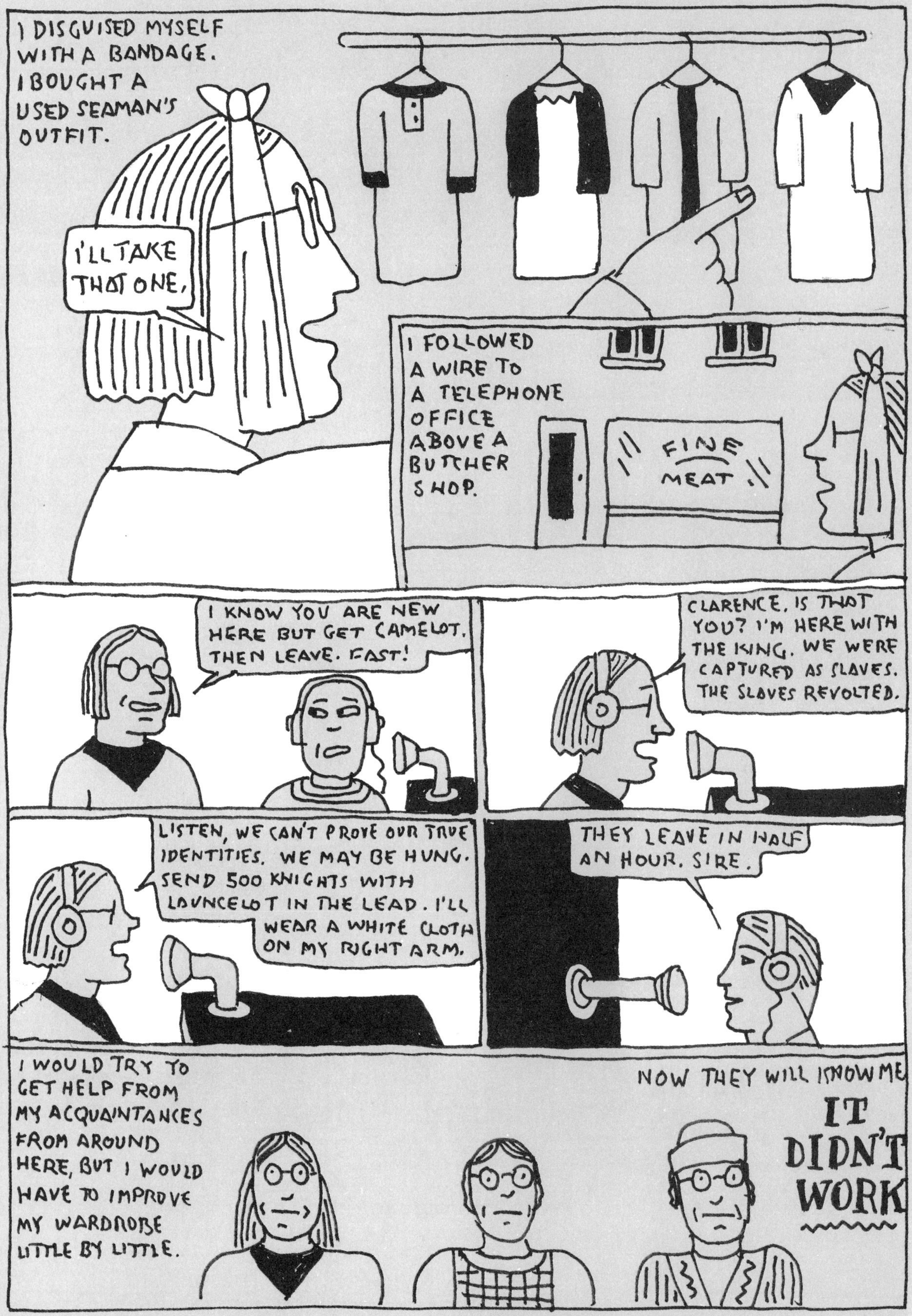
I DISGUISED MYSELF WITH A BANDAGE. I BOUGHT A USED SEAMAN'S OUTFIT.
I'LL TAKE THAT ONE,
I FOLLOWED A WIRE TO A TELEPHONE OFFICE ABOVE A BUTCHER SHOP.
FINE MEAT
I KNOW YOU ARE NEW HERE BUT GET CAMELOT. THEN LEAVE. FAST!
CLARENCE, IS THAT YOU? I'M HERE WITH THE KING. WE WERE CAPTURED AS SLAVES. THE SLAVES REVOLTED.
LISTEN, WE CAN'T PROVE OUR TRUE IDENTITIES. WE MAY BE HUNG. SEND 500 KNIGHTS WITH LAUNCELOT IN THE LEAD. I'LL WEAR A WHITE CLOTH ON MY RIGHT ARM.
THEY LEAVE IN HALF AN HOUR, SIRE.
I WOULD TRY TO GET HELP FROM MY ACQUAINTANCES FROM AROUND HERE, BUT I WOULD HAVE TO IMPROVE MY WARDROBE LITTLE BY LITTLE.
NOW THEY WILL KNOW ME.
IT DIDN'T WORK

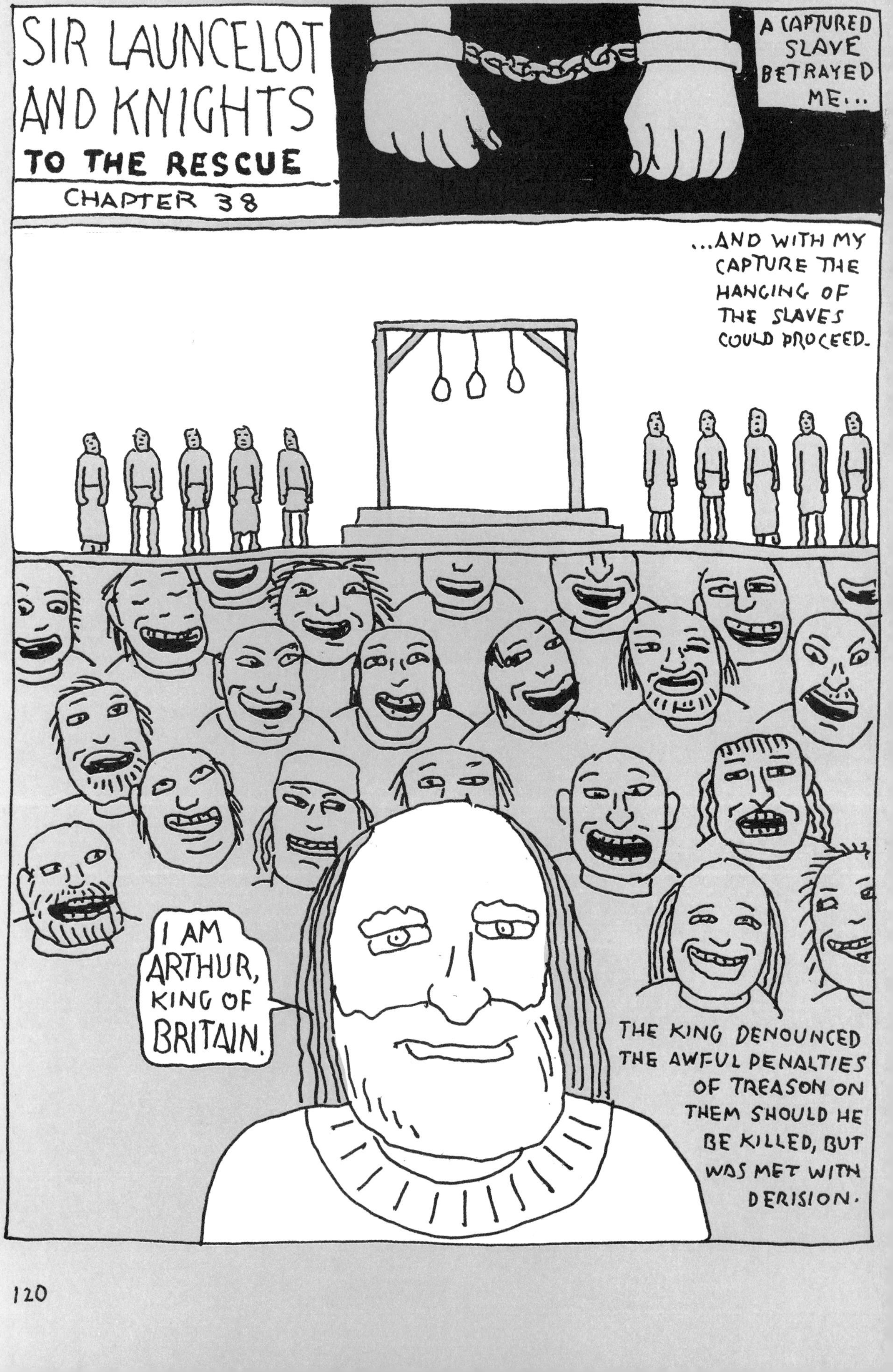
SIR LAUNCELOT AND KNIGHTS
TO THE RESCUE
CHAPTER 38
A CAPTURED SLAVE BETRAYED ME...
...AND WITH MY CAPTURE THE HANGING OF THE SLAVES COULD PROCEED.
I AM ARTHUR, KING OF BRITAIN.
THE KING DENOUNCED THE AWFUL PENALTIES OF TREASON ON THEM SHOULD HE BE KILLED, BUT WAS MET WITH DERISION.

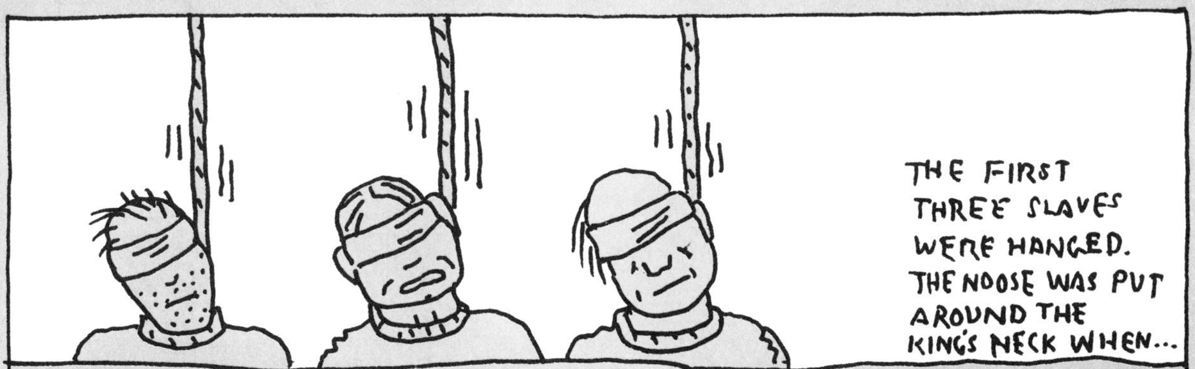
THE FIRST THREE SLAVES WERE HANGED. THE NOOSE WAS PUT AROUND THE KING'S NECK WHEN...

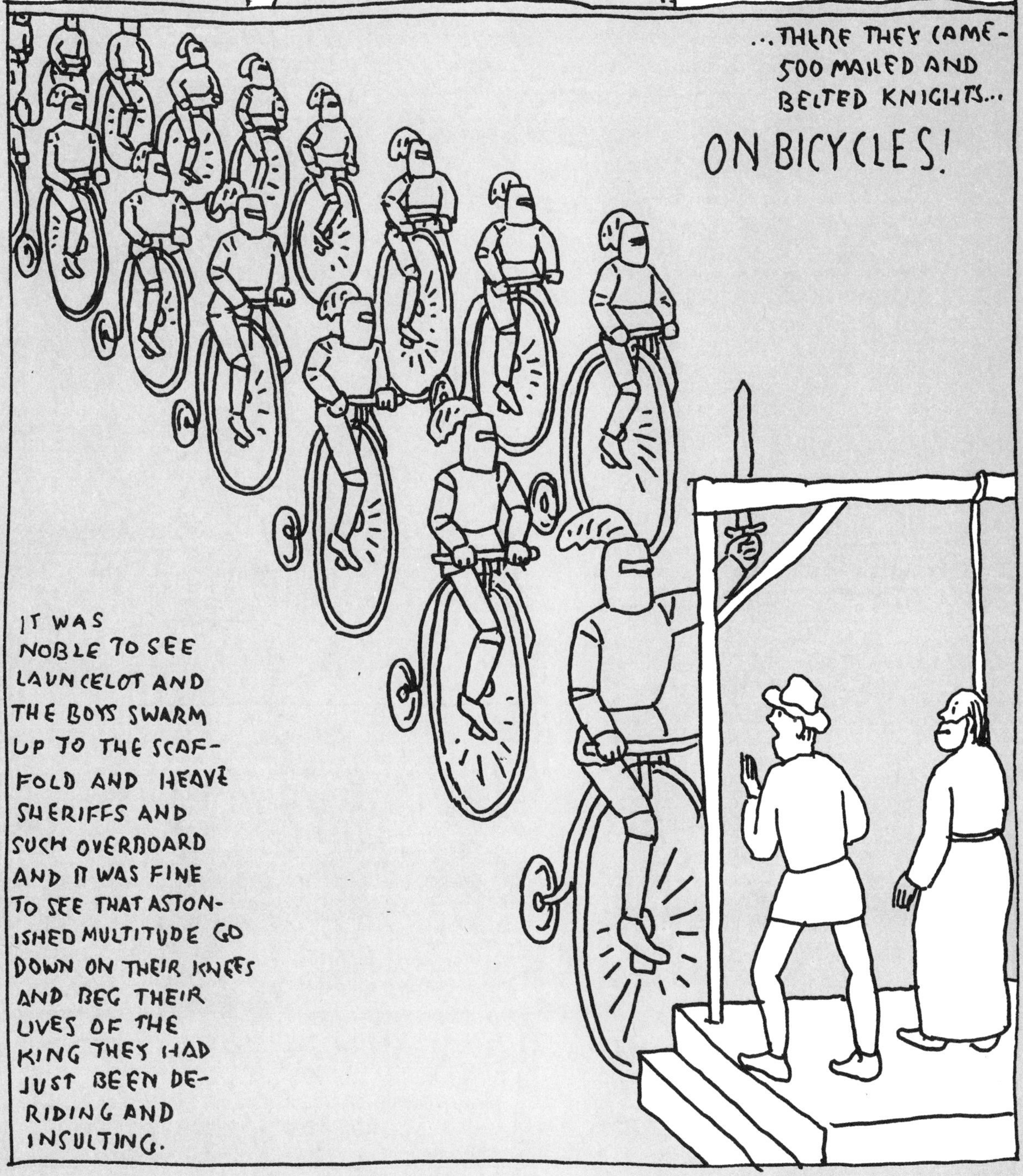
...THERE THEY CAME- 500 MAILED AND BELTED KNIGHTS...
ON BICYCLES!
IT WAS NOBLE TO SEE LAUNCELOT AND THE BOYS SWARM UP TO THE SCAF- FOLD AND HEAVE SHERIFFS AND SUCH OVERBOARD AND IT WAS FINE TO SEE THAT ASTON- ISHED MULTITUDE GO DOWN ON THEIR KNEES AND BEG THEIR LIVES OF THE KING THEY HAD JUST BEEN DE- RIDING AND INSULTING.

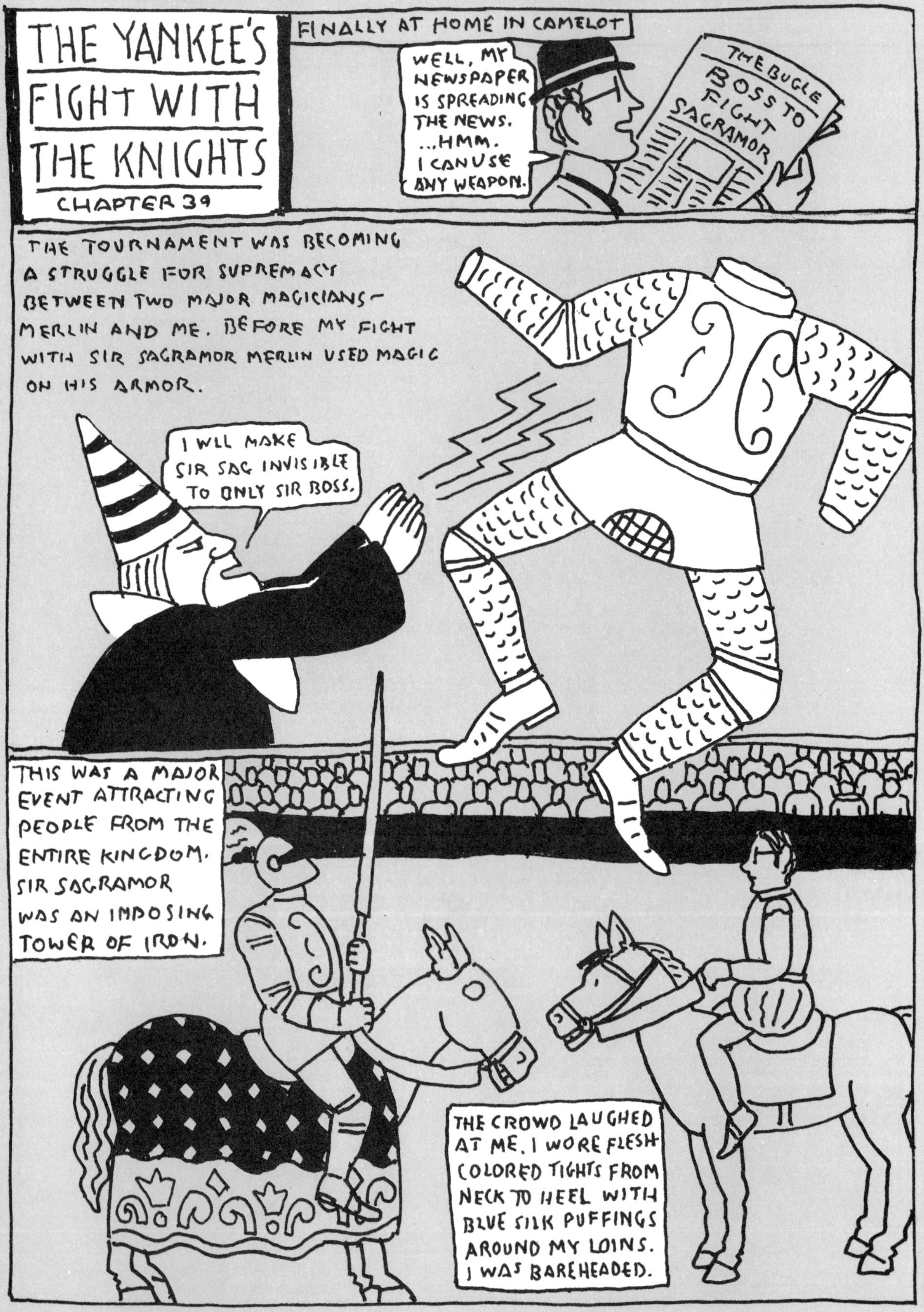
THE YANKEE'S FIGHT WITH THE KNIGHTS
CHAPTER 39
FINALLY AT HOME IN CAMELOT
WELL, MY NEWSPAPER IS SPREADING THE NEWS. ...HMM. I CAN USE ANY WEAPON.
THE BUGLE
BOSS TO FIGHT SAGRAMOR
THE TOURNAMENT WAS BECOMING A STRUGGLE FOR SUPREMACY BETWEEN TWO MAJOR MAGICIANS— MERLIN AND ME. BEFORE MY FIGHT WITH SIR SAGRAMOR MERLIN USED MAGIC ON HIS ARMOR.
I WLL MAKE SIR SAG INVISIBLE TO ONLY SIR BOSS.
THIS WAS A MAJOR EVENT ATTRACTING PEOPLE FROM THE ENTIRE KINGDOM. SIR SAGRAMOR WAS AN IMPOSING TOWER OF IRON.
THE CROWD LAUGHED AT ME. I WORE FLESH COLORED TIGHTS FROM NECK TO HEEL WITH BLUE SILK PUFFINGS AROUND MY LOINS. I WAS BAREHEADED.

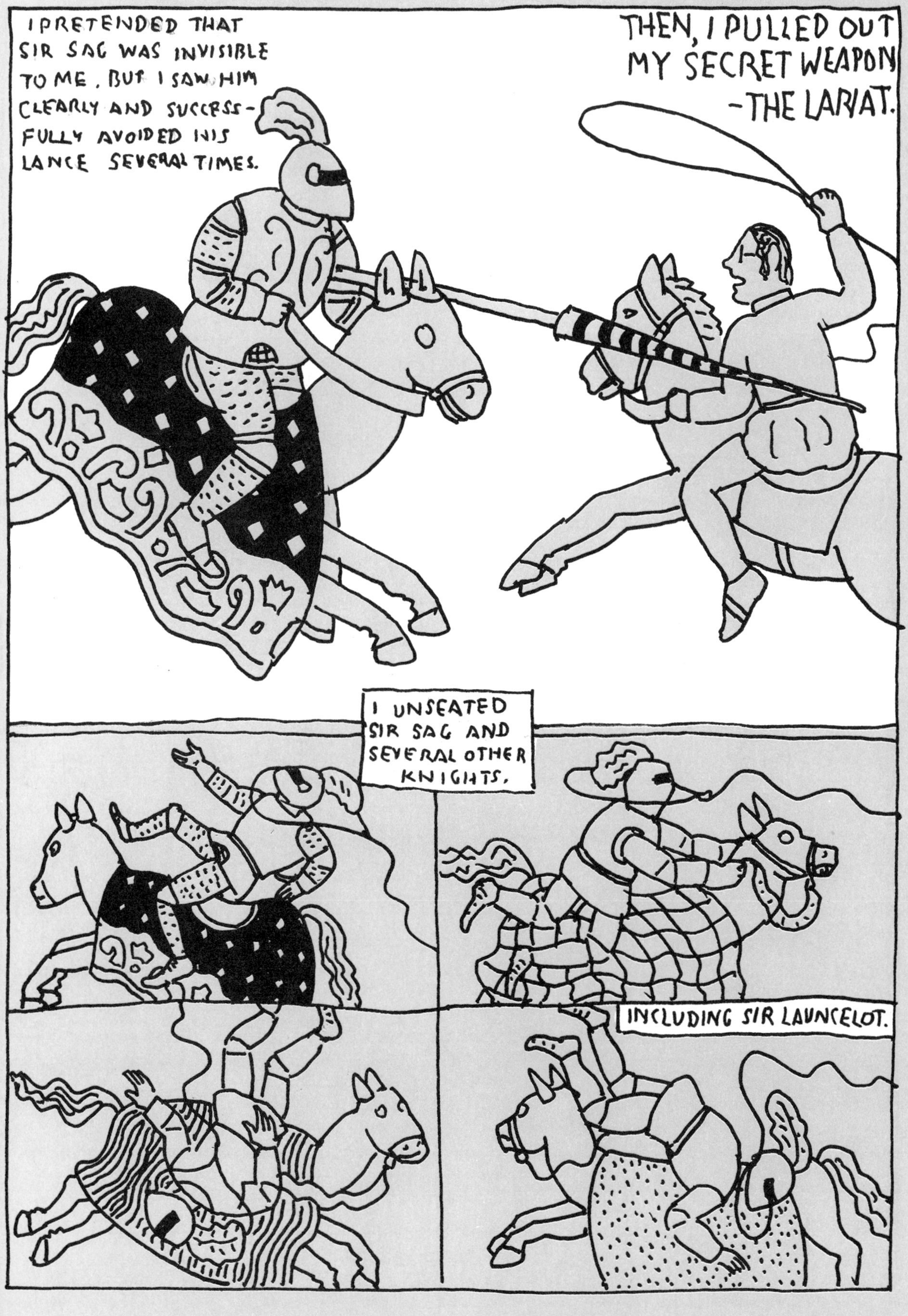
I PRETENDED THAT SIR SAG WAS INVISIBLE TO ME. BUT I SAW HIM CLEARLY AND SUCCESS-FULLY AVOIDED HIS LANCE SEVERAL TIMES.
THEN, I PULLED OUT MY SECRET WEAPON -THE LARIAT.
I UNSEATED SIR SAG AND SEVERAL OTHER KNIGHTS,
INCLUDING SIR LAUNCELOT.

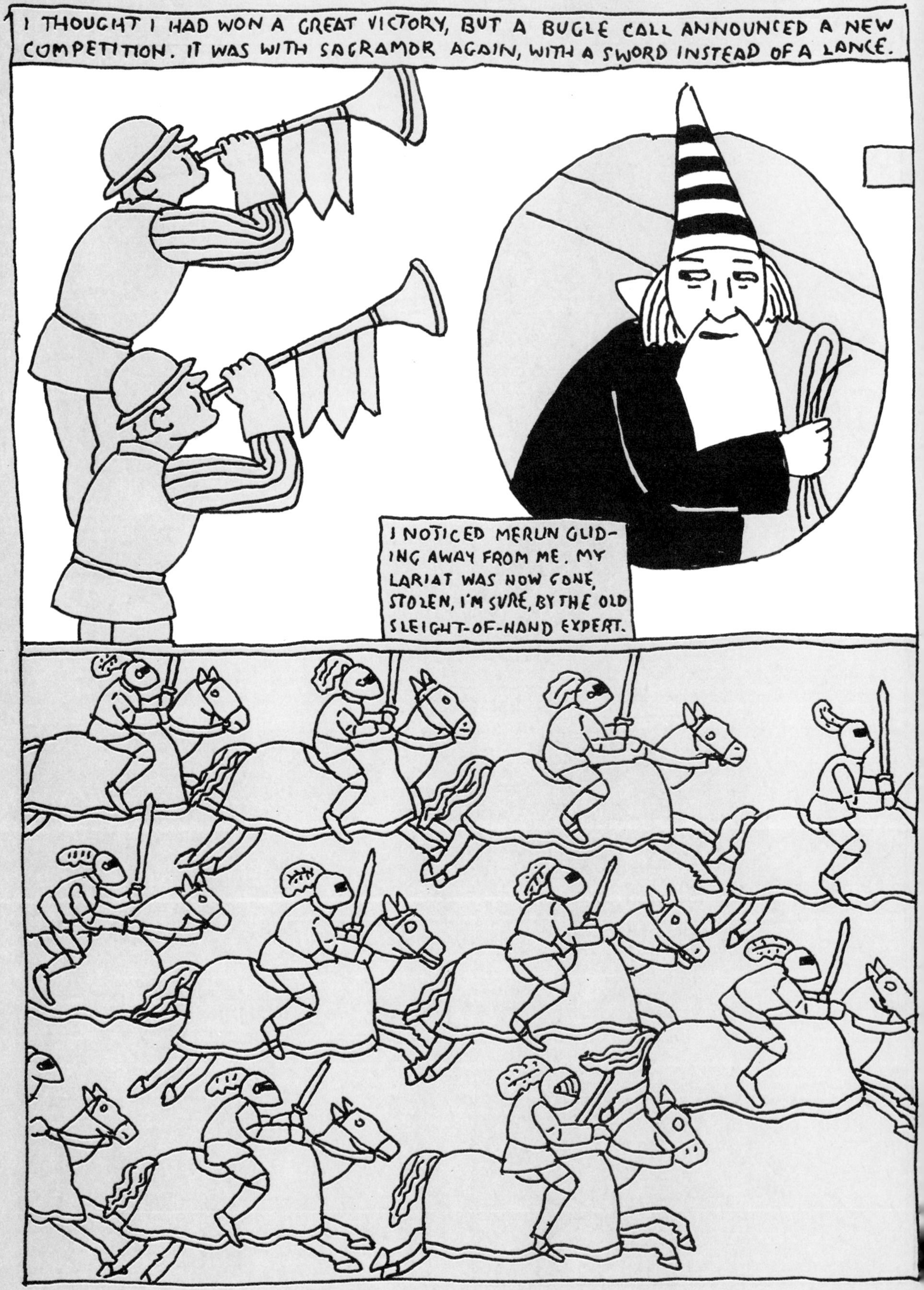
I THOUGHT I HAD WON A GREAT VICTORY, BUT A BUGLE CALL ANNOUNCED A NEW COMPETITION. IT WAS WITH SAGRAMOR AGAIN, WITH A SWORD INSTEAD OF A LANCE.
I NOTICED MERLIN GLIDING AWAY FROM ME. MY LARIAT WAS NOW GONE, STOLEN, I'M SURE, BY THE OLD SLEIGHT-OF-HAND EXPERT.

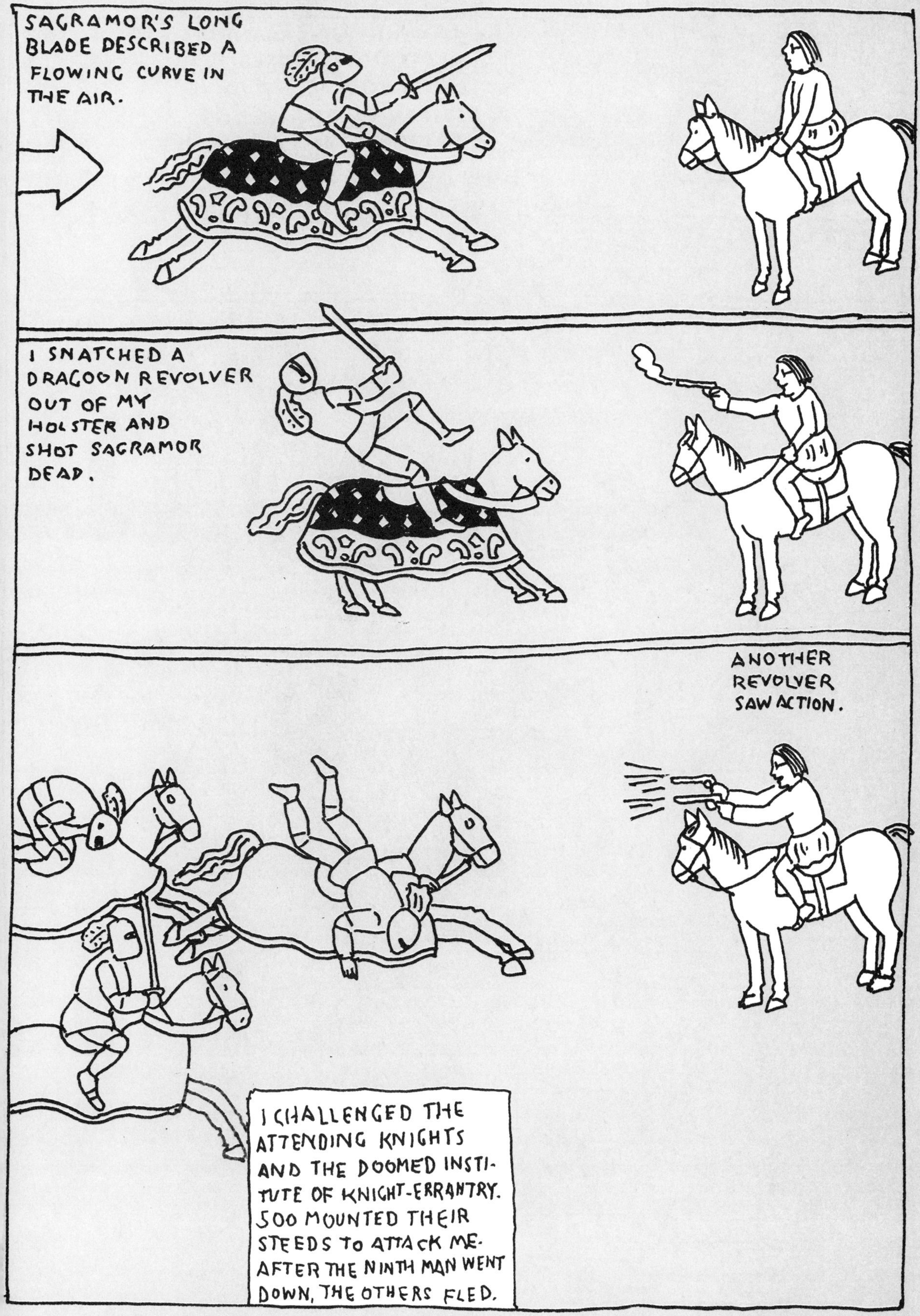
SAGRAMOR'S LONG BLADE DESCRIBED A FLOWING CURVE IN THE AIR.
I SNATCHED A DRAGOON REVOLVER OUT OF MY HOLSTER AND SHOT SAGRAMOR DEAD.
ANOTHER REVOLVER SAW ACTION.
I CHALLENGED THE ATTENDING KNIGHTS AND THE DOOMED INSTITUTE OF KNIGHT-ERRANTRY. 500 MOUNTED THEIR STEEDS TO ATTACK ME. AFTER THE NINTH MAN WENT DOWN, THE OTHERS FLED.

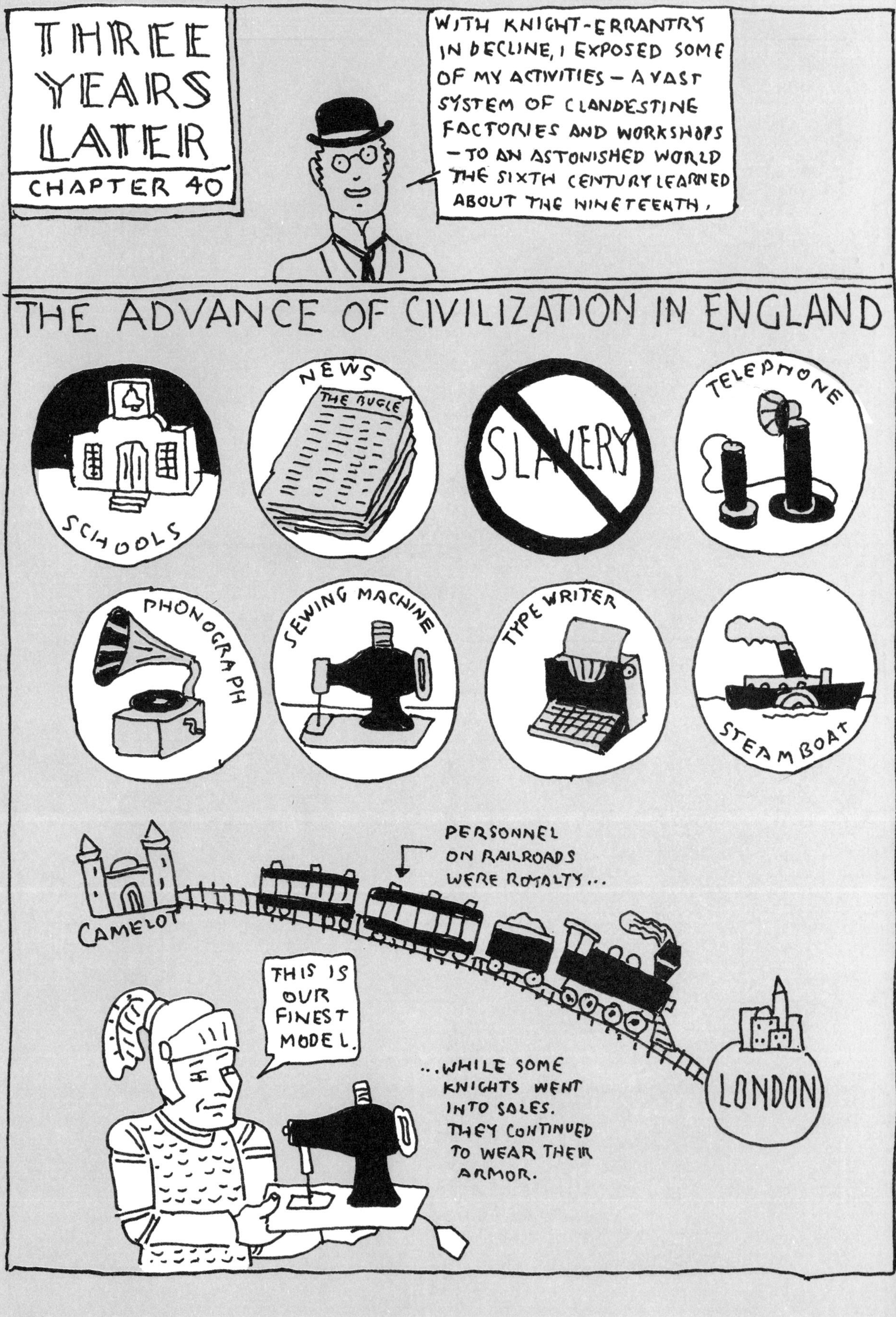
THREE YEARS LATER
CHAPTER 40
WITH KNIGHT-ERRANTRY IN DECLINE, I EXPOSED SOME OF MY ACTIVITIES — A VAST SYSTEM OF CLANDESTINE FACTORIES AND WORKSHOPS — TO AN ASTONISHED WORLD THE SIXTH CENTURY LEARNED ABOUT THE NINETEENTH.
THE ADVANCE OF CIVILIZATION IN ENGLAND
SCHOOLS
NEWS
THE BUGLE
SLAVERY
TELEPHONE
PHONOGRAPH
SEWING MACHINE
TYPE WRITER
STEAMBOAT
PERSONNEL ON RAILROADS WERE ROYALTY...
CAMELOT
LONDON
THIS IS OUR FINEST MODEL.
...WHILE SOME KNIGHTS WENT INTO SALES. THEY CONTINUED TO WEAR THEIR ARMOR.

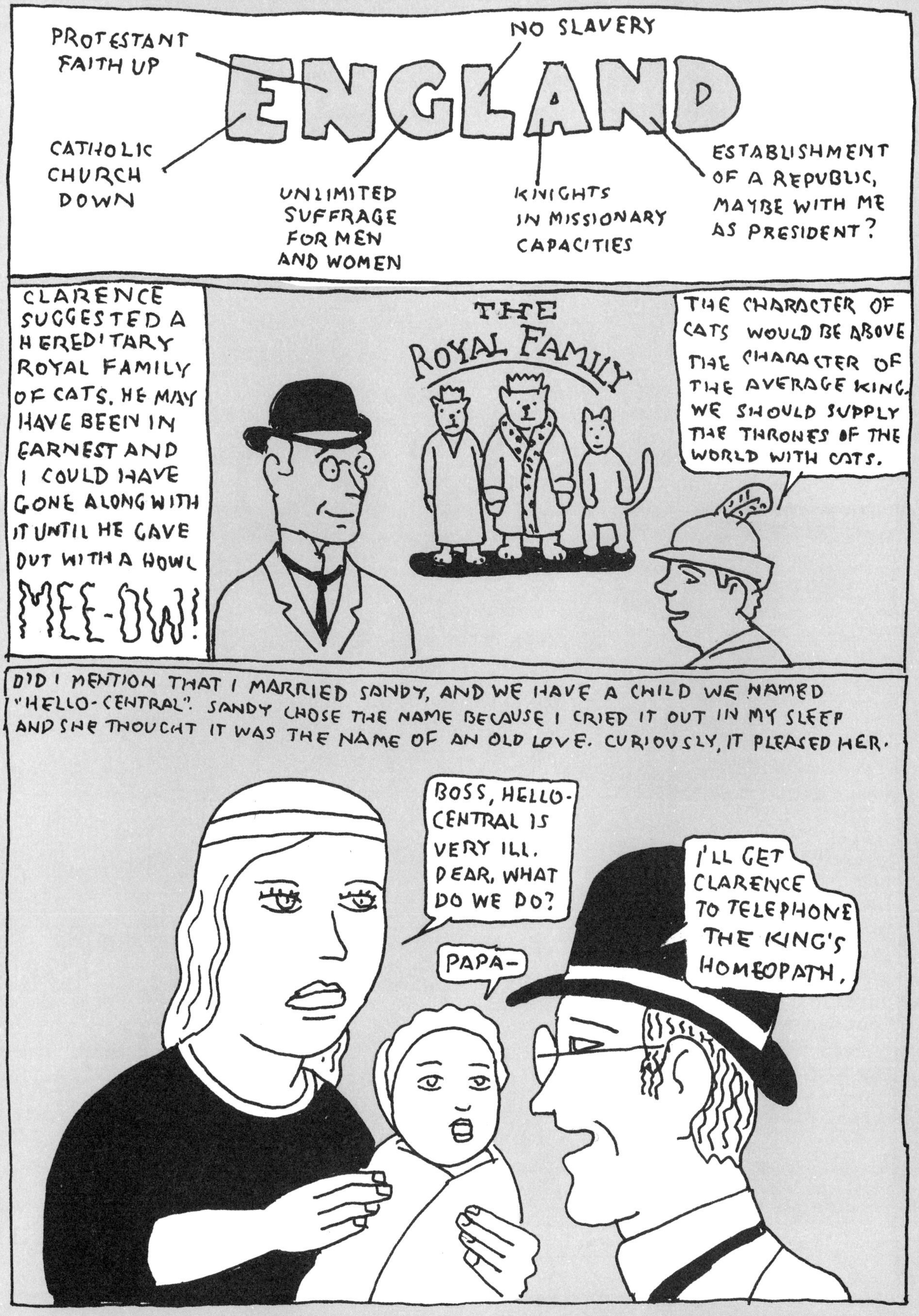
ENGLAND
PROTESTANT FAITH UP
NO SLAVERY
CATHOLIC CHURCH DOWN
UNLIMITED SUFFRAGE FOR MEN AND WOMEN
KNIGHTS IN MISSIONARY CAPACITIES
ESTABLISHMENT OF A REPUBLIC, MAYBE WITH ME AS PRESIDENT?
CLARENCE SUGGESTED A HEREDITARY ROYAL FAMILY OF CATS. HE MAY HAVE BEEN IN EARNEST AND I COULD HAVE GONE ALONG WITH IT UNTIL HE GAVE OUT WITH A HOWL
MEE-OW!
THE ROYAL FAMILY
THE CHARACTER OF CATS WOULD BE ABOVE THE CHARACTER OF THE AVERAGE KING. WE SHOULD SUPPLY THE THRONES OF THE WORLD WITH CATS.
DID I MENTION THAT I MARRIED SANDY, AND WE HAVE A CHILD WE NAMED "HELLO-CENTRAL". SANDY CHOSE THE NAME BECAUSE I CRIED IT OUT IN MY SLEEP AND SHE THOUGHT IT WAS THE NAME OF AN OLD LOVE. CURIOUSLY, IT PLEASED HER.
BOSS, HELLO-CENTRAL IS VERY ILL. DEAR, WHAT DO WE DO?
PAPA-
I'LL GET CLARENCE TO TELEPHONE THE KING'S HOMEOPATH.

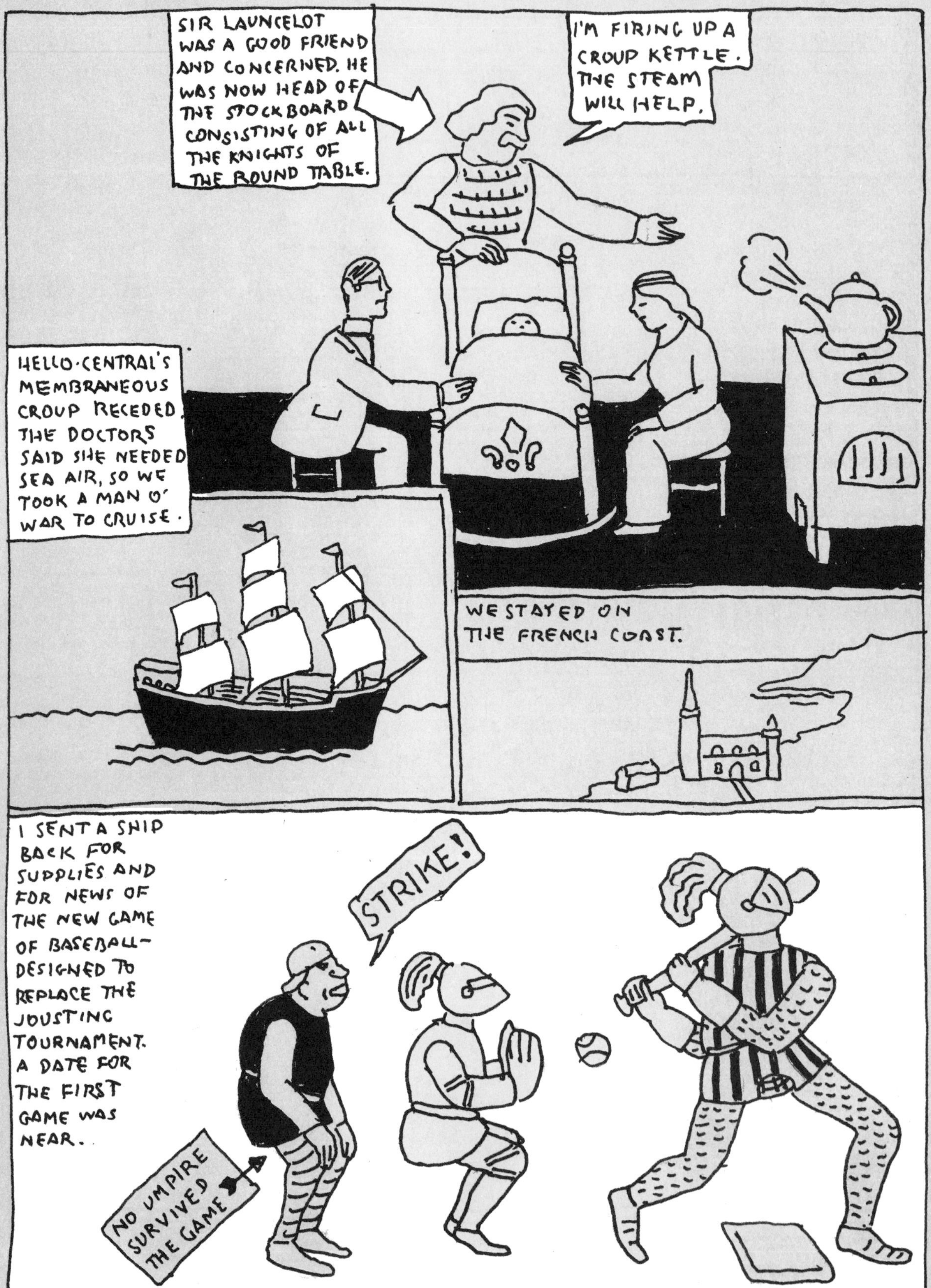
SIR LAUNCELOT WAS A GOOD FRIEND AND CONCERNED. HE WAS NOW HEAD OF THE STOCKBOARD CONSISTING OF ALL THE KNIGHTS OF THE ROUND TABLE.
I'M FIRING UP A CROUP KETTLE. THE STEAM WILL HELP.
HELLO-CENTRAL'S MEMBRANEOUS CROUP RECEDED. THE DOCTORS SAID SHE NEEDED SEA AIR, SO WE TOOK A MAN O' WAR TO CRUISE.
WE STAYED ON THE FRENCH COAST.
I SENT A SHIP BACK FOR SUPPLIES AND FOR NEWS OF THE NEW GAME OF BASEBALL- DESIGNED TO REPLACE THE JOUSTING TOURNAMENT. A DATE FOR THE FIRST GAME WAS NEAR.
STRIKE!
NO UMPIRE SURVIVED THE GAME

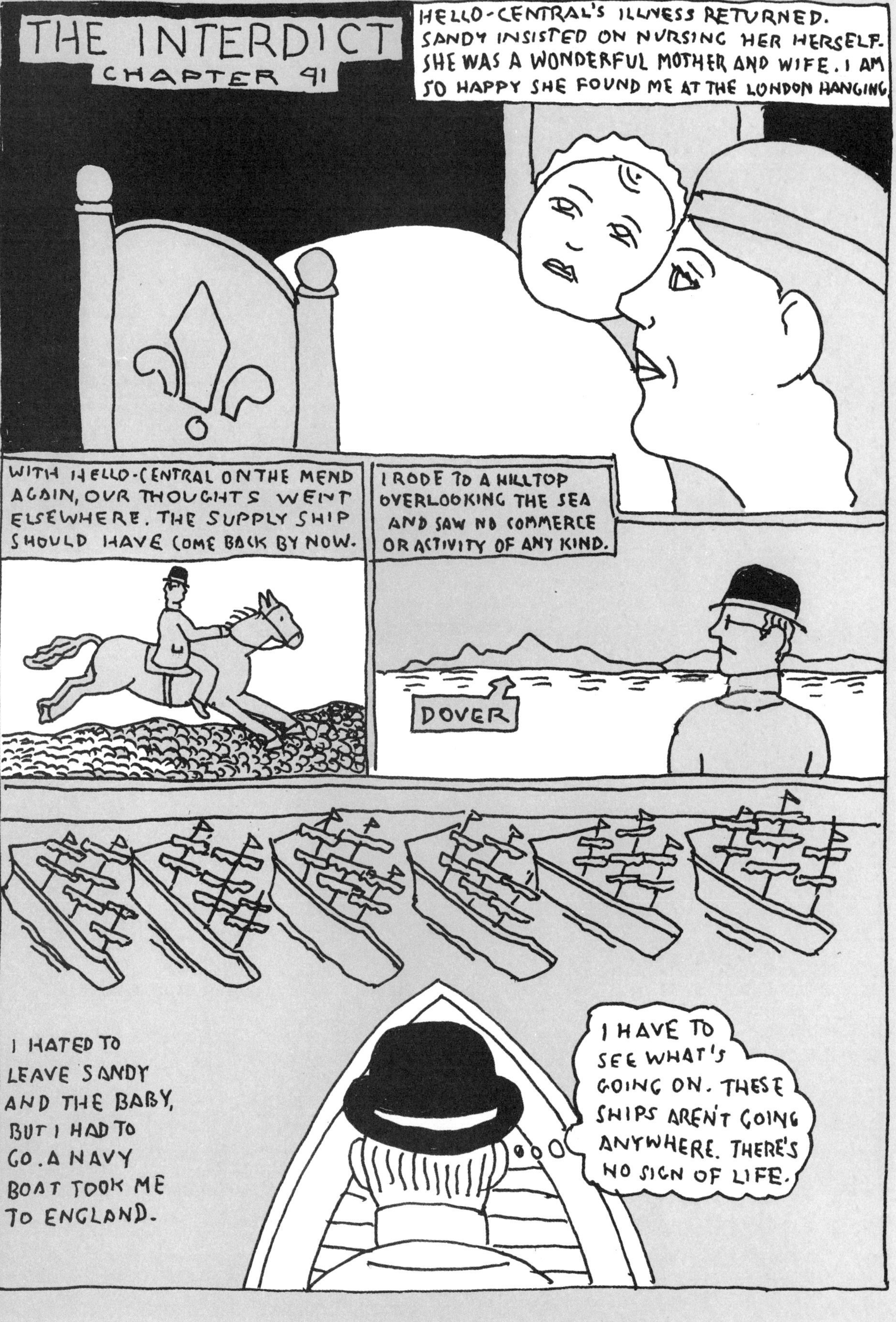
THE INTERDICT
CHAPTER 91
HELLO-CENTRAL'S ILLNESS RETURNED. SANDY INSISTED ON NURSING HER HERSELF. SHE WAS A WONDERFUL MOTHER AND WIFE. I AM SO HAPPY SHE FOUND ME AT THE LONDON HANGING.
WITH HELLO-CENTRAL ON THE MEND AGAIN, OUR THOUGHTS WENT ELSEWHERE. THE SUPPLY SHIP SHOULD HAVE COME BACK BY NOW.
I RODE TO A HILLTOP OVERLOOKING THE SEA AND SAW NO COMMERCE OR ACTIVITY OF ANY KIND.
DOVER
I HATED TO LEAVE SANDY AND THE BABY, BUT I HAD TO GO. A NAVY BOAT TOOK ME TO ENGLAND.
I HAVE TO SEE WHAT'S GOING ON. THESE SHIPS AREN'T GOING ANYWHERE. THERE'S NO SIGN OF LIFE.

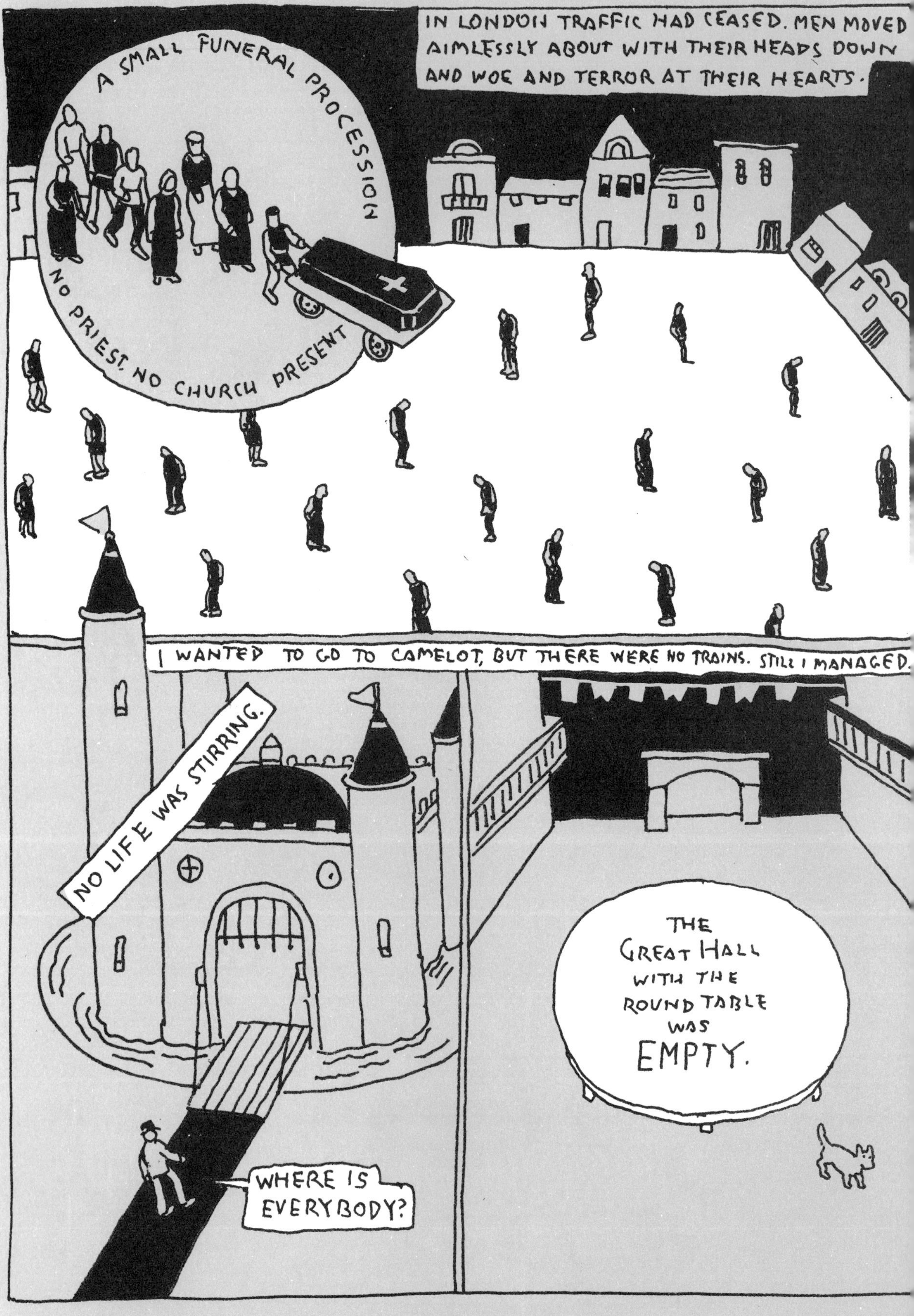
IN LONDON TRAFFIC HAD CEASED. MEN MOVED AIMLESSLY ABOUT WITH THEIR HEADS DOWN AND WOE AND TERROR AT THEIR HEARTS.
A SMALL FUNERAL PROCESSION
NO PRIEST, NO CHURCH PRESENT
I WANTED TO GO TO CAMELOT, BUT THERE WERE NO TRAINS. STILL I MANAGED.
NO LIFE WAS STIRRING.
WHERE IS EVERYBODY?
THE GREAT HALL WITH THE ROUND TABLE WAS EMPTY.

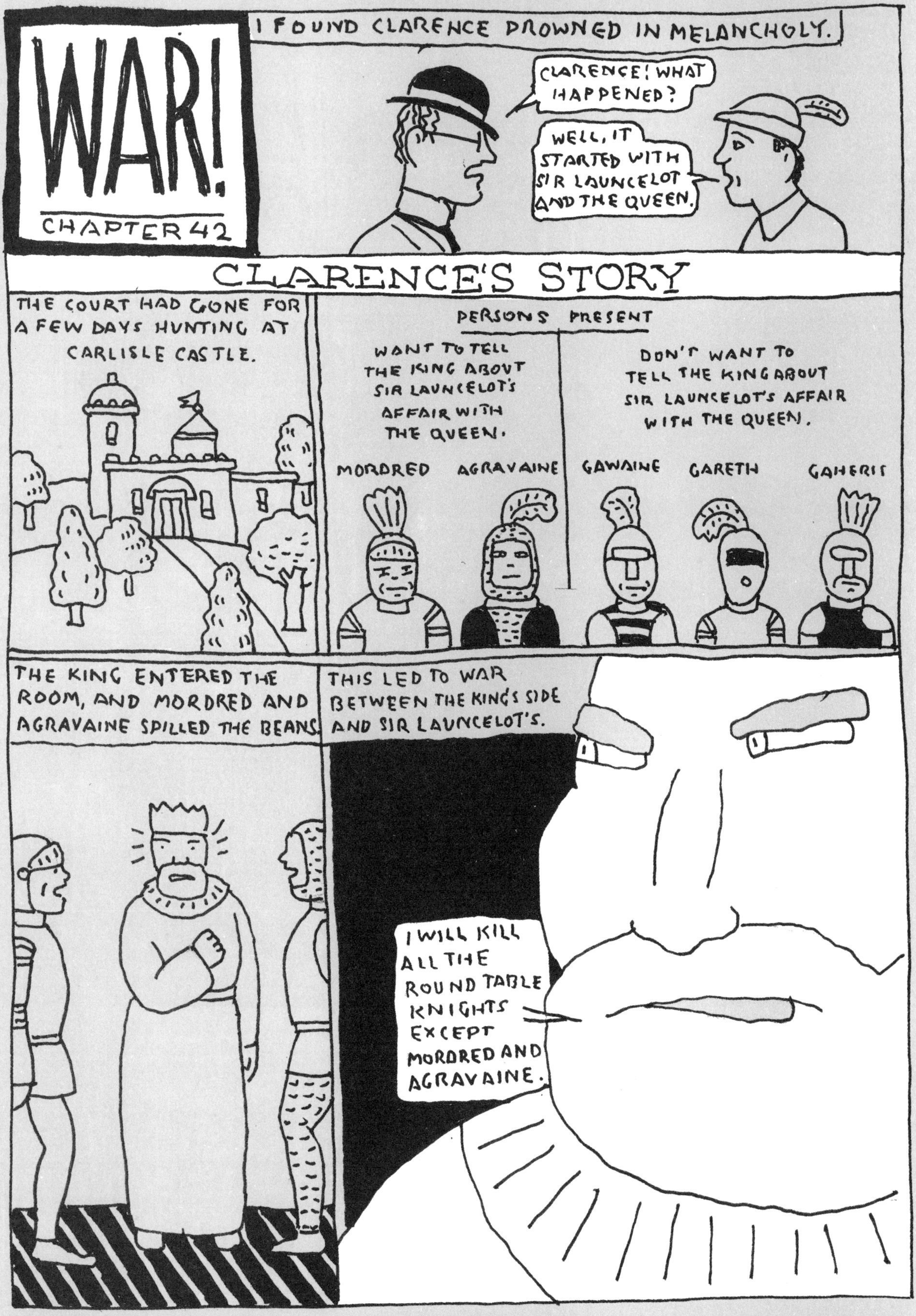
WAR!
CHAPTER 42
I FOUND CLARENCE DROWNED IN MELANCHOLY.
CLARENCE! WHAT HAPPENED?
WELL, IT STARTED WITH SIR LAUNCELOT AND THE QUEEN.
CLARENCE'S STORY
THE COURT HAD GONE FOR A FEW DAYS HUNTING AT CARLISLE CASTLE.
PERSONS PRESENT
WANT TO TELL THE KING ABOUT SIR LAUNCELOT'S AFFAIR WITH THE QUEEN.
DON'T WANT TO TELL THE KING ABOUT SIR LAUNCELOT'S AFFAIR WITH THE QUEEN.
MORDRED
AGRAVAINE
GAWAINE
GARETH
GAHERIS
THE KING ENTERED THE ROOM, AND MORDRED AND AGRAVAINE SPILLED THE BEANS.
THIS LED TO WAR BETWEEN THE KING'S SIDE AND SIR LAUNCELOT'S.
I WILL KILL ALL THE ROUND TABLE KNIGHTS EXCEPT MORDRED AND AGRAVAINE.

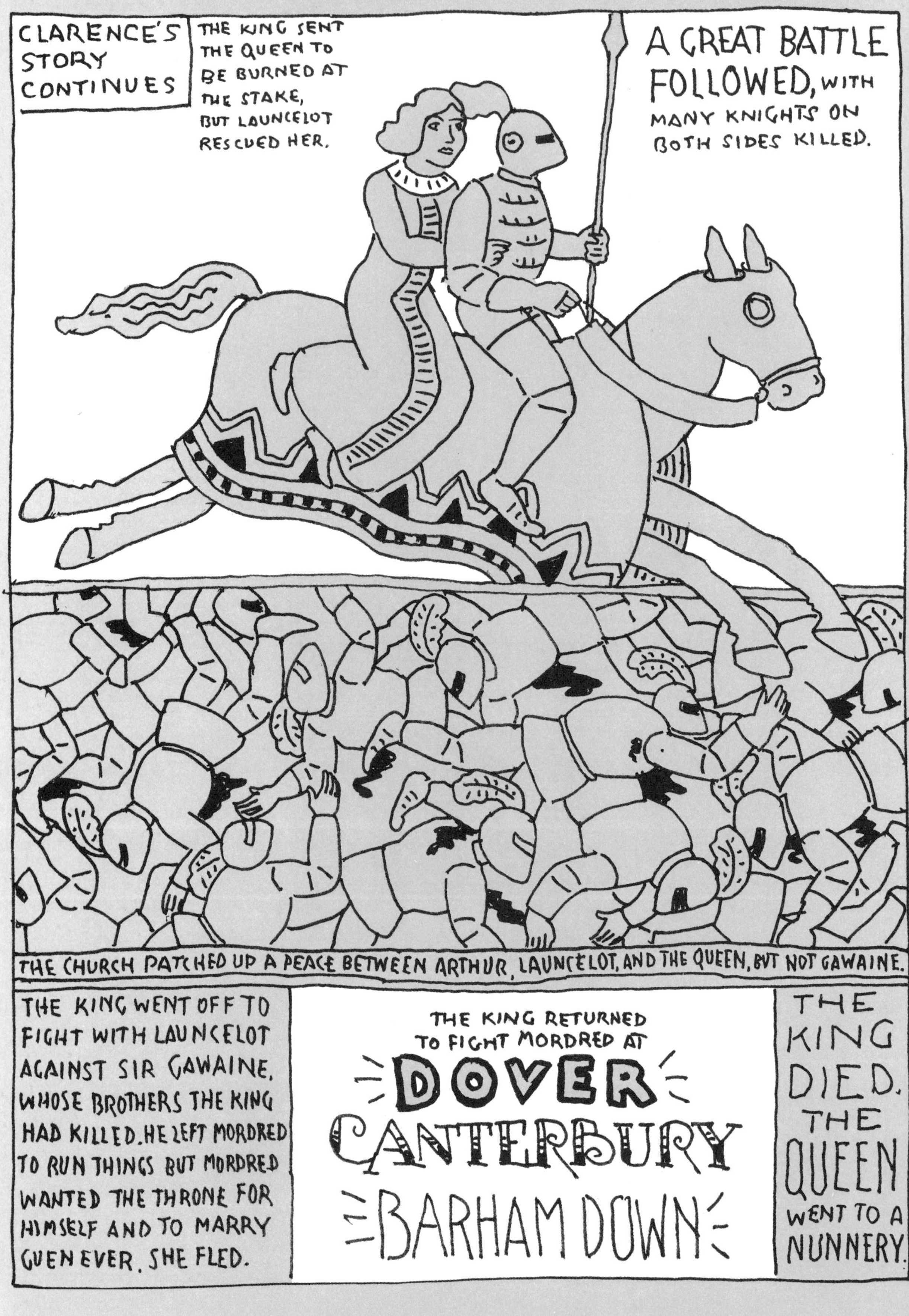
CLARENCE'S STORY CONTINUES
THE KING SENT THE QUEEN TO BE BURNED AT THE STAKE, BUT LAUNCELOT RESCUED HER.
A GREAT BATTLE FOLLOWED, WITH MANY KNIGHTS ON BOTH SIDES KILLED.
THE CHURCH PATCHED UP A PEACE BETWEEN ARTHUR, LAUNCELOT, AND THE QUEEN, BUT NOT GAWAINE.
THE KING WENT OFF TO FIGHT WITH LAUNCELOT AGAINST SIR GAWAINE, WHOSE BROTHERS THE KING HAD KILLED. HE LEFT MORDRED TO RUN THINGS BUT MORDRED WANTED THE THRONE FOR HIMSELF AND TO MARRY GUENEVER. SHE FLED.
THE KING RETURNED TO FIGHT MORDRED AT
DOVER
CANTERBURY
BARHAM DOWN
THE KING DIED. THE QUEEN WENT TO A NUNNERY.

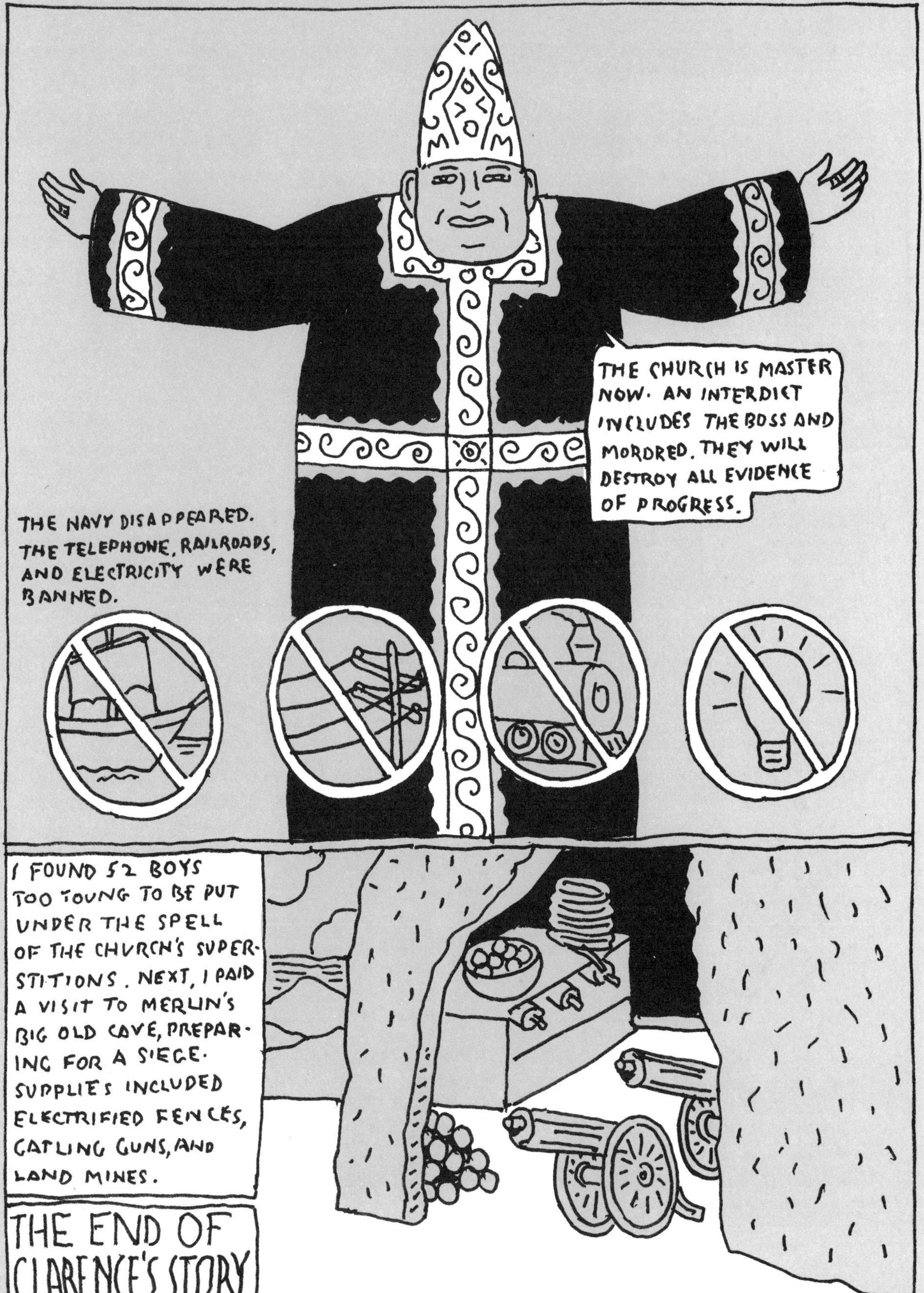
THE CHURCH IS MASTER NOW. AN INTERDICT INCLUDES THE BOSS AND MORDRED. THEY WILL DESTROY ALL EVIDENCE OF PROGRESS.
THE NAVY DISAPPEARED. THE TELEPHONE, RAILROADS, AND ELECTRICITY WERE BANNED.
I FOUND 52 BOYS TOO YOUNG TO BE PUT UNDER THE SPELL OF THE CHURCH'S SUPERSTITIONS. NEXT, I PAID A VISIT TO MERLIN'S BIG OLD CAVE, PREPARING FOR A SIEGE. SUPPLIES INCLUDED ELECTRIFIED FENCES, GATLING GUNS, AND LAND MINES.
THE END OF CLARENCE'S STORY

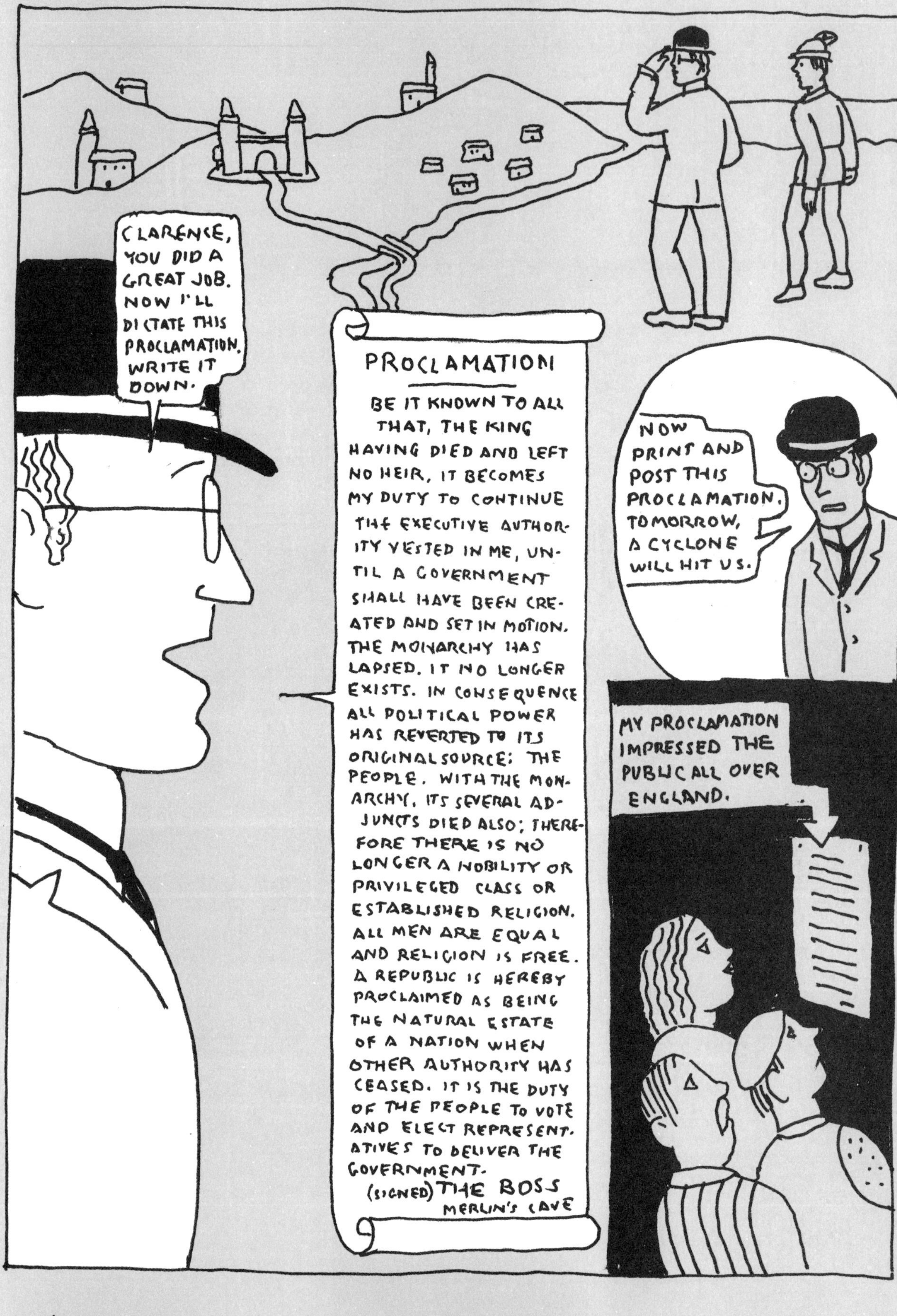

CLARENCE, YOU DID A GREAT JOB. NOW I'LL DICTATE THIS PROCLAMATION. WRITE IT DOWN.
PROCLAMATION
BE IT KNOWN TO ALL THAT, THE KING HAVING DIED AND LEFT NO HEIR, IT BECOMES MY DUTY TO CONTINUE THE EXECUTIVE AUTHORITY VESTED IN ME, UNTIL A GOVERNMENT SHALL HAVE BEEN CREATED AND SET IN MOTION. THE MONARCHY HAS LAPSED. IT NO LONGER EXISTS. IN CONSEQUENCE ALL POLITICAL POWER HAS REVERTED TO ITS ORIGINAL SOURCE: THE PEOPLE. WITH THE MONARCHY, ITS SEVERAL ADJUNCTS DIED ALSO; THEREFORE THERE IS NO LONGER A NOBILITY OR PRIVILEGED CLASS OR ESTABLISHED RELIGION. ALL MEN ARE EQUAL AND RELIGION IS FREE. A REPUBLIC IS HEREBY PROCLAIMED AS BEING THE NATURAL ESTATE OF A NATION WHEN OTHER AUTHORITY HAS CEASED. IT IS THE DUTY OF THE PEOPLE TO VOTE AND ELECT REPRESENTATIVES TO DELIVER THE GOVERNMENT.
(SIGNED) THE BOSS
MERLIN'S CAVE
NOW PRINT AND POST THIS PROCLAMATION. TOMORROW, A CYCLONE WILL HIT US.
MY PROCLAMATION IMPRESSED THE PUBLIC ALL OVER ENGLAND.

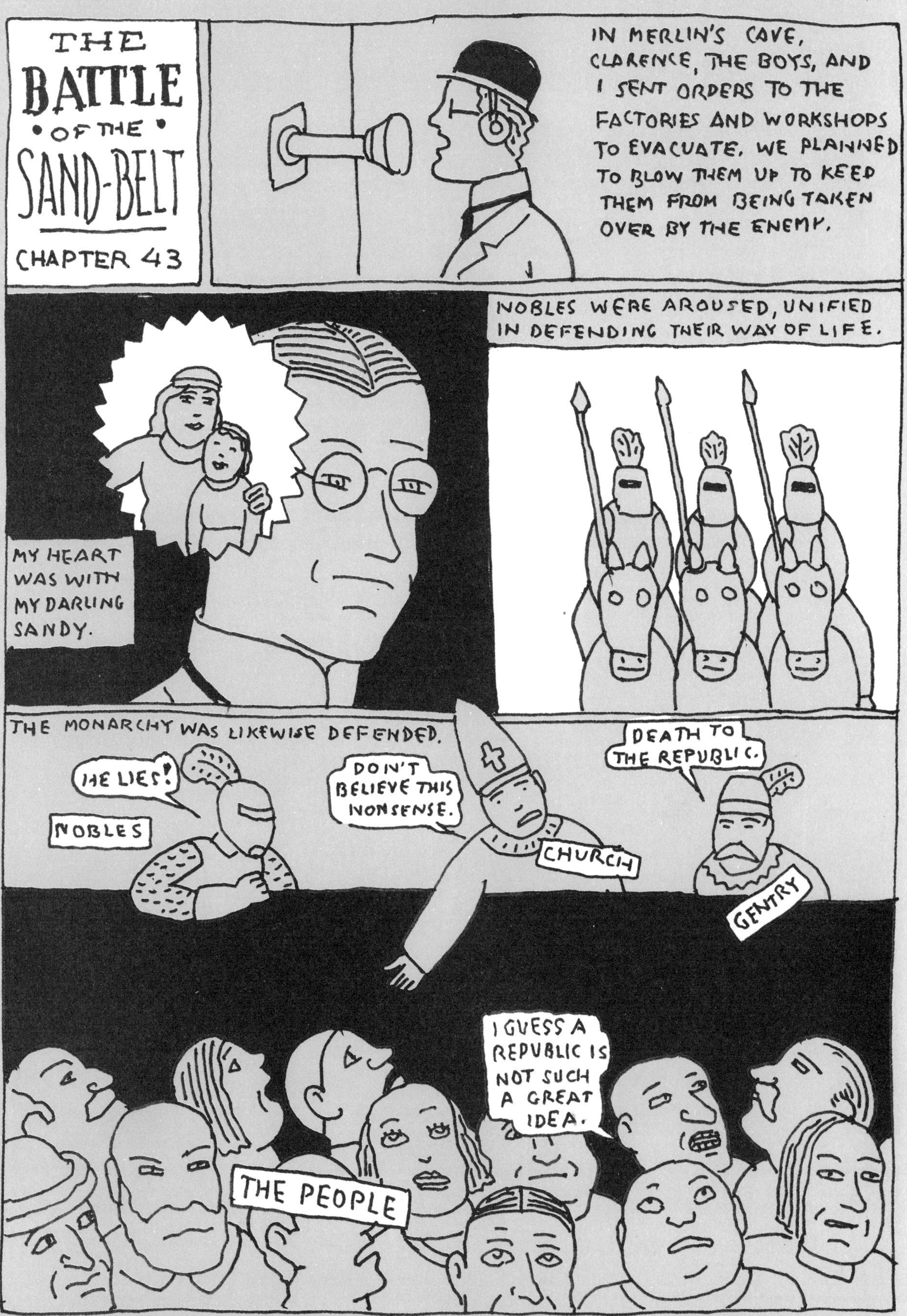
THE BATTLE OF THE SAND-BELT
CHAPTER 43
IN MERLIN'S CAVE, CLARENCE, THE BOYS, AND I SENT ORDERS TO THE FACTORIES AND WORKSHOPS TO EVACUATE. WE PLANNED TO BLOW THEM UP TO KEEP THEM FROM BEING TAKEN OVER BY THE ENEMY.
MY HEART WAS WITH MY DARLING SANDY.
NOBLES WERE AROUSED, UNIFIED IN DEFENDING THEIR WAY OF LIFE.
THE MONARCHY WAS LIKEWISE DEFENDED.
HE LIES!
NOBLES
DON'T BELIEVE THIS NONSENSE.
CHURCH
DEATH TO THE REPUBLIC.
GENTRY
I GUESS A REPUBLIC IS NOT SUCH A GREAT IDEA.
THE PEOPLE

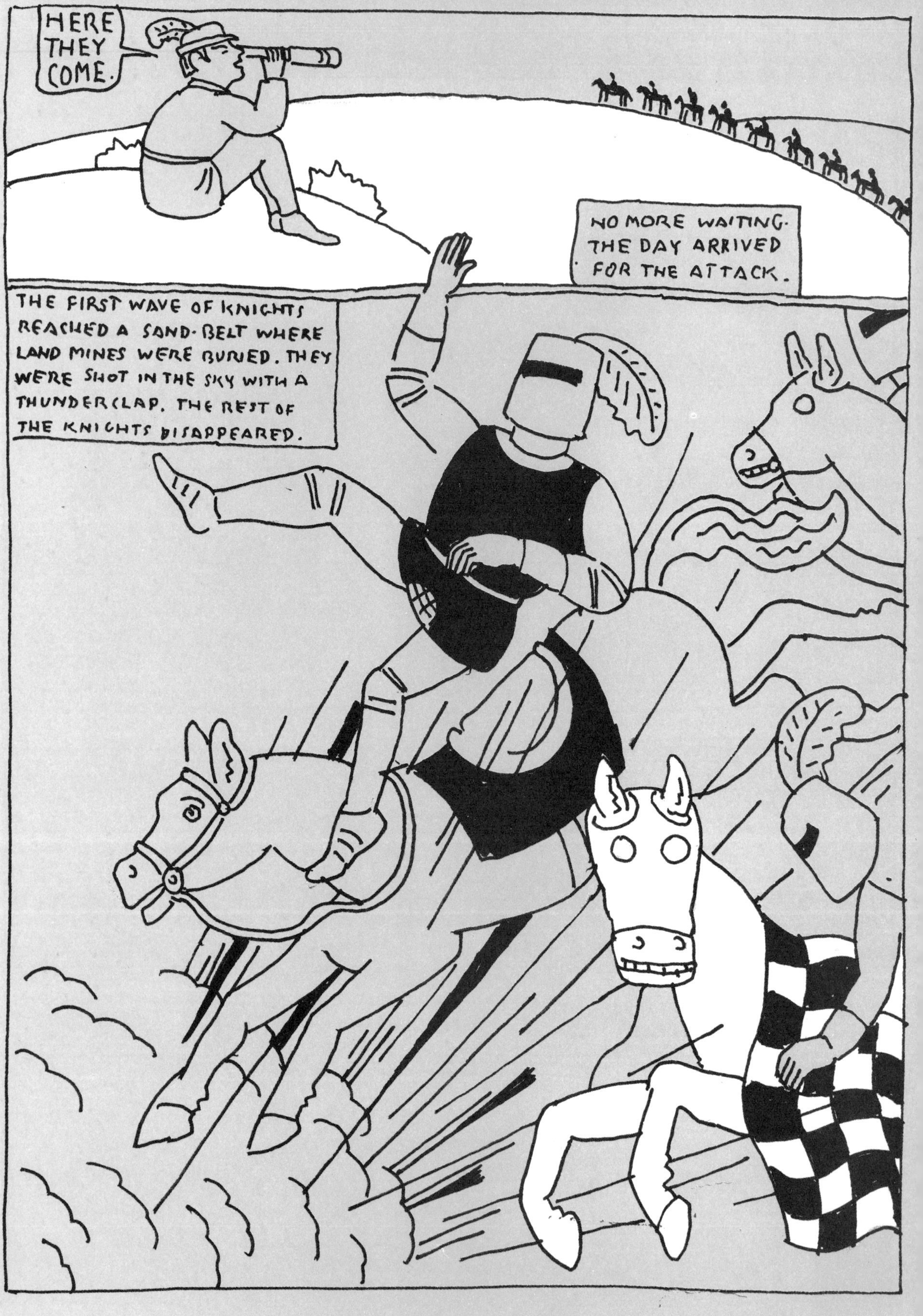
HERE THEY COME.
NO MORE WAITING. THE DAY ARRIVED FOR THE ATTACK.
THE FIRST WAVE OF KNIGHTS REACHED A SAND-BELT WHERE LAND MINES WERE BURIED. THEY WERE SHOT IN THE SKY WITH A THUNDERCLAP. THE REST OF THE KNIGHTS DISAPPEARED.

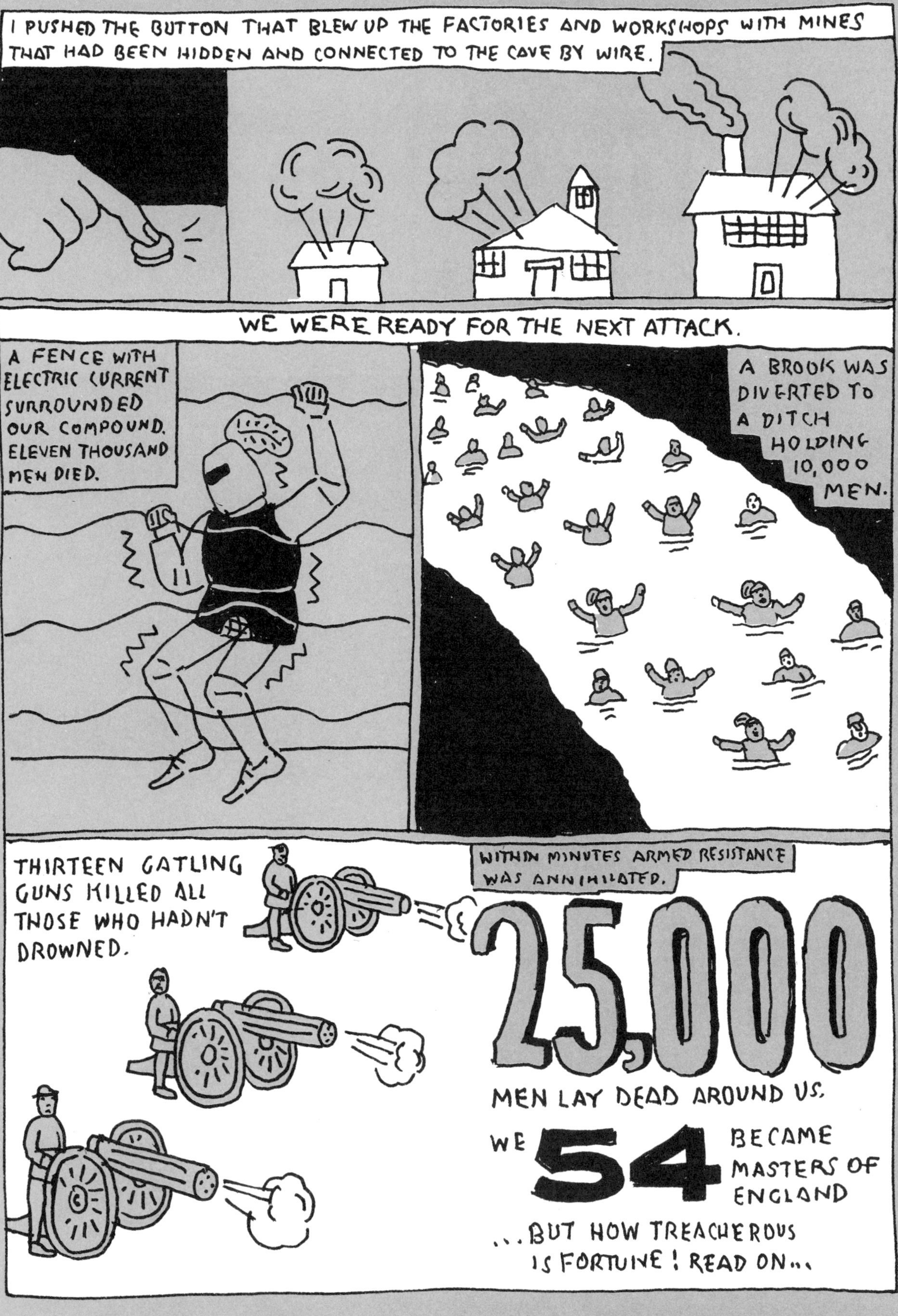
I PUSHED THE BUTTON THAT BLEW UP THE FACTORIES AND WORKSHOPS WITH MINES THAT HAD BEEN HIDDEN AND CONNECTED TO THE CAVE BY WIRE.
WE WERE READY FOR THE NEXT ATTACK.
A FENCE WITH ELECTRIC CURRENT SURROUNDED OUR COMPOUND. ELEVEN THOUSAND MEN DIED.
A BROOK WAS DIVERTED TO A DITCH HOLDING 10,000 MEN.
THIRTEEN GATLING GUNS KILLED ALL THOSE WHO HADN'T DROWNED.
WITHIN MINUTES ARMED RESISTANCE WAS ANNIHILATED.
25,000
MEN LAY DEAD AROUND US.
WE 54 BECAME MASTERS OF ENGLAND
...BUT HOW TREACHEROUS IS FORTUNE! READ ON...

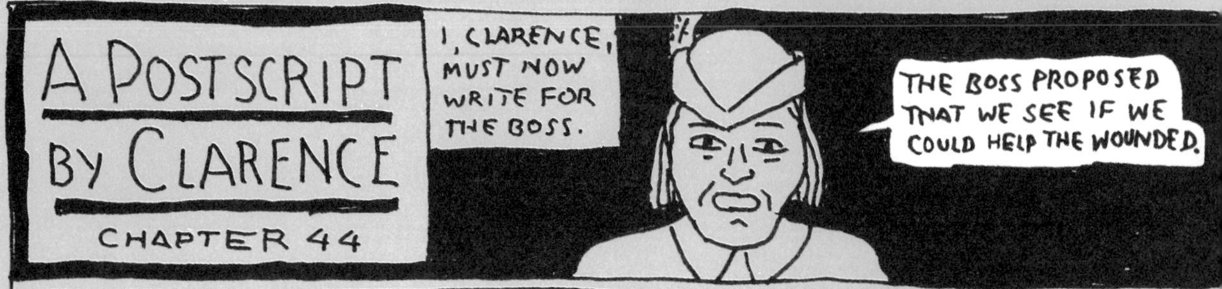
A POSTSCRIPT BY CLARENCE
CHAPTER 44
I, CLARENCE, MUST NOW WRITE FOR THE BOSS.
THE BOSS PROPOSED THAT WE SEE IF WE COULD HELP THE WOUNDED.

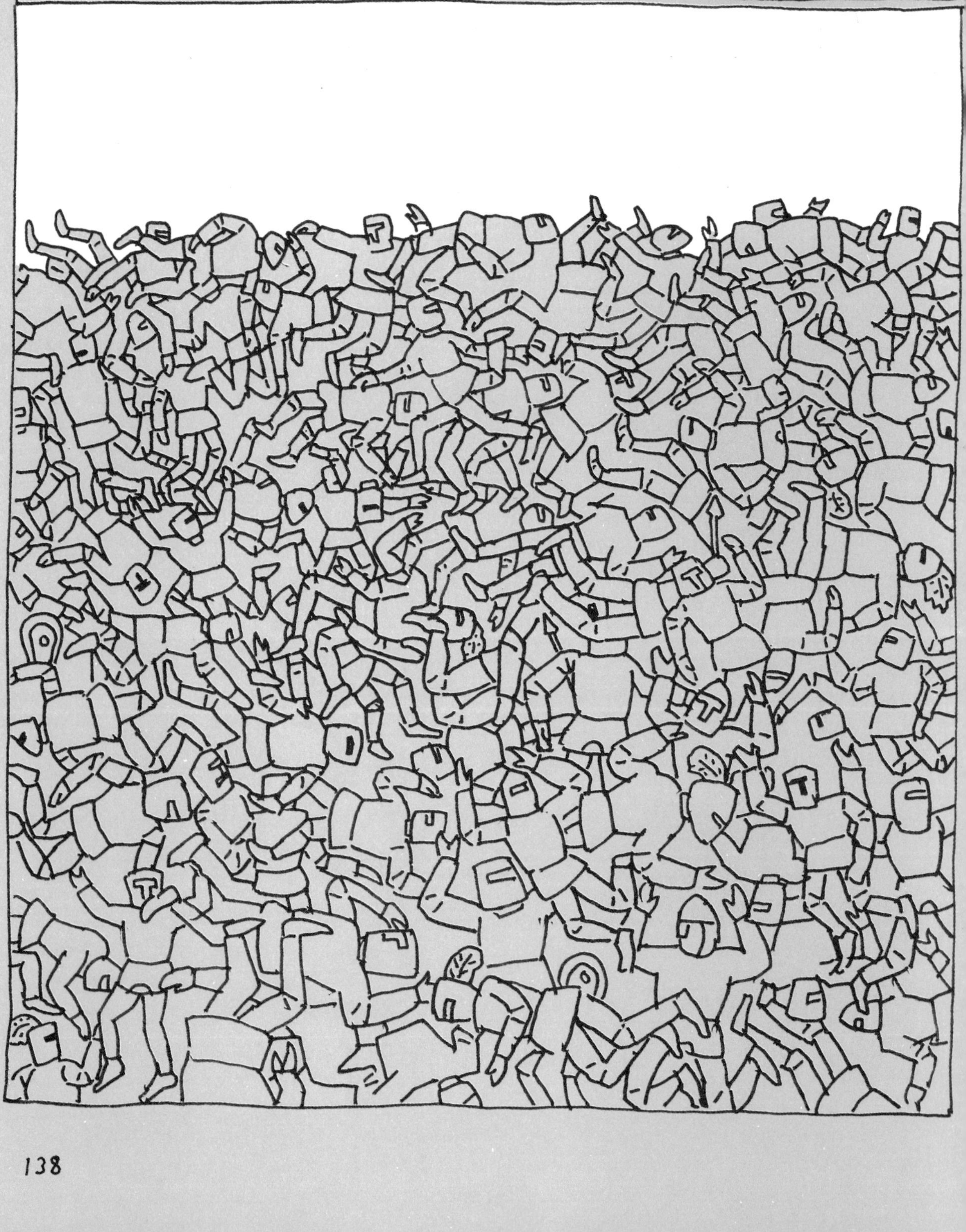

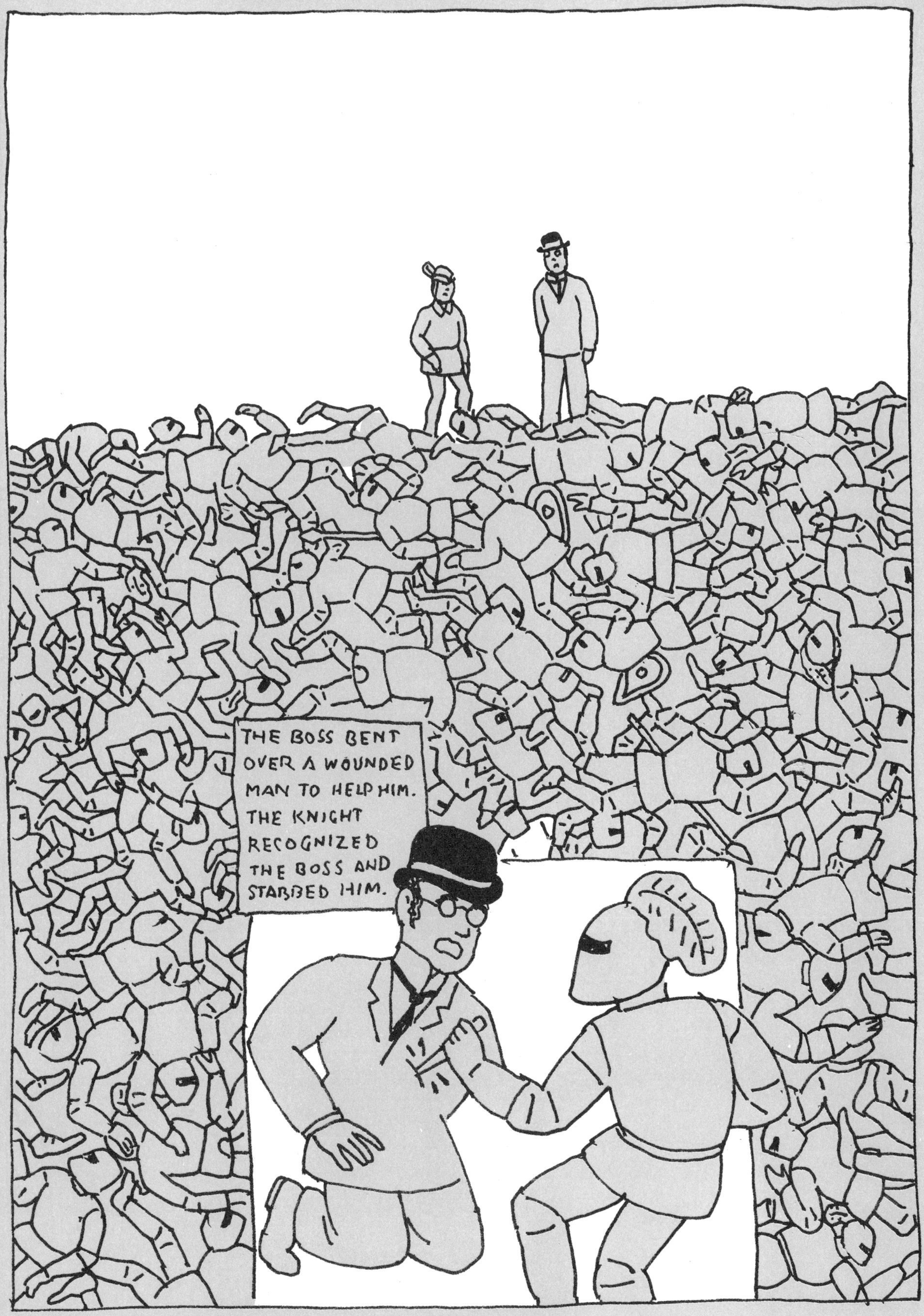
THE BOSS BENT OVER A WOUNDED MAN TO HELP HIM. THE KNIGHT RECOGNIZED THE BOSS AND STABBED HIM.

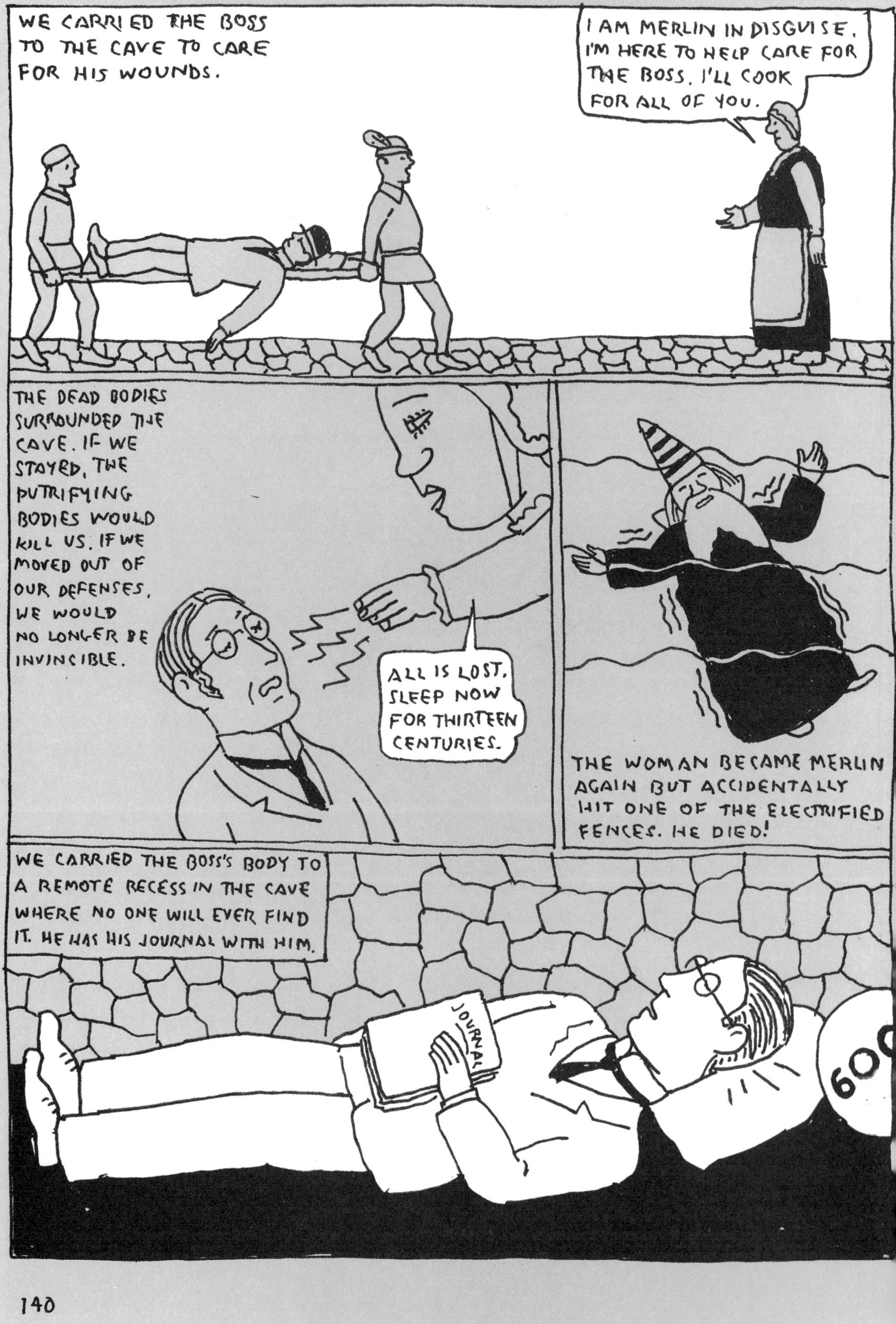
WE CARRIED THE BOSS TO THE CAVE TO CARE FOR HIS WOUNDS.
I AM MERLIN IN DISGUISE. I'M HERE TO HELP CARE FOR THE BOSS. I'LL COOK FOR ALL OF YOU.
THE DEAD BODIES SURROUNDED THE CAVE. IF WE STAYED, THE PUTRIFYING BODIES WOULD KILL US. IF WE MOVED OUT OF OUR DEFENSES, WE WOULD NO LONGER BE INVINCIBLE.
ALL IS LOST. SLEEP NOW FOR THIRTEEN CENTURIES.
THE WOMAN BECAME MERLIN AGAIN BUT ACCIDENTALLY HIT ONE OF THE ELECTRIFIED FENCES. HE DIED!
WE CARRIED THE BOSS'S BODY TO A REMOTE RECESS IN THE CAVE WHERE NO ONE WILL EVER FIND IT. HE HAS HIS JOURNAL WITH HIM.
JOURNAL
600

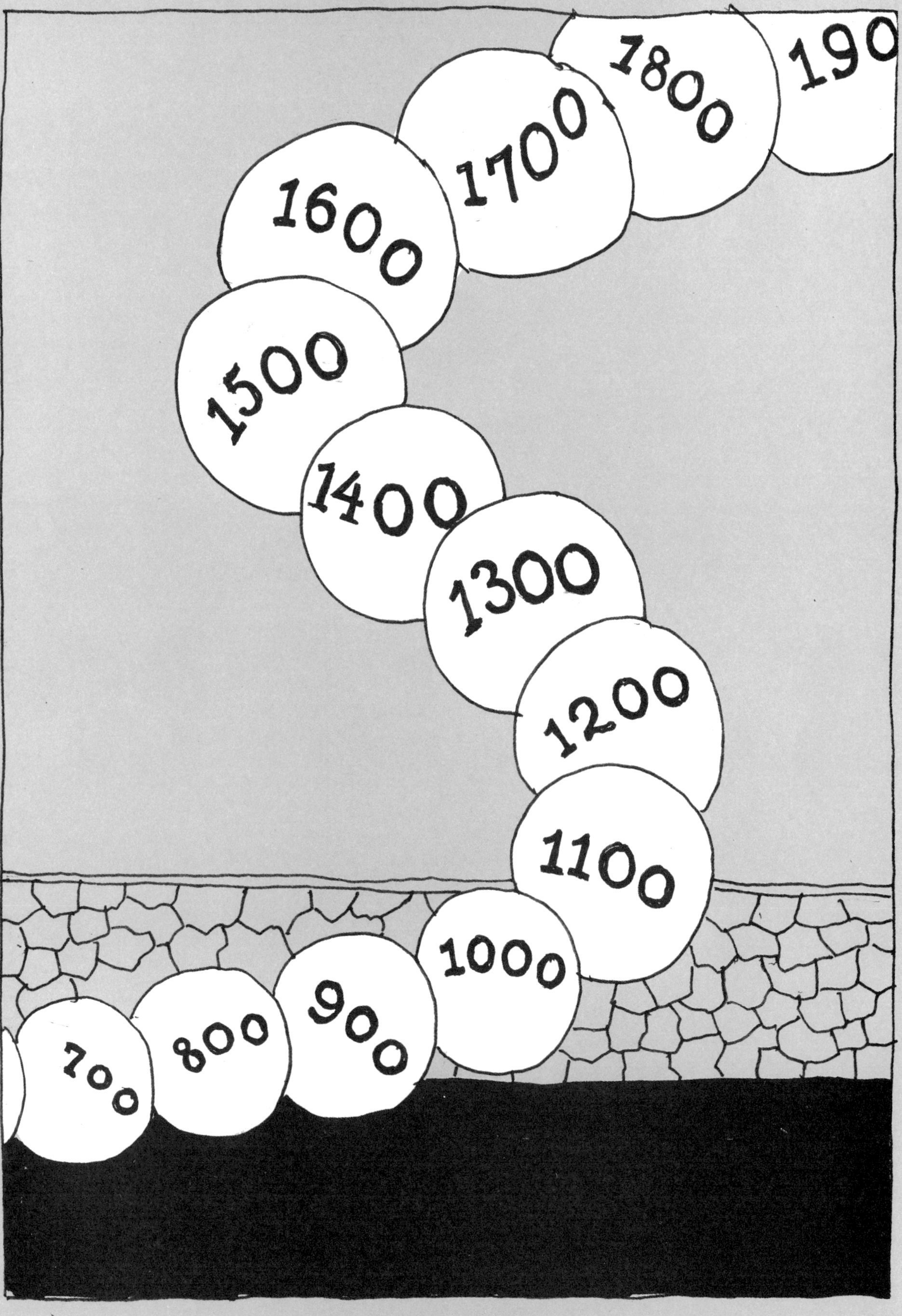
190
1800
1700
1600
1500
1400
1300
1200
1100
1000
900
800
700

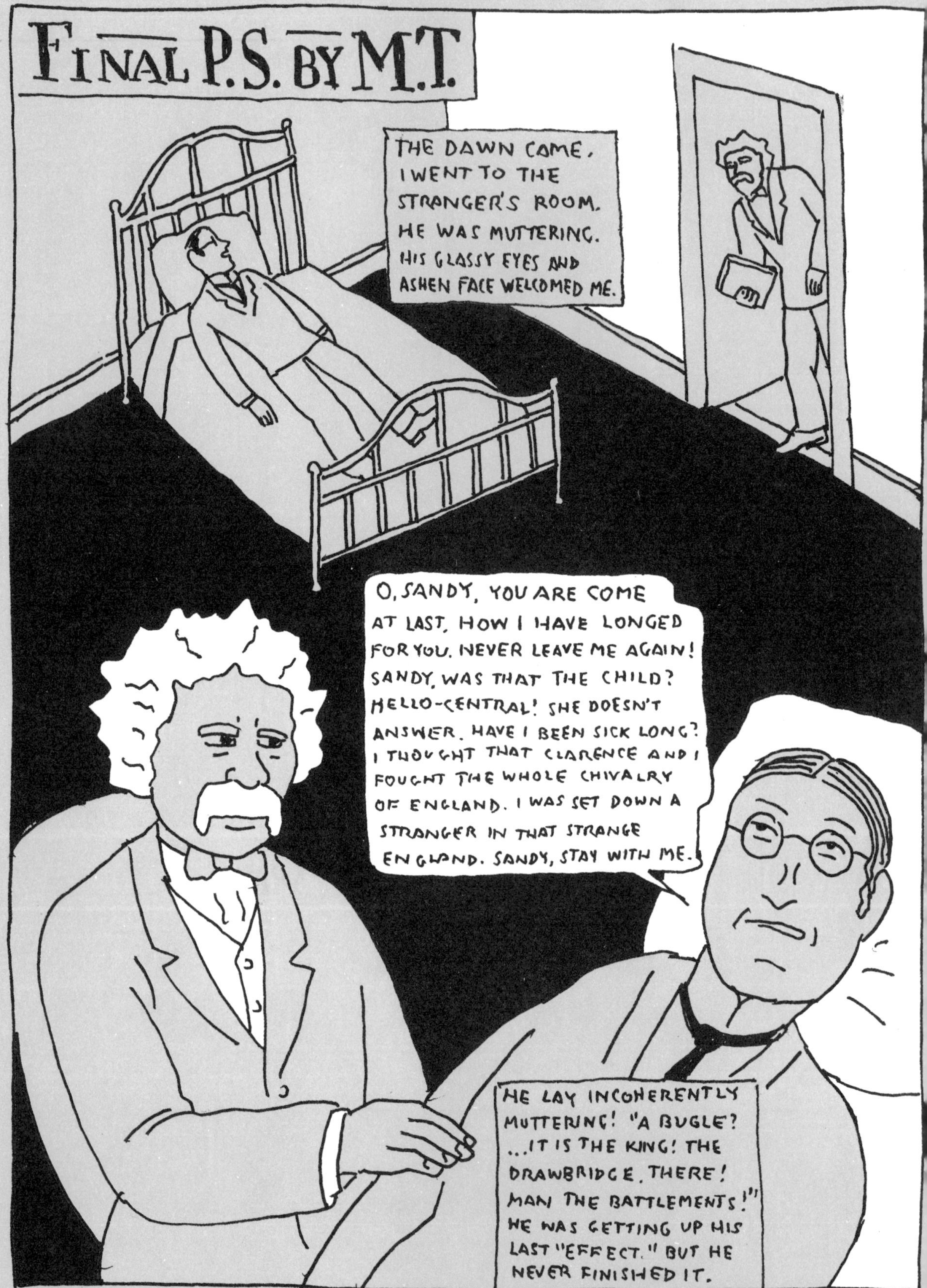
FINAL P.S. BY M.T.
THE DAWN COME, I WENT TO THE STRANGER'S ROOM. HE WAS MUTTERING. HIS GLASSY EYES AND ASHEN FACE WELCOMED ME.
O, SANDY, YOU ARE COME AT LAST, HOW I HAVE LONGED FOR YOU. NEVER LEAVE ME AGAIN! SANDY, WAS THAT THE CHILD? HELLO-CENTRAL! SHE DOESN'T ANSWER. HAVE I BEEN SICK LONG? I THOUGHT THAT CLARENCE AND I FOUGHT THE WHOLE CHIVALRY OF ENGLAND. I WAS SET DOWN A STRANGER IN THAT STRANGE ENGLAND. SANDY, STAY WITH ME.
HE LAY INCOHERENTLY MUTTERING! "A BUGLE? ...IT IS THE KING! THE DRAWBRIDGE, THERE! MAN THE BATTLEMENTS!" HE WAS GETTING UP HIS LAST "EFFECT." BUT HE NEVER FINISHED IT.

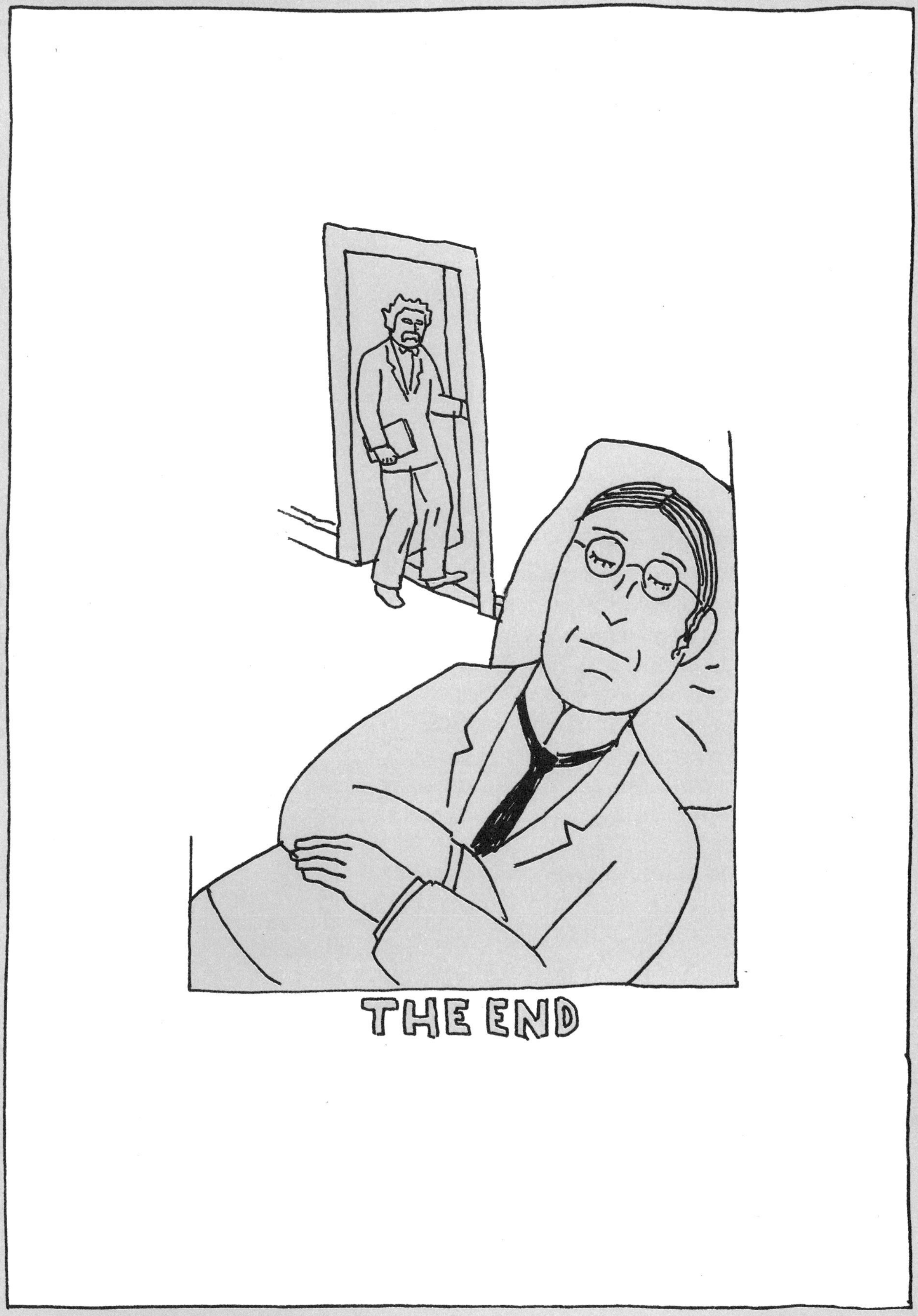
THE END

A NOTE ON THE AUTHOR

SEYMOUR CHWAST'S AWARD-WINNING WORK
HAS INFLUENCED TWO GENERATIONS OF
DESIGNERS AND ILLUSTRATORS.
    HE COFOUNDED *PUSH PIN* STUDIOS, WHICH
RAPIDLY GAINED AN INTERNATIONAL REPUTATION
FOR INNOVATIVE DESIGN AND ILLUSTRATION.
PUSH PIN'S VISUAL LANGUAGE (WHICH REFERENCES
CULTURE AND LITERATURE) AROSE FROM ITS
PASSION FOR HISTORICAL DESIGN MOVEMENTS
AND HELPED REVOLUTIONIZE THE WAY PEOPLE
LOOK AT DESIGN.
    CHWAST IS A RECIPIENT OF THE A.I.G.A.
MEDAL, WAS INDUCTED INTO THE ART DIRECTORS
HALL OF FAME, AND HAS HONORARY PH.D.s
IN FINE ART FROM THE PARSONS SCHOOL OF
DESIGN AND THE RHODE ISLAND SCHOOL OF
DESIGN. HIS WORK IS IN THE COLLECTIONS OF THE
MUSEUM OF MODERN ART AND THE METROPOLITAN
MUSEUM OF ART AND HAS BEEN COLLECTED IN
THE LEFT-HANDED DESIGNER AND SEYMOUR:
THE OBSESSIVE IMAGES OF SEYMOUR CHWAST.
    CHWAST'S PREVIOUS GRAPHIC NOVELS
ARE DANTE'S DIVINE COMEDY, THE CANTURBURY
TALES, AND HOMER'S ODYSSEY.
    HE LIVES IN NEW YORK WITH HIS WIFE,
THE GRAPHIC DESIGNER AND PAINTER PAULA SCHER.